## BEASTSLAYER

FELIX WATCHED THE Chaos horde begin its advance. It was all he could do to keep himself from whimpering with fear like some of those around him. He wondered whether he would survive an hour. Massive metal siege towers carved with the effigies of hideous daemons began to rumble forward. Teams of sweating, near-naked men drew some of them. Others moved under their own sorcerous power, rumbling ever closer to the walls. Huge trebuchet arms swung backwards and forwards sending loads of massive stones tumbling towards the walls. Felix heard screams and shrieks from a distant section of the line as their cargo of death descended among the defenders.

'Ask them to keep the noise down. Snorri has a bit of a hangover,' said Snorri.

*Also from the Black Library*

## · GOTREK & FELIX ·

TROLLSLAYER by William King

SKAVENSLAYER by William King

DAEMONSLAYER by William King

DRAGONSLAYER by William King

## · OTHER WARHAMMER TITLES ·

HAMMERS OF ULRIC by Dan Abnett,
Nik Vincent & James Wallis

THE WINE OF DREAMS by Brian Craig

REALM OF CHAOS eds. Marc Gascoigne & Andy Jones

## · GAUNT'S GHOSTS ·

FIRST & ONLY by Dan Abnett

GHOSTMAKER by Dan Abnett

NECROPOLIS by Dan Abnett

## · SPACE WOLF ·

SPACE WOLF by William King

RAGNAR'S CLAW by William King

## · OTHER WARHAMMER 40,000 TITLES ·

13TH LEGION by Gav Thorpe

EYE OF TERROR by Barrington J. Bayley

INTO THE MAELSTROM eds. Marc Gascoigne & Andy Jones

STATUS: DEADZONE eds. Marc Gascoigne & Andy Jones

DARK IMPERIUM eds. Marc Gascoigne & Andy Jones

# A WARHAMMER NOVEL

## Gotrek and Felix

# BEASTSLAYER

## By William King

A BLACK LIBRARY PUBLICATION

Games Workshop Publishing
Willow Road, Lenton,
Nottingham, NG7 2WS, UK

First US edition, March 2001

10 9 8 7 6 5 4 3 2 1

Distributed by Simon & Schuster
1230 Avenue of the Americas
New York, NY 10020

Cover illustration by Adrian Smith

ISBN 0-7434-1161-7

Set in ITC Giovanni

Printed and bound in Great Britain by
Omnia Books Ltd, Glasgow, UK

See the Black Library on the Internet at
**www.blacklibrary.co.uk**

Find out more about Games Workshop
and the world of Warhammer at
**www.games-workshop.com**

'**O**ur battle with the dragon Skjalandir left me incapacitated for many days. The events of the particular few weeks that follow it are mercifully vague. I know we brought word of the arrival of the Chaos horde to the Tzarina of Kislev. I know we flew on to the city of Praag where my companion and his dwarf compatriots thought they would meet their dooms. I know we were welcomed in the City of Heroes by the duke himself, who turned out to be a distant cousin of my fair companion, Ulrika. Of the detail of these matters, however, I remember very little, possibly because they are overwhelmed in my memory by the apocalyptic events that were to follow them.

'What happened in those following weeks caused me to plumb new depths of horror and despair. In my entire long and sorry career as the Trollslayer's amanuensis, I have found myself in few more desperate places. Even today, I shudder when I recall the madness and turmoil of those dreadful days...'

— From *My Travels With Gotrek*, Vol IV. by Herr Felix Jaeger (Altdorf Press, 2505)

# ONE

FELIX JAEGER LOOKED northwards from the gate tower high above the outer wall of Praag. As if for reassurance, his hands rested atop the carved head of one of the huge sculptures that gave the Gate of Gargoyles its name. From his high vantage point, he had a perfectly clear view for leagues. Only the long snaky curve of the river looping off to the west broke the monotony of the endless plains surrounding the city.

In the distance he could see the smoke of burning villages. It was war coming closer and it would reach the city in less than a day. He shivered and drew his tattered red cloak around his tall, lean form although it was not cold yet. If truth be told it was unnaturally hot. These last days of autumn had been warmer in Kislev than many a summer in his homeland, the Empire.

It was the first time in his life he had ever prayed for the onset of snow. Winter was deadly here, an untiring ally who slaughtered the foes of Kislev, or so the locals claimed. Lord Winter was their greatest general, worth a legion of armed men. He wondered whether he would live to see winter's arrival. Even Lord Winter might prove powerless against the Chaos warriors and their evil magic.

The warriors of the advancing army out there were not mere mortals, but worshippers of Chaos fresh from the Northern Wastes. Of all the foolish things he had done in his career as Gotrek Gurnisson's henchman, putting himself in the way of the armies of the Dark Powers was conceivably the most foolish.

Felix had barely recovered from wounds taken in the battle with the dragon Skjalandir, and the orcish armies that had tried to take the dragon's treasure. The wizard Max Schreiber had healed him and had done the work well, but still Felix was not sure that he felt as strong as he had before. He hoped he could wield his sword with his customary skill when the Chaos warriors came. He would need to. If he could not, he would die. Most likely he would die anyway. The black-armoured riders and their brutal followers were not famous for their mercy. They were unrelentingly savage and lived only to kill and conquer in the name of the daemonic powers they worshipped. Even the massively thick walls of Praag would not hold them back for long. If those wicked warriors failed, then the dark magic of their sorcerous allies would surely succeed.

Not for the first time, Felix wondered exactly what he was doing here, standing on the chilly walls of a fortified city, hundreds of leagues from home. He could be in Altdorf right now, sitting in the offices of the family business, haggling with wool traders and counting gold. Instead he was readying himself to face the greatest invasion the world had seen in two hundred years, since the time when Magnus the Pious had driven back the legions of the damned, and reunited the Empire. He glanced over at his companion.

As ever it was impossible to tell what the Slayer was thinking. The dwarf looked even more brutish and sullen than usual. He was short, the tip of the crest of red-dyed hair that rose above his tattooed and shaven head barely reached Felix's chest, but he was more than twice as broad as the man. In one hand he held an axe that Felix would have struggled to lift with both his hands, and Felix was a strong man. The Slayer shook his head, and the gold chain that ran from ear to nostril jingled. He knuckled the patch that covered his empty eye socket, and spat over the wall.

'They will be here by nightfall, manling,' said Gotrek. 'Or my father was an orc.'

'You think so? The scouts say they are burning the villages as they come. Surely so great a horde could not move so quickly.'

Felix had a better idea of the size of the horde than almost any man in Kislev. He had flown over it in the airship, *Spirit of Grungni*, when he and the Slayer and their dwarf companions had returned from the lost city of Karag Dum. It seemed half a lifetime ago but was scant months in the past. Felix shook his head, amazed at how much his life had changed in that month, more than at any time since he had sworn his oath to follow the Slayer and record his doom in an epic poem.

In that time, he had ridden in a flying ship, visited a buried dwarf city in the blighted wastes of Chaos, fought with daemons, and dragons and orcs and beastmen. He had fallen in love and pursued a troubled affair with the Kislevite noblewoman Ulrika Magdova. He had almost died of wounds. He had journeyed to the court of the Ice Queen, the Tzarina Katarin, bringing word of the enemy army to that fearsome ruler, and then he had come here with Gotrek and the others to help resist the invasion. It seemed as if he had barely time to catch his breath, and now he was caught up in a full-scale war with the assembled powers of Darkness.

He wondered again at his reasons for being here. Certainly he still held to his oath to Gotrek. And Ulrika was here, waiting to see if her father and his men would make it to Praag before the Chaos horde. Felix knew she was going to be disappointed there.

He brushed a lock of long blond hair from his eyes, then shielded them with his hand. In the distance he thought he could make out flashes of eerie red and gold light. Sorcery, he thought. The daemon worshippers are using their forbidden magic. He shivered again, thinking that perhaps it would be better to be in the counting house back in Altdorf.

He could not quite bring himself to believe it though. He knew he had become accustomed to a life of adventure. Even before his travels with Gotrek, life in the capital had seemed unbearably dull. He knew that no matter how often he thought a little dullness might improve his life, he could not go back to being what he had once been. Not that there was much chance of that anyway. He was in disgrace for killing a fellow student at the university in a duel. And he and Gotrek were wanted by the law for their part in the window tax riots.

'Do you think that the Kislevites are the only ones who have scouts, manling?' Gotrek asked. 'The Chaos warriors will have outriders too. Not even they are mad enough to ride without them. They will be here soon.'

Felix did not like to speculate on what the followers of the Dark Powers were mad enough to do. To him it seemed madness enough to want to worship daemons anyway. Who could tell what else they were capable of? On the other hand, when it came to making war, it did not matter how crazed they were. They were as deadly as any other army, far more so than most. In this, the Slayer was most likely right. He said so. Gotrek sucked his blackened teeth.

'Tis late in the year for an army to be marching,' he said. 'The warlords must be confident they can take Praag before winter sets in. Either that or they don't care.'

'Thanks,' said Felix sourly. 'Always look at the bright side, don't you?'

Gotrek cocked his head to one side, and spat over the wall. 'They must be planning some trick.'

'Maybe they have magic. Maybe the prophets of doom back there in the city are right. Maybe winter will not come this year. It is unseasonably warm.'

The words came out quickly and with less calm than he would have liked. He knew he was half hoping the Slayer would contradict him. After all, the dwarf had more experience of this than he did.

Gotrek grinned, showing the blackened stumps of most of his teeth. 'Now who is looking on the bright side, manling?'

Sombre silence fell between them. Felix scanned the horizon. Dust and smoke clouds continued to rise. Way off in the distance, he could swear he heard the sound of horns, the clash of weapons, the screams of dying men. Only your imagination, he told himself.

Down below them, workers slaved away driving more sharpened stakes into the great pit that now lined the base of the walls. Behind them, more labourers reinforced the outer wall of the city with buttresses. Gotrek had done more than his share of supervising them. Under normal circumstances, Felix would have been hard put to believe these massive fortifications needed any augmenting. The walls of Praag were ten times as high as a man and so wide you could drive a wagon along the top. Towers bristling with siege engines spiked the walls every hundred paces or so. Felix could smell the acrid reek of alchemical fire coming from some of the towers. He shivered to think there was a weapon nearly as dangerous to its user as any enemy, but so desperate were the Kislevites that their alchemists guild had been producing it night and day since news of the invasion arrived. They were preparing containers of it for the siege engines.

To their credit, Felix thought, the Praagers and their duke had taken the news seriously. They had done everything in their power to reinforce the strength of a fortress city many thought impregnable. These monstrous outer walls were but the first line of defence. Within the city was another wall, higher and even more formidable, and above that, on a massive spike of rock jutting out of the endless plains, loomed the titanic fortress that was at once the citadel and the duke's palace.

Felix glanced back over his shoulder. That citadel was a thing to give anyone nightmares and did as much as anything to maintain the reputation of Praag as a haunted city. Its walls were as strong as those of any Imperial fortress but they had been carved with many strange figures. Leering monstrous heads emerged from the stone. Massive tormented figures supported buttresses. Titanic dragon heads tipped tower tops. It was a work of art created by an insane sculptor. What sort of mind could have conceived and executed such a design, Felix wondered?

After the citadel, the whitewashed walls and red-tiled roofs of the rest of the city came as a relief. Even they looked strange and foreboding to Felix. The roofs were higher and steeply sloped, doubtless to let the snows of Lord Winter slide more easily off them. The temple spires were topped by minarets and onion domes. This was not the architecture of the Empire. The sight as much as the guttural accents of the soldiers around them told Felix that he was a long way from home. He felt like an outsider here. The strangeness of the city allowed his mind to give credence to the tales of horror about the place.

It was said that ever since the last siege of Praag, when the city had been sacked by the forces of Chaos, that the place had been haunted, that all manner of eerie things happened here. It was said that on certain nights when Morrslieb was full that the spirits of the dead walked the streets and that sometimes the stones of the buildings could become animated. New statues could emerge from the stone. New gargoyles appeared where none had been before. Under normal circumstances, Felix would have found this hard to believe, but there was something about the atmosphere here that told him that there was at least some truth in these old tales. Swiftly he looked away from the city.

In the fields covering the vast plain around the city, peasants still worked, gathering their crops from the long strips of cultivated land, driving their beasts towards the city. There was a sense of feverish industry down there, of folk frantically gathering the last meagre scraps of the harvest. They worked as if their efforts might make the difference between life and death. Felix supposed it was true. If a siege came – no, when a siege came – every last bite of food would be precious. These Kislevites knew that. They had spent their entire lives here on the borderlands between the lands of men, and the lands occupied by the powers of Darkness.

Felix wondered if any peasants in the Empire could have remained so calmly at work. He doubted it. Most likely they would be long gone, their fields abandoned, their crops left to rot. Parts of the Empire were a long way from the war against Chaos, and Kislev stood as a bulwark between the nearest provinces and the eternal enemy. Some in the Empire doubted the very existence of the Chaos warriors. It was a luxury that was not available here.

Another glance around reassured him a little. Huge cauldrons for the burning oil were already in position along the walkways. Massive ballistae bristled from towers along the walls. Felix doubted that any army the Empire had ever mustered could take the city but the horde approaching was far from an ordinary mortal army. He knew it contained monsters and beastmen and evil magicians as well as crazed warriors gifted by the Dark Powers. Where the armies of Chaos rode, evil magic, plague and festering corruption were ever their allies.

Worse yet, Felix knew that within the city itself the approaching enemy most likely had powerful allies. The worshippers of Chaos were numerous and not all of them were mutants or wore the ornate black armour of the Chaos warrior. Some of those workmen there might be plotting to open the gates one dark night. One of those noble captains might well be plotting to poison his own men or lead them into an ambush. From his own experience, Felix knew that such things were far from uncommon. He pushed the gloomy thoughts aside. Now was not a good time to be thinking them.

He looked down at his hand and was surprised to see how steady it was. He had changed since he and the Slayer had started their wanderings. There was a time when simply knowing what was out there on the plain burning those little towns would have turned his bowels to water. Now he was capable of standing here and discussing it calmly with the dwarf. Maybe it's not the Chaos worshippers who are mad. Maybe it's me.

His keen blue eyes picked up a disturbance on the horizon. Dust clouds, he thought. Men riding fast and coming closer. He glanced up at the guard tower overlooking the gate. Up there were hawk-eyed men with telescopes. One of them lifted a horn to his lips and blew a long blast. It was echoed by calls from other towers.

As soon as the call sounded, bells began to ring deeper in the city. The workmen down below calmly picked up their tools and made their way to the gates. Out in the fields, the peasants gathered the last turnips into their baskets, hoisted them and turned towards the gates. The speed of the people driving their flocks into the city increased perceptibly. From behind him, Felix could hear the sound of armed men racing for the walls.

'This duke might be mad, but there's nothing wrong with the efficiency of his guard,' Felix said, and then wished he hadn't. Questioning the sanity of the ruler of a city at war was not a sensible thing, even if he was only repeating what most people said. What was acceptable in war and what was acceptable in peace were two different things.

'If you say so, manling,' said Gotrek. He did not sound very impressed, but then he never was by anything human. The elder race were like that. They would never admit that there was anything today that was not worse than it had been two thousand years ago. A very insular, backward-looking proud people, thought Felix.

Soldiers swarmed past them onto the walls. Most of them carried bows, a few of the higher ranks brandished swords as they shouted orders. All of them were garbed in the winged lion tabards that were the symbol of Praag. The same sign blazed on a hundred banners about them. An officer came rushing up to them, looking as if he was about to order them to leave. One look at Gotrek convinced him otherwise. No one knew who the Slayer really was, but it was well known that he and his companion had come to Praag on that mighty flying ship bringing word of the invasion and orders from the Ice Queen herself. Felix had heard rumours that Gotrek and the other Slayers were emissaries from Karak Kadrin, the vanguard of a mighty horde of dwarfs come to aid Kislev in its hour of need. Felix fervently hoped it was true. From what he had seen of their enemies, the northerners were going to need all the help they could get.

He wondered when the *Spirit of Grungni* would return, and what aid it would bring with it. Malakai Makaisson's airship was a mighty weapon but he was not sure what it could do against the army that was coming against them. Malakai had promised to return bearing soldiers but it was not really up to him. He was a Slayer and an engineer, not a king. Help would only come from the dwarfs if their rulers sent it. Or maybe not, Felix thought. In Karak Kadrin there were hundreds of Slayers. The members of that death-seeking cult would most likely come whether ordered to or not. After all, where else were they more likely to find a heroic death than here in Kislev? If anything could atone for whatever sins had turned them into Slayers, surely falling in battle with the hordes of Chaos could.

Felix looked around to see if there were any of the other dwarfs present. None were that he could see. Snorri and Ulli and Bjorni were most likely still in the White Bear, throwing as much ale down their throats as they could manage while regaling each other with complaints about the weakness of human beer. Old Borek, the loremaster, had gone back to Kadrin with Malakai Makaisson. He still mourned the loss of his nephew, Varek. Felix did not blame him. There were times when he missed the quiet young scholar himself. It was a pity Varek had given his life saving the airship from the dragon Skjalandir. Better him than you, part of him thought. Shame filled him. He knew he should not think such things.

The dust clouds grew larger. Felix made out mounted men. To each rider's back was attached a feathered pole that looked like a bird's wing. Felix had no idea of the deeper significance of this emblem but he knew that it was the mark of the elite Kislevite cavalry. At this moment, they did not look very elite. He could see that they looked battered and weary. If there had been a battle he would wager that they had come out on the losing side. Behind them he could see other riders, garbed in black armour, mounted on black steeds. He did not need Gotrek's muttered oath to tell him what they were. He too had fought Chaos warriors in his time.

Even as he spat out another curse, Gotrek moved towards the stairway. If the daemon worshippers reached the gate, he intended to be there to meet them. Felix followed him, loosening his sword in his scabbard. He did not know whether to be disappointed or glad that it showed no signs of mystical energy about to be unleashed. It appeared that the weapon had fulfilled its purpose when he had used it to slay the dragon. From behind him, he heard warriors roaring battle cries and challenges and encouragement to the winged lancers. It appeared that they too had realised who pursued their countrymen.

As he reached the bottom of the tower, he saw more winged lancers riding out through the gate. He had to huddle in the doorway at the foot of the stairwell to avoid being ridden down. As the horsemen raced by, he saw their faces were grim. He could understand – the prospect of facing Chaos warriors was not one he relished himself.

As soon as the riders passed, the peasants started to stream in again. Felix found himself pushing against a tide of sweaty, dirty bodies. If it had not been for the presence of the Slayer ahead of him, he probably would have been swept back into the city by the crush. As it was the crowd parted around the Slayer like a stream swirling round a rock. Felix followed the eddy out across the packed earth bridge over the ditch surrounding the city walls and then ran. A few strides brought him abreast of the Slayer and he slowed his pace.

'No need to run so hard. It looks like the battle will come to us,' he said. It was true. The approaching Kislevites raced ahead of their pursuers, heading for the gates. The Kislevite reinforcements were spreading out into a long line, readying themselves to charge. Their change of formation swiftly blocked Felix's view of the action. He could still hear screams and war cries and the sounds of blades impacting on flesh from ahead of him. Perhaps, he thought, this is not such a good idea. Waiting to meet a charging cavalryman on open ground did not seem like a very clever plan. He wondered if he should mention this to Gotrek. Probably not. The Slayer had redoubled his efforts to get to the battle.

Ahead of them, the first of the fleeing cavalrymen had passed around those who came to relieve them. Felix could see the fear written on their faces. They galloped like men who had seen the gates of hell open behind them. Given how tough Felix knew Kislevite cavalrymen to be, this was not a reassuring thought. Anything that could make winged lancers break and run was most likely something to dismay the bravest. He glanced back over his shoulders at the walls lined with warriors. He was surprised how small a distance they had come from the city, and how much ground the pursuit had covered while he and Gotrek descended from the tower. It was all too possible that if the cavalry ahead of them broke and ran then the Chaos warriors might make it through the gates. Felix suddenly realised that he had no idea of how many of them there really were. He did not think it was likely that they could take the city, but perhaps they might be able to hold the gates until reinforcements came. Stranger things had happened in times of war. Anyway, it would not be good for morale if the daemon worshippers set foot in the city so early in the siege.

Ahead of them the captain of the riders gave the order to charge. Felix watched horses rear and then race towards their foe. War cries split the air. Moments later came the clash of lance on shield. He saw sparks fly, heard metal spear-tip screech against armour. Screams and bestial roars filled his ears. One man was tossed from his saddle. Horses reared. Ahead of them, men died. Just as suddenly, the Kislevites were broken. The lightly armoured lancers were no match for the heavily armoured Chaos warriors.

Knowledge of this did not affect Gotrek's determination to be part of the combat. With a mighty roar, he threw himself forward, diving into the battle like a swimmer leaping from rocks into dangerous water. Felix followed, knowing that his own chances of surviving the fray would be greatly increased if he stayed close to the Slayer. A black-armoured figure broke through the mass, cleaving the skull of a Kislevite rider with a massive ebony rune sword, and came racing towards them. Gotrek laughed and bellowed a challenge in dwarfish. The rider seemed to understand and touched spurs to the armoured flanks of his mount, goading it directly at the Slayer.

In the brief moments it took the rider to close the gap between them, time seemed to stretch for Felix. Everything appeared to happen with acute slowness, like in a nightmare. He picked out the elaborate metalwork on the Chaos warrior's armour, depicting the snarling heads of beastmen and daemons. He saw the strange evil runes blazing along its blade, and the ruddy molten glow from inside its elaborate bat-winged helmet that illuminated the space where eyes should have been. Small jets of sorcerous flame emerged from his steed's nostrils, reminding Felix all too uncomfortably of the dragon he had so recently faced. Its eyes glowed red.

The Chaos warrior raced towards them. Felix did not think he had ever seen a horse that looked quite so big. It looked more like a moving hill of muscle than a riding beast. He could see enormous sinews contract and twist beneath its night-dark skin as it raced towards them. Small clouds of dust erupted from under its hooves. Sparks flew where its black-iron shoes struck pebbles. Somehow, Felix found his blade already in his hand. He felt all the strength was draining out of him, but he had been in enough battles to know that this was an illusion. He knew that when the time came, he would move as quickly and forcefully as he needed to. At least he hoped he would.

Gotrek stood slightly ahead of him, axe raised high, glaring fearlessly at their oncoming foe. The rider laughed contemptuously as he saw the two of them attempt to bar his way. His horse thundered closer. Bloody foam erupted from its lips. Its yellow teeth were stained red, and Felix could see that they were not horse's teeth, they were sharp like the fangs of wolves. He did not know why that surprised him. He had seen far stranger mutations among the followers of Chaos. As the rider swept closer, he leaned sideways in his saddle in order to make a better strike against Gotrek. The Slayer stood still as a statue, waiting. At least, Felix hoped he was waiting. He had never known Gotrek to freeze in battle but there was a first time for everything.

At the last second before impact, the Slayer moved. He lashed out with his axe. A blow, swift and irresistible as a thunderbolt, struck the Chaos steed's legs. The beast tumbled, blood fountaining from its sheared limbs. Its rider cartwheeled from the saddle and skidded across the hard-packed earth to land at Felix's feet with a crash like an earthquake hitting an ironmonger's shop. Almost without thinking, Felix lashed out with his blade, driving it into the man's throat, smashing through the chainmail links that covered the flesh between helmet and breastplate. The Chaos warrior gurgled. Bloody froth bubbled through the hole in the armour. Felix withdrew his sword and chopped again, severing head from torso. He passed the fallen steed, feeling no sadness. The mount might be a dumb beast, but then again it might not. Some such creatures were preternaturally intelligent. All were fell foes.

He and Gotrek raced further into the battle. It was like being caught in a whirlwind of flesh. All around them, horses reared and pawed at each other. Lancers stabbed at armoured cultists. Men fought with unrestrained savagery. Gotrek moved with deadly power, lashing out to left and right, killing everything that got in his path. Felix moved behind him, watching the Slayer's back, stabbing at anyone who tried to encircle him. Within heartbeats, they stood behind a barrier of dead horseflesh and dying men. Felix heard more war cries from behind them and knew that soldiers were emerging from the city to join the fray. The clatter of hooves told him that some of the winged lancers had rallied and were coming back to join the fight. Within moments, the balance of the battle had changed, and the Chaos warriors were in retreat with the Kislevites in pursuit. From the walls behind them came the sound of cheering.

Felix found himself looking up at one young Kislevite noble, mounted on a fine white steed. His hair and eyebrows were almost as white as his horse. His eyes were a chilly blue. The man's armour was heavier and more costly than that of any mere trooper. The gold-hilted blade he wielded in his right hand spoke of considerable wealth. Felix thought he recognised him from his brief audience with the duke. It was the ruler's brother Villem.

'Not many men would have left the safety of the city to face a charge from the accursed ones,' he said, stroking the long pale moustache that drooped down past his chin. It was a fashion among young Kislevite nobles. 'It seems we owe you for more than bringing a warning from our fair ruler, the tzarina.'

'I am not a man,' said Gotrek. 'As any fool can plainly see, I am a dwarf.' The warriors around the noblemen flinched and brought their weapons to the ready position. Good, thought Felix, it's not enough that we have enemies outside the city. Let's have some inside too. To his surprise, the newcomer merely laughed. Felix had heard that the duke's brother, like most of the ruling family, was mad. Apparently the madness went as far as tolerating behaviour that others might have taken as grievous insults. Whatever the reason, Felix was grateful for it. 'I had heard that the elder race were proud and touchy, and Slayers most of all,' he said.

'No Slayer has anything to be proud of,' said Gotrek.

'As you say,' said the stranger, although his jocular tone implied that he did not quite believe it. 'Let all here bear witness that, I, Villem, of the House of Kozinski, am grateful to you for your bravery, and would see it rewarded.'

'The only reward I require is a place in the forefront of the coming battle.'

'That should be easy enough to arrange, my friend.'

Felix prayed that the Slayer would not make some sort of sarcastic remark. After all, this was no mere noble; Gotrek was halfway to picking a fight with the brother of the ruling duke.

'I shall make sure my brother and liege hears of your brave deeds.'

'Thank you, milord,' Felix said.

'No, it is I who should thank you. You are an Empire man. Not many would come all this way to fight and perhaps die in defence of our lands. Such bravery should be rewarded.'

Felix looked up at him. Villem seemed a fair-spoken and pleasant-looking young man, but Felix had learned to mistrust noblemen, no matter how polite they were. Now did not seem like a good time to say this, however. Rumour had it that Villem could be a particularly unpleasant enemy.

'All we wanted was a good fight,' Gotrek said, disgruntled. 'And one thing's certain. We didn't get it here.'

'Wait a few more days, my friend,' said Villem. 'Then the fighting will be as hot and hard as any could wish, even a Slayer.' The noble's entourage nodded their agreement. Felix saw no reason to doubt his words either. Gotrek merely spat on the ground and glared into the distance, looking at the plumes of smoke rising on the horizon.

'Bring them on,' he said.

Villem laughed easily. 'It is good that at least one warrior in the city is keen to face the foe,' he said. 'You are an inspiration to us all, Gotrek, son of Gurni.'

'Just what I've always wanted,' Gotrek said sourly. If he noticed the barbed glances of the nobleman's lackeys, he gave no sign. The Slayer barely showed any respect for the rulers of his own people; he showed none whatsoever for humans.

Felix wondered whether this was a trait that was going to get them both killed one day. He felt like apologising for the Slayer's attitude but he knew that Gotrek would more than likely just contradict him anyway, so he kept his mouth shut and prayed that Villem was as tolerant as he appeared to be.

The nobleman gave no sign of taking offence, which was good, Felix decided, considering there were thousands of soldiers sworn to the defence of his person and city within easy call.

'I must go now, but you will be welcome at the palace, should you decide to visit,' he said, sweeping away.

'That's an invitation I will be sure to take up,' Gotrek muttered sarcastically to his departing back.

One of the advisors turned and glared at him. There was murder in the man's eyes.

*I wonder who will kill us quicker,* Felix thought, *the Kislevites or the Chaos worshippers?*

# TWO

THE WHITE BOAR WAS crowded. The air stank of beer, stale sweat and pipeweed smoke. The bellowed conversation of drunks and the boasting of newly arrived warriors threatened to deafen Felix. He was not complaining. Right at this moment, he needed the cheery warmth of the tavern to help him forget the sight of the Chaos warriors. In some ways they were even more frightening in retrospect than they had been at the time.

He could not deny to himself that they were there now, outside the city. He had seen them, fought them. It was one thing to imagine their presence, to know that soon you would have to fight them. It was another thing entirely to know with certainty that a vast army of the evil warriors was approaching the city.

He glanced around wondering if Ulrika were present. Part of him hoped that she was not. Recently they had returned to their old pattern of fighting bitterly and making up passionately. The making up was just fine, but Felix felt like he could live without the conflicts. There was going to be enough of that in his life soon anyway, without it being present in his love life. Right now, all he wanted was some peace and quiet before the inevitable storm.

At the same time, part of him was disappointed that she was not there. Was she with Max again, he wondered? And if so, was this just some attempt to make him jealous or was there something more serious going on? He smiled ruefully. If it was the former, he had to admit that it was working. On the other hand, he could not really say that was what she was doing. Ulrika was not particularly guileful. Still, she was a woman, and Felix sometimes thought that women did these things almost by instinct. Now was not the time for worrying about it, he decided. Now was the time for drinking.

As he had suspected, Snorri Nosebiter and the other dwarfs were present, and all of them looked far from sober. It was quite possible they had been drinking ever since they got up this morning. Dwarfs took beer the way fish took water. Snorri was a massive dwarf, even more frightening-looking than Gotrek. His nose had been broken and reset countless times, and one of his ears had been ripped clean off. His head was shaven and three painted nails had been driven right into his skull. Felix wasn't sure how this had been done without infection setting in, but it had. Right at this moment, Snorri was arm wrestling with another dwarf Slayer and it looked as if he was winning.

Snorri's opponent was a young dwarf who seemed to shout rather than speak. His head was completely shaved to show his new tattoos and his beard had been clipped so close there was only stubble. Felix doubted that Ulli's had ever been very long anyway. He could probably grow a better beard himself.

Nearby another Slayer, quite possibly the ugliest dwarf Felix had ever seen, bounced a tavern wench upon his knees, apparently unaware that all the men and not a few of the dwarfs were glaring at him. Felix was amazed that the girl would even touch someone so repulsive. Bjorni had a truly gruesome collection of warts on his face, and together with his missing teeth they made him as repellent as any gargoyle. Noticing that Felix was looking at him, he gave him a wink and a leer and then placed his head between the bargirl's breasts and rubbed his beard backwards and forwards. She giggled. Felix looked away. Bjorni was incorrigible.

Looking around, Felix could see a group of massive men, armoured in heavy plate, with cloaks of white wolfskin hanging around their shoulders. They sat at their own table and bellowed drinking songs as they threw back jack after jack of ale. One of them caught Felix's eye and glared at him. Felix shrugged and looked away. He was no keener on White Wolf templars than they were on anybody who did not follow Ulric. A bunch of fanatic bigots, was Felix's opinion, but he knew enough to keep it to himself. Nasty as they might be, they were deadly warriors, and with the huge Chaos army approaching every blade was going to be needed. He could not afford to be too choosy about the men he fought alongside. Hopefully, they would soon come to the same realisation.

There were many others present: Kislevite horse soldiers, mercenaries from all over the Empire and beyond. He thought he heard the babble of Tilean voices and the slurred accent of Bretonnia. It seemed that there were warriors present from all over the Old World. He wondered how they had got here so quickly. It hardly seemed possible that the rumour of war had reached the Empire, and yet...

He told himself not to be so foolish. These men had not come here because of the invasion. They had come because this was the wild frontier and there was always work for hired blades so close to the Chaos Wastes. Most of them were probably caravan guards or attached to the private armies of some Kislevite noble. Looking across at one haughty, well-dressed man surrounded by burly thugs, Felix felt sure that some of them were bodyguards to travelling nobles from his own land. Why were they here, he wondered? Who knew? There were always wealthy men who liked to travel and scholars and mages in search of new knowledge. Most of them came from the ruling classes. Who else had the money to pursue such interests? He tried to dismiss the idea that some of these men could be spies for the Chaos cults. He knew that it was all too likely, but he did not want to deal with the thought right now.

Eventually, just when he had about given up, he saw the face he wanted to see. Ulrika Magdova entered the tavern, her face a mask of worry. Even so she was still beautiful. Tall, slender yet as strong as steel, her ash blonde hair cut short. Her clear blue eyes fixed on his own and she gave him a tight-lipped smile. Ignoring the leers of the mercenaries she walked straight over to him. He took her hand and pulled her to him, feeling only the slightest resistance. Not a good sign. Ulrika was one of the most unpredictable women he had ever met, hard when he expected her to be soft, soft when he thought she would be hard. He had almost given up trying to understand her, but at least, at this moment, he thought he had some idea of what troubled her.

'Still no word?' he enquired, using as gentle a tone as he could muster.

'None,' she said in a voice that was flat and purposefully devoid of emotion. He knew that she had been doing the rounds of the guardhouses and taverns, and various noble relatives, hoping for some word of her father. She had not seen or heard from Ivan Petrovich Straghov since they had boarded the *Spirit of Grungni* and headed south. It was not a good sign. Even allowing for the vast distances that separated the Marchlands from Praag, the old boyar should have been here by now. Unless something terrible had happened.

'I am sure he is all right,' Felix said. He tried to make his tone comforting. 'He is a hardy man, and he had over fifty lancers with him. He will make it through if anyone can.'

'I know. I know. It's just… I have heard what the outriders have been saying about the size of the Chaos army. They liken it to a plague of locusts. No force such as this has emerged from the Wastes in two centuries. This one may be even larger than the one that faced Magnus the Pious and Tzar Alexander.'

'That will just make it easier to avoid.'

'You don't know my father, Felix. He is not a man to run from a fight. He may have done something foolish.' She glanced around, tight-lipped. He sat down on the nearest chair, put his arm around her waist and drew her down onto his knee.

'I am sure he would not. Have a drink. That might help calm your nerves.'

She gave him an angry glare. 'You have been drinking too much since we got here.'

It was the old argument. She always brought it up. Compared to most of the people they travelled with, he hardly drank at all. Of course, most of them were dwarfs, so perhaps that did not mean too much.

'Well, I have not been drinking today,' he said. 'I have been at the Gate of Gargoyles, fighting.'

She looked at him slantwise. 'I saw wounded being taken from there to the Temple of Shallya for healing. They say a thousand Chaos warriors attacked.'

'More like twenty. Outriders. The horde has not arrived yet.' Felix raised his hand and gestured for a barmaid. The woman sauntered over and put down two jacks of ale on the table without being asked, then moved on. Felix lifted his to his lips and took a sip. It tasted sour compared to what he was used to. Goat's water, Snorri called it. Felix suspected that he knew enough to make the comparison exact. Snorri would drink anything.

Ulrika lifted a jack and slugged some back herself. He would never quite get used to this. Kislevite noblewomen drank as hard as any of their menfolk. When they drank at all.

'You were at the gate?' a man asked from the next table.

'Yes,' Felix replied.

'They say you could see the army of Darkness from the gate. They say it is ten thousand strong. Twice ten thousand strong.' The man was drunk and rambling.

'It does not matter,' said a swarthy man with the drooping moustaches of a Kislevite horse soldier. 'They will break against the walls of Praag as they did two hundred years ago!'

That brought a roar of approval from the surrounding tables. This was the sort of talk men liked to hear in taverns on the night before a battle. Felix had seen too many real battles to think it would be like the books and poems he had read as a lad. On the other hand, these men looked the same, and still they talked as if they were in a story. Maybe they were just whistling in the dark. Maybe just trying to keep their spirits up. If they had seen what Felix had seen flying back from the Chaos Wastes they would not sound so cheery at this moment. He tried to push those depressing thoughts aside.

'I don't know,' a thin weasel-faced man said from the doorway. 'My caravan just got in, and we faced beastmen and

Chaos riders on the way here. They were tough. Even if they were Chaos spawn they were tough. Never seen anything that died so hard as those beastmen.'

Felix was inclined to believe it. A glance at Ulrika told him so was she, but the warriors in the tavern wanted none of it.

'What sort of Chaos-loving talk is that?' a huge, fat man demanded, slamming a chicken leg down on the tabletop. 'Beastmen and Chaos riders die just as quick as any other living thing – if you stick two foot of good Imperial steel in them!'

More roars of approval. More laughter. More boasts about how many of the enemy were going to die in the days to come. More talk of how they would all be heroes in the song of the siege of Praag. Felix looked around again. He could see that there were plenty who disagreed with these sentiments. Many men looked worried, and they were the sort of men who looked as if they knew there was something to be worried about. Hard-faced men, wearing well-worn armour and carrying weapons they appeared to know how to use. Felix knew that the sort of boasting he was hearing was stupid, but he did not want to contradict it. He did not want to be the one to bring the spirits of all these people down. The weasel-faced man was apparently having second thoughts too. A city soon to be under siege by the powers of Darkness was no place to be suspected of being a Chaos worshipper.

'Aye, you're right,' he said. 'They died quick enough when me and my boys stuck steel in them.' Even so he still could not manage to get much enthusiasm into his voice. Felix looked at him sympathetically. It was obvious this man had faced beastmen before and knew what he was talking about. It was just that no one wanted to listen. By the way Ulrika was shaking her head, he could tell that she agreed with the weasel-faced man.

'Soft southerners don't know what they are talking about,' she muttered. 'A gor would eat that fat pig like he's gobbling down that chicken.'

Felix smiled sourly. For him the folk of Kislev were a byword for hardiness, a people who lived in a dangerous land of constant warfare. It never occurred to him that they might look down on each other. Of course, Ulrika had grown up on the northern marches, the very boundary of human territory and Chaos. If anyone in this room knew about such things it was her. She rose smoothly from his knee. 'I am going upstairs. To our room.'

Her tone made it obvious that he was supposed to follow. Under the circumstances, given a choice between doing that and staying downstairs to listen to this chatter of war, it seemed like the sensible thing to do.

IVAN PETROVICH STRAGHOV stared off into the distance. He was a big man and he had once been fat. The past few weeks had burned most of that off him. They had been weeks spent in the saddle, snatching sleep and meals where he could, fighting desperate battles against overwhelming numbers of beastmen, and retreating at the last second so that he could fight another day. He tried to tell himself he was harrying the flanks of the Chaos army, slowing its advance, giving its generals something to worry about to their rear. He suspected that his attacks worried that mighty force the way a flea's bites worried a mastodon.

He rubbed the bandage around his head. The wound itched again. He supposed he had nothing to complain about. If the beastman had been just a fraction stronger or his parry just a split second slower, his brains would have been decorating the monster's axe. The healing salves seemed to have done their work though, and there appeared to be no infection. He felt a bit feverish sometimes, that was all.

He glanced around at his riders. Thirty men, all veterans. He had started out with over fifty, survivors of the skaven attack on his mansion, and he had gathered over a hundred lancers more on the ride south. He had sent fifty to escort the women and wagons, heading south-west away from the main track to Praag. Hopefully that way some of his people would escape the advance of the horde. The rest he had led into battle, harrying the invaders in the time-honoured Kislevite fashion. Hit and run raids, savage night attacks, swift ambushes. His men had done well. They must have killed well over three times the number of casualties they had taken, but it was not enough. It was a drop of water in that great ocean of Chaos filth. The Wastes must be emptied, he thought. Who would have guessed so many could dwell in that pitiless land?

Like all his people, he had studied the old records of the ancient wars against Chaos. He knew the ballads and epic poems by heart. The Deed of Magnus had spoken of an army as numberless as the blades of grass on the great northern plain. He had always thought the poets had exaggerated. Now, he suspected that perhaps they had underestimated.

You're getting old, he told himself, to let such thoughts fill your head when you have a horse beneath you, a lance in your hand and a foe before you. There could be no such defeatist thoughts now. Too many men depended on him. He glanced around, and saw determination on every face. He was proud. These were not men who would give up. He knew they would follow him to the gates of hell itself if he asked. They were a finely honed blade. All he needed to do was wield them well, point them in the right direction, and they would do what he asked or die trying. Most likely the latter. He pushed that thought aside.

He was glad Ulrika was not here. He hoped she was somewhere safe now. He hoped she had delivered his warning to the Ice Queen and had sense enough to remain behind in the capital. Most likely not though. She had always been wilful, just like her mother, and, if he was honest, just like him. She had most likely followed that young Felix Jaeger, and since he followed Gotrek Gurnisson that meant she had most likely marched straight into trouble again. All he could do was pray to the gods to watch over her and hope Ulric was not too busy to listen to an old man's prayers.

'We go south,' he said in his most determined voice. 'We'll hit these blue-furred bastards as they try to cross the Urskoy and then head on. The Ice Queen must have sounded the assembly horn by now and be heading north to Praag. We'll meet her there and drive the Chaos worshipping scum back to the desert from which they came.'

His men cheered raggedly, almost as if they believed his every word. Once again, he was proud of them. Like him they had seen the true size of the horde – and, like him, they must know it was invincible.

MAX SCHREIBER LOOKED out from the walls of Praag into the gloom. Out there, he knew, the greatest army assembled by the forces of Darkness in two hundred years was waiting, readying itself to sweep over the lands of humanity in a tide of blood and fire. Perhaps this time, the Chaos worshippers would succeed. The gods knew how close they had come in times past, far closer than most men alive today would believe possible. Every time in the past they had been pushed back, at high cost, but every time the Chaos Wastes had advanced a little further, and had not retreated. Every time the world had become a little more corrupt, the hidden followers of Darkness a little stronger.

Max knew about such things. He had spent most of life studying them when he had not been studying magic. He had sworn an oath to oppose the worshippers of the Ruinous Powers however he could when he had joined his secret brotherhood. At this exact moment, he was wondering whether that oath had led him to the place of his death. Looking out into the night he could see the vast cloud of dark magic hovering over that distant army. To his sorcerously trained senses, the currents of power flowing through it were evident. There were powerful mages at work out there, he knew, and they were mobilising forces that should have been too great for any mortal sorcerer to control.

Who said they were mortal, Max thought sourly? They did not have to be. Time flowed queerly in the Wastes, and one of the most common reasons men submitted themselves to the Darkness was that they sometimes granted immortality or something close to it. And not eternal life in some distant paradise where you went after death either, but real eternal youth in the flesh, in this world. Eternal life and power. Two things many men had no qualms about giving up their souls for.

Max knew too that they were fools. Nothing came without its price, particularly not power borrowed from the Dark Lords of Chaos. They were like money lenders who charged ruinous interest. You gave up your soul, a small intangible thing that many people truly did not believe existed, and by doing so, you gave up everything. You surrendered your life and your will to the Dark Ones. You ceased to be yourself. You ended up a mere puppet, dancing on the strings of powers far greater than yourself.

Or so Max had been taught. He had seen nothing to make him doubt it, but if ever there was a time to want to, he thought wryly, this was it. When your choice came down to painful death or eternal damnation, it did not seem like there was much to choose between them. Certainly the priests of Sigmar and Taal and Ulric and Morr had their texts, and could tell you what waited for you beyond the grave. Still, none of them seemed too keen to leave the flesh behind either no matter what paradise they were certain awaited them. Max was not an ignorant peasant. He did not necessarily believe that the magical powers priests wielded were granted to them by the gods. He had wielded too much power himself to believe that. The temples did not like the fact their long monopoly on magic had been broken. That was why they still persecuted wizards like Max when they could.

He shook his head, trying to dismiss his dark mood, trying to blame it on the presence of all that dark magic swirling in the distance. Here he was ready to disbelieve in the existence of the benevolent gods, yet he was all too willing to believe in the Powers of Chaos. He told himself that the gods existed and some of them aided mankind. He had best believe that, and keep his doubts to himself, or the witch hunters would come calling.

Such men were not at all thrilled by the fact he was a mage. It was not all that long ago that wizards had been burned at the stake as followers of Chaos and forced to practice their arts in secret. And there were plenty of people in the city who were still more than willing to do a little wizard-cooking. He could tell by the way people muttered at the sight of him in his long robes and staff.

Well, let them. In the days to come they would need his powers, and would be grateful for them whether they thought they came straight from hell or not. When a man was wounded unto death and his only hope was magic, they swiftly rethought their prejudices. Most men, anyway.

He gave his attention back to the currents of magic. He could sense power pulsing through the stones beneath him. Dwarf work or the work of the ancient priests, it did not really matter. The spells were strong, reinforced over centuries by people who knew how to work protective enchantments. Max was grateful for that. At least the city had some protection against evil magic. The same runes guarded the inner walls and something stronger still protected the citadel.

He doubted even a greater daemon of Chaos could pass through the spell walls surrounding Praag. Of course, he could not be absolutely certain. No mortal man really knew what the mightiest servants of the Darkness were capable of. They were strong beyond measure. Perhaps he would soon be measuring that strength. All he could do was pray that it was not the case.

An enormous amount of mystical power and energy had gone into shielding this place, and Max wondered why. By common consent it was an accursed spot. Any folk less stubborn that the Kislevites would have abandoned it long ago. Not them. This was the Hero City, symbol of their eternal struggle with the forces of Chaos; they would never give it up as long as one citizen still breathed.

He leaned on his staff and drew a deep breath into his lungs. The spellwalls would hold for as long as the walls themselves did. If the stones were cast down, he doubted that the magic they contained would endure. The real threat would be that. Siege engines could destroy the stonework and the spells they held would simply unravel. He wondered if the defenders around him had any idea of what horrors might ensue if that happened. Better if they did not really. There was no need to spread despair.

Max knew that despite the desperate nature of the situation, he was really only trying to distract himself from the real problem. Ulrika. He loved her desperately and to distraction, and he knew he could not have her. She was with Felix Jaeger and that seemed to be what she wanted. Of course there were times when the two of them weren't happy together, which gave Max some hope if the two of them split up she might turn to him for comfort. It was depressing and not a little embarrassing that his hopes were so slight, but it was really all he could pray for.

It was ironic really. Here he was, a man privy to many of the darkest secrets of magic, a sorcerer capable of binding daemons and monsters, and he could not stop thinking about one woman. She bound him as strongly as any pentagram had ever bound a daemon, and she did not even seem aware of it. He had even confessed his infatuation to her one drunken night in Karak Kadrin, and she had ignored it, had treated him with nothing but friendliness ever since. In a way, it was humiliating.

He was a good-looking man, and a powerful one, modestly wealthy from his practice of sorcery. Many women had found him attractive although in his earlier years he had been too wrapped up in his studies and his pursuit of magical knowledge to pay them much attention. Now he had finally found one he wanted, and she would not even give him a second glance. Part of him was wise enough to wonder whether this was part of the attraction. Part of him wondered whether, if she had wanted him from the first, he would still have wanted her so badly. He knew enough of the human heart to know how perverse it could be.

Not that it mattered. He was hooked now, and he knew it. He spent as much time in daydreams of saving her life and earning her gratitude as he did in studying. He knew that it did not matter if the four great Powers of Chaos manifested themselves outside the city, he would remain here for as long as she did. It was annoying, for he felt himself to have reached a new plateau of power, and he knew he should be concentrating all his efforts into his studies. He was certain now that he was a match for any of his old masters when it came to sheer magical power, and he had come into his mastery while still young. Perhaps it was all the adventuring he had done recently, all the stress he had endured, all the spells he had cast under difficult circumstances, but he felt he had gained enormous strength in the past few months.

He shook his head wondering why he was spending so much time worrying about one woman while the whole world was on the verge of being shattered into pieces. Within the last season he had witnessed skaven attacks in the north, dragon raids in the mountains, orc tribes on the march. It seemed like a whole hornet's nest of evil forces was being stirred up. Was there any connection between these things? Instinct and experience told him that there most likely was.

\* \* \*

GREY SEER THANQUOL glared around the chamber. He was outraged. How dare those Clan Moulder imbeciles accuse him of fomenting this absurd rebellion? If they were incapable of keeping their own slaves obedient, it was no fault of his. He stared around the chamber that was his prison, taking in the strange living furnishings that were the hallmarks of the clan that held him captive. There was the fur-covered chair that shaped itself to him when he crouched in it, and the bloated balloon-like creature that pissed fungusberry wine. There was the carpet that writhed like a living thing beneath his paws, and the odd windows of translucent membrane that opened when he clapped his paws. Most of the time. When the Moulders did not think he would try to escape.

*Escape!* The very suggestion annoyed him. He was a grey seer, one of the Chosen of the Horned Rat, second only to the Council of Thirteen itself in power and influence. He did not need to escape. He could come and go as he pleased without any need to explain himself to lesser beings. He lashed his tail and twitched his snout, then rubbed the curling goat horns protruding from the side of his head. That was the theory anyway. The Moulders did not seem to agree.

It was all that buffoon Lurk's fault. Thanquol knew it. He was behind this. That obese monstrosity Izak Grottle had hinted as much during their last meeting. Somehow, showing a daemonic cunning Thanquol would never have suspected he possessed, his former minion had escaped from captivity and roused the skavenslaves to rebellion against their masters. Apparently, he claimed the mutations that had erupted from his twisted form during his sojourn in the Chaos Wastes were some sort of blessing from the Horned Rat, and that he was a prophet destined to lead the skaven race to even greater glories. Thanquol did not know what outraged him most: the thought of his own captivity or the fact that his worthless lackey was claiming authority greater even than that of a grey seer. Somehow it did not surprise him that even Lurk had managed to find enough dullards witless enough to believe such obvious lies here among the oafs of Moulder. A people whose leaders were foolish enough to imprison Grey Seer Thanquol were doubtless idiotic enough to believe anything.

The door parted, and a low chuckle announced the presence of Izak Grottle. Thanquol studied his old underling and rival from the fiasco at Nuln with a cold eye. There had never been any love lost between them, and Thanquol's captivity had done little to improve the situation. The Moulder licked his snout with a long pinkish tongue before stuffing a small living thing into his mouth. The creature shrieked as it died. Grottle emitted a loud belch. Blood stained his fangs. It was a disconcerting sight even for a skaven as hardened as Thanquol. He did not think he could ever remember seeing a ratman quite as fat as Izak Grottle, nor one so sleekly full of himself.

'Are you ready to confess your part in this nefarious scheme?' Grottle asked. Thanquol glared at him. He considered summoning the winds of magic and blasting the fat skaven where he stood, but dismissed the idea. He needed to hoard his power the way a miser hoarded warp-tokens. He had no idea when he might need it to escape. If only that ball of strange warpstone the Chaos mages had given him had not mysteriously evaporated before the rebellions began, he would have had more than enough sorcerous energy to manage his escape. Sometimes, Thanquol wondered if there was some connection between the two events, but he had decided that would have meant he had been outsmarted by two humans, clearly an impossibility, so he had dismissed the ludicrous idea.

'I told you I know nothing of any scheme,' squeaked Thanquol angrily. Grottle waddled forward and slumped down on the living chair. Its legs flexed and it gave an anguished groan as it subsided under his weight. 'This is nonsense. Nonsense. The Council of Thirteen will hear of this insolence. They brook no disrespect to one dispatched on their business.'

That was certainly true. Only a fool intervened in any affair sanctioned by the hidden masters of the skaven race. Unfortunately, it was obvious that Clan Moulder was full of fools.

'And what exactly was this mission for the Council?' asked Grottle, dismissing Thanquol's anger the way he might ignore the angry complaints of a runt. 'If you were on a mission in

Moulder's territory, why were not the Masters of Hell Pit informed?'

'You know full well what my mission was. I was sent to claim the dwarf airship for the Council that they might study it, and learn its secrets.'

Well, it was almost the truth, Thanquol thought. He was a representative of the Council, and he had come north on his own initiative to try and capture the airship. And he would have succeeded too had it not been for the incompetence of his lackeys, and the intervention of that accursed pair, Gotrek Gurnisson and Felix Jaeger. Why did those two always appear to thwart his best-laid plans?

'So you claimed, but the elders sense something hidden at work here. Surely it is no coincidence that since you arrived there has been nothing but an uninterrupted series of disasters for Clan Moulder?'

'Don't blame me if you cannot keep your own slaves under control,' chittered Thanquol testily. He lashed his tail and extended one of his claws menacingly to emphasise his point. Grottle did not flinch. Instead he scratched his long snout with one of his own much larger talons, and continued to speak as if Thanquol had not already answered him.

'No sooner did you arrive than we lost a mighty force of our best stormvermin attacking the horsesoldiers' burrow. Then a huge horde of Chaos warriors erupts from the North and starts laying waste to everything in its path. As if that were not bad enough, since your arrival none of our experiments has gone right, and during one of them, the strange mutant accompanying you breaks free and begins to organise our own lackeys against us. The elders feel that this cannot be coincidence.'

Thanquol considered the Moulder's words. There did seem to be a sinister pattern there, which would appear to minds less enlightened than Thanquol's own to implicate him in something. But he knew that for once in his long and intrigue-filled life he was not responsible. He had done nothing, had not even spoken to Lurk since they arrived in the great crater of Hell Pit.

He considered his words with care. 'Perhaps your elders have done something to displease the Horned Rat. Perhaps he has withdrawn his favour from them.'

Grottle chuckled again. 'This echoes rather too accurately what your partner has been telling our skavenslaves.'

Thanquol was outraged. How dare this fat fool suggest there might be anything like equality between himself and a mere skaven warrior? 'Lurk Snitchtongue is not my partner. He is my *minion*.'

'So, you admit that you are the mastermind behind this agitator then?' Izak Grottle said, nodding his head as if this merely confirmed his suspicions.

Thanquol bit his tongue. He had walked right into that trap. What was going on here? Why was his mind so cloudy? Why did he lack his usual cunning? It was almost as if he were under some spell. His thoughts had been a bit muddy since his capture by the Chaos horde. An enchanter whose mind was less well protected than Thanquol knew his to be would have suspected he had been ensorcelled. Fortunately in Thanquol's case this was an impossibility. No mere humans could possibly have warped his thoughts... could they?

'No! No! My former lackey!' he said. 'I have nothing to do with this uprising.'

Grottle gave him a look that combined frank disbelief and culinary appraisal. Thanquol shuddered. Surely not even Izak Grottle would dare devour a grey seer? The massive skaven moved ever closer. Thanquol did not like the glint in his eye. But just as Grottle came within striking distance the door to the chamber opened and a group of wizened, ancient-looking skaven strode in. Instantly Grey Seer Thanquol and Izak Grottle threw themselves onto their bellies and abased themselves.

One of the ancient skaven's voices rasped out. 'Grey Seer Thanquol, get up! You have much to explain and little time to do so. Your former minion has brought our city to the brink of civil war, and we have need of your counsel in dealing with him.'

Thanquol trembled and tried to restrain himself from squirting the musk of fear. Then the ancient one's words sank in. They needed his help. Their city seethed on the verge of anarchy. Here was a lever that might be used to open the doors of his prison, a key which he might use to get his freedom.

Suddenly, the situation seemed very promising.

# THREE

Felix clambered to the top of the watchtower near the Gargoyle Gate. He was surprised no one tried to stop him. The guards recognised him from the fight at the gate, and his association with Gotrek, and they did not mind him being here. A gold crown slipped to their commander had ensured that.

Gotrek and Ulrika were right behind him. They were just as interested in the arrival of the Chaos horde as he was. Looking around he saw they were not the only ones. The flat landing at the tower's top was packed with people, not all of them soldiers by any stretch of the imagination. He saw men in the thick sable furs favoured by merchants, and women in the heavy velvet gowns currently fashionable at the duke's court. Felix did not feel too out of place. He had grown up around such people. His father was one of the wealthiest merchants in Altdorf. He could tell Ulrika felt the same way. She was the daughter of a noble. Gotrek did not give a damn about what anybody thought. Seeing that they behaved as if they had every right to be there, no one gave them a second glance.

Looking around he could see that there was a picnic hamper and wine. The fat merchant held a silver goblet in his hand. Felix shook his head. These people seemed determined to treat the arrival of their foe as if it were some sort of entertainment. Felix was not sure whether it was bravado or pure mule-headed stupidity.

'By Ulric, look at that,' he heard one fat man mutter. The man had a spyglass jammed to one eye. He did not sound as if he were being entertained. Glancing out over the rooftops Felix could see the cause of the man's disquiet.

The Chaos horde covered the plains beyond Praag for as far as the eye could see. It was an inexorable black tide of steel and flesh flowing in to drown the world. In the lead were the riders, massive men mounted on monstrous black or red fleshed chargers. Those riders belonged in the haunted lands of the Chaos Wastes; it was a nightmare to see them here on the grasslands of Kislev. From the sea of armoured figures rose hundreds of rune-covered banners, cloth ensigns whipping in the breeze. Behind the riders were more heavily armoured infantry. And behind those were countless hideously mutated beastmen, foul creatures that walked upright like men but whose heads were horned, and who had the muzzles of animals. Scattered throughout the vast host were tens of thousands of barbarically clad men, feared marauders from the northern Wastes. He doubted that if every soldier in the Empire was mustered they could match the numbers of beastmen out there. Huge clouds of dust rose up where they marched, obscuring the more distant figures. Somehow Felix knew that if he could see them, the monsters would stretch to the horizon.

'Could be worse,' Ulrika said. All the wealthy folk on the tower top turned to look at her. Some shook their heads in disbelief.

'And what would you know about it, my dear?' said the fat merchant patronisingly. He sounded like he was suggesting that she should go home and play with her dolls. Gotrek grunted ominously. The guards shifted their attention to him, looking worried.

'Far more than you, sir,' replied Ulrika with bare civility. The merchant's heavy-set bodyguards gave her a warning glance. Ulrika merely smiled coldly at them, and her hand toyed with the pommel of her sword. Neither of the two big men looked worried, which was not too bright. Felix had seen Ulrika fight with that blade and would have backed her against most men. 'I am the daughter of Ivan Petrovich Straghov.'

'The march boyar,' said the fat man with more respect. His bodyguards relaxed a little, like attack dogs whose master has given them a sign not to attack just yet. 'Perhaps you would care to explain what you mean. I am sure everyone here would give ear to a discourse from the daughter of the man who has guarded our frontier with Chaos Wastes for the past twenty years.'

'There are no daemons,' she said, 'no flamers. None of the more exotic monsters that sometimes come down from the Wastes to ravage and burn.'

'Why is that?' the merchant asked.

'I don't know,' Ulrika said.

'Perhaps I can explain,' said a familiar voice. Felix turned to see that Max Schreiber had made his way to the roof. Was he following them, Felix wondered? It was fairly obvious that Max was enamoured of Ulrika, which was not good. Felix liked the man well enough but he was a little annoyed by his persistence in seeking Ulrika's affections. Felix felt that soon he might have to say something. He wasn't looking forward to the prospect. Having a wizard for an enemy was rarely a good thing, as Felix had found out to his cost in the past.

'And who are you, sir?'

'Max Schreiber, an Imperial wizard, formerly in the service of the Elector Count of Middenheim.'

If Max had announced that he was the chief baby eater at the court of the Lords of Chaos he could scarcely have got a colder response. Everyone glared at him suspiciously, as if he were in some way connected with the vast attacking army down below. Felix was torn between satisfaction at his rival's discomfiture and sympathy for a man who had been his comrade on a dangerous quest. Max had obviously forgotten he was not in the Empire for a moment. Even there magicians were only tolerated, not popular. In Kislev, they still burned mages in the more isolated areas. If Max was embarrassed, he

gave no sign of it. Felix supposed he was used to frosty recep-
tions by now. The wizard kept speaking as if his audience
were enthralled by his every word, which in a way, Felix supposed they were.

'The winds of magic blow stronger and darker up by the
Chaos Wastes. Many supernatural beings such as those of
which Ulrika spoke need the presence of strong magic in
order to manifest themselves for any length of time. The
winds of magic, particularly those associated with Chaos, are
much less strong this far south.'

'So you are saying that we are safe from daemons at least,'
said the fat merchant. His words were almost a snarl.

'No.'

'Then what are you saying?'

'I am saying the reason you can't see them is because they
have not been summoned yet. The winds of magic are strong
enough here to support such beings only for a short time, say
for the length of a battle. I have no doubt that there are Chaos
sorcerers down there powerful enough to summon them.'

'You seem very knowledgeable about these matters, young
man,' said one of the noblewomen, backing as far away from
Max as possible.

'Suspiciously so,' said the fat merchant. Felix did not like
the way the merchant's men were staring at Max. It would not
take much to drive these people to violence, he realised. And
that would not do them much good either. If anything, Max
was even more dangerous than Ulrika.

'I have trained at the Imperial College of Magicians in
Altdorf,' said Max. 'I am merely telling you what any competent magician can tell you about these things. If you are so
suspicious of the art that you believe that I could be a follower of Chaos, then more fool you.'

Very good, Max, Felix thought. Very diplomatic. That will
help solve everything won't it? Felix wondered what had
come over the magician. Did the presence of Ulrika really
affect him so badly? Was he really so desperate to impress
her? He seemed unable to think clearly when she was around.
Normally he was a very mild mannered and diplomatic man.
There were mutterings from the throng in the watchtower.
Felix wondered if Max had any idea how close he was coming

to provoking these people to violence. They were scared and afraid, and they were just looking for someone to vent their fear on.

And they had every right to be afraid, Felix realised. That army out there was enough to terrify any sane person witless. Felix had seen such forces before, when he had flown over the Chaos Wastes, but there was a huge difference between that, and knowing that he was in its path and that there was no escape. As he stood there, he felt a growing sense of claustrophobia. Until that very moment, the whole situation had seemed slightly unreal. In his mind, he had known what they faced, but emotionally it had not quite registered. Now, it was as if he felt the jaws of some great trap slamming shut round about him. Even as he watched, more and more Chaos warriors flowed into position around the city. Behind them came those endless ranks of beastmen.

He knew now he was trapped. There was no escape from Praag, unless the *Spirit of Grungni* returned, and even then it might not be possible to get away. There was no way out of Praag unless that mighty force down there was defeated, which meant, most likely, there was no way out of Praag alive. Judging from the spreading silence all around, he was not the only one to have come to this conclusion.

The fat merchant and his bodyguards stared at Max as if trying to decide what to do. They might want to burn him at the stake but he was a magician and none of them had any real idea of what he was capable of. He might be able to blast them to cinders with a wave of his hand or turn them into some sort of loathsome beast at a whim. Felix knew Max could do the former.

'I ought to have you horsewhipped,' said the fat merchant.

'And how are you going to do that with your fat head separated from your shoulders?' asked Gotrek. His tone was conversational but his expression was serious. Clearly he was no more pleased than Felix to have one of his comrades threatened. The merchant's guards looked distinctly queasy now.

'Why are you taking this Chaos lover's side?' stuttered the fat man.

'Are you suggesting that I would side with any follower of the Dark Powers?' Gotrek asked. His tone was dangerous now. The expression on the face of the merchant showed he understood he was a heartbeat away from death. Felix kept his hand on the hilt of his sword. He did not doubt that if Gotrek decided to kill the man, he would, and that the bodyguards would not be able to stop him. After that carnage would erupt on the tower top. The bodyguards obviously understood this too. They had started to back away. The merchant shot them a look that suggested their employment had just been terminated. Gotrek's growl got his attention.

'Of course not. None of the elder race would ever do such a thing.' Gotrek gave him a cold smile that revealed the blackened stumps of his teeth. The merchant looked as if he wanted to try and squeeze past the Slayer and hurry down the stair but couldn't quite summon the courage to do so.

At that moment a blare of trumpets and a thunderous roll of drums attracted everybody's attention. A rider emerged from the throng of Chaos warriors. He was a huge man on the largest steed Felix had ever seen. His armour was incredibly ornate and blazed with magical runes whose internal illumination hurt the eye to look upon. He seemed almost to shimmer, like a mirage seen in the desert, yet there was a solid deadliness about his presence that made him seem all too real. In one hand he held a massive lance upon which was a banner depicting a monstrous claw holding a glowing sphere. In the other hand he brandished a mighty runesword. A big war-axe hung from the pommel of his saddle. Fierce-looking as that malevolent steed was it gave its rider no trouble whatsoever. The rider stopped just out of bowshot and spread wide his arms and the whole vast horde behind him fell silent.

'He's going to tell us that if we surrender he will spare our lives,' said the fat man. He tried to make it sound like a sneer but that moment he sounded as if he would gratefully accept such an offer. Felix felt much the same way.

The huge Chaos warrior turned his attention to the people crowding the towers and battlements of Praag. Felix shivered as that burning gaze passed over him. For a second he felt as if the man, if that was what he was, had looked right at him, and stared directly into his soul. He tried telling himself that it was impossible, but he was not certain. Who knew what those creatures down there were truly capable of?

'I am Arek Daemonclaw,' said the Chaos warrior. By some magical trick his voice carried clearly over the distance separating him from the walls. It was a powerful voice, suggesting one used to instant obedience to his every command, and there was something in it that compelled belief. Not sincerity, just raw certainty. 'I have come to kill you all.'

Such was the force of that voice that a woman near to Felix screamed and fainted. The fat merchant moaned. Felix felt his hand tense around the pommel of his sword.

'I will build a pile of skulls higher than those walls you cower behind, and I will offer up your souls to the gods of Chaos. The Time of Changes is here. The false dominion of your petty kings is over. Now the true rulers of the world will stand revealed. Think on this and tremble.'

He glared around one last time. 'Now, prepare to die!'

Arek Daemonclaw brought his sword forward. As one the mighty Chaos horde advanced. Beastmen swarmed forward in their thousands. Some carried ladders. The defenders on the wall watched as if paralysed. Felix wondered if the Chaos worshipper had cast some sort of spell.

Inexorable as the tide, the beastmen advanced. Felix gave up trying to estimate how many of them there were. He had never seen so many monstrosities gathered in one place before. There were creatures with the heads of goats and rams attached to the bodies of massively muscled men. There were towering bull-headed monsters armed with axes that made Gotrek's look small. There were leering abominations from the darkest pits of hell. They howled, cursed and chanted in their foul tongue as they advanced. Their red eyes glittered with unquenchable malice. There were so many of them, and they came on with such insensate fury, that he wondered how they were ever going to be stopped. Even the mighty walls of Praag seemed like a flimsy barrier when confronted with so much hatred and power. Fear filled Felix. He glanced around and saw it written on every other face.

Before the attackers were half way to the walls the city's defenders responded. Catapults hurled huge boulders out into the oncoming ranks, smashing the spawn of Chaos to bloody pulp. Mages sent fireballs arcing outwards to explode among the tightly packed bodies. Thousands of arrows darkened the sky. The beastmen roared defiance, trampling their fallen comrades under their hooves in their determination to get within the walls of Praag. They brandished their weapons and bellowed challenges at the defenders. Even as they died, they howled obscene prayers to their dark gods. Felix felt sure they were crying out for vengeance.

The twang of mighty catapult arms surging forward filled the air. More beastmen died. Their masters looked on. From the Chaos army came answering balls of fire, and great glowing snakes of monstrous energy. Felix flinched when he saw them, knowing that dark magic was at work. A few of the others in the watchtower groaned, as if expecting death to descend upon them at any moment.

The fireballs disintegrated in a shower of sparks mere inches from the walls. The streamers of energy unravelled. The lightning bolts arced into the stonework causing no damage. The stink of sulphur and ozone filled the air. 'What happened?' Felix asked. 'Why didn't their magic work?'

'The defensive enchantments in the walls held firm,' said Max. 'They cannot be penetrated by such spells as those.'

'Then we are safe from magic at least,' Felix said. Max nodded slowly.

'Perhaps. As long as we stay within the walls, and none of their magicians get inside, and as long as no truly great magical powers are brought to bear. The spell walls of Praag are very strong but they are not unbreakable. I doubt master wizards cast those spells. They would know they were wasting their strength. Most likely those enchantments were the work of novices showing off.'

'You're not reassuring me, Max.'

'I'm sorry, but there is little about this situation that is reassuring.'

The horde came on, racing forward, brandishing their weapons. The Chaos warriors watched calmly. Seemingly they were taking no part in this assault. Max looked at them. 'Why are their warlords not attacking? Why is no one supporting those beastmen? This inaction worries me.'

'They are not attacking because they do not expect this assault to succeed,' Gotrek said. 'This is not an assault. It is merely a test.'

Looking at those thousands of charging monsters, Felix muttered, 'Some test.'

'We shall see,' Gotrek said. 'I know nothing of spell walls but the stone walls of Praag are also strong.'

'For human work,' he added almost as an afterthought.

The beastmen reached the great pit at the foot of the walls and halted for a moment. The mass of their comrades rushing behind them drove the leaders forward once more, so that they stumbled into the stake-lined pit at the foot of the walls. Roaring and screaming, they died, but still their comrades advanced, until the pit was so filled with squirming bodies that the remainder of the force could trample over them and reach the base of the wall.

What sort of madmen would throw away so many lives just to achieve a path to the walls, Felix wondered? And that only for a test. A glance back at the rows of Chaos warriors sitting impassively on horseback gave him his answer. The madmen they faced. Now more than ever, he was worried. Suddenly desperate for a closer look at their foe he snatched the spyglass from the merchant's hand and focused it upon Arek Daemonclaw. If the merchant had any objections to this a glance from Gotrek was enough to quell them.

Felix shivered as the Chaos warlord leapt into view. He was a massive figure in incredibly ornate armour. His eyes glowed balefully within his full-face helmet. Two massive horns curled from the lower part of the helmet, like the mandibles of some huge insect. The runes of Tzeentch, the Great Mutator, the Lord of Changes, blazed upon the warlord's breastplate. His banner rippled in the wind. He was flanked on either side by two figures that grabbed Felix's attention.

They were lean, vulture-like men, unarmoured and wrapped in huge cloaks whose folds gave them a resemblance to wings. Their skin was a pale corpse-like white. Odd runes were painted on their cheeks and foreheads that resembled those on the Chaos warrior's armour. Their eyes glowed with a baleful red light. They were twins, identical in all ways except one. The one on the warlord's right hand side held a golden staff in his right hand. The other twin bore a staff of ebony and silver in his left hand. The hand holding the gold-sheathed staff had long talon-like nails of gold. Silver encased the talons of the one on the left.

One glance at them was enough to tell Felix that these were sorcerers. They had an air of power about them that was indisputable. Even as Felix watched one of them leaned forward and whispered something into the ear of the warlord. The other smiled a sinister smile that revealed two prominent fang-like canine teeth.

Felix wondered what they were saying.

'IT GOES BADLY,' Kelmain Blackstaff said. 'As we told you it would.'

Arek Daemonclaw glared out at his forces as they assaulted Praag, then he glared at the sorcerer. He was getting a little tired of his wizards' admonitions. Had they not warned him against heading south so late in the summer? Had they not warned him against attacking Praag? Had they not advised him to join forces with the other great warlords instead of striking out on his own?

Recently they always had this aura of superior knowledge about them that Arek found intensely aggravating. Could they not see that the other warlords were treacherous fools? That taking Praag before winter set in would give his army a secure base of operations in the southlands? Late summer was the perfect time for a surprise attack since no one expected armies to move then. They had quite missed the point that it was impossible to keep from moving in that direction. Some instinct appeared to be driving every follower of the Great Powers south. Every seer and tribal shaman in the Wastes was prophesying that the Time of Changes had come. Every oracle that spoke claimed the four Great Powers were, for once, united in their determination to cleanse the lands of men. His wizards had not seen that if Arek had not come south his followers would have deserted him and flocked to the banners of some bolder chieftain. As it was marching now, his army was being swollen by tens of thousands of tribesmen and beastman, all answering a call that sounded deep in their souls.

Arek studied the mage. He could see the aura of power shimmer around the albino. It was one of the many gifts

Tzeentch had granted him. Blackstaff was a mighty mage. Tzeentch had granted him powers greater than any mage save his twin but it was obvious he was no warrior. 'It is a beginning.'

'Aye, that it is,' agreed Lhoigor Goldenrod, flexing his yellow talons. His giggle was high-pitched and irritating. Arek longed for the day when he would no longer need their services and could offer the mages' souls up to his patron. 'And what a beginning!'

Like his twin, he could not resist allowing just a hint of irony to show in his voice. Arek looked to see who had taken note of their exchange. Bubar Stinkbreath, the bloated follower of Nurgle, was watching them. His pustulent face showed no sign of having overheard anything, but then it wouldn't. Bubar was as wily as he was diseased. Lothar Firefist, the chief follower of the Blood God in Arek's army was too busy cheering on his fellow Khorne worshippers to pay any attention to what Arek and his wizards were saying. Most of the time, he could barely keep his contempt from showing anyway. Sirena Amberhair, the hermaphrodite warlord of Slaanesh, was licking her lips at the sight of the combat. It was hard to tell if she had noticed anything. She was nearly as crafty as Bubar, when not lost in the drug dreams the black lotus brought her.

Watching the beastmen charge forward to certain death, Arek felt nothing but contempt. Foul, idiotic, weak creatures, he thought. Brutish and stupid. Fit only to die in the service of their lords and masters. Plenty more where they came from at least. Tens of thousands of them were drifting down from the Wastes, drawn to Arek's banner by the promise of plunder and carnage. Still, he thought, even such petty creatures can be the agents of destiny, even if they don't know it.

One of the many differences between Arek and those brutes was that he knew who he was. He had always known even centuries ago, when he had a different name, and a different life, as a young lord in the Empire. He had known he was destined for greater things than other men. He had not let the fact he was not the eldest of his line stand in his way. He had made sure he had acquired the power he deserved. Poison, convenient accidents and sorcery had ensured he inherited all of his late and unlamented father's estates. For a while that had been enough. He had riches, he had power, and he had women. But it had not been enough. Even then unconsciously he heard the call of greater things. His fate would not let him live as other men lived, or die like any mere mortal.

The sorcerer who had first seen to the disposal of a jealous brother had proven a rich source of other knowledge, of other boons. He was a weak man who had thought the worship of Chaos an easier path to the wealth and respect he craved than study and hardship. Still, weak as he was, he had served his purpose. His grimoires had revealed certain ancient truths to Arek. They had taught him that it was possible for certain worthy men to transcend mortality, to acquire almost limitless power, if only they would agree to serve the hidden Powers of Chaos, the powers which Arek now knew secretly ruled the universe. The man had been a fool but Arek still felt a certain gratitude to him.

It had taken Arek years to learn more. He had infiltrated certain hidden cults, fools who believed they knew the truth about the Powers of Chaos and who sought to advance themselves using its influence. Down the years, despite investigations by witch hunters, and secret wars with rival cults, Arek had slowly found out what he needed. He had learned that in order to find the power and longevity he needed to achieve his destiny, he would have to visit the Chaos Wastes, and dedicate himself to the Changer of the Ways at his shrine there.

It had been a long hard journey, but Arek knew now that it had to be, for the journey was a test, intended to weed out those not strong enough, or dedicated enough or clever enough to enjoy the blessings of the supreme lords of Chaos. Just as the cults had been a proving ground where only those who really sought for the knowledge they needed would ever find the truth. Of course, it had not seemed that way to him then, but over the years he had learned the truth for himself. A lesser man would not have survived the trials Arek had endured, but that was only just. Lesser men did not deserve the rewards that Arek had received.

At first he had not possessed the wisdom to see them as rewards. Then he had been horrified by what he had seen as the stigmata of Chaos appearing on his body. Now he knew the stigmata had been granted to him for a reason. He had always been vain of his personal appearance, had always revelled in the good looks that made him attractive to women. When his features started to melt and run, after the first warp storm he endured in the Wastes, he had thought that he would go mad. He had not been able to look at his reflection without shivering. It was a weakness of course, one that he had soon overcome.

And he had been rewarded. The Great Mutator had gifted him with increased insight and wisdom. Many of the hidden secrets of the universe had been revealed to him.

When he had found the hidden shrine to Tzeentch, buried deep in a crystal cave in the Mountains of Madness, he had been judged worthy to become a Chaos warrior. The black armour had been grafted to his body. Its gifts of increased strength and resilience had become his, and he had ridden out into the world to spread change and terror in the name of his master. He had joined a warband, and fought his way to leadership, for as all the great powers, Tzeentch liked to pit his worshippers against each other so that they could prove their worthiness for his favour.

Arek had been worthy indeed. He had led his followers to victory after victory, showing a deep shrewd grasp of the tactics needed for victory and the political insight needed to rise within the ranks of the chosen. In quick succession he had bested the bellowing Khornate warrior Belal, the foul disease-ridden champion of Nurgle, Klublub, and the decadent perfumed but deadly pleasure-knight of Slaanesh, Lady Silenfleur. He had made pilgrimages to all the sacred Tzeentchian sites within the Wastes, and acquired greater knowledge and magical power, as well as many runic refinements to his armour and weapons.

It was during this period that he had first encountered the twin wizards who were to be so instrumental to his rise to power, Kelmain Blackstaff and Lhoigor Goldenrod. They had first met in the caverns of Nul deep beneath the Mountains of Madness when Arek had made his offering of thirteen captured souls of champions of rival powers to Lord Tzeentch. During his vigil daemons had whispered many secrets to him, and the twins had helped him interpret those cryptic warnings. One of those secrets had brought them all here today. For he knew the reason why Skathloc had tried so hard to take the citadel of Praag, and what lay concealed there still.

The twins had recognised his great destiny and aligned themselves with him, lending him their sorcerous powers, advising him on matters magical and occasionally about other things. He had usually followed their advice, and since they never challenged his decisions, never disobeyed his orders, he had been happy to have them in his warband. Indeed, their powers of divination and prophecy had proven so accurate that he had found them to be his most useful servants.

They became good luck charms, in a way, for soon after they joined him, Arek began to enjoy even greater success than he had before. His forces swelled as beastmen and lesser champions swarmed to his banner. Their magic had helped him acquire the first of his fortresses within the Chaos Wastes when their spells had opened the gates to the Citadel of Ardun on the rocky crags above the Vale of Desolation. Of course, he had led the warriors within and had slain the Ancient of Ardun with his own hands but they had certainly been helpful.

They had been more than helpful when he retrieved his invincible armour from the Vaults of Ardun. They had somehow known the spells that would unlock the armour and then bind it to his body. Since that day, as they had prophesied, he had proven invulnerable to every weapon forged by mortal or daemon.

Their advice had helped him form his great coalition of the followers of Tzeentch. They had told him who was trustworthy and who was treacherous, and they seemed to have infallible noses for sniffing out those who plotted against him. It was they who warned him that his trusted lieutenant Mikal the Lion-Headed plotted to have him assassinated and overthrown. He had swiftly turned the tables on his treacherous follower when they were alone in his throne room, and Mikal sought to take him by surprise.

They had forewarned him of the great ambush planned for his forces at Khaine's Defile, and allowed him to surprise those would-be ambushers in turn. Their spells had turned the sky red with magical energy and helped him win a victory against a force ten times the size of his own.

They had woven him around with spells that had made him invulnerable to sorcerous attack and that had allowed him victory even over daemons. Over the centuries they had helped him acquire the power and prestige that had eventually enabled him to forge this grand coalition consisting even of followers of the other three great powers. Arek knew that this was the final culmination of his destiny.

Over the long millennia very few warlords had the charisma, the military skill, the drive and the sheer ability to forge such a coalition. Skathloc Ironclaw had made the last one over two centuries ago, and Arek knew that he was the first man since then to have welded such a force together. True, at least three other warlords had forged forces of similar size and had now emerged from the Wastes, but in the end, it would be Arek who would prove triumphant. Victory here at Praag would give him the prestige to unite all of the Chaos worshippers behind him.

If everything went according to his plans, he would also be the last. For he intended to bring the entire world under the sway of his power, and extend the Chaos Wastes from pole to pole. He knew that given time he could do it.

The twins had certainly been useful, but it seemed now to Arek that their usefulness was coming to an end. They had resisted his plan to come south so soon. They had wanted him to wait longer, acquire even more force. They had muttered their usual cryptic warnings about the omens not being right. They had claimed that the paths of the Old Ones would soon be open, and there would be no need for these great marches. They had not seen that the assembled warleaders were already chafing at the bit, eager to be started and needing a campaign of conquest to keep them unified. For the first time since they had acknowledged his destiny to rule, Arek had found himself at odds with his pet wizards.

It was a situation that would swiftly be rectified. Powerful as they were, there were plenty more sorcerers willing to follow Tzeentch's favoured champion. Once this city was taken, and the great campaign launched with a resounding victory that would weld his horde together, Arek vowed he would see to the troublesome wizards' replacement.

Right now he returned his attention to the ongoing battle. The beastmen were falling in their thousands to the human war engines. It did not matter. Arek did not seriously believe they had any chance of taking the city. He merely wanted the defenders to realise the strength of the foe they faced, that he could afford to squander ten thousand such lackeys if he wanted to, and it would not put the slightest dent in the numbers of his horde. It would demoralise the defenders when they realised the sheer scale of the opposition they faced. In a prolonged siege it would affect the outcome significantly.

Besides, all of the attacking beastmen were followers of Khorne. They had been desperate for battle, and Arek doubted that he could restrain them or Lothar Firefist, the warlord who led them, much longer without them turning on the rest of the host. It was the main difficulty leading a coalition like this. Giving them a common foe was sometimes more important than mere military utility.

Even as he watched he saw that the attackers had reached the wall. Boiling oil splashed their fur, as the defenders upended cauldrons of it onto the beastmen. Ever-burning alchemical fire turned them into blazing humanoid torches. Even so a few ladders still reached the wall, and a few beastmen swarmed up them. For a moment it looked like some of them would succeed in clearing a space on the battlements and allow their brethren to swarm over. By sheer berserk fury, it looked like they might carry the day. That would be good, Arek decided.

Then he saw a dwarf and some humans appear from the base of one of the towers. A bolt of lightning danced along the walls, slaying beastmen. There was something about that dwarf, an aura of power, of destiny that was obvious to Arek's altered vision. One of the men who followed him had the same aura, although to a lesser degree. With a shock Arek realised that he recognised the axe carried by the dwarf. He had seen it wielded once before, during the assault on the citadel of Karag Dum. It was a potent thing, woven round with baneful runes, and perhaps powerful enough to breach even Arek's armour. The sight of it filled him with foreboding.

Perhaps he should consult with his pet wizards about this, Arek decided. He had a reason to let them live for just a little while longer.

FELIX SMASHED HIS sword through the skull of the beastman, and looked around. The battlements were clear. All of the beastmen had either been cast down to the ground below, or were dead. He glanced over at Gotrek. The Slayer stood nearby covered in filth and matted gore, a sour expression on his face. He looked surprised and disappointed at finding himself still alive, hardly surprising since his avowed intention in life was to find a heroic death in battle. Nearby, Ulrika and Max Schreiber stood blinking in the gloom. Sweat ran down their faces. Ulrika looked as if she had been working in a butcher's shop. Small clouds of smoke drifted up from Max's hands. Felix was glad to see that they were all still alive.

It had been touch and go there for a while. Even given the huge numbers of beastmen in the assault, upon seeing the carnage wreaked on them by archers and siege engines, Felix had been surprised that any had reached the walls. It was a testimony to the sheer strength and ferocity of the Chaos worshippers that they had managed to do so. That they had come so close to sweeping over the outer walls on the first day of the battle was a scary thought. Even more terrifying was the memory of the sheer fury and utter lack of concern for their own safety with which they had thrown themselves forward.

From the faces of the defenders visible all around him, he could see that they were just as concerned as he was. They had not expected this. They had considered their city walls impregnable and with some justification. Archers looked out of every gap in the battlements. Beside them were well-armoured men-at-arms. Heated pots of boiling oil stood ready to be poured down on the attackers. Engines to lob pots of alchemical fire into the enemy stood on every tower top. And all of these preparations had proven barely sufficient. They had almost been swept away by the sheer fury of the attackers. Felix shuddered. If it was like this on the first day, what was it going to be like once the siege was in full swing, and the attackers had time to raise war engines, and bring foul sorcery to bear?

And there was still the possibility of treachery. Looking at the seething mass of Chaos worshippers out there, Felix didn't even want to consider this. It was frightening enough having them outside the city. The prospect that some of them might already be within was a fearsome one.

AREK STRODE CONFIDENTLY into the magicians' tent. It was quiet inside. Somehow all the roars and shouts and bellows of the horde were left behind as soon as he entered. The air stank of the hallucinogenic incense pouring from the brazier near the entrance. He looked around and noted all the massive chests and intricate paraphernalia of sorcery. He saw sandalwood caskets from far Cathay, and strange dragon-inscribed lanterns from legendary Nippon. The skeleton of a mastodon loomed in the darkness. Shadowy presences flickered just under the drooping canvas of the roof. Not for the first time, he wondered how Kelmain and Lhoigor fitted all of this stuff into their pavilion. It sometimes seemed to him that it was larger on the inside than it was on the outside. Arek supposed it was possible. They were after all mighty mages.

The twin sorcerers sat cross-legged, floating a hand's breadth above an Arabian carpet. Their eyes were closed. Pieces on the chessboard in front of them moved without a hand being laid on them. Arek glanced at the position. From where he stood it was obvious that the game was going to be a win for white. It always was when the twins played. They were so well matched that whoever held that slight advantage inevitably won. He reached down and moved the pieces through the combination that led to inevitable victory.

'Why do you always do that?' Kelmain asked, smiling sardonically.

'I fail to understand why you play each other at all,' Arek said. He had always found the twins' good humour vaguely annoying. They seemed to share some secret that they did not want to tell the world, but which caused them great amusement. It was a testimony to their great power that they still lived. Men had died for a lot less than that in the Chaos Wastes.

'One day we hope to establish which of us is the better player.'

'How many games have you played now?'

'Close on ten thousand.'

'What's the score?'

'Kelmain's victory, which you foresaw, puts him one ahead.'

Arek shook his head and surveyed the blazing auras of his pet sorcerers. There was mockery there for certain.

'You did not come here to discuss our chess playing, fascinating as it doubtless is,' said Lhoigor.

'What do you require of us?'

'What I always do – information, prophesy, knowledge.'

'Tzeentch has granted us a great deal of the latter.'

'Sometimes too much I think,' Kelmain said.

Arek was in no mood for the mages' banter. Swiftly he outlined what he had seen on the walls today. He spoke of his presentiment of danger. He asked the mages to grant him a vision.

'Your forebodings are doubtless justified,' Kelmain said.

'Sometimes Lord Tzeentch chooses to send warnings in just this manner,' Lhoigor added.

'I require more specific information than this,' said Arek.

'Of course,' Kelmain said.

'You wish to learn more of this axe and its bearer,' Lhoigor said.

'Naturally.'

'You wish us to invoke the name of the Lord of Change and ask of him to grant you the boon of a vision,' Lhoigor said. His voice had taken on the quality and rhythm of a priest intoning a ritual. Arek nodded.

Kelmain gestured and an enormous metal sphere floated over to the centre of the tent. It hovered over the table. Lhoigor passed his hand over it, and the sphere split into two halves. They floated away from the mages, revealing the gigantic crystal orb that had rested within. 'Look into the Eye of the Lord, and gain wisdom then,' he said.

Arek *looked*.

IN THE DEPTHS of the sphere he saw a flickering light, the merest pinpoint, a distant flame that grew brighter as he watched. In it he thought he caught sight of a swirling distant realm that he recognised from his most troubled dreams, a place

that had appeared to him in visions before at sites sacred to
Lord Tzeentch. It was a place where the sky constantly
changed colour as ripples of red and green passed across the
cloudless firmament, where huge winged shapes with the
bodies of men and the heads of predatory birds pursued the
souls of their victims over an endless landscape, a land in the
centre of which his god sat enthroned.

He felt other presences with him now, which he recognised
as the souls of his magicians. He could hear their voices, far
off in the distance, chanting the words of eldritch incanta-
tions. He saw as from afar a scene in the primordial dawn of
time. A massive dwarf who somehow seemed more than a
dwarf forged an axe that he recognised. The ancient dwarf
beat the blade on an anvil through which the power of magic
flowed strongly, patiently inscribed runes of surpassing might
to be the bane of daemons. At the final stages of the ritual he
invoked protective spells and the scene shimmered and vanished.

*He sensed us*, said the voice of Kelmain in his mind.

*Nonsense, brother, the spell he invoked wards out all external
magic, including ours.*

*I suppose you are right.*

Arek wondered what they were talking about, and who they
were watching. The scene shimmered and shifted, and he saw
a huge dwarf similar to the first bearing two axes, the one he
had seen forged and another that was akin to it. His head was
shaved, tattoos covered his skin. He fought endlessly against
the hordes of Chaos in a world where the sky was the colour
of blood, and the sorcerer's moon, Morrslieb, glared down
huge and baleful from the skies.

*The first great incursion*, Kelmain's voice whispered.

*When the Lords of Chaos first gained entrance to this world*,
added Lhoigor.

Arek saw the dwarf lead armies from the fortress cities of
the dwarfs. He saw the endless doomed campaign waged
against the armies of Darkness. He saw the axe-bearer eventually depart into the Wastes on a quest to deny the Lords of
Chaos entry into his world. He saw him cast away the axe,
before his final doomed battle with the daemonic hordes.

\* \* \*

THE SCENE SHIFTED once more. A young dwarf retrieved the axe and bore it to the great citadel of Karag Dum far to the north. The spell walls of that vast city blocked any further vision for millennia. Then the tides of Chaos advanced once more, in a time that Arek recognised. He saw Karag Dum encircled by the Wastes, and laid siege to by a mighty host of beastmen and daemons. He saw the spell walls broached by a great bloodthirster of Khorne, and viewed inside the city. He saw the bloodthirster vanquished by a distant descendant of the original axe wielder, who died even as he defeated the mighty winged daemon. He saw the axe being picked up by the son of the king who headed out into the Chaos Wastes to bring aid to his people. Arek witnessed his quest's failure and the young dwarf dying alone and far from home, fighting his final battle against an army of beastmen after taking refuge in a cave.

THE VISION SHIMMERED. A convoy of strange armoured vehicles moved across the Wastes. Wagons encased in steel, powered by muscles of the dwarfs within them.

*Some sort of expedition, brother, to find the city of Karag Dum.*

*Doomed, of course*, came the reply.

Arek saw the wagons being destroyed one by one, and their crews turning back, until one alone continued onwards. Eventually even that steel wagon was attacked and crippled by beastmen, and from it emerged three dwarfs: one an ancient with his long beard braided into two forks, one a huge brutish and very dim-looking warrior, the third a dwarf of stern visage.

*Gotrek Gurnisson*, he heard Kelmain whisper.

*Yes, brother*, came the reply.

All three were armed and armoured with potent weapons, and shielded by runic talismans. They fought their way clear of their destroyed wagon and began the long trudge back towards their so-called civilisation.

A storm sprang up, dust clouds rising from the Wastes. The three were separated. The one named Gotrek took shelter in the cave, until the huge mutant beastman within discovered him. Chased deep into the caves, he found the body of the young prince and the axe. He picked it up, and a link was forged between him and the weapon. Armed with its ancient might, he slew the beastman, and rejoined his two companions.

ANOTHER TRANSITION. Mountains. Blue skies. A long valley. The dwarf known as Gotrek was there. He was larger, more muscular and somehow grimmer.

*The axe changes its wielder, brother. See, how he has grown.*

The Slayer entered the valley; he looked happy to be there. In the valley, a burned village and many dead dwarfs. The dwarf entered one stone house. Within was sprawled the wretched body of a dwarf woman and her small baby.

The dwarf bowed his head. Perhaps he wept.

A FURTHER CHANGE. The hall of a dwarf lord. Gotrek Gurnisson was there once more, arguing passionately with a long-bearded noble on a throne. There was a sneer on the noble's lips. He spoke mockingly, it seemed, and then made a chopping gesture with his hand, perhaps forbidding Gotrek to do whatever it was he wished to do, perhaps even ordering his death.

The other dwarf shook his head and grinned darkly. The lord ordered his troops to seize the axe-bearer. It is a mistake. A vast brawl began. Soon everyone in the hall save Gotrek was dead or fled. Dwarf corpses were lying everywhere.

The dwarf took up a knife and hacked away at his hair. Soon his head was shaved bare, save for a small rough strip. He strode out into the world, to do whatever it was he had to do.

A VAST HUMAN city. Perhaps Altdorf, the Imperial capital.

A tavern. A tall blond-haired man, clearly drunk, was sitting down at the table with the dwarf who was obviously as drunk as he. The dwarf was older now. His hair was a huge crest, dyed orange. Tattoos covered his shaven head. He was scarred and there was a cynical twist to his mouth. The tall man was obviously distressed by something. They talked. And as they spoke the human became more and more excited. They drank more. The dwarf took up a knife and the unlikely pair swore some sort of blood-brothership oath.

* * *

SCENES CAME NOW in quick succession. Crypts beneath the Imperial city. A magician performed a ritual of cosmic evil only to be interrupted by the pair. A small village in the wilds, terrorised by a winged daemon until the two of them ended its reign of terror. A forest at night; Morrslieb grinned down. The two did battle with mutants and cultists, eventually rescuing a small child from their clutches. A wagon train headed south, fighting goblins and undead monsters as it went. The pair were there always, fighting like devils. At the gate of a burning fort, the Slayer defeated a whole tribe of wolf riders, losing an eye in the process. Arek saw a ruined dwarf city and battles with monsters, and meetings with ghosts.

An accelerating succession of scenes blurred by. Encounters with mages and werewolves and wicked men. Buildings burned in another Imperial city as an army of ratmen stalked the streets. A massive airship crossed the Chaos Wastes and arrived at Karag Dum. The bloodthirster returned, only to be defeated once more by the pair of adventurers. They encountered a mighty dragon and slew it. They battled with an army of orcs and somehow survived.

As he watched, it became obvious to Arek that whatever else the pair are, they are heroes, and somehow it is their destiny to oppose Chaos. Or perhaps it is not their doom, but that of the axe. He cannot tell. It is something to discuss with his pet wizards.

SUDDENLY THE CASCADE of visions stopped. One further change charged the air. A deep sense of foreboding filled Arek. The scene went black and he was confronted for the briefest of instants by a gigantic face whose features appeared to shimmer and change, sometimes resembling a bird-headed daemon, sometimes resembling an incredibly beautiful man with eyes of glowing light. He knew at once that he was gazing on Lord Tzeentch. The being smiled mockingly at him, and a last scene appeared before his eyes.

Buildings burned. Horned warriors clashed with humans in the street. He saw himself lying on the ground, his armour breached and broken, his headless corpse sprawled in the snow. All around were the mangled bodies of beastmen and Chaos warriors. He saw himself locked in combat with the dwarf. Arek found himself enthralled waiting for the moment of his inevitable triumph.

The scene went blank to be replaced by another. He saw the axe flashing in to sever his head.

A third moment of vision appalled him: Gotrek Gurnisson and his human companion standing over his corpse, wounded but triumphant, Arek's severed head held in the man's hand. Arek stared in shock at the picture, and it began to fade. He stood stunned in the centre of the wizards' tent.

'Your visions have done nothing to reassure me,' he said eventually. Kelmain looked at Lhoigor. Once again Arek was uncomfortably aware that some sort of voiceless communication was taking place between them.

'Such visions are not always accurate,' Kelmain said eventually, stroking his pale temple with his golden nails.

'Sometimes malicious daemons interfere for their own purposes. They have a strange sense of humour, our elder brothers,' added Lhoigor.

'Did you see what I saw?' Arek asked.

'We saw one of the dwarf ancestor gods making the axe. We saw much of its history. We saw the siege of Karag Dum. We saw Gotrek Gurnisson receive the axe. We saw... your death.'

'How is that possible? I thought the Eye was supposed only to show the past.'

'The Eye is a peculiar artefact. It can only reveal certain things–' began Lhoigor.

'It normally shows only the past,' Kelmain interrupted. 'Or what people think is the past.'

'What do you mean?' asked Arek. Kelmain looked at Lhoigor. Arek knew they were trying to decide which of them would explain things to him.

'The realm of Chaos from which all magic eventually flows is another plane roughly contiguous with this one–' Lhoigor began.

'It is composed entirely of energy–' Kelmain interrupted again.

'Which can be drawn on by those who are gifted,' finished Lhoigor.

'So?' asked Arek.

'There are links between the two planes. Strong emotions, hopes, dreams, fears, all stir the seething sea of energy which is the true realm of Chaos,' Kelmain said.

'Events that create those strong emotions can leave an impression on the plane of Chaos. Battles, murders and such like. So can dreams and fears. These impressions float around like–'

'Like bubbles,' Lhoigor said. 'The Eye can draw those impressions to us, if invoked correctly. It takes an artefact of such power to sift through the swirling vortices of energy and select the ones the wielder wants.'

'You are saying though that what we saw is not necessarily true.'

'I believe most of it is true in the essentials. It may not be entirely accurate but it is accurate enough in most respects.'

'What about the final vision?'

'That might have been something you brought to the ritual yourself,' said Kelmain.

'A projection of your own hidden fears,' Lhoigor added mockingly.

'Or it might have been a warning sent by Lord Tzeentch, foretelling what will happen if you continue down this path.'

'It is difficult to know. Such visions are always cryptic.'

'So are your interpretations, it seems.'

'We are only humble servants of our esteemed Lord,' said Lhoigor. Arek was never sure whether he meant Tzeentch or himself when he spoke this way. He suspected the ambiguity was deliberate.

'You know this dwarf,' said Arek.

'We know of him,' Kelmain corrected. 'He has inadvertently foiled some of our schemes in the past.'

'We suspect he is, however unwittingly, a chosen champion of the enemies of our cause.'

'Certainly, he has been warped by that potent weapon he carries.'

'If the dwarf were dead that future can never happen,' Arek said. 'Without him to wield the axe, it cannot slay me.'

'Perhaps. Perhaps the axe will find another wielder.' Arek considered this for a moment then came to a decision. The dwarf would have to be eliminated, and that axe would need to vanish.

'You have agents in the city?'

'Many.'

'See to it the dwarf and his human henchman die. See that the axe is lost and not found again soon.'

'We shall do our best,' Kelmain said, his mocking smile widening.

'If the vision really came from Lord Tzeentch it would be blasphemy to try and interfere with the destiny he plans for you.'

'Nonetheless do it.'

'As you wish.'

# FOUR

ULRIKA GLANCED AROUND the chamber in disgust. It was not her surroundings that she found intolerable, it was the people in them, or most of them anyway. The chamber was far more austerely furnished than anything she would have expected from a decadent southern noble. There were none of the elaborate carvings and gargoyles that covered the walls of so many of the buildings in the city, only weapons and banners.

The duke himself cut a fine martial figure as he sat upright on the polished wooden throne. He was a handsome slender man in early middle age. He had black hair going to grey. On his face, the long drooping moustaches favoured by the southern aristocracy actually looked fine. They made him look like one of the wild riders of Gospodar legend. He had a disconcerting intensity to his stare but Ulrika could see nothing to give credence to the rumours that he was mad.

Some people claimed that Duke Enrik's tendency to see the worshippers of Chaos everywhere was a sign that he had inherited his father's insanity. To Ulrika his support of witch hunters and constant persecution of mutants seemed only sensible precautions against the Great Enemy. Perhaps it was true. Perhaps decadent Imperial customs were taking root even here in the great citadels of Kislev. She smiled ironically at her thoughts. She herself was no better. Hadn't she taken a decadent southerner for a lover? Hadn't she taken advice from Max Schreiber, a wizard, a man who only a few months ago she would have been willing to bet was a worshipper of Chaos himself? No, she was in no position to criticise these people. She knew that intellectually. It was not going to stop her from doing it though.

Beside the prince's throne was a large stove that radiated heat against the autumnal chill. A long bearded chamberlain carrying a heavy wooden staff stood to the left of the ducal throne. Slightly in front of the throne stood two armoured giants of the ducal guard, each armed with a halberd, and a head taller than any other man in the room. Ten strides ahead of the throne was a rope barrier behind which waited petitioners. They were a motley crew, wealthy merchants, lesser nobles and a few ragged-looking men of indeterminate profession. They might have been wizards, or priests or professional agitators for all Ulrika knew.

Looking around at the others in the chamber, she wondered how Enrik put up with it. The behaviour of these people was enough to drive the sanest man crazy. At the front of the room were a group of men from the merchant's guild protesting about the latest ducal command to freeze prices. It seemed that not even the presence of that vast Chaos horde outside the gates was to be allowed to interfere with a man's right to seek the best price his goods might command. The fact that exercising that right might lead to starvation for the majority of the people and food riots did not appear to concern them. Ulrika recognised the fat man from the watchtower among the merchants. He seemed to have gotten over his fears now, and was far more concerned that he was not being allowed to sell his grain for ten times the price it had commanded a month ago. Merchants, thought Ulrika, with the warrior-nobles' usual contempt for the rising middle class. They had no honour. Even with the city enmeshed in a life or death struggle they thought only of their own profits.

Duke Enrik seemed to share her opinion. 'It seems to me,' he said in his high-pitched voice, 'that keeping our men in the field and our population content and supportive of their duke is far more important at this moment than the profits of the guild.'

'But your grace–' the fat merchant began.

'And furthermore,' the duke continued as if the merchant had never spoken, 'it seems to me that the people who are most likely to think otherwise are Chaos worshippers and followers of the Dark Powers themselves.'

That shut the merchants up, Ulrika thought with some satisfaction. They could see the not-so-veiled threat as well as she.

The duke continued to speak in a slightly more reasonable tone of voice. 'And after all, Osrik, what do profits matter if the city falls? Gold is only useful to those who are alive to spend it. If those beasts break into our noble city I am sure they will spare no one no matter how wealthy... except perhaps a few Chaos worshippers.'

The duke's meaning was only too clear to the merchants now. Most were looking around shiftily, hoping only to make a graceful retreat from the chamber. The duke's remark about gold only being useful to the living was not lost on them. It applied just as much to those hung as traitors as to those slain by Chaos warriors.

'I am sure there are no Chaos worshippers here, brother,' said Villem suavely. He looked up at his brother, winked and then turned and gave the merchants a friendly smile. The iron hand and the velvet glove, Ulrika saw. In a way it was sad. By temperament, Enrik was far more suited to be a hatchetman, and his brother a conciliator. It might have been better for the popularity of the ruling house if the two men's positions had been reversed; that way the duke could have stood apart with his hands clean and been more popular. Still, it was not to be. Birth had made them what they were, and neither brother seemed uncomfortable with their roles, if roles they were. Perhaps the brothers were simply doing what came naturally. On the other hand, she had heard rumours about Villem too. He was something of a scholar, dabbled in alchemy and was said to read books brought all the way from the Empire. This would have made him a figure of suspicion to members of the old Kislevite aristocracy too.

The merchants nodded agreement. 'Is there anything else you want to discuss?' asked Enrik icily. The merchants shook their heads and were granted the ducal permission to withdraw. More petitioners approached the throne. Lesser nobles, by their garb, wanting the duke to settle some small dispute between them. Ulrika soon lost the point of the discussion and gave her attention to the audience chamber.

It was quite small, and the walls were covered in thick tapestries showing scenes from ancient battles. Depictions of the last Great War against Chaos were displayed prominently. There was Skathloc Ironclaw mounted on his mighty wyvern, Doomfang. There was Magnus the Pious, resplendent in his heavy plate mail, a halo of sanctity playing around his head, the great warhammer that was the mark of the Emperor held in one hand. There was the Tzar Alexander, a mortal god in his gilded armour. Beastmen leered from the thick woollen weaving. Noble knights and winged lancers rode to meet them. The Chaos moon glared balefully in the sky, looking larger than it had at any time in Ulrika's lifetime save the last few weeks.

Not for the first time, she wished she had taken advantage of her relationship with the ducal family. They were distant cousins related by marriage, and she might have presumed on that for a private audience, but she had not. Her native sense of fairness forbade it. Her business was important to her, but not important enough to anyone else to interfere with matters of state. She had resolved to use the public audience time for it. After all, all she really wanted to do was learn if there was any news of her father. There was only a slim chance the duke might know something. She shivered and tried to keep her worry under control. Her father would be all right. He had lived through war and famine and plague for nearly half a century. He would survive this. He was indestructible. At least, she hoped he was. He was all the real family she had left in this world.

The sound of the duke's voice being raised broke into her reverie. He had lost all patience with the nobles and was shouting at them as if they were naughty children in need of stern discipline. 'And if either of you dare come here, and waste my time again, I will see you are both flogged and denied a place in the battle lines. Is that clear enough for you?'

Ulrika was shocked. These men might be petty and mean-spirited but they were nobles. It was most unusual for anyone to speak to them like that. Like all Kislevite nobles they would be touchy and they would have their own private armies and assassins. Such open rudeness was usually cause for a duel. One of the nobles pointed this out.

'When this battle is over, Count Mikal, I will gladly give you satisfaction,' sneered the duke, in a tone that left no doubt whom he thought would be the victor in any duel. 'But right at this moment, in case you had not noticed, we have slightly more important things to concern us. Even more important than the question of which of you takes precedence in choosing their position on the outer wall. Still, if you wait long enough, those beastmen beyond the walls might make the question academic by lopping of your fool heads. That's if I don't have my guardsmen do it first. You may leave the ducal presence. Now!'

The anger in the duke's voice was quite unfeigned, and Ulrika had no doubt that Enrik meant what he said. Even so, she thought, he was being foolish. In the days to come he would need the willing support of both those men and their troops. Villem also saw this, for after a quiet word in his brother's ear, he hurried after the two to speak some concil-iatory words to them. The chamberlain studied his list, stamped his staff on the ground and commanded two more men to stride forward.

They were big men, garbed in well-used armour, with long cowled cloaks and wolf-head amulets at their throats. On each of their gaunt faces was a look of blazing fanaticism. Without being told, and even before they spoke, Ulrika knew what they were. Witch hunters.

'Your grace, there are depraved worshippers of the Dark Powers within the walls of Praag. We must make examples of them. Burning a few will set a good example for the citizens.'

'And of course you know exactly who needs burning, Ulgo?' The sneer was evident in the duke's voice. Ulrika was sur-prised; Enrik had a reputation for being sympathetic to witch hunters, and a harsh enemy of Chaos. It was one of the few things that made him popular with his people. She watched closely. Perhaps he simply did not like these two. It was the second witch hunter who replied, and his voice was smooth and sophisticated, not unlike Felix's, in fact.

'We have taken the liberty of preparing a list, your grace,' he said. The duke beckoned him forward, took the scroll from his outstretched hand, studied it for a moment and began to laugh.

'Your grace finds something amusing?' purred the man. There was a dangerous note in his voice. He was not someone used to being mocked.

'Only you, Petr, could find half the hierarchy of the temple of Ulric to be heretics.'

'Your grace, they do not prosecute the search for the dupes of Darkness with anything like sufficient zeal. Any priest of Ulric who behaves this way must be a traitor to the cause of humanity, and therefore a heretic.'

'I am sure the Archprelate would disagree with your assessment, Petr. Which may be why he expelled you from the priesthood.'

'My expulsion was the work of hidden heretics, your grace, who feared exposure to the shining light of truth, and who knew they must see me disgraced or be revealed as the foul spawn of daemons that they are. They–'

'Enough, Petr!' the duke said quietly but threateningly. 'We are at war now, and I will explain this only once. I summoned you here to tell you something – not to listen to your ranting. So listen carefully, and listen well.

'There will be no further persecution of those you deem heretics by you or your men… unless I command it! There will be no exhorting the populace to burn the homes of those you deem to be lacking in zeal… unless I give you permission! You and your private army of zealots will be useful in the coming fight, but I will not tolerate you taking the law into your own hands. If you disobey me on this I will have your head on a spike before you have time to speak. Do you understand me?'

'But your grace–'

'I said: do you understand me?' The duke's voice was cold and deadly.

Ulrika looked on, unsure of whether she approved or not. It was good that Enrik was taking a firm hand with any unruly elements of the population, particularly troublemakers like Ulgo and Petr appeared to be. Still these were powerful men, and their cause was just, and he should not have offended them by taking this high-handed tone. She began to understand why Enrik was not as popular as his brother.

'Yes, your grace,' said Petr. His tone was dangerously close to disrespectful. Ulrika began to suspect that the duke's intervention here might be counter-productive. It was not unknown for witch hunters and their minions to go about their business masked.

'You may go then,' said the duke.

Ulrika was paying such close attention to the way the witch hunters departed that she almost missed her own name. Hastily she strode forward and made her obeisances.

'Cousin,' the duke said. 'What can I do for you?'

'I wish to know if there has been any word of my father, your grace.'

'I regret to inform you there has been none. If any message is received I will have you informed at once. My chamberlain knows where to find you, I trust?'

'Yes, your grace.'

'Good. Then you may go.'

Ulrika flushed. Even by the standards of Kislevite nobility, this was a peremptory dismissal. She turned to leave. Anger ate her. When she felt a hand on her shoulder, she whirled, almost ready to do violence. She halted when she saw Villem smiling at her.

'You must forgive the duke,' he said. 'He is not a patient man, and there have been many things to vex him recently. These are not easy times, for any of us.'

'He is the ruler here. This is war. There is nothing to forgive.'

'I am sure Enrik would agree with you, but still it is never good to forget the courtesies, particularly not when dealing with blood relatives. I am sorry we have not heard from your father. Still, there is always hope. Messenger pigeons go astray, and couriers have been known to go missing or get themselves killed. I would not despair. Looking at that horde

out there, I doubt any messengers could have got through
from the north in quite some time.'

Sensing the concern in Villem's voice, Ulrika started to
thaw a little. She already felt a bit better. 'Thank you,' she said,
and meant it.

'Please, think nothing of it. It is a pleasure to be of service.
Don't worry – we will pull through this. I understand you
arrived with the dwarf Slayer and his companions, the wizard
and the swordsman. Fascinating people and very heroic, I am
sure. I would like you all to have dinner with me some
evening here at the palace. I would like the opportunity to
talk about that wonderful flying ship and get to know so fair
a cousin better.'

Ulrika tried to picture Gotrek at table with this urbane man
and could not. Felix and Max were a different matter however.
'I would like that,' she said.

'I will see that an invitation is dispatched. Till then…'

GREY SEER THANQUOL glared into his scrying crystal. He was
feeling the strain. All around the elders of Moulder looked at
him as if he were something good to eat. He forced himself
to ignore this distraction and concentrate on working his sorcery. He let his mind descend into the trance he had first
learned when barely out of runthood, and just beginning his
apprenticeship as a grey seer. He let his spirit float free and
gather the energies of dark magic and then he shunted them
into the crystal.

As he did so, his point of view shifted. It was as if the crystal had been transformed into the eye of a watching god, an
analogy that gave Thanquol a warm feeling in the base of his
stomach. He saw his own body from above. He saw the grey-
furred oddly mutated Moulder elders glaring at him, and he
saw Izak Grottle looking on hungrily from the chamber's
edge. Grottle ran a long pink tongue over his yellowing fangs,
and then began to gnaw his tail. It was a gesture that made
Thanquol fear for his own safety. Still, there was nothing for
it, he had volunteered for this. Helping the Moulders put
down Lurk's rebellion was the quickest and surest way of getting himself back into their good books, and the sooner he
did that, the sooner he would be out of this death-trap. Hell

Pit was the last place he wanted to be with that huge Chaos army on the march.

Even as the thought entered his mind, he cursed. The merest notion of the army instantly conjured a vivid image of it in his mind, and in his hyper-sensitised state this was enough to send the crystal vision racing outwards. The crater of Hell Pit was suddenly below him, monstrously fleshy buildings looming over the site of the ancient starfall. The streets filled with fighting skaven as Lurk's followers warred with troops still loyal to Clan Moulder. Just for a heartbeat he had a glimpse of the brutal conflict and then his mind's eye swung to bear on the huge dustcloud in the distance.

In an instant he was there, looking down on it. He saw rank upon serried rank of beastmen, a howling mass of fur-clad and near bestial humans, hundreds upon hundreds of black-armoured Chaos warriors mounted on their huge and deadly steeds. Beneath him marched monstrous creatures half gigantic humanoid, half dragon. Alongside them strolled mutated trolls. Flocks of bat-winged humanoids darkened the sky. It was a vast host and the worst thing about it was the fact that Thanquol knew that it was only part of the huge Chaos armies that were on the march. Something had certainly gotten the worshippers of the lesser powers worked up, and Thanquol had no great desire to find out what. Looking at this army through his scrying crystal was as close as he ever cared to get to it.

He growled, and forced himself to discipline. This was all very well, but it was nothing to do with his mission. He needed to know what Lurk was planning. He needed to find out some way to give the Moulders an advantage in the civil war that was tearing their fortified city apart before the oncoming horde managed to find a way to take advantage of the strife. He concentrated on Lurk. Immediately he had a sense of his treacherous former minion's presence. The jewel Thanquol had forced upon Lurk long ago still served its function of linking them.

With the speed of thought, his point of view shifted. He was now in a vast chamber, looking down on a seething mass of determined and desperate-looking skaven. Most of them were not large. They were slaves, the lowest of the low in the hierarchy of skavendom, ratmen too weak and too stupid to claw their way to power like their betters. Their only strength lay in their numbers. Unfortunately those were great. Here and there throughout the crowd though were larger and better armed skaven. Thanquol did his best to quiet the rage that seethed within him. It was the skaven way. There were always those who changed sides whenever expediency dictated, aligning themselves with those they thought would come out on the winning side of any struggle. What alarmed Thanquol most was how many Moulders seemed to think this. There were even huge black-furred stormvermin in this crowd, and many warriors in the livery of the clan. Suddenly Thanquol understood why he was being given this chance to work his way back into favour with the elders. Somehow, impossible as it might seem, Lurk had managed to stage quite a successful little rebellion. More and more loyalist troops were swarming to his banner, and if the process continued their numbers would tip the balance of power in Lurk's favour.

Briefly Grey Seer Thanquol paused to consider this. If so many were siding with his former minion, perhaps he should too. Or rather he should consider siding with those who were behind Lurk, for surely Lurk himself did not have the intelligence to be running the show. Somewhere out there a keen intelligence was masterminding this. Perhaps with suitable guidance from an experienced skaven like Thanquol, it could establish a new power base for itself and its loyal advisors here in Hell Pit.

Lurk stood on a high podium looking down on the masses. He was even bigger than Thanquol remembered. Now he was larger than a rat ogre by far, almost twice as tall as Felix Jaeger was, and far heavier. His long worm-like tail ended in a massive spiked club of bone. His eyes gleamed with red madness. Most frightening of all were the curling horns, so like Thanquol's own, that protruded from the side of Lurk's skull. It was true, he did bear an uncanny likeness to all the effigies of the Horned Rat that Thanquol had ever seen. Indeed he bore an uncanny likeness to the Horned Rat with whom Thanquol had communed in his initiation rituals. Could it be possible? Could the Rat God himself really have chosen Lurk as his emissary? Thanquol immediately dismissed the thought.

*Impossible.*

Lurk had begun to speak. 'Oppressed skaven-brothers! Children of the Horned Rat! The hour of liberation is at hand. The time of changes is here.'

The time of changes? That was a familiar phrase. Thanquol wondered where he had heard it before.

'The world is changing. The lowest shall become highest. The high shall be laid low. Thus my father, the Horned Rat has promised me.'

Thanquol's heart almost stopped with outrage. His father? How dare that pitiful mutated excuse for a skaven make such blasphemous claims? The depths of his own feelings in this matter astonished Thanquol. Lurk was claiming a kinship to the greatest of gods even closer than that enjoyed by the grey seers. He was taking upon himself the mantle of a religious leader. Thanquol was surprised that the Horned Rat did not strike him down on the spot. Unless... *No.* It was impossible. There was no way that what Lurk claimed could be true.

'Those of you who follow me will be rewarded big-big! Those who do not, or those who betray me, will be punished in ways that you cannot imagine. Except if you think about being peeled alive, over a very big, warpstone-fuelled bonfire while two clanrat torturers poke your musk glands with a red hot branding iron and then...'

Lurk went on to describe a range of tortures that were impressively imaginative and quite excruciating. Even at this distance Thanquol felt his musk glands tighten as he listened to the descriptions.

'...up your back passage!' finished Lurk.

Stunned silence ensued. Thanquol had to admit that Lurk appeared to have learned something from their long association. His oratory was certainly impressive, and succeeded in that most cherished of all skaven goals: inspiring fear in his minions.

'Now, listen-listen!' continued Lurk. 'To succeed in our great crusade we must first take Hell Pit. To take Hell Pit we must seize control of the breeding vats and the council chambers as well as the warpstone refinery. To do this we will split our force into three.'

As Thanquol listened, Lurk outlined his plan. It was one of great boldness. It relied on speed, surprise and feints within feints. Thanquol knew he could barely have conceived of a better one himself, and that it would almost certainly succeed if Thanquol did not release its details to the elders of Moulder.

*If.*

Thanquol's keen skaven mind considered his options. He knew there must be some way he could personally take advantage of the situation. Even as he did so, part of him wondered how or if his brutishly stupid minion could have come up with such a scheme. Surely so intricate and subtle a plan could not be Lurk's own work? It could only be the work of an intellect almost as towering as Thanquol's own. Thanquol began to consider how he could unearth the mastermind behind his minion.

Some vast treachery must be involved, he was certain. Who among his enemies was devious enough to subvert such a closely observed lackey as Lurk?

LURK LOOKED OUT at his followers and bathed in their adoration. It was only his due, he knew. Long years of hiding his light under a bushel, of failing to get the recognition that was rightfully his, were finally being made up for, and the taste was sweet. Lurk smiled, revealing his fangs and revelled in the cringing awe the gesture evoked. Surely this must be how his former so-called master, Grey Seer Thanquol, must have felt when he stood before the skaven army at Nuln. This was the feeling that in his secret heart every skaven craved.

Lurk filed the thought away for later consideration. He knew that with every day that passed he was becoming cleverer and cleverer. To his vastly powerful brain, it was obvious what was happening. As soon as his body had stopped mutating, his mind had started to. The process that had changed him from a small, but not unimpressive, skaven warrior, to a towering engine of destruction, was now starting to reshape his mind, changing him from an incredibly clever skaven to a being of god-like intellect.

To Lurk's new greatly enhanced mind, this was a significant fact. His mind was being changed in the same way his body had been into a mirror-image of the Great Father of All Skavendom's. And Lurk knew that this had happened for a reason. He knew it had happened because he was the chosen one, the one destined to be the new supreme leader of the skaven race, the being destined to lead them to a thousand-year reign of glory.

It was all so clear when you looked at it. It was obvious that the Horned Rat had chosen him for a reason. He knew that he was the Horned Rat's anointed, his new prophet, the leader that all the skaven had been waiting for to unite them, and lead them to inevitable victory.

Of course, the visions helped. He had started having them back in the camp of the Chaos horde after he had spoken with those two strangely similar-looking human mages who had almost immediately recognised his near divinity. He remembered with something like fondness the way they had bowed before him in secret and then began chanting his praises in those almost hypnotic voices. He remembered how they had spoken to him respectfully, prevailing on him to continue to play the part of prisoner so that he could gain admittance to the citadels of his enemies and raise his own banner among them. They had told him that his mind was becoming stronger than any skaven's just as his body has already become so. Soon, he thought, he would gain sorcerous powers greater than any grey seer's, and then he would be the mightiest skaven who ever bestrode the face of this terrified world.

Even the foolish Moulders had recognised his uniqueness, his superiority. Had they not tried to imprison him within their vile alchemical laboratories? Had they not sought to learn the secrets of that which separated him from all other skaven?

He supposed he should thank them really. They had bathed him in those strange nutrient fluids and exposed him to ever greater amounts of warpstone dust. He could still remember how his flesh had tingled and his mind had gone blank. It was possible, but not really likely, that he had perhaps babbled and begged for mercy as they did so. He knew now that if he had, and he was not admitting to it, that it was merely a sign that his brainpower was increasing. Even then, he had known enough to deceive his enemies about his true nature and schemes, and lull them into a false sense of security, so that when the moment had come for him to effect his escape, he had been able to take his persecutors off-guard.

It was fortunate indeed that he had found the city already a seething cauldron of rebellion. Many of the skavenslaves believed that the increased size of the Chaos moon, Morrslieb, was a sign that something was about to happen. They believed the increasing number of warpstone meteors falling to earth in the region were a portent of mighty events to come. It had not taken much for him to convince them that he was the thing they portended, that his arrival was the event long foretold. They had swiftly flocked to his banner against the oppression of their Moulder masters. It was almost as if they had been forewarned, as if secret cabals had been preparing for just such an event for weeks. And why not, Lurk thought? He was the chosen of the Horned Rat; certainly there were those who must have been given foreknowledge of his coming.

At first he had been surprised that the grey seers had not prophesied his arrival, but his incredibly keen mind had soon provided him with the insight needed to understand what had happened. Contemplation of the nature of his former so-called master, Grey Seer Thanquol, had shown him the hideous truth. The grey seers were corrupt, they had failed the Horned Rat, and he had withdrawn his favour. They were no longer the true guardians of the skaven race. A new day had dawned, a new leader had emerged, one whose glorious reign would last a thousand years, at least. Today was the day of Lurk, once known as Snitchtongue, now known simply as Lurk the Magnificent.

Instantly he communicated this knowledge to the cabal of grovelling followers who surrounded him. Their worshipful squeaks of obeisance were music to his ears.

Today, Hell Pit, he thought – *tomorrow the world!*

# FIVE

FELIX LOOKED DOWN at the oncoming Chaos horde. It had grown no less terrifying in the last few days. It seemed to stretch as far as the horizon in every direction, and clouds of dust in the distance told of more and more troops arriving every day.

He raised the spyglass to his eye and studied the lines of the Chaos army. Their position was a strong one. Most of their camp was protected from attack by the curve of the river. Hordes of skin-clad barbarians worked frantically, erecting earthworks and excavating trenches facing the city. He could see lines of sharpened stakes jutting from the base of the earthen walls. The Chaos worshippers were taking no chances with the riders of Kislev sallying forth from Praag to engage them.

Over the past few days, hit and run raids by Kislevite horsemen had taken quite a toll on the attackers. A toll that was a mere drop in the ocean of their numbers but one that had been good for the morale of the defenders. Knowing many in the city shared the despair he felt at the sight of this massive force, Felix decided that those small victories were as important as food to the defenders.

What was worse was that, as the numbers of besiegers increased, the portents and omens had got worse. Apparitions were sighted nightly stalking the streets of the city. Last night in the White Boar, Felix had heard two drunken Tilean mercenaries describe how they had encountered the ghost of a headless woman in the street near their lodgings. Most outlanders had tried to dismiss it as a product of the cheap rotgut brandy the Tileans had been drinking, but the locals had merely nodded sagely and sadly and returned to their drinks. He supposed that a lifetime of familiarity with such apparitions might have helped inure the locals to their horror, but he knew he could never rest easy in a city where such things were relatively commonplace.

He wondered if the increasing number of apparitions had anything to do with the presence of the army outside the walls.

'It might,' said the familiar voice of Max Schreiber. Felix was surprised to realise he had spoken aloud. He was equally surprised to see Max here.

'Max! What are you doing on the walls?'

'Same thing as you, Felix. Looking at that army out there and wondering how we will survive this siege.'

Felix glanced around and was glad the nearest soldiers were five strides away. They might not have heard. Expressing such defeatist sentiments was not a popular thing to be heard doing in Praag these days. Felix shrugged. Max was the man doing the talking, not him.

'You think these reports of apparitions in the streets are connected with that army out there?'

'I am certain of it.' A number of soldiers were looking on now. The conversation had all of their attention.

'How? I thought I heard you say that the spell walls around the city are strong, and the power of Chaos cannot penetrate them.'

Max drew his gold and brown wizard's robes tight around him. Today he had donned a strange pointed helmet-like hat, which towered over his head and made him look taller. The stubble on his face was beginning to look suspiciously like a beard. He leaned his full weight upon his staff, gazed thoughtfully out at the horde for a moment, and then spoke.

'I said there was a connection. I did not say that those Dark worshippers out there were responsible.'

Felix looked at the wizard. Max was a friend, in his way, but he was still a magician, and they were sometimes inscrutable to mere mortals like him. 'What do you mean?'

'I mean all of this is connected. The massive skaven attack on Nuln. The way Morrslieb has grown larger over the past years. The way the forces of Chaos are on the march. The increasing number of starfalls, mutations and magical mishaps. The way the ghosts are stirring in this city. It's all part of the same thing.'

'Are you saying the Powers of Chaos are behind all of these things, Max? You don't have to be a great sorcerer to work that out.'

'No, Felix. I mean that there's a huge pattern here. It may be that there is some monstrous intelligence at work or it may be something different, something more akin to a natural phenomenon.'

'I am not sure natural is the word I would choose to use under the circumstances.'

'I mean something like the tides of the sea, or the turning of the seasons.'

'I don't get you.'

'Think of it this way, Felix. Magic is a force, like the wind or the rain or the tides. Sometimes it is strong. Sometimes it is weaker, but it is always there, just like the air we breathe. It permeates the world in which we live. Wizards call the flow of this energy the winds of magic.'

'Yes. So?'

'Perhaps there are seasons of magic like there are seasons of weather. Perhaps we are entering a season when the winds of magic blow stronger, and the power of magic increases. Perhaps that is what happened two hundred years ago.'

'That's a long season.'

'Don't be deliberately obtuse, Felix. You are a clever man. I know you understand an analogy when you hear one.'

Felix flinched at Max's tone. He knew that the wizard was right. Perhaps his jealousy over Ulrika was making him want to pick an argument with the mage. 'Fine. Go on,' Felix said, a little sulkily.

'The forces of Chaos are strongly associated with magic – perhaps their power waxes and wanes with these seasons. Perhaps this is the start of a time when they are stronger. And perhaps this same increase in energy is increasing the number of apparitions in Praag, and driving the skaven wild too.'

Felix considered the mage's argument, turning it over in his mind. It was logical and it made a certain sense from whatever angle he looked at it, but that meant nothing. In the courtyards of Altdorf university Felix had heard learned scholars prove the most blatantly ludicrous theories through the rigorous application of logic. 'It's an interesting theory, Max, but I've heard other theories. There was a man outside the White Boar this morning shouting that this was the punishment of the gods for our sins, and that the end of the world was coming.'

Max smiled a little nastily. 'These two theories are not necessarily mutually exclusive,' he said. 'What happened to this prophet?'

'The town watch hit him over the head with clubs and dragged him away.'

'My theory may not be quite so dangerous to your health in these times.'

'It has that to recommend it, certainly,' said Felix, turning his attention back to the Chaos horde. There seemed to be some sort of activity around the monstrous black pavilion that had been erected in the centre of the army.

FROM THE HILLTOP, Ivan Petrovitch Straghov watched the horde of Chaos marauders march along the plain. March was the wrong word. It suggested a discipline that these wild tribesmen simply did not possess. Not that it mattered. They had the numbers, and they had their unshakeable faith in their dark gods. His long years as march boyar had given Ivan plenty of experience of their sort. These ones marched along under the banner of the Skinless Man.

'There must be a thousand of them at least, Lord Ivan,' muttered Petrov. Ivan turned and looked at his youngest lancer. The boy was barely more than fifteen but his eyes were those of a much older man. Dark shadows had gathered below them, and his face was creased by fatigue, too much riding and too little food.

'Careful, lad. Remember a retreating man counts every foe twice. Let's not make things out to be worse than they are.' Ivan kept his voice cheerful and confident but he did not feel that way himself. It was possible that the boy's estimate was a good one. It looked like the Wastes had disgorged their entire tainted population. For two days now Ivan and his men had been encountering their scouts, big fur-clad men who spoke a harsh tongue, their skins stained by the stigmata of early mutation or strange Chaos rune tattoos. It was not good to find so many of them so far south. They were not even part of the great Chaos army, Ivan guessed, just tribes-men driven by some dark inner urge to come south and plunder. Not that it mattered. There were enough to tell him something big was happening. In the past few days, he had encountered warriors bearing the tattoos of Scar Raiders, Ice Marauders and Blood Screamers. It looked like every tribe in the Wastes was heading south.

His riders took up position along the brow of the ridge. They were making themselves plainly visible, hoping to taunt the marauders into coming at them. In the centre of the barbarian mass, a white-haired ancient carrying a skull-tipped staff that marked him as a shaman exhorted the tribesmen to attack. Ivan waited confidently. While the Chaos worshippers wasted time ploughing up the slope, they would be subjected to a rain of arrows, and a host of flank attacks by the reserves Ivan had kept out of sight behind the hill. The tribesmen would most likely fall for it. Many of them would die. It was a small con-solation to him, but it was one, knowing that he was making them pay in blood for every pace they marched into Kislev.

At that moment, the thunder of hooves behind them got Ivan's attention. He turned to see two of his men escorting a blue-cloaked rider up the hill. Ivan smiled, recognising the tall white-haired man at once. It was Radek Lazlo, one of the Ice Queen's couriers.

'Well met, Radek!' Ivan bellowed. 'You're just in time to see me and the lads kill some more Chaos scum.'

'Much as I would enjoy that,' said Radek, a cold smile twist-ing his thin lips, 'I don't have time. Neither do you. The Ice

Queen commands your presence at Mikal's Ford. The Gospodar Host is mustering there.'

Ivan considered the courier's words. Mikal's Ford was a week's hard riding away but it was much closer than the Host would be if it had not received some warning of the impending invasion. That must mean that Ulrika had got through!

'We will ride. What of you? Will you accompany us?'

'No. I must keep moving through these lands bringing the word to any other march lords who I can find.'

Ivan shook his head wonderingly. Radek had been given a near suicidal task, riding alone through these over-run lands. 'I can detail a lance of my lads to accompany you,' he offered.

'No. The tzarina needs ever spear at the Ford. I tell you, Ivan, in all my years I have never seen anything like this.'

'It gets worse,' Ivan said. 'We have come from the north. I swear it seems like the very gates of Hell have been opened. It will be the Great War all over again before we are done, mark my words.'

'You're not reassuring me, old friend,' Radek said, casting his eye on the tribesmen advancing towards the hill. He could gauge the distance as well as any of Ivan's men, and knew they still had some time left for their discussions.

'Any word of my daughter?'

'I saw her briefly at court. It was she who gave the Ice Queen word of the invasion. She arrived on that great flying ship of the dwarfs.'

Parental pride touched Ivan's heart. 'She rides with the Host then?'

Radek shook her head. 'No, lord. She accompanied the dwarfs to Praag.'

'That's right in the path of the invasion. The Chaos worshippers always strike the great fortress there first.'

'Aye, old friend, it is. But your path lies south now, to Mikal's Ford and war. Do not worry. Doubtless the Ice Queen's first move will be to relieve the city.'

Briefly love and duty warred within Ivan and he considered riding directly to Praag. His only child would be in danger there. Yet he knew there was little he could do to aid her, and there was no way his small force of lancers could do anything but die, if it encountered the main strength of the Chaos horde at the city. It made more sense to join the muster and then ride with the full armed might of Kislev to the rescue of the capital. Part of him feared, though, that even that mighty army would not be enough to defeat what they now faced.

He sighed quietly to himself, then gave the command to his warriors. 'To Mikal's Ford. We ride!'

As one, with disciplined precision the lancers and horse archers turned and trotted down the hill. Behind them the disappointed howling of the wild tribesmen sounded like the cries of hungry wolves.

OUTSIDE NIGHT GATHERED, bringing with it the chill. The streets were filled with marching men and drilling troops. Down here, the cellar was dark and warm and quiet. A single lantern illuminated the cowled and cloaked figures meeting in secret to discuss the fate of the city. The man known to his four fellow conspirators as Halek looked around, knowing that if he were found here by the witch hunters, not even his exalted position would save him. Death by fire would be the most merciful fate he could expect.

He told himself that there was no chance of that happening. He was within the home of one of the wealthiest merchants in Praag, doubtless one of the other masked men sitting around the table. Or perhaps not, perhaps it was simply one of the man's servants. Only the High Priest of the Great Mutator, sitting at the head of the table, the man who had recruited them all, would know for certain.

Why am I here, he asked himself? How did it come to this? What started off as a search for knowledge had ended up with him sitting here surrounded by the enemies of Man. He took a deep breath and reminded himself that he was one of those enemies now. There were no excuses for what he had become, not here in Praag, probably not anywhere. He tried to reassure himself. At least he had picked the winning side.

It was obvious to any with eyes to see that there could only be one victor in the coming battle. The Powers of Chaos would prove too strong for Praag, just as they would prove too strong for the world. They were destined to inherit the earth. Chaos was like death or time; in the end it would always triumph, eroding its foes over the long years.

As the High Priest droned on with the opening invocations, Halek forced himself to control his thoughts. Such thinking was dangerous, close to madness. He was enough of a scholar to know that there had been setbacks, sometimes on the heels of great triumphs. It might not matter to the four Great Powers whether victory came now, or in several centuries, but it would matter to him. The penalty for failure now was death, or worse than death, since his masters were not kind to the souls of those who failed them. It was all very well convincing yourself of the inevitable victory of Chaos, but it was all rather pointless if you were not around to enjoy the fruits of that victory. He smiled behind his simple cloth mask. It helped to keep things in perspective.

Here in Praag just two centuries ago, mere weeks after the city had fallen, the forces of the so-called Ruinous Powers had been thrown back into the Wastes by the forces of Magnus the Pious. How his fellow Kislevites liked to boast about that. How truly characteristic of them, and how truly stupid. They could not take the long view, as he could. They could not see that it did not matter whether Chaos was thrown back once, or a hundred times. It always returned, and returned stronger. He knew that it was in part despair at this knowledge that had eventually made him decide to throw in his lot with Chaos. That and the fact that he had already gotten in too deep to get safely out. By the time he had realised that the society he had joined was not simply another secret fellowship devoted to the pursuit of alchemical and mystical knowledge, it had been too late. He knew his fellow cultists would kill him rather than let him go free. And there was nothing he could do to them without exposing himself to the world for what he was. It would have made no difference what he did. They were already too strong to be defeated. No, the best thing he could do was what he had done, stick with the cult of the Changer of Ways, and do his best to rise within it.

What heart would not leap at the prospect of sharing the spoils of that triumph? All his life, Halek, close to the seat of power but not on it, had coveted power. And temporal power was the least of what the Lord Tzeentch offered. The promises included so much more: life eternal, and not in some dull fairytale hereafter, but here and now in this sweet mortal realm. Power over the forces of magic. The ability to fulfil any and all of your desires, no matter how dark or depraved society deemed them to be.

Not that Halek was one of those weaklings drawn by that promise. He desired to serve the Lord Tzeentch for the simple reason that the god would reward him with knowledge and satisfy his curiosity about all things. And allow him to live through the coming end of the world as he knew it, he added sourly. All he had to do was betray those who loved and trusted him. He tried to control his bitterness. Those people would not love or trust him for one heartbeat if they knew he was here, or knew of the stigma of mutation that had started to appear on his body. There was no way he could conceal them for much longer. This invasion had come at the right time for him. Another few months and he would have had to flee the city anyway.

The prayers and invocations that would seal the chamber against prying sorcery ended, and the true business of the meeting proceeded. Halek looked at the other four men around the table, all swathed in their bulky robes, and listened to what they had to say.

'The Time of Changes approaches, brothers,' said the one known as Alrik, their leader. He had a coarse accent like a common merchant, but Halek knew that he was anything but a brutish commoner. His wits were keen, his intellect swift. If Halek had to guess, he would have said that Alrik was a man who the world had refused to acknowledge, who after what he would have called the accident of his lowly birth had found in Lord Tzeentch the way to advance himself.

'Are all things in readiness?' asked the one called Karl. Halek recognised the accents of the nobility there. Karl was of the same class as himself. He had often grumbled within hearing of the others about injustices done to him by the damn duke, and how he would make him pay. Karl was in this for vengeance. It was a simple understandable motive. Halek thought if Karl ever moved directly against the duke, he would kill him. He was not sure whether this was because he wanted to spare the duke or kill him himself. His relationship with the ruler had always been a complex one.

'You would know as well as I, brothers,' said Alrik. 'If all your cells have done their work, we are ready.'

Each of the men here was in charge of his own cell of cultists, whose members were known only to him. It meant that, in the unlikely event of any of them falling into the clutches of witch hunters, they could only betray those people they knew from their own cells. It was ingenious, but then such was the way of Lord Tzeentch. Khorne, the Blood God, might rely on brute strength but the followers of the Changer of the Ways preferred to use their intelligence. All of them knew that one well-placed conspirator could be more dangerous than a hundred men with swords.

'Mine certainly have,' lisped the man called Victor. His accent was that of an outlander, Bretonnian perhaps. Or it might just be a cunning ruse, designed to keep anyone here from suspecting his true identity. Halek had known Victor long enough to understand how his devious mind worked. Victor was one of those who liked convoluted things for the sake of convolution. He liked to plot and scheme just for the sake of it. He was a natural follower of the Prince of Schemers.

'Halek?' the high priest asked.

'The poison is ready. It can be distributed any night.'

'Are you sure it is necessary for us to go over this?' Damien said suspiciously. 'It is surely for the best if all of us know only what we need to know.'

'The Great Day approaches,' Alrik said. 'We cannot afford any of our people to be at cross-purposes.'

Halek smiled behind his mask. He understood what Alrik meant. It was not uncommon for their various groups to interfere in each other's plots. Sometimes it was accidental. Sometimes it was not. He knew each of the men present spent as much time trying to keep tabs on the others as they did on Lord Tzeentch's business. It was one of the hazards of what they did. All were rivals for their lord's favour, just as much as they were enemies of society at large.

'Must we bicker like this always,' Halek said. 'We all serve Lord Tzeentch. We are all trustworthy here.' He was sure Alrik caught the irony in his voice. He was not so sure about the others.

'Some of us are more diligent in our lord's service than others, and more careful,' Damien said nastily.

'It could have happened to anybody,' said Karl defensively, taking Damien's remark personally. He was a fool, he should have just ignored the bait. Men like Damien thrived on any revealed weakness. 'Even the clumsiest of witch hunters gets lucky sometimes.'

'It's funny how they always get lucky with members of your cell,' said Damien. 'We were lucky that we managed to silence our sister before she could speak. Perhaps next time our lord will not be so kind to us.'

Halek had ensured that Katrin had been silenced. He had not known that she was part of Karl's cell, it had been simple caution that made him ensure that one brought to the duke's dungeons who might really be a sister was silenced. Silence filled the chamber for a moment.

'I have received word from outside of a task that needs to be carried out,' Alrik said. All of them glanced at him with renewed interest. They knew what was meant by 'outside'. The high priest had been in communication with the leader of the army out there. Halek would have given a lot to know how that communication had been achieved. Not by magic, he was sure, he had heard often enough that the spell walls of Praag were unbreachable, and he believed it to be true. Perhaps messengers came and went by secret ways, or by pigeon or bat, or perhaps those outside communicated through dreams. Halek dismissed this idle speculation, and listened to what Alrik had to say.

'There are present in this city two warriors who have interfered in our lord's plans before, albeit unknowingly. He would ensure that this does not happen again, and he would be certain that their previous interference is rewarded with death.'

Halek had a feeling he knew who was going to be mentioned, and he was not disappointed.

'This pair, a dwarf and a man, are deadly foes, and they bear weapons of considerable power. More than that, they seem blessed by the other Powers, who are ranged against our master. He will reward any who slays them, and he will doubly reward any who present those weapons to him. Their names are Gotrek Gurnisson and Felix Jaeger. It is your appointed task to see that they do not live out this week. Halek, I would like you to see to this personally, but should the opportunity arise to kill these men, any of you must take it.'

Halek pushed away his qualms. He had never much cared for murder but needs must when daemons drive. In a way, it was a pity. He had liked young Jaeger when he had met him but he was not going to allow that fact to stand in the way of his personal immortality. What could the pair possibly have done to arouse the enmity of their lord, he wondered?

The meeting degenerated, into petty political squabbles and discussions of logistics. Halek could not wait for it to end.

AREK LEANED FORWARD on his huge throne, his massive helmeted head rested on one iron gauntleted fist, which in turn rested on the arm of the throne. He was not in a good mood. The vision his mages had granted him, combined with his impatience for the siege to begin, had not put him in the best of tempers. He glared balefully down at the Champion of Nurgle, hating the man with a bitter passion. He had never cared for the festering followers of the Lord of Pestilence.

'I tell you, great Warlord, it will work, or my name is not Bubar Stinkbreath. The magic of great Nurgle will give you certain victory.' The man, if you could still apply that word to a human form that was a walking pestilence of buboes, sounded far too pleased with himself for Arek's liking.

'Our victory is already certain,' Arek said. 'That pitiful city cannot resist the might of my horde!'

'Meaning no disrespect, great Warlord, but why throw away troops assaulting those huge walls when Nurgle's way is so much easier and faster. Why not let plague slay your enemies and pestilence reduce their defence to nothing?'

Discontented rumblings filled the air. Bubar's words had not pleased the other warleaders. All were keen to have some share in the glory of reducing Praag, a city which had long held a special place of enmity in the heart of every Chaos worshipper. If Bubar really could do what he claimed, their victory would be a hollow one, and any glory gained would be a sham. Still, Arek had to admit, the nasty-smelling, grossly obese man had a point. There was a world out there to be conquered. Why wait any longer than he had to, in order to take it?

In the distance he could hear the sound of sawing and hammering as the northern tribesmen began to build their enormous battering rams, weapons that might prove unnecessary if what Bubar claimed was true. Arek swatted away one of the flies that buzzed up from the plague worshipper and thought for a moment. In one ear Kelmain Blackstaff whispered. 'Let him try it, great Warlord. What have you got to lose?'

*What indeed*? thought Arek. All the construction would continue as Bubar worked on his rituals. No time need be lost if the Nurgleite failed. And if he succeeded weeks might be gained. Those might be important weeks with winter fast approaching.

'Very well, Bubar Stinkbreath. Conduct your rituals. Spread the plague.'

Bubar bowed. The buzzing of the cloud of flies surrounding him increased a hundredfold. 'Thank you, great warlord. You will not regret this.'

'See that I do not,' Arek said as he rose from his throne and retired within his pavilion.

'YOU'VE BEEN HERE all day, manling,' said Gotrek Gurnisson. He leaned on the wall and stared at the camp of the Chaos worshippers. Felix tore his gaze away from the assembled horde, and looked at the Slayer.

'Yes. Did Max tell you I was here?'

'Aye.'

'What brings you here?'

'I wanted to look upon our enemies and take their measure.' Gotrek fell into moody silence. Felix glanced out into the gloom, and looked upon the horde once more. Just the sight of it filled him with many questions.

Where had all those warriors come from? He had always known that the Chaos Wastes were full of enemies but he had never guessed that they could have supported an army on anything like this scale. As well as horror, the army inspired a kind of appalling wonder. At this distance the sound of the horde was like the breaking of ocean waves. Occasionally chanting or the screams of tortured victims could be heard above the bellows of beastmen and the shouts of evil men.

Felix could see massive siege towers starting to rise in the enemy ranks. Hundreds of fur-clad barbarians swarmed over the huge black iron war engines, assembling them from parts brought on monster-drawn wagons. Massive scaffolds were erected around them. The engines looked more like statues of great daemons than siege machines. They were covered in hideous ironwork, leering daemonic faces. Rams like the fists of evil gods protruded from their bellies. These mighty towers looked as if they might overbear the walls. It was not a reassuring sight.

Massive catapults, long-armed trebuchets taller even than the towers, were starting to tower above the massed horde. Long low-wheeled rams lay beside them.

'Somebody out there knows what they are doing,' said Felix.

'Aye, manling,' replied Gotrek. 'This is an attack long prepared for. This is not the work of some warlord who simply decided to come south with his followers.'

'Even the host that faced Magnus the Pious was not this well-organised.'

'No, but it was even more numerous, and the power of Chaos itself waxed stronger then. The raw stuff of the Wastes flowed over Praag and changed the very buildings and people.'

Felix considered this for a minute, and looked up at the moons. Morrslieb, the Chaos moon, was larger than ever. It shimmered with an evil greenish light. Who knew what was going to happen? Perhaps the full power of Chaos had not yet been sent forth. Perhaps this army, with all its hellish weaponry and evil soldiers, was but a foretaste of what was to come. In the dreadful light, looking on that vast host, it looked all too possible to Felix that the end of the world was coming.

Already in the streets, people whispered that the dread Lords of Chaos were soon going to manifest themselves. Not all the fury of the witch hunters had managed to quiet these rumours. This was not the only manifestation of religious mania. Zealots had begun to take to the streets scourging themselves with whips till the blood flowed down their backs in penance for their sins and the sins of mankind. Once Felix would have thought it was a kind of madness but now he wondered if there was any sane response to that huge army out there, and the evil it represented.

'What's that?' Gotrek asked suddenly. Felix looked in the direction he pointed. A crowd of weary, ragged beggars was emerging from the body of the host. They were being driven forward by a group of obese men in soiled, cowled robes. The drivers leaned on huge skull-tipped staffs whose eyes glowed greenly in the gloom. Even from this distance, Felix caught a whiff of their foul scent and almost gagged. It was an odour of rot and corruption worse than anything he had encountered since he fought the plague monks of Clan Pestilens in the gardens of Morr in Nuln.

'I don't know,' said Felix, 'but I am willing to bet it's nothing good.'

As the crowd of beggars approached, Felix could hear their pitiful weeping. *Save us. Help us. Have mercy on us.* The cries were heart rending, and never for a moment did Felix doubt their sincerity. Even as he watched the robed slave drivers began to back away, and the beggars raced towards the walls of Praag. *Open the gates! Let us in! Don't leave us in the hands of these daemon worshippers!*

Even as they raced forward, their cries were answered but not in the way Felix would have expected. Archers on the walls opened fire. Arrows whined through the air, piercing the bodies of the leading fugitives. Some of them stopped and shrieked; others continued on, towards inevitable death from missile fire.

'What are they doing?' Felix asked, appalled.

'It's some devilish trick, manling,' said Gotrek. 'These Kislevites are responding to it in the only way possible.'

He sounded as if he approved of the slaughter. Even as Felix watched the last of the fugitives was cut down. The only response from the Chaos host was cruel laughter. 'What was that all about?' Felix asked.

'Doubtless tomorrow will reveal all,' said Gotrek. 'Come, it's time to go and get a drink – if there's any decent ale to be had in this city.'

* * *

TOMORROW DID INDEED reveal what had happened. The bodies of the fugitives had swollen and turned black overnight. Through the spyglass Felix saw with horror that the bodies of the beggars were marked with the signs of disease. Massive blisters full of pus were raised off their skin. The smell was awful. Felix covered his nose. He did not know if there was any truth in the idea that plagues could be spread by their stench but he was not taking any chances.

'The guards did the right thing,' Gotrek said. 'Letting those refugees in would have brought the plague here. This is Nurgle's work. The followers of the Plague Lord did this.'

'But that must mean they were probably just innocent peasants, captured when the Chaos horde advanced,' Felix said with a shudder.

'Aye,' Gotrek replied darkly. 'Most likely.'

'This is a most ignoble way of fighting a war,' said Felix.

'Take your complaints to them, manling,' said Gotrek pointing out into the sea of Chaos scum. 'They are the ones doing it, not me.'

Felix could hear the anger in the dwarf's voice. Gotrek was no happier about this than he was. Another thought occurred to him. The guards ,too, must know that they shot down some of their innocent kinsfolk. It was all part of a simple ploy to help break down the morale of the defenders. And Felix knew that it would most likely work. Plague was a thing against which there was no defence.

'What can we do?' Felix asked.

'I will get Snorri and some of the lads and we'll haul the bodies away for burning.'

'You might get the plague too then,' said Felix.

'Dwarfs don't suffer human diseases, manling. We're too tough for it.'

Felix sincerely hoped he was correct.

THE WHITE BOAR was packed. The dwarfs all sat apart in one corner. No one was speaking to them, since they had come back from burning the bodies at the gate. No one wanted to take the chance of catching the plague. Felix, Max and Ulrika were the only people who would even take a table by them. If the dwarfs were offended, they gave no sign. Well, they were all Slayers, Felix thought, they probably didn't see anything unusual in people avoiding them.

'I can't wait for the Chaos warriors to attack,' bellowed Ulli. 'I am going to kill at least a hundred of them.'

The other Slayers looked at the youth with mild incredulity. He did not seem to notice but just kept on boasting. 'I will chop them to bits! Then I'll jump up and down on the pieces.'

'Snorri doesn't see much point,' said Snorri drunkenly. 'They'll be dead by then.'

'You can never tell with Chaos worshippers!' Ulli shouted. 'They have all those magical powers.'

'You'd be an expert on that,' Gotrek said with heavy irony.

'No! I just know what my old granddad used to say about Chaos worshippers. He was here in Praag. The last time they attacked.'

A murmur of disbelief rose from the other tables. Ulli's shouts were too loud to be ignored by anyone in the bar. It wasn't crowded enough for the general hubbub to drown him out.

'Is that possible?' Ulrika asked in a low voice. Felix nodded. It certainly was. Before he could say anything more, Max spoke eagerly.

'Yes. Dwarfs live far longer than most humans. They are different from us. Even an average dwarf can live to be 250 years old quite easily. There are records of some dwarfs reaching 400, and legends of some of them living for over a millennia.'

'I doubt any of those dwarfs will live to be two centuries old,' Felix said sourly. 'They are all Slayers.'

Max looked at Felix with a superior smile that he was starting to resent. 'In that case, Felix,' he said pedantically, 'they will be the exception rather than the rule. I believe dwarfs suffer far less from disease than us, and the effects of ageing only appear to make them stronger and hardier for a long time. It is only in the very last stages of their lives that they begin to show any signs of decrepitude.'

'Fascinating,' said Felix, reaching over and squeezing Ulrika's hand just to annoy him.

A frown passed over Max's face. Ulrika withdrew her hand. It was Felix's turn to be annoyed. He wondered if she understood what was going on, was even, perhaps, in some ways encouraging it. The frown vanished from Max's brow.

'You've heard of longbeards. They're the toughest dwarf warriors,' Max said. Perhaps it was the beer, but his tone was starting to annoy Felix unreasonably.

'Believe me, I have travelled long enough with Gotrek to be more familiar with the nature of longbeards than most men.'

Max nodded, seeming to accept this. Felix noticed he wasn't drinking. In fact, Felix had not seen him drink since they had left Karak Kadrin. 'Would you like some wine, Max?' he asked. 'I can order you some. I'll pay.'

'No thanks,' Max said. 'I don't drink any more.'

'Why not?'

'It interferes with my magical abilities.'

'That's a pity. Still, we're going to need those abilities soon.'

'We're going to need every man who can wield a blade soon too. That army is not going to stand back forever.'

Suddenly the doors of the White Boar crashed open. A gang of very marked, very nasty-looking men entered. They were all wearing stained white tabards with the sign of an eye. White hoods were flung back from their faces. Their leader was a tall, gaunt fanatical-looking man.

'Why is this licentiousness continuing?' he bellowed. There was a brief silence and then some of the mercenaries at the tables started asking each other what 'licentiousness' meant. This only seemed to enrage the fanatic more.

'The armies of Chaos stand beyond our gates. They are poised to sweep over the lands of men with fire and sword and yet here we find men drinking, whoring and gambling and engaging in every form of vice.'

As he spoke his burning eyes came to rest on Ulrika. Her face flushed. Her hand went to the hilt of her sword. Felix could understand. She did not like being mistaken for a tavern wench.

'Get lost!' Ulli bellowed.

'Can't you see Snorri has some serious drinking to do?' shouted Snorri.

'And I have a couple of these wenches to bounce,' Bjorni added, a wicked leer contorting his repulsively ugly face.

'Silence, subhuman scum!' bellowed the witch hunter. 'You are in league with the foul daemons beyond.'

Felix shook his head, knowing only too well what was about to happen. There was a brief appalled silence from the Slayers' table. The dwarfs all glanced at one another as if unable to believe anyone would be stupid enough to insult them in this fashion. Felix could not quite believe anyone could be that stupid himself. Oh well, this loud-mouthed fanatic and his bully boys were going to learn the hard way.

'I suggest you leave now,' said Max rising from the table, and clutching his staff. It was obvious to all that he was a wizard. Being ordered to go by a mage was not a thing calculated to calm a Kislevite bigot, Felix judged. If anything, Max's attempt to calm things was somewhat akin to trying to put out a fire by pouring oil on it.

'Take this daemon-loving wretch outside and teach him a lesson,' the witch hunter shouted. Felix wasn't feeling too fond of Max at the moment but he was not about to let that happen. Max had been a comrade on many dangerous adventures. Felix stood up, and put his hand on his sword hilt too.

'Why don't you head out the main gate?' he suggested softly. 'You'll find plenty of Chaos worshippers there. You're rather too quick with your accusations in here for my liking.'

'And who are you to speak so knowledgeably about the Darkness?' asked the leader of the witch hunters. He looked closely at Felix and then at Gotrek. He seemed to recognise them. It was hardly surprising. They had become very well known since the fight at the gate. Still, there was something in this recognition that Felix did not like.

'Who are you to be asking my name?' countered Felix.

'His name is Ulgo,' Ulrika said softly. 'I have seen him before.'

'And why have you been spying on me, slut?' asked Ulgo nastily. Something had hardened in the man's attitude. He seemed determined to provoke a fight.

Felix was tired of this now. He was tired of these men who obviously did not have enough enemies to fight outside the city. 'Get out!' he said. 'The laughter of the Dark Ones will be your only reward if you start a fight in here. We are all enemies of Chaos here.'

'That remains to be proven,' Ulgo pronounced with the blazing certainty of the fanatic. He drew his blade. 'Take them outside and burn them,' he told his men. The bully boys looked only too pleased with this order. They drew their weapons too.

'If you are not out of here by the time I count to three, you will all die,' said Gotrek. Even Felix was shocked by the menace in his voice. The Slayer was as angry as Felix had ever seen him, and was obviously not in the mood to put up with these fanatics. 'One.'

'You cannot tell me what to do, Chaos lover,' said Ulgo, brandishing his blade menacingly.

'Two,' said Gotrek. He ran his thumb along the blade of his axe. A bead of bright red blood appeared. Looking at his squat muscular form, the witch hunters behind Ulgo began to get nervous. Ulgo obviously did not realise his peril. He strode forward to loom over Gotrek menacingly. His sword was drawn back to strike. Here was a man too foolish to live, thought Felix. One who was more used to intimidating people than to being intimidated.

'Don't think you frighten me, I'll–' Ulgo began to lunge forward.

'Three.'

The axe flashed forward.

Ulgo's head rolled on the floor. Blood spattered everywhere. Droplets of it landed in Felix's beer.

Gotrek sprang lightly over the corpse and moved towards the doorway. The remaining witch hunters turned and fled. Deathly silence fell over the tavern.

'You probably should not have done that,' said Felix.

'He interrupted my drinking, manling. And I gave him fair warning.'

'I hope the city watch thinks the same way as you do.'

'The city watch have better things to do.' The Slayer stooped and picked up the corpse of the dead witch hunter. Effortlessly he threw it across his shoulders, and made his way to the door, kicking the head in front of him as he went. As he strode out into the darkness, Felix found himself thinking, there's another one who does not care how many enemies he makes. Felix did not doubt that after this night they would have many enemies inside the city themselves. Witch hunters were not usually partial to those who killed their leaders. Gotrek returned.

'It's your round, Snorri,' he said. 'And hurry it up. Killing loudmouths is thirsty work.'

A barmaid had already thrown sawdust on the blood. Half a dozen customers departed, doubtless to make reports to whomever they thought would pay them most for the information. Once again, Felix found himself wondering why he had ever come to this place.

Gotrek slumped down at his table. 'Interesting,' he said.

'What's interesting?' Felix asked.

'The loudmouth's head was not the only one in the street.'

'What?'

'It seems our daemon-worshipping friends outside the city are firing the severed heads of their prisoners over the walls. Corpses too.'

'Why would they do that?'

'Tomorrow will doubtless tell us more, manling. Right now I want my beer.'

Felix was getting a little sick of being told that tomorrow he would find out more, but there did not seem to be much he could do about it. He shook his head. He noticed that Max was giving him a troubled look.

'What is it?' Felix asked.

'That witch hunter seemed in an awful hurry to pick a fight.'

'That sort always is.'

'Yes, but why with Gotrek?'

Felix could not answer that question.

# SIX

THE STINK MADE Felix sick. He had seen plagues before. He had seen the horror of a city besieged before. In Nuln, the dead had fallen in the streets where they lay from diseases bred by the foul Plague Monks of Clan Pestilens. But he had never quite witnessed anything like this. It was as Gotrek said. The Chaos forces were firing corpses over the walls using those monstrous trebuchets and catapults they had built. The bodies fell from hundreds of feet, and, already bloated and rotten exploded on impact with the cobbles sending great belches of corpse gas and pus everywhere, leaving yellowing bones and skulls exposed to sight.

What manner of being could fight a war in this fashion, Felix wondered, as he made his way through the haunted streets towards the White Boar? In all his reading, he had never even seen hints of this foul tactic. Yet he knew it was an effective one. People were vomiting and retching at the sight of the corpses. Worse, some of them were starting to cough. Felix knew that this was just the first, and doubtless the least, symptom of what was to follow. Already rumours of plague were everywhere.

He glanced over at Ulrika. She too looked grim. Of course their surroundings would depress a drunken jester. Praag was not a cheerful city at the best of times. The architecture was sombre. Horned gargoyles clutched the eaves of buildings. Hideous leering faces were carved on the walls, mementoes of the long war fought two centuries ago against the forebears of the army that now waited outside the gate. And there was worse. There was an atmosphere of brooding gloom, that seemed to have intensified with the presence of the Chaos horde, that responded to it being there. Sometimes out of the corner of his eyes, Felix thought he saw strange shapes moving in doorways, in alleyways, across roofs. Whenever he looked though, there was nothing there. He was left with the sense that something had just ducked out of sight, but he could never quite see what it was.

He smiled at Ulrika. She did not smile back. Her face was pale and drawn. She coughed. She was like the city, becoming gloomier by the day. It was like sharing a bed with a stranger these days. They did not seem to be able to find anything to talk about. They could not find much joy in anything. And yet, every time he thought about ending things, he could not. It was as if he were tied with invisible chains.

He understood she was worried. Under the circumstances who would not be? Both their lives were in danger. And, bad as it was for him, this must be harder for her. Her whole life had been uprooted. Her father was missing. Her country was invaded. She was threatened by plague and dark sorcery as well as with slaughter. It was not quite the same for him. He shook his head and almost laughed.

He was starting to realise how much he had changed during his wanderings with Gotrek. He was afraid, but his terror was a controlled thing, bubbling along just beneath the surface of his consciousness. The rest of his life was pretty much business as usual, as his father might have described it. Years of wandering had left him inured to hardship and hunger. The experience of dozens of dangerous adventures left him able to ignore the danger they were in until the very last moment. He had learned a little about pushing worries away until a time when they could be dealt with. Even the plague did not terrify him quite as much as it might once have done.

He had survived plagues before, and somehow, he expected to survive this one as well.

In any case, he told himself, whether he worried about it or not, it would make little difference. If it was his destiny to die of plague, he would rather not know it, at least until he had to. Part of him knew that he was kidding himself. Deep in his brain part of him was all too aware of what was going on, and did worry about it, but right at this moment, he found he could ignore it.

'Under the circumstances you seem unnaturally cheerful,' said Ulrika.

They entered the main square, just outside the inner wall. This was still a place of business where dozens of merchant stalls could be found selling everything from leather goods to food. Only now soldiers of the ducal guard were doling out rations of corn to the poor, a leather cup the size of a small tankard going to each person. They carried it away in jugs, sacks, or rolled up bits of cloth. Felix could not help but notice that not all of those present looked poor. Some wore the clothes of artisans or merchants. The guard turned most of these away unless coin changed hands which it quite often did. Felix shrugged. Everybody had to eat. These people were most likely only doing their best for their families. Perhaps he should do the same. That was the way his father would look at these things, he thought.

'It's a lovely morning and we are still alive,' he said. It was true too. The sky overhead was a perfect blue, almost untouched by cloud. The cool was more pleasant than the stifling blast of high summer. If you could ignore the stink of decomposing bodies it brought, the breeze was almost refreshing.

'Make the most of it,' said Ulrika, coughing. 'Winter comes quickly here.'

'You are a ray of sunshine today, aren't you.'

'It is our main hope,' she said as if answering the question of a fool.

'Why?'

'Winter in Kislev is fierce. It is not a time to be outside the gates of a city. It is a time to be indoors, beside a fire, with plenty of provisions.'

There was something about her tone that goaded him, as he guessed she intended. 'Perhaps Warlord Arek and his minions intend to be inside the walls by then, warming their hands on the burning buildings.'

'Now who is not being cheerful?'

'Watch out below!' Felix leapt to one side to avoid being splattered by the contents of a chamber pot being emptied into the street. His leap almost carried him into a dung heap. He rocked back on his heels and nearly overbalanced. Ulrika caught him by the shoulder and laughed.

'Perhaps you should have been a tumbler, or a clown,' she suggested. Her tone was friendlier than it had been in days.

'Perhaps,' he said. They turned the corner and the apothecary's shop was just ahead. Felix recognised it by the sign of the mortar and pestle hanging over the door. Even if he had not the long queue of glum-looking people outside would have been a give-away. The plague had made everybody worried about their health. Felix groaned. The last thing he wanted today was to be standing in a long line of folk waiting to be served.

'Why can't Max get his own herbs?' he asked plaintively.

'Max has other things to do. He needs to prepare his magic. To protect us all from the plague.'

'I have other things to do as well.'

'Like drink, you mean?' Her tone told him she was not about to accept any argument. He was starting to wish he had never offered to accompany her on this errand. Still, after the events of last night it seemed like a good idea. The witch hunter's friends might come back, looking for vengeance. Not that Gotrek or any of the other Slayers were too worried by the prospect.

So far, he had to admit that their attitude seemed well justified. The authorities did not appear at all bothered by the death of one man amid so many, and Ulgo's companions had not come back seeking vengeance. But it was early days yet.

They joined the line of people outside the apothecary's. All of them seemed to be coughing or scratching or somewhat the worse for wear. Felix hoped that they were not already going down to the plague magic. Somehow he knew that the plague was only the beginning of their troubles.

He wondered what new deviltry the Chaos worshippers were working on.

AREK INSPECTED THE walls. As far as he could see there were no changes. The defenders still waited, weapons ready. He could make out faint plumes of smoke rising from beneath the cauldrons of boiling oil. The ballistae were all manned. The catapults looked ready. The massive walls looked as if it would take the fist of a god to smash through them. In a way, he was glad. He wanted a battle. He wanted to crush his foes beneath the hooves of his steed. He wanted to ride in triumph through the gates of a conquered city. He did not want his inevitable victory to be the work of those festering fools who served the Plague god.

Be careful, he told himself. Victory is victory no matter how it is achieved, and you have a whole world to conquer. If Bubar Stinkbreath and his lackeys can deliver an easy conquest, why worry? There will be plenty more battles before this is through. Part of him, the part that craved the eye of Tzeentch to turn fully on him, rejected this idea, and wanted to deny any but himself part of the glory. Another part of him, the part that schemed eternally for his patron's favour, weighed the options.

A victory for Bubar might alienate all the other warlords, and he needed their support. It might even give the Nurgleite ideas above his station, unlikely as that now seemed. And there was always the possibility of something going wrong. Plague was ever a treacherous weapon. It would not affect him, or the Chaos warriors or those sorcerers who enjoyed the favour of their powers, but it might kill large numbers of the tribesmen and beastmen if they were not careful. Bubar assured him that the protection of Lord Nurgle extended over the horde, but, perhaps, the Spewer of Vileness might withdraw his protection. After all, such things had happened in the past.

Arek considered all of this in a heartbeat. Best to attack now while Nurgle still extended his favour. After all, gods were notoriously temperamental and who knew when he might change his mind. And it might be a good idea to order Bubar to discontinue his spells now. Why give him time to brew a truly lethal plague?

Arek turned to Lhoigor and his twin. 'The other plans are proceeding apace?' he asked.

'Yes, great one,' replied Lhoigor almost sneering. 'The rune-stones now almost ring the city and our acolytes are near enough ready to begin the ritual of power. Soon the stars will be aligned correctly and Morrslieb will reach the proper phase.'

Arek thought about this for a moment. 'Well done, Bubar,' he said. 'I am sure that your plagues will weaken the defenders sufficiently for our purposes. You may discontinue your rituals.'

'But, great one–'

'I said you may discontinue your rituals. It's time to give others their chance now.' His tone brooked no disagreement. Bubar grovelled and withdrew.

'Most wise,' said Kelmain.

'How long will your rituals take?' Arek asked brusquely.

'The stars must be right, master, and the moons in the proper conjunction. If you remember, that is why we advised…'

'I said how long?'

'The omens are auspicious now. If we begin immediately a great vortex may be completed within the week.'

'See that it is so.'

'As you wish, master.' Arek wondered if he heard just a hint of rebellion in his minion's voice.

GREY SEER THANQUOL strode through the streets of Hell Pit. All around was howling madness. Skaven fought skaven. Moulder fought Moulder. Stormvermin hacked at clanrat warrior. Rat-ogre disembowelled skavenslave. Monsters, their handlers dead, ran wild in the streets killing and feasting where they could. Lurk had a lot to answer for, Thanquol thought. Not that these idiotic Moulders did not deserve it.

Still, things were bubbling along nicely. Careful reflection, and the fact that he was still in their power, had eventually decided Thanquol to reveal Lurk's plans to the elders of the clan. Forewarned, they had been able to place their forces to the best advantage and were now slowly but surely gaining the upper hand. Thanquol's reward had been to be released from captivity and given his own troop to lead in the fighting. It was not much of a reward really. He was expected to endanger his own precious pelt to secure the fiefdom of Clan Moulder. All things considered however, he had managed to look suitably grateful. Later there would be time to extract a reckoning for this indignity.

Burly stormvermin carrying his own personal banner hacked a path for him towards the great warpstone refinery. It was a dangerous place for him to be. Lurk's army had managed to fight its way through stiff resistance and seize the massive structure. They had held it against all the Moulder counter-offensives. Under normal circumstances Thanquol would never have gone near it while the war raged but these were hardly normal circumstances. He knew that if he could fight his way into the refinery he could get his paws on a huge stock of purified warpstone, just the substance he needed and craved. The lack of it for the past few days was starting to give him terrible headaches and shaking spasms. The want of it made him feel weak.

And, of course, with it his sorcerous powers would once again be boundless. He was going to need that if he was ever to win his way free from these cursed northlands and make his way back to the security of Skavenblight. For many reasons, he needed the stuff, and he was going to make sure he got it.

A howling blood-mad pack of clanrats, red scarves tied around their foreheads in a way that marked their allegiance to Lurk, crashed into his bodyguard. Thanquol felt his musk glands tighten as they hacked down the clawleader of the stormvermin. A frothing beast chopped his way almost to Thanquol's feet. Thanquol met him blade to blade and cut him down. He was only slightly helped by the fact that the clanrat had got his paws entangled in the ropes of a disembowelled stormvermin's gut. Not that it mattered anyway. Thanquol was sure that he could have taken him in any sort of fight. It was just the Horned Rat's way of showing that Grey Seer Thanquol was restored to his favour.

*Lurk*, thought Thanquol, *when I get my paws on you, you are going to pay for this!*

* * *

THINGS WERE NOT going very well, Lurk thought, peering down through the arched window of the refinery onto the battle in the streets below. He could make out the horned head of Grey Seer Thanquol as he fought his way forward. Things must be going badly indeed for his side, Lurk realised, if that cowardly monster had dared show his face. Lurk found it all very discouraging.

Things had been going so right, for a while. His worshippers, driven by sheer fanatic fury, had managed to overcome their oppressors, despite the uncanny knowledge the Moulders appeared to possess of his plans. Lurk knew beyond a shadow of a doubt that this proved there were traitors among his followers. His swift execution of all his highest-ranking followers had somehow failed to restore morale as it should have, and the enemy still appeared to know his plans. The slaughter of a hundred more suspiciously co-operative followers had done nothing to halt this treachery, and inexplicably, even appeared to have had a deleterious effect on the morale of his worshippers.

Despite all of this, they had managed to hold on to most of their early gains, until defections back to the Moulder ranks had weakened the forces. Now it looked like all of Lurk's mighty plans were crumbling. It looked like it would soon be time to bolt. Fortunately he had long since taken the precaution of snooping out the secret escape tunnels from the refinery and from the city. After all, it was just sound skaven common sense. He was not the first skaven in history to be let down by the inferior quality of those who followed him.

Yes, thought Lurk, it would soon be time to go. He who fights and scurries away lives to conquer another day. And perhaps there might be a place for him in that great army of conquest heading south.

FELIX CLUTCHED THE packet of herbs in his hand and looked at Ulrika worriedly. She was not looking well, he thought. Her face was even paler. Sweat beaded her brow, and she was starting to shiver.

'Are you all right?' he asked. She shook her head.

'I do not feel so well.'

'We'd best get you home and to bed then.'

'Always thinking of bed,' she said, and tried to smile. If anything the feebleness of her smile made Felix fear the worst. Supporting her with one hand he strode out into the street. It was a long way back to the White Boar, and by the time they got there, Ulrika could barely walk.

'It does not look good,' Max said softly. Felix looked at Ulrika. She lay on the bed shivering, yet her brow felt red-hot. 'She shows all the signs of the new plague.'

'Are you sure?' Felix asked. Suddenly all of the fighting and all his other problems seemed irrelevant. He realised that he did not want her to die.

'I am not a physician, Felix, nor am I a priest of Shallya, but I do possess some skill at healing, and some understanding of what is at work here. This is not a natural disease. I have wrought some divining spells and the foul talons of the cult of Nurgle are at work here.'

'Is there nothing you can do?'

'I have already started. I have given her the herbal admixture, and as soon as you give me some peace, I will work the best healing spells I know.'

It dawned on Felix that he might well be interfering with Ulrika's best chance of survival. 'I will go,' he said.

'It would be for the best.'

Felix made his way towards the door of the small chamber he shared with Ulrika and opened it. As he did so, Max spoke.

'Don't worry, Felix, I will not let her die.' He looked at the mage and saw the pain in his eyes. Understanding passed between them.

'Thank you,' he said and strode down into the crowded tavern.

The wine tasted bitter. The jests of the warriors failed to amuse him. Felix stared moodily into his goblet and pondered on the vagaries of fate.

Why had he been spared so far? Why had the plague not struck him down? Or was it only a matter of time before it did? Who could tell? He remembered that once a famous physician had told him that there were many factors involved in such things. Perhaps the strain of worrying about her father had made her more vulnerable than he. All that mattered was that she got better again.

Now all of their arguments and disagreements seemed trivial. Now he struggled to remember even a harsh word. Now all he could remember was the way she had looked the first time he had seen her in the Elector's throne room in Middenheim. Unbidden a host of memories and images flickered through his mind. He remembered her riding alongside him one sunny morning in Kislev before he departed for the Chaos Wastes. He could picture her exactly: the wide cheekbones, the slight bump in her nose, the fine web of lines around her eyes as she smiled, the characteristic way she had of smoothing her hair. He could remember waking beside her on a dozen mornings, and the world seeming brighter for her presence. He remembered holding her hand as they walked through the peaks on their way to Dragon Mountain. Suddenly he wanted to go upstairs and demand that Max make her live. He knew that it would be counter-productive, that all he would achieve would be to interrupt Max as he wove his spells, possibly to the detriment of Ulrika's chances of survival. He cursed the fact that there was nothing else he could do. Except pray. Maybe he should find a temple of Shallya and make an offering.

He glanced around wondering when the dwarfs would get back. They had headed for the walls hoping for a fight, and to see if they could be of any help shoring the defences. Now the horde had its own siege engines in place they had started to pound at the walls with more than just rotting corpses. Now they flung huge boulders, capable of crushing men and smashing stone. The battle had entered a new phase.

Suddenly he could not bear to be in this dark smoky common room any more. He wanted to be outside, on his own, in the relatively clean night air. Perhaps he could find a temple that was still open.

He rose and strode out through the swinging door, into the muddy street. Outside, it was dark and chill. The temperature had started to drop with astonishing swiftness. Overhead, Morrslieb glared down. A greenish glow surrounded it, and more than ever its blotched surface looked like a sinister leering face. It was as if one of the dark gods of Chaos had ascended into the sky and glared down on the helpless world.

A faint mist filled the streets and the tang of woodsmoke was in the air. Felix imagined that he could smell the stink of the horde outside, of overflowing latrines and cooking fires and unclean roasting meat. He told himself it was just his imagination turning the smell of nightsoil and local chimneys into something they were not, and lengthening his stride, walked off into the gathering gloom.

The cold night air made him feel almost sober. Now, more than ever, he understood why they called Praag the haunted city. By night the buildings looked fearful. The gargoyles clutching their sides looked almost alive, and every shadow seemed to whisper. All the old stories came back to him, of how the city had been rebuilt after the last siege, using stones corrupted by the taint of Chaos, of how the spirits of those slain by Skathloc Ironclaw's horde could be seen stalking the streets on those anniversaries of the battle when the Chaos moon was full, of how sometimes men would suffer strange dreams that drove them mad. And there were other tales, of covens who gathered in dark cellars and sacrificed children for dreadful feasts.

Tonight, it all seemed dreadfully plausible. Tonight, the monstrous bulk of the city walls provided no comfort. Tonight, it felt like they were part of a huge trap, penning him in this fearful place. Tonight the citadel loomed over the city like some ogre's tower. Even the lights on the huge inner wall looked threatening

He walked swiftly, his hands on the hilt of his sword, trying to avoid thinking of Ulrika and Max and the plague. He felt as helpless as a child. This was a situation in which he could do nothing. Ulrika's fate was in Max's hands, and the hands of the gods, and the powers had not seemed too kind of late.

The mist gathered around him, making the familiar streets seem strange. His own shadow loomed ahead of him like the outline of some spectral monster. Footsteps rang strangely in the damp darkness. The distant call of the night watchman counting the hours was anything but reassuring. Far off he could hear the drumming, and the howling and the noise of endless infernal labour coming from the Chaos horde.

His boots scuffed the cobbles, and he paused for a moment, thinking he heard stealthy footsteps behind him.

He listened, but the sound had stopped, if indeed it was not something he had imagined. He waited for a moment anyway, knowing that sometimes, if he was patient, a pursuer might start moving again, and give himself away. Nothing.

Part of him half-hoped there was someone there. A fight would be just the thing to distract him from his dark thoughts, and let him work off the fear and tension and anger he felt. The more cautious part of his mind told him not to be stupid. He had no idea who his pursuers might be or how many of them there were. If he was being followed the best thing would be to head back to the White Boar. At least there he would find some comrades who could help him.

He heard a ringing of metal, as of a dagger being drawn. He froze back into the doorway. Footpads! Probably hungry men after some silver, hoping to find a drunk and part him from his money. If he had any sense, Felix knew, he would run, but now it was a little too late for that. He could hear the footsteps coming closer. And they belonged to more than one man.

'I'm sure he went this way,' he heard someone mutter. It was a high thin voice, and there was a note of complaint in it, as if the owner believed that the world were out to cheat him, and had just found another way.

'Are you sure it was him?' asked a second voice, deeper, gruffer.

Felix felt certain this man was the less intelligent of the two. His mind conjured up the picture of a hulking bruiser. His mouth suddenly felt dry. His heartbeat sounded loud in his ears.

'Oh, it was him all right, I saw him when he came out of the inn. Tall skinny fellow, blond-haired like a lot of them Imperials. Red cloak. Dragon head hilt on his sword.'

Felix froze. That was a fairly good description of him. Was it possible that these men were looking for him specifically? Why? Were they witch hunters?

'Jaeger – that's his name.' The two men were almost abreast of the doorway now. He could see that one of them was indeed a big man, massively built. The other was short and very broad. He looked fat but moved lightly all the same. 'Felix Jaeger. Don't know why his nibs wants him dead now.

The Time of Changes is almost here. Most likely he'll go down under a beastman axe in the not too distant future.'

'Ours is not to reason why,' said the larger man, the one with the deeper voice. 'The high-ups want him and the dwarf dead, and that axe out of the way. It falls to us to see that orders is carried out. Let's hope we do better than that fool witch hunter.'

Felix felt held his breath. These men were not witch hunters. They sounded more like professional assassins or cult members. He was sure he had heard the phrase about the time of changes before, and in no wholesome context. Someone wanted Gotrek and him dead, and they wanted rid of the Slayer's axe. He wondered why. More to the point, what was he going to do now? He did not fancy taking on this pair in hand-to-hand combat. Except perhaps with the advantage of surprise. Maybe he could spring from his hiding place and have his sword in one of their backs before they realised it. It hardly seemed fair or chivalrous but then these men probably weren't going to ask him to joust either. Alternatively, he could try and follow them, and see where they had come from. That was not a particularly appealing idea either. After all, he had heard them and waited in ambush for them. Who was to say they could not do the same thing to him?

The easiest thing would be to simply wait for them to disappear down the street, and then head back to the inn. He could tell the Slayer what had happened. If it came to violence, he was certain that Gotrek could handle this pair or any dozen like them. Provided he had warning. That seemed like the best plan.

'I tell you, Olaf, we missed him. He went into one of those doors back there.' It was the big man speaking.

'Nah, he couldn't have. And why? Who'd he know in those buildings?'

The voices were coming closer again. It sounded as if the men were stopping for a moment to check the doorways as they went. Felix wondered if he could make a break for it. It was dark and misty so he reckoned he had a good chance. But if the men were faster runners than he, or knew the area better, or if one of them simply had a knife and made a lucky throw then things might go badly for him. They did not look like men he wanted to turn his back on. Perhaps he could shout for help. If the watch came these thugs would surely run.

If the watch came, he thought, and if these men did not have confederates nearby who were attracted to the noise. Calm yourself, Felix told himself. There are only two of them here for certain, don't let your imagination populate the night with killers, or fear might keep you from doing anything. He felt the familiar sense of weakness in his limbs he always got before a fight and ignored it. His mind seemed to be working with great clarity now, ignoring his fear, considering his options.

If these two men were professional sell-swords, his chances were slim. Felix knew he was a good swordsman, but he was outnumbered, and if they were competent they would make the most of that advantage. All it would take would be one well-placed or lucky blow, and life would be over. He would never see Ulrika again. Suddenly the threat of the Chaos army and all his other worries seemed to recede to a great distance, to become petty and unimportant. The necessary thing was simply to live through the next few minutes, then he would deal with any other problems life presented. Suddenly, living was desperately important to him. It did not matter whether the Chaos army swarmed across the wall in the next day or the next hour. He wanted that time, no matter how little it might prove to be, and these men wanted to rob him of it.

A clear, cold anger filled him. He was not going to let them do that. Not without a fight at least. If he needed to do murder here so be it. It was his life or theirs and he had no doubt whose was most important, at least to him. Slowly, knowing he would need to seize whatever small advantages he could, he unbuckled the clasp of his cloak and slipped it off, holding it wadded up in his right hand. As stealthily as he could he began to withdraw the blade from the scabbard, and he was grateful that the magical blade slid near silently out.

'Hush!' said the big man. 'I thought I heard something.'

Best take him first, thought Felix. He is the more dangerous of the two.

'Most likely a rat. The city's full of them. Maybe there'll be some of those ratmen. I heard they had problems with them down in Nuln. Damn. I wish Halek would do his own dirty work instead of sending us out on a night like this. I can almost smell winter.'

'Be grateful to the Great One that you will be alive to see winter. Most in this city won't.'

'Well Felix Jaeger won't be for sure if I get my hands on him. I intend to make sure he pays dearly for making me miss my kip. I could be in a warm bed with a warm whore in the Red Rose if it wasn't for him.'

'There'll be time enough for that later. Once the business is done.'

'Aye, if we don't get sent out again after the dwarf. I heard he's a right hard bastard.'

'Poisoned knife will do for him same as anybody else,' said the big man. He sounded like he was almost on top of Felix now. A shiver of fear passed through Felix at the mention of the word poison. These men weren't taking any chances. He could not afford to either. Even the slightest slip might be his last. His knuckles tightened around his cloak. It was nearly time.

'If it weren't for this mist I would wait across from the inn and put a crossbow bolt into him,' said the fat man.

'And how would you do that without being noticed,' asked the big man. His shadow was right in front of Felix now. 'That's just the sort of dumb idea that I would–'

Felix leapt from his concealment and tossed his cloak. It billowed outwards as he threw it and covered the big man's head. Even as it entangled him, Felix struck, viper-fast. His blade passed right through the big man's stomach and out of his back. Felix twisted the blade as he pulled it free. Poison, he thought, fuelled with desperate rage and fear. Try and use poison on me, would you. The big man's scream rang through the night.

His partner might have been fat but he was fast. He lashed out almost instinctively and only a swift leap backwards got Felix out of the way of the knife. He could not be sure, but he thought he saw a smear of sticky black substance on the blade. The big man fell forward. His weight twisted the sword out of Felix's grip. Damn, he thought. Things weren't going quite according to plan. He backed off quickly, fumbling for his own dagger as he kept his eyes on the outline of the fat man. He didn't want to risk even the slightest cut from that weapon.

'Bastard! You've done for Sergei, by the looks of it. Well, don't matter. Means I'll stand higher in favour with his nibs when I bring back your head.'

Felix was grateful when his dagger cleared the scabbard. Now he had a chance, albeit a slim one. The fat man was holding the knife with a professional's poise. Felix was a swordsman, and had little experience with anything but throwing knives. On the other hand, he thought, backing away from the assassin, he had killed two men with those and now might be a good time to try for a third.

He drew back his arm and made the toss. It was a tricky throw in the darkness against a shadowy moving target and even as he made the cast he knew it wasn't going to work. All he had done was disarm himself. The man ducked, but Felix was in that heightened state of alertness where thought and action were almost one. Even as he realised his cast had gone astray some part of his mind, quicker than rational thought had reacted. It had known the assassin would be distracted for a fraction of a second, which would give Felix an opening in which to attack.

He threw himself forward, bunching his fist and connecting a solid blow to the man's chin. The pain in his hand was excruciating and he knew that in the morning he was going to suffer from bruised knuckles at the very least. Not that it mattered right now. If he survived he would worry about that tomorrow. The man grunted and swung upward with the knife. It was a professional's blow, aimed in a short stabbing motion intended to bury the blade in Felix's gut.

It was only the fact that he expected it that allowed Felix to block the blow, more by luck than judgement. Reaching down he caught the sell-sword's wrist. It was thick and slippery with sweat and it took a near superhuman effort for Felix to stop the knife. The fat man was stronger than he looked and obviously experienced in close quarter combat. He twisted his knife arm, trying to break free and at the same time tried to knee Felix in the groin.

Felix shifted his weight so that the knee jabbed his thigh, and then did the unexpected, he kept twisting away and pulled the man forward at the same time, using his own weight and motion against him. The man fell sprawling and landed face down in the muck and cobbles. A long agonised groan burst from his lips, then he spasmed and lay still. Half expecting it to be some sort of trick, Felix kicked him in the head. There was no response, but anger and fear drove Felix to kick him again and again. After a minute he realised that the man was not feigning anything. He turned him over and saw that he had fallen on his own knife. It had not been a bad fall by the look of it. The blade had gone in only partially. Under normal circumstances it would have only been a nick really, not a fatal wound, but the poison the man was using must have been a strong one, for it had certainly sent him headlong into the realm of Morr, or whatever daemon god he had followed.

Spitefully Felix hoped the Powers of Chaos would punish him for his failure, then sanity returned and he retrieved his knife, sword and cloak. Looking at it, he thought the cloak was ruined but it still wasn't a good idea to leave it lying around near the scene of a killing. You never knew, it might be recognised as his. He wadded it up and moved off into the night, walking quickly and purposefully, and trying not to look like someone who had just killed two men.

Prayers at the temple of Shallya could wait till he had cleaned the blood from his hands, he reasoned. He had better warn Gotrek that hired killers were after them. Not that the Slayer was likely to care.

MAX LOOKED DOWN at Ulrika as she lay on the bed. Her face was pale. Sweat poured from her brow. Her eyes were wide and unseeing. Strange red blotches marked her beautiful face. His magical senses told him that she was failing fast. Her life force was draining away; her spirit was becoming separated from her body. Max shook his head and took a deep breath, trying to calm himself. It was difficult. He felt that if anything happened to her he would die.

Calm yourself, he thought. Now is not a good time to be thinking like a schoolboy. Now is a time to concentrate all your resources on being a magician. Don't let your personal feelings interfere with what you need to do here. He took another calming breath, and repeated one of the chants he had learned in his early apprenticeship, a meaningless rhythmic verse intended to soothe the mind and calm the senses. He opened his mind to the winds of magic and felt them respond to his call.

Max had been trained extensively in protective magics. Of necessity these included healing spells and spells intended to counteract diseases. It was not an area he had specialised in though, and he knew that plagues in particular were a tricky thing neutralise. Nurgle was strong and there were too many other factors that could affect the outcome.

Fortunately, most of the ones he was familiar with were in Ulrika's favour. She was young and healthy and had everything to live for. She was not starving. Her surroundings were clean. She had been in good health previously. He hoped that these things would make the difference.

He closed his eyes and drew on the winds of magic. Instantly he sensed something wrong. There was far more dark magic about than there should be and it was getting stronger. Of all the types of energy that the winds of magic carried it was the worst, and carried with it the promise of corruption, mutation, and undeath. He had thought he was prepared for this. After all, the Chaos army outside was drawing heavily on the evil power, but just the sheer amount of dark magic present was almost overwhelming. The touch of it was sickening. He breathed out and expelled the energy as quickly as he could. By focusing his mind he could draw on the other sorts; for this he needed a mixture of gold and grey. It was harder to get at now with all the dark magic in the air, but he knew he could do it.

Slowly, carefully, making sure to avoid any touch of the taint of Darkness, he plaited together the power. Opening all of his mage senses he gazed down on Ulrika. He could still see her on the bed, but now he could also see her aura, the reflection of her spirit. Things did not look good. An unhealthy green surrounded her, and he sensed the taint of dark magic within her. That was hardly surprising since the plague was magically generated by the followers of Nurgle.

He began to speak the incantation that would let him expel that dark energy. The tendrils of power he wove around her slowly began to seep through her skin. She stirred in her sleep, moaning. Max kept the flow of power strong, joining the magical energy to her spirit, feeding her life force drawn partially from himself and partially from the winds of magic. For a moment he felt he was being sucked down into the dark whirlpool of death. He felt the tug of that infinite vacuum, and his own skin became cold and clammy. He poured more power into her, but it was like dropping water onto the sands of a desert.

He felt his own life draining away, and fought against it. This was one of the dangers of magical healing of this type. When the subject was close to death, the life of the healer was in equal peril. A small panicked part of his mind fought against the current, desiring him to break the contact and save himself. He refused to listen to it, and he refused to give in. Like a swimmer fighting against a powerful undertow, he struggled on, fighting for his own life and Ulrika's. He offered up a prayer to Shallya, and found some more energy within him, then he realised that something within the woman herself had awoken and was helping him. Suddenly the moment of crisis was past. He no longer felt as if he was drowning. The constriction in his chest was gone.

That was the hard part, he told himself, knowing it was not quite true. He had stabilised her condition and he could keep it that way for as long as he provided the energy, but his power was not infinite, and he doubted he could maintain the link for as long as she needed to heal. Her body was going to need help. Slowly he extended the tendrils of power once more, feeling for the pockets of dark magical energy within her. One by one he struck at them, lancing them as a surgeon would lance a boil, expelling the dark magic from her. It emerged from her mouth and nostrils like a noxious cloud of dark green smoke.

Next, he sent the energy seeking out the tiny daemons of disease that infected her, entities so small that they were invisible to the naked eye but not to the sorcerous senses he was using. The tide of magic raced through her bloodstream and internal organs cleansing them. It was hard, tiring work requiring the highest level of concentration. Max already felt as tired as he had after his sorcerous duel with the skaven grey

seer but he kept at it, kept his mind focused. It was a long
time before he felt sure he had exterminated every one of the
loathsome plague-bearing entities.

The final stage now, he thought wearily, drawing on the last
of his energies. He sent out the command to sleep, to heal,
and to replace the vital force that had been lost. Then having
done it, he closed his eyes and offered up another prayer of
thanks. He touched her brow. The fever had broken. The
sweating was subsiding. He hoped he had done enough.
There was no way to tell. Then he fell asleep in the chair
beside the bed.

FELIX FOUND HIM there minutes later when he came in to get a
new cloak and clothing. He had paused by the well outside to
cast a bucket of water over himself and get the worst of the
blood off. He doubted that any of the guards would come to
the White Boar in search of the sell-swords' killers but he was
doing his best to cover his tracks. The jokes about rain that
had greeted him when he entered he had countered with a
tale of dumping a bucket of water over his head to sober himself up.

As he entered the room, he could tell from Ulrika's breathing that she was starting to recover, and he thanked Shallya
for her mercy. As quietly as he could, he changed his clothes
and went back downstairs to see if he could find the dwarfs
and warn them. Even as he entered the common room, he
could hear Ulli and Bjorni bellowing out some old dwarf
drinking song. Behind them came Gotrek and Snorri. None
of the Slayers looked any too sober.

'I was attacked,' he said.

'You don't say, young Felix,' replied Snorri. 'Did we miss a
good fight?'

He knew it would be a long time before he could get them
to take this seriously.

# SEVEN

IVAN PETROVICH STRAGHOV looked up and laughed. White flakes of snow mingled with the rain. The cold northern wind threatened to freeze his old bones. Good, he thought. It looks like winter will come early this year. The earlier the better. Blizzards would slow the army pouring out of the north. Frostbite would freeze fingers from hands. Exposed flesh would stick to metal. He doubted an army of any size could move through the Kislevite winter.

Slowly his good humour waned. Who knew what these Chaos worshipping bastards were capable of? Maybe they had magic to protect them. In any case, even if the marauding tribes were cut down by hunger, he did not doubt that the Chaos warriors and the beastmen would survive. He had encountered them before coming down out of the Troll Country in the depths of winter. The beastmen would most likely eat their human allies. The black-armoured warriors did not seem to need food or water or shelter, a trait they shared with their inhuman steeds.

He told himself not to be so gloomy. Every little helped, and if Lord Winter and his icy troops destroyed a few thousand of the daemon lovers he would be grateful. Right now, Kislev needed all the help it could get.

He urged his horse to greater efforts. It was only a couple of hours, ride now to Mikal's Ford and the Gospodar muster. He was looking forward to joining it. He did not doubt that if it descended on the Chaos horde, win or lose there would be a mighty killing.

FELIX JAEGER RACED across the battlements of Praag. Snow fell all around. Chill wind cut at his face. The monstrous siege engine crashed into the wall. The stones shook beneath the impact of the massive ram. Chains clanked as a huge ramp descended from the top of the tower. With a roar, fur-garbed tribesmen emerged. Their leader was a black-armoured Chaos warrior, seven feet tall, an enormous mace clamped in one hand, a huge broadsword held firmly in the other.

Even before the Chaos worshippers could move, Gotrek was among them, followed by Snorri and Bjorni. The dwarfs carved a path though the Chaos lovers straight at the leader. Felix was right behind them, Ulli at his side. The demoralised human defenders took heart and threw themselves back into the struggle.

Felix felt the ramp flex beneath the weight of the mass of warriors upon it. He hacked at the shield of one of the marauders and kicked another one off the ramp to fall to his doom in the spike-filled trench below. Ahead of him, he could hear Gotrek's bellowed war cry as the Slayer chopped down the leader of the attackers and hacked his way through the followers. At times like this the dwarf seemed unstoppable, an ancient war god of his people returned to wreak havoc on their enemies.

Felix chopped and chopped again, and then realised that the whole enormous structure was shaking. 'Back off,' he shouted. 'The whole thing is going to come down.'

Immediately he retreated to the wall, defending himself as he went. He parried the blow of a massive beastman and took off its hand with his counter-stroke. Even as he watched, he saw that the whole infernal engine was shaking and starting to lean to one side. Gotrek and the other Slayers were moving back now, reluctantly, having driven their prey back into the innards of the tower. Felix could smell burning, and saw flames beginning to leap up over the battlements. It seemed like the siege tower was on fire. How this had happened he had no idea. A spell, alchemical fire, burning oil, it did not matter. He was grateful for the respite.

There was a cheer from the defenders as the tower heeled over like a foundering ship and then crashed to the ground below. It died away as the watchers glared off into the distance and saw dozens more towers taking shape out there. This was hardly a victory, Felix realised, because this was hardly an assault. The tower had rolled forward with no support. It was obviously the work of a few crazed madmen desperate for glory, rather than part of a massive overall attack. Felix wondered what would happen when all of the towers rolled forward, supported by sorcery and those huge trebuchets. It did not bear thinking about.

Suddenly, he was very tired. He felt drained and exhausted and he slumped down with his back to the wall to snatch some rest. Gotrek stomped over. He left huge prints in the thin carpet of snow. Felix rubbed his hands together to warm them. Now that the fight was over the sweat was starting to cool on his body. He knew he would need to change out of these clothes soon or risk a fever or worse. He wondered at this snowfall. It seemed unnatural; by all accounts it was too early in the year for snow. The Kislevites had cheered it, claiming it was the work of Ulric, and that Lord Winter was fighting on their side. Felix was not so sure.

'Hardly worth the effort today. We should have stayed in the White Boar and let your people get on with it.'

'Why didn't you?' Felix gasped.

'Killing a few beastmen is better than killing none at all.'

'You may have a point there, but if it's all the same to you, you can take my share in the future.'

'Best get up, manling. We have business to be about this evening.'

'Don't think I have forgotten,' said Felix. Privately, he wished he could.

THIS LOOKS LIKE my kind of place,' Bjorni said with a cackle. He rubbed his hands together and made an obscene pumping motion with his arm. Small flakes of snow caught in his short beard. Felix wondered if it would ever stop. He had heard tales of the Kislev winter. Some said it started snowing at the end of the summer, and didn't stop till spring. He hoped this was not true.

'Somehow, I thought it might be,' Felix muttered.

Just looking out of the alley mouth at the Red Rose made him glad Bjorni was there. It had not been hard to find, since it was one of the biggest whorehouses in the whole city. Judging by the way lights blazed within, it was doing a roaring business. It was hardly surprising really. With the Chaos horde outside everyone who could afford a little forgetfulness in the pleasures of the flesh was seeking it. The inclement weather didn't seem to have discouraged any customers.

'That's not why we're here,' Gotrek said.

'Speak for yourself,' Bjorni replied cheerily. 'I hear they have a halfling girl here who can–'

'I don't want to hear it,' Gotrek said dangerously. Bjorni fell to silent muttering.

'I think I should do the talking,' Felix said. 'Why don't you just get a drink, and stay within call, in case of trouble?'

'Snorri thinks that's a good idea, young Felix,' said Snorri. The rest of the Slayers seemed to go along with this.

Felix wondered whether this was such a great plan. Showing up at the Red Rose at the same time as the four Slayers was not going to make him inconspicuous, but he felt a lot better going into the place knowing help was at hand. His encounter with Olaf and Sergei had not left him with any great desire to go into the joyhouse on his own. Still, it was the only lead on the two assassins they had at this moment, and he was keen to follow it up. Better to be the hunter than the hunted, he thought.

'Right, you lot go in, and I'll follow in a few minutes.'

'Fair enough, manling.' The Slayers stumped out of the alley, towards the joyhouse, Gotrek in the lead, Bjorni almost running beside him. If he had not known better, Felix might have sworn Ulli was blushing. Trick of the light, he thought.

Gotrek glared at the bouncers, who made way for him as he walked up to them. They obviously understood the dangers involved in trying to part four Slayers from their weapons in these troubled times. Lots of other people were going in with their swords anyway. Rough place, Felix decided, as the dwarfs disappeared inside. He gave them a few minutes, all the while praying that they did not start any trouble. He felt in his purse. He still had some gold left which was good, since he was going to have to spend it to find out what he needed to know.

Idly he speculated on whether Olaf and Sergei were Slaanesh worshippers. This looked like just the sort of place where the deranged followers of the Pleasure Daemon might hang out. He wished he knew more. Just enquiring about them might be enough to warn the people they were looking for, or it might trigger another attack if this place were some sort of secret temple. He told himself not to let his imagination run away with him. This was not a Detlief Sierck melodrama. There would be no hidden temples in this place. At least he hoped not.

He realised that he was just dragging this out now, not wanting to proceed. He took a deep breath, offered up a prayer to Sigmar that Ulrika never found out where he was this evening, as she lay recovering in their room, and strode forward. The bouncers didn't give him a second look as he marched up the stairs and through the swing doors. A wave of warmth flowed over him. He blinked as his eyes adjusted to the sudden bright lights. Dozens of candles glowed in the massive chandeliers above. A small lantern illuminated every booth around the walls. It was still dim compared to daylight, but it was much brighter than the night he had just left behind.

The smell of beer and strong perfume struck him as soon as he entered. It looked like the Red Rose was packed to capacity this evening. There was barely enough room to stand. Good, he thought, less likely that anyone will try anything nasty. Then the thought of someone scratching him with a poison blade and walking away into the crowd struck him, and made his flesh creep. He told himself that it was the melting snow running from his hair that sent a chill down his spine, but he knew it was not true. He shouldered his way through the crowd towards the bar. As he did so a couple of heavily rouged women thrust themselves towards him.

'Hello, handsome. Looking for a good time?' one of them asked.

'Maybe later,' he replied, as one of them linked her arm with his. He tried shaking it off, but she just clung tighter. Oh well, he thought, and pushed on. A quick glance revealed that the Slayers were at a table near the bar which commanded a fine view of the massive staircase that ran up to the chambers above. A constant stream of drunken men and scantily clad women headed up and down the steps. A short stocky Kislevite rider barged into Felix and reeled past. Felix felt hands clutch at his belt, and was suddenly glad he had placed his purse inside his jerkin.

'Buy a girl a drink?' said the woman on his arm.

'If we ever get to the bar,' he replied, shoving forward again. Ahead of him a crowd of mercenaries gathered round a table where a young woman garbed like an Arabian harem girl slowly removed her veils. She had an interesting selection of tattoos and piercings, Felix thought.

'I have a ring like that, through my belly button,' the girl said. 'I'll show it to you it if you like… upstairs…'

'Let's get something to drink first,' Felix said.

They got through to the bar. It was packed. Felix was forced to elbow his way between two big men in the tabards of Imperial halberdiers and ordered two beers.

'I don't want beer,' the girl announced. 'I want wine.'

'Make that a Tilean red as well,' Felix added. He was a bit annoyed now. He had hoped to make some enquiries among the bar staff concerning Olaf and Sergei, but it was obvious that things were way too busy right now to do any questioning. This was proving more difficult than he had thought already. On the plus side, nobody except the girl accompanying him appeared to be paying him the slightest attention. The place was so packed you'd have to be a Slayer or an elf prince to stand out in the crowd.

'Let's find a place to sit,' Felix said. 'I need a rest.'

'Hope you're not too tired, handsome.'

'Spent most of this afternoon on the walls,' he said. 'It takes it out of a man.'

'You don't sound like a guardsman or one of the duke's soldiers. You a mercenary?

'Something like that.'

'You either are or you aren't.'

'I got stuck here when the Chaos horde showed up.'

'Caravan guard then?'

He nodded as they shouldered their way towards a booth. It seemed a better idea than telling her the truth. If anyone was looking for Felix Jaeger, the man who had arrived on the airship, the fewer here who knew who he was the better. Felix studied the woman. She was small, and he suspected she looked older than she really was. Her skin was pale, her hair curly and bright as gold. Her face while pretty, had a worn-out look. Her features looked slightly puffy. Still, there was a quick, malicious intelligence in her eyes. Her smile was professional but pleasant. The hand working its way up his thigh was practised.

'You don't sound like a caravan guard. More like a priest or a clerk.'

'You get a lot of priests in here, do you?'

'You'd be surprised who we get in here. Elves, dwarfs, magicians, nobles... all sorts.'

'Ever see a pair of tough lads called Olaf and Sergei?' he asked, taking a chance that she might know something about his quarry. He put his hand down on hers. The creeping massage stopped. 'One's a big guy, craggy looking, and hard, very hard. The other looks fat but he's quick on his feet and good with a knife.'

'They friends of yours?' she asked warily. The smile seemed fixed on her face now, frozen almost.

'Not exactly.'

'What's the connection then?'

'I'm looking for them.'

'You want somebody hurt?' The hesitant way she said it made it sound like she was going to say something other than hurt then thought the better of it. 'I'm surprised – you look like someone who could do that yourself.' Her fingers had started moving again. He immobilised her hand.

'You know where I might find them?'

'What's it worth?' An appraising glint appeared in her eye.

He showed her his purse, holding the mouth of it open so she could see the glitter of gold and the shimmer of silver.

'Depends what you tell me.'

'They were here last night.'

'I know that much.'

'They told Sasha they would be back, but they never returned. Probably went somewhere else. The Gilded Tree maybe.'

'Sasha?'

'Tall girl, black hair. She had a thing with them.'

'Both?'

'It takes all sorts.'

'Where might I find Sasha? I would like to talk to her.'

'If you spare me some of that coin I might find her for you. I might even persuade her to talk.'

'Why might she need persuading?'

'Your friends are bad men to cross.'

'Then maybe you'd better remember something as well.'

'What's that?'

'I am a bad man to cross too.'

'I was starting to suspect that.'

'Go get her, and if you bring her here, there's gold in it for you.'

'I'd rather have it now.'

'I'm sure you would. Here's silver to keep your interest.'

'You already have my interest, handsome, but the silver's always welcome.'

Felix watched her vanish into the crowd, not quite sure what he was getting into, but determined to proceed anyway. He really wanted to find out all he could about his attackers of the previous evening. He wasn't hopeful but it was just possible that he might be able to find out who was behind them. Taking any chance to find that out, however slim, seemed preferable to waiting for a poison dagger in the back.

He took a sip of the beer, determined to stay sober. He might need all his wits about him soon. If the girl didn't just run off with his money. Or if her friend didn't just warn this Great One Olaf and Sergei had talked about. Damn, he wished he had bothered to find out her name. There was every chance that she would just take his money and never come back. Even as the thought occurred to him, he saw the golden-haired girl returning, alone.

'She'll talk to you, but she won't do it here.'

'Where then?'

'Upstairs, where else? You'll need to pay the house for the room and her time. That's on top of what you owe her and me.'

'Fine. Let's go.'

Felix rose and followed her, still clutching one of the beers to make himself look inconspicuous. As he reached the stairs, he turned and looked at the Slayers. Gotrek met his gaze and nodded. Felix was reassured by his presence. He held up all five fingers of his free hand. He hoped Gotrek understood he meant five minutes. The Slayer nodded once more. Felix went on up the stairs, suddenly feeling all too vulnerable. If there was any sort of trap being laid here he could be dead in five minutes.

THE ROOM WAS LARGE. On the walls was an interesting selection of whips and chains. The bed was well used. The girl on it looked the same way. She was tall and slim, but her eyes had an odd quality, the look of one not quite sane, or, more likely, addicted to weirdroot. She was dressed in nothing more than a thin shift.

Felix sniffed – the air smelled of stale sweat and other secretions, heavy perfume, and incense. The way his nose tingled and his throat felt tight told him that someone had been smoking weirdroot in here, mingled with something else, something he had no experience of. He moved over and opened a window. It looked down onto the street. It was a long drop. They were on the third floor of the cathouse.

'If you're looking to make a quick getaway that's not the way,' the girl said with an eerie high-pitched giggle. 'All you'll get is a broken neck. Believe me, it's been tried before.'

Felix looked at her and then back at the little blonde. 'You think I might need to make a quick getaway, do you?'

'If you're looking for Olaf and Sergei and they don't like you, like Mona says, you might have no choice. You might sort of accidentally fall out.'

'They're bad men those pair,' Felix said.

'Yes, they are. Why are you interested? Mona said something about gold.'

'Depends what you have to tell me. Depends on whether I believe what you say. Depends on a lot of things.'

'You looking to waste our time. You one of those strange ones who just wants to talk to a girl. Or is this the lead-in to something weird?'

'Nothing like that. I was just wondering why Olaf and Sergei might want to kill… a friend of mine.'

'This friend – he sent you to straighten things out, did he?'

'Something like that.'

'You look the sort. First time I hear you speak I think you talk like a priest. Looking at you I think you might be like one of those templars, the holy boys who'd cut your throat quick as look at you.'

'You have a lot of experience with templars, do you?' Felix asked with a smile, thinking of the only one he had ever known, Aldred. He had certainly fitted that description.

'You get all sorts in here, handsome,' Mona said, looking at Felix's purse meaningfully. She obviously wanted the money she had been promised.

'I haven't heard anything I wanted to know yet.'

'If I tell you where Olaf and Sergei are, what will you do?' asked Sasha. I'll be very surprised, thought Felix, considering I left them dead in an alley last night.

'Depends,' he said.

'On what?'

'On whether I can persuade them to leave my friends alone.'

'That might be difficult, unless you're tougher than you look.'

'I have friends who make me look like a priest of Shallya,' said Felix, knowing he was speaking nothing less than the truth. The sincerity of his tone must have convinced them. The girl's response surprised him. She burst into tears.

'I told them they should never have got involved. I told them to leave well enough alone. They wouldn't listen.'

Felix schooled his face to immobility, wondering exactly what the crying woman meant. Instinct told him to keep quiet, to just let her speak, to see what he could pick up. He stared at her as coldly as he could manage. He noticed that Mona had become fidgety, nervous, as if she did not like the direction the conversation was taking. It seemed that she too knew something. It looked like there was some truth in the aphorism his father used to spout crudely when drunk with his merchant friends: no place like a joyhouse when it comes to overhearing secrets. The girl was looking at him again, tears running down her face. It was hard to believe anybody could feel any tender emotion for two brutes like Olaf and Sergei, but she apparently did. Or maybe it was just the weirdroot, he told himself cynically. The girl looked at him, as if expecting some response. He decided to bluff this one out.

'What exactly did they tell you about us?' he asked, keeping his voice as soft and polite as possible. It was amazing how menacing he could sound under the right circumstances.

'Not much. Not much. I don't know much of anything recently. They talked about it sometimes when they thought I couldn't hear, and it was some sort of joke with them. They had found some sort of new… patron, one who was giving them plenty of work, and who was going to give them all sorts of special rewards.'

'By work, you mean…'

'Muscle work. Silencing them that needed silenced. At first I thought it was the usual stuff, nobles settling grudges, merchants burning out rivals but then…'

'Then what?'

'They started acting weird, coming and going at strange hours. They talked about blackmailing some folks. Seems they thought they had something on some of the nobles.'

Felix looked at Mona. 'You sure you want to hear the rest of this? There are some things that it's not worth your life to overhear.'

She looked at him, then looked at the purse. She understood but greed was warring with fear, and it did not take him long to work out which one would win. He tossed her a gold coin.

'I'll wait for you downstairs,' she said.

'You do that.' She opened the door and stepped outside.

'What else did they tell you?'

'They didn't tell me anything.'

'What else did you overhear then?'

'Nothing. Nothing.'

'You ever see this new patron of theirs?' Felix realised his speech patterns were starting to echo the girls'. 'Did you ever see this new patron of theirs?'

'Sometimes a big man would come in looking for them. A noble, I guess from his speech.'

'Did you ever see him?'

'No.'

'No?'

'He always wore a cloak with a cowl, kept a scarf wrapped round his face.'

'Isn't that a little unusual.' To his surprise, she laughed.

'Here? Gods, no! Plenty of folk, 'specially the nobs, don't want folk to know they come here. They have wives, mistresses, rivals. You get that, don't you?'

'Know anything else about this man. Did they call him the Great One or something like that?'

Suddenly whatever fit had taken her seemed to pass, and she seemed to realise what she had been saying. 'Olaf and Sergei would kill me if they knew I was telling you this.'

'I wouldn't worry about them, if I were you. They won't be troubling anybody ever again.'

The girl's eyes went wide. She looked as if she were about to scream. Felix put his hand over her mouth, and silenced her. She squirmed weakly as if she expected him to attack her, or carry her to the window and throw her out. Felix cursed. He had learned nothing from her he had not already guessed except that some unidentified patron had actually met them here at the Red Rose a few times.

'Listen to me,' he said. 'I won't hurt you. I just want answers to my questions and then I'll go. Just don't scream or do anything to attract attention, and there will be gold in this for you. Do you understand?'

She nodded. He wondered as to the wisdom of letting her go, but could see no other option. He could hardly carry her out into the corridor with her mouth covered. Even in the Red Rose that might attract the very eyes he wished to avoid. He uncovered her mouth. She breathed a bit more easily. It did not look like she was taking a breath to scream.

'Anything else about this patron? A name? A meeting place? Anything?'

'I know they followed him once, to see where he came from. Said he was a slippery customer but they were good at not being seen when they wanted to be.'

Not that good, thought Felix, remembering the previous evening. 'Where did he go?'

'The palace.'

Wonderful, thought Felix, just what I wanted to hear. He studied the girl, hoping for some sign that she was lying. He could not see any. She seemed sincere, and a little addled from the drugs once more.

'Is that all?' he asked.

'I heard them mention a name once.'

'Who?'

'Halek.'

Felix began to wonder how much time had passed and whether Gotrek and the Slayers were about to come looking for him. That was the last thing he wanted under the circumstances. He took some gold from the pouch and tossed it to the girl.

'Here, this is yours. If you see this man again, or hear anything else about him, ask for Felix Jaeger at the White Boar. There will be more gold in it for you.'

'I'll remember,' she said, and turned and buried her face in the pillow. He could hear her sobbing as he went out the door.

'I'M STAYING HERE,' said Bjorni. 'You can go if you like.'

'Suit yourself,' Gotrek said.

'I think... I will stay too,' Ulli said quietly, shuffling his feet with embarrassment.

'It's up to you, youth.'

Felix and Gotrek strode out into the street. Swiftly Felix outlined what he had learned. It seemed like even less than it had done at the time.

'We're no closer to finding this Great One behind those assassins than we were, manling.'

'No. I wish I knew why they wanted us dead. Could it be some old enemy come back for revenge?'

'We killed most of those.'

'There's a few left. Like that skaven grey seer, for example.'

'I doubt that he could pass himself off as a noble and sneak into the palace, manling, no matter how potent his sorcery.'

'He's used human agents in the past.'

'Aye, true enough.'

'Or it may be connected with the Chaos horde out there.'

'Seems more likely to me,' said the Slayer, pausing for a moment to listen to the night.

'You hear something?'

'Footsteps, trying to be stealthy. Might be footpads.' The Slayer raised his axe. Felix almost felt sorry for any would-be robbers that came on them out of the darkness. Almost. Then he remembered the assassins and their poisoned knives. He was suddenly glad of the chainmail shirt he was wearing. He held his breath for a moment, willing himself to silence. Two young men emerged from the mist, their faces masked, clubs held in their hands. They took one look at the Slayer, shrieked with fear, and turned and fled into the night. Gotrek shrugged and didn't bother to pursue them. Felix felt that was wise.

'If the girl was telling the truth then there's a traitor in the palace, manling,' said Gotrek conversationally.

'What can we do about it? March up to the duke and tell him there may be a Chaos cultist in his employ. We're sorry we don't know who, he'll just have to take our word for it. Or maybe we should start asking the staff about this Halek. It's probably a false name anyway.'

The Slayer shrugged and turned to stalk along the street. The Chaos moon gleamed balefully in the sky. Felix could have sworn that the gargoyles on the buildings had started to move. A trick of the light he told himself, hurrying after the Slayer. At moments like this he wished that he was anywhere else than Praag. It was not a comfortable city to be in, even without a Chaos army outside its gates.

MAX SCHREIBER GOT up and pulled the curtains fully closed over the shuttered windows, trying to block out the chilly draught. For a moment, through the gap in the shutters, he caught sight of the white snow-covered roof of the building opposite. He did not like it. It was too early in the year for snow. Something was affecting the weather. The fact that it was happening just as the Chaos horde approached could not be a coincidence.

He looked over at Ulrika, where she lay wrapped in a thick quilt. If this cold snap continued she would need more than one or a chill might undo all of Max's work. Right now though, she slept the healthy sleep of someone recovering from an illness. The crisis was past, and really he was no longer needed here. He stood there anyway, looking at her sleeping form, and offered up a prayer of gratitude to Shallya for sparing her life. Even if she would never be his, he was glad she had survived. He walked over, stroked her head, and tiptoed quietly to the door.

He was as drained of energy as if he had walked for days without food, and he knew he needed to replenish his strength both physical and magical. He headed downstairs into the tavern. Men looked at him with new respect, wonder and even fear. Somehow word had got out that he had saved Ulrika from the plague. No one wanted to offend him now. After all, he might be able to save them if they went down with the disease.

Max knew that sooner or later this was going to cause problems. Much as he would have liked to, he simply did not have the strength to save so many people. Saving Ulrika had almost killed him, and he doubted there was anybody in the city he cared enough about to make him want to risk his life again. Of course, that was easy to think now, sitting here among these rough hard-faced men, but what if tomorrow some teary-eyed mother came to him and asked him to save her child? That was a plea he would find much harder to resist. Well, he would worry about that when it happened. There was no sense in borrowing trouble from tomorrow.

He ordered food from the serving wench, and some tea, and then returned to the room. He did not feel like facing the stares of the men in the common room, and he did not feel at all like drinking wine. He wanted a clear head and nothing to distort his powers. He wondered where Felix and the Slayer were. Out hunting for the man who sent those hired killers last night, most likely. Max wondered if there was anything he could do to help. Not likely at the moment. He needed to husband every iota of his strength until he recovered. Even

then it was unlikely he could do much if the man they sought
was a cultist. Such people were usually well protected against
scrying spells. They needed to be.

Max wondered if assassins would come looking for him and
Ulrika or whether it was just Felix and Gotrek they were after.
Given the power of the Slayer's axe, there might be some reason for getting rid of him, but what reason could there be for
seeking out anybody else? Why even bother trying to understand the reasoning of the worshippers of Chaos, Max thought.
Too much effort in that direction might end up warping your
own mind. It had happened before, he knew. Those who tried
to understand the ways of Chaos were often seduced by them.
It was a thing he had been often warned against.

Even as these thoughts churned through his mind, he felt a
sudden vast change in the winds of magic. If it had been the
distant rumble of a thunderstorm it could not have been
more obvious. He glanced out of the window and invoked
his mage sight. At once, he saw his suspicions were correct.
Great turbulent currents were starting to affect the massive
cloud of dark magic above the Chaos army. Huge vortexes of
magical energy swirled downwards into it, funnelling all that
power somewhere. What was going on, he wondered?
Nothing good, that was for certain.

There was a knock at the door. Max moved cautiously and
checked the bar. It was still in place. 'Who is it?' he asked.

'Are you Herr Schreiber?' The voice was calm, and held a
great deal of authority.

Max wondered who it was. Was this some sort of trap? He
used some of his carefully husbanded power and risked a
scrying spell. A vision of the man beyond the door flickered
into his mind. He was a tall soldierly figure in a tabard that
bore the winged lion of Praag. The chevrons that marked him
as a sergeant-at-arms were on his sleeves. Two other soldiers
waited with him. Max wondered whether the duke had sent
these men. It was likely enough. Still, it would not be the first
time Chaos cultists had impersonated those in authority. He
wanted to take no risks with Ulrika in her weakened state.

'Why do you ask?'

'I bear a summons from the duke.' That at least appeared to
be true. The man held a rolled-up piece of parchment in his

hands. Still, how much did parchment cost, Max asked himself. He prepared a potent offensive spell in his mind, drawing the winds of magic to himself. If these men were assassins they would not find him unready.

He opened the door a crack. No knife was pushed through. The sergeant-at-arms looked at him oddly, as if his behaviour were somehow a little cracked. If the man were what he seemed, Max supposed it would seem that way to him.

'I have a patient in here who may still carry the plague. It would be best if you passed me the message and waited downstairs,' Max said. This was the moment of truth. If these men were hired killers now was the moment when they would attack.

He saw the sergeant's face blanch, and the scroll was swiftly thrust through the crack in the door. 'Right you are, sir,' said the sergeant.

Max inspected the paper. It certainly looked authentic enough, and it bore a winged lion seal. He sensed no magical energies laid on it, so, as far as he could tell, it was not some sort of magical trap. Working on the theory that you could never be too careful he probed it with his mage senses, and came up with nothing. He shrugged, closed the door and cracked the seal.

Swiftly, he read the message within. It was a simple request for his presence at the palace. It was addressed to Herr Max Schreiber of the Imperial College of Magicians. It appeared that the ruling house of Kislev wished to hire his services. Most likely they wanted an extra healer on hand in case of plague, Max thought cynically.

He looked around at Ulrika. He did not want to leave her now with no one to protect her, but Praag was a city at war, under martial law; refusing a request by the ruler might be construed as treason. He studied the message once more. It did not say when he had to report to the palace, and the hour was certainly late. He considered this for a moment, looked over at Ulrika's sleeping form, and decided that he would risk offending the duke. There would be time enough to go see him in the morning. He scribbled out a hasty reply, and went downstairs to hand it to the sergeant.

\* \* \*

GREY SEER THANQUOL looked around at the elders of Clan Moulder. He was enjoying himself now. Since the defeat of Lurk's forces, they looked at him with new respect tempered by a healthy amount of fear. That was good.

In some ways this council chamber was a blasphemous echo of the Chamber of the Thirteen back in Skavenblight. The elders sat on a great rotunda roughly the shape of a horseshoe. There were thirteen of them, which was unsurprising, since that was one of the holy numbers of skaven cosmology. There were representatives of each of the Moulder clan-guilds, a group so interbred that it made even Thanquol's mighty mind swim trying to understand the complexity of their relationships. He guessed that, as in Skavenblight, status was reflected by their representative's position on the horseshoe: the closer to the centre and the further from the wings, the more powerful the skaven. The clan's High Packmaster sat in the centre, at the fulcrum. Grey Seer Thanquol stood before him, in the space enclosed by the horseshoe, confronting thirteen pairs of fitfully gleaming red eyes. His paws rested on the rune of Clan Moulder tiled on the floor. He was not intimidated by his position. Not in the slightest. The faint tightening in his musk glands merely indicated excitement.

'Your former minion has vanished, Grey Seer Thanquol,' squeaked the High Packmaster. Thanquol saw notes being passed from paw to paw around the table edge. This was never a good sign.

'The traitor Lurk has eluded Clan Moulder once more,' sneered Thanquol, more to have something to say than for any other reason. 'Why does this not surprise me?'

'We had hoped that you would use your powers to locate him. Clan Moulder has a score to settle with that deviant creature.'

'I have done my best,' chittered Thanquol, 'but he appears to have left the city.'

'What has that got to do with it, grey seer?'

Thanquol watched the note slowly make its way from the outer left hand edge of the horseshoe to the centre. What information did it contain, he wondered, even as he spoke.

'There are great disturbances in the flow of mystical energies,' Thanquol said in his best oracular manner. This was true. In the past few days the winds of magic had blown stronger than ever before. Scrying through such a mage storm was like trying to see in a blizzard. Finding Lurk was all but impossible under the circumstances.

'So? So?'

'These disturbances interfere with my vision, and disrupt all forms of scrying.'

'Have you given thought to what causes these disturbances? Could it be the powers behind the menace of Lurk?'

That was a disturbing thought, and all too likely. Not that Thanquol suspected the powers of Chaos would aid a creature as lowly as Lurk. It was more likely that this was some mystical phenomenon occurring simultaneously with the march of the Chaos horde. There was perhaps the vanishingly small possibility that the spellcasters of the horde were drawing energy from the Wastes to aid their magic. Even as the thought crossed Thanquol's mind, he felt his musk glands tighten almost to bursting point. Just the chance that it might be so was terrifying. It spoke of a power almost beyond belief.

Of course, thought Thanquol, if there was a way to tap into that mystical energy before it reached the Chaos horde, the sorcerer who managed it would be powerful beyond belief.

Suddenly Thanquol knew it was imperative that he get out of Hell Pit and begin investigating that possibility. All he needed now was an excuse. At that point the note reached the High Packmaster and he opened it, read it and frowned.

'We have received word from Skavenblight. You are to return there at once, and explain your actions to the Council of Thirteen, Grey Seer Thanquol. We will, of course, provide an escort to see you through these troubled lands.'

Normally the prospect of such a trip would have made Thanquol queasy with justifiable skaven caution. Now he almost looked forward to it.

'I will depart at once!' Thanquol declared.

He could tell the Moulders were puzzled, and not a little frightened, by his enthusiasm.

FELIX WONDERED WHAT was going on. His skin crawled. The hairs on the back of his neck had risen. There seemed to be a peculiar glow in the night sky, a shimmering over the army outside the city. He had sensed such things just before dark magic had been unleashed. It was not a feeling he enjoyed. Perhaps it had something to do with the early snowfall.

The White Boar was just ahead of them, lights blazing cheerily through the constant drift of snowflakes. Even as he watched three men in the uniforms of the ducal guard emerged. He fought down an urge to duck into an alley. Surely they had not come to investigate the deaths of Olaf and Sergei? Surely they could not be looking for him? Gotrek showed no sign of any concern whatsoever. He strode forward, ignoring the guardsmen as if they were not there.

The guardsmen obviously knew who he was, for he gave him a wide berth. As he walked past Felix heard the soldiers whispering about the day's battle. It seemed their exploits on the walls were well known.

*Fine*, thought Felix. It might not do them much good to be the heroes of the hour, but every little helped. While they were useful fighters in the defence of the city, he doubted anyone would look too closely at their other activities.

He entered the tavern and immediately headed upstairs, leaving Gotrek to his solitary drinking in the bar.

'How is she?' Felix asked nervously. Max sat in the chair next to the bed. Felix was not sure how he felt about the wizard being here. He was at once jealous and grateful.

'She will be fine,' Max said softly. 'She just needs rest and time to recover.'

'How are you? Feeling any better?'

'I've been less tired, but I'll live. Find out anything interesting?'

Felix risked a look at Ulrika to make sure she was asleep and then explained where he had been and what he had learned.

'It's not much, but it's better than nothing,' Max said. 'Did you really expect to uncover the name of the assassin's master?'

'No, but sometimes you get lucky. If you don't try, you never get anywhere, and then we might as well all go back to waiting for a poisoned knife in the back some dark night. Can you think of anything?'

'No. I am worried though. It's not a reassuring thought that there may be traitors in the palace. I can't say I am surprised though.'

'Nor can I.'

'Really? You say that with some authority, Felix.'

'It won't be the first time I have encountered traitors in high places.' Max just looked at him. Without knowing why, Felix found himself telling the tale of his encounter with Fritz von Halstadt, chief of the Elector Countess Emmanuelle's secret police, and an agent of the skaven. Max was a good listener, nodding and smiling and asking intelligent questions when he needed a point clarified.

'You think the traitor might be just as highly placed?' Max asked eventually.

'No reason why he might not be even more highly placed. High birth is no guarantee that a man is not corrupt.'

'I am sure many of our ruling class might violently disagree with that,' said Max. 'But I won't. Even in Middenheim I saw evidence of that. I can remember...'

As Max spoke a look of pure fear passed across his face. His features went pale. His hands shook. He looked like he had just been struck by a thunderbolt.

'What is it?' asked Felix.

'We must go to the wall! Now! Get the Slayer!'

# EIGHT

THE MAN CALLED Halek stood on the topmost tower of the citadel and gazed off into the night. Below him he could see the snow-covered roofs of the inner town, the towering temple tops, the maze-like pattern of streets, and the enormous inner wall. The houses and tenements beyond that looked tiny in the distance. Only the massive outer wall appeared to have any substance. In the far distance, he could see out into the vast sea of campfires that surrounded the city, the silhouettes of the monstrous daemonic war-engines, dark metal leering out through their covering of snow. He could see other things now too.

His master had granted him a gift recently. He had been changed. His eyes could see more than mortal eyes now, could see the powers of his master, Tzeentch, Lord of Magic, as it ebbed and flowed around him. He knew that soon his eyes would start to change, and would show the stigmata of mutation, but it did not matter now. By the time any of the people around him realised he was one of the Gifted, it would be far too late to do anything about it. They, and their whole city, would be crushed beneath the iron heel of Chaos.

Halek knew he had to stop thinking like this. He knew that with the change he was becoming unduly sensitive to the currents of magic being summoned by the master magicians out there among the Chaos horde. He knew that it was starting to affect his mind. Soon it would not matter. Soon he would be free to revel in unfettered worship of his master, the Changer of Ways, but now things were at a delicate juncture, and might still go wrong. As he had so often reminded himself, there was no point in Chaos triumphing if he himself was not there to witness it. He did not want to risk exposure so soon before the glorious day when the Time of Changes arrived.

Part of him was still unsure whether he wished to see the triumph of Chaos at all. Part of him was still loyal to the city and the people and the duke. Part of him wished he had never attended that first meeting, never allowed himself to be seduced into the quest for forbidden knowledge. Too late now, he told himself, trying to submerge the side of himself that felt guilt and weariness and pain. Too late for anything except to play his planned part.

He tried to tell himself that the changes were for the better. He could feel his master's gifts wakening within him, as they would soon be doing among all the chosen of the Old World. With his new sensitivity to the winds of magic had come the first hints of the ability to wield it. He could with an effort of will now shape the raw stuff of magic itself. To prove it to himself, he concentrated on making light appear around his hand. By dint of prodigious effort he made a faint nebulous glow appear about him. Astonishing, what it took most magicians years of study and intensive training to master was coming to him through nothing more than the force of his own will. If he could do this now, after only a few days, what else might be possible in a few years?

He glanced out into the distance, his attention suddenly caught by the vast skein of magic woven around the city. Tonight it blazed with astonishing brightness. Tonight as Morrslieb blazed down in all its glory, the final rituals were taking place to seal the circle around the city, and move the great scheme forward. He could see the webs of force shimmering through the lines of the Chaos army, running from sacred obelisk to sacred obelisk, as the sorcerers in the service of Tzeentch summoned the winds of magic and channelled them to their own purposes. Each of those great, carved standing stones had been brought down from the Chaos Wastes borne by hundreds of sanctified slaves. He could not yet guess what the purpose of them was, but he knew it must be mighty. When the time was right, he would know.

He forced his enraptured mind away from the contemplation of the infinite beauty of the magical weaving, and back to matters at hand. It was a pity Olaf and Sergei had failed in their assigned task. They had been good servants in their way, and he was sorry they would not be around to claim their rewards on the great day. Felix Jaeger must have been very lucky or very tough to survive that encounter, for the pair had been formidable killers. It was not a reassuring thought, for he had counted Jaeger as the less formidable of the pair it was his assigned task to see killed.

If it took this much effort to kill the man, it was going to take much more to get rid of the Slayer. Still, he knew with patience, persistence and a painstaking determination to learn from one's mistakes, all setbacks could be overcome. He would just have to find another way forward, that was all. He felt sure that he would fulfil his part in the Great Scheme before too long. He always had before.

Right now there were other things to concern him. His agents must have poisoned the Watergate granary by now. It would be the first of many if all went well. He shuddered. He did not like doing these things. It went against all he had been brought up to believe. He did not like thinking of himself as a traitor. Even as this thought crossed his mind, he was granted a flash of insight. Part of him did feel guilty, it was true, but another part of him revelled in the wickedness of it all. He was taking his revenge for a lifetime of being in second place, for all those little slights that had been heaped on him. He was breaking free from the straightjacket of honour and responsibility. In a way it was a good thing. Then why do I feel like I stand on the brink of an abyss, he thought.

Even as he watched he sensed a change coming over the city in response to the flow of power in the distance. It sounded like a high-pitched keening wail. The sort of sound a soul in torment might make when plunged into Tzeentch's deepest hells. What was going on, Halek wondered? Was this some part of the Great Scheme of which he had not been warned?

As THEY RACED through the snow, shapes emerged from the gloom. At first, Felix could not believe his eyes. He thought he was just seeing gusts of snow, being driven into odd forms, but as he watched it became obvious that it was not so.

The outlines took on a misty nebulous substance that looked like the silhouettes of men but had the faces of souls in torment. They howled and wailed thinly, their spectral voices rising above the wind in a terrifying shriek. One of them came straight at Gotrek, gibbering insanely, long trails of faintly glowing ectoplasm swirling out behind it as it flowed through the air. The Slayer raised his axe, and his blow passed through the ghastly creature as if it were made of mist. As it did so, the creature lost coherence and dissolved into invisibility. All around them the wailing intensified, and a sense of terrible presence thickened.

Looking around him, Felix could see that thousands of the creatures swam through the air of the city, shrieking and howling and gibbering. One of them flashed directly at him. He raised his sword to block it, the way Gotrek had blocked his. As the creature came closer, he could see that it was almost transparent. It glowed green in the light of Morrslieb. Snowflakes passed through it, as if it were not really there. It did not seem quite real. As he watched he saw more and more of the things were emerging from the very stones of the city. What new Chaos-spawned evil was this, he wondered? What had the forces of Darkness unleashed this night?

With appalling speed the creature swerved around his blade. It reached out and clasped his face with its eldritchly glowing fingers. At the instant of contact a shock passed through Felix, potent as if he had been struck by lightning. The shock was not physical but emotional. It was a jolt of pure undiluted terror. Felix felt his blood run cold as fear entered his mind, and threatened to bury his mind under an avalanche of pure dread.

A flood of images flickered through his mind, threatening to drown his brain. He saw the city of Praag, oddly changed. He saw a vast Chaos army outside the gates, and a leering hungry face glowing in the moon. He saw a pitiful army of human defenders cut down by the warriors of evil. He saw the city raised and the army of Darkness move off leaving only the spirits of the restless dead. Later he saw the city rebuilt, and the eerie consciences of the slain seeping into its very stones, to be poisoned and corrupted by the warping energies that surrounded them.

Instantly he realised what the thing was. It was a ghost of one of those warriors who had fallen two centuries ago, in the Great War against Chaos. Once it had been a man like him, now it had been reduced to a near mindless hungry echo of what it once was. The fear it projected into him was its own fear, a thing that had consumed its consciousness over the long decades of imprisonment in the stones. It was an all-consuming horror that threatened to kill him with its sheer power. His heart raced until he felt it would burst. His nerve endings screamed. Something deep within his brain shrieked and gibbered in primal terror. He felt as if his mind would crumble under the sheer intensity of the feeling, and as sanity receded he felt tendrils of alien thought begin to invade his brain. He had a sense of a bottomless hunger, and a mindless lust to take on flesh once more, and slake desires that had not been gratified in centuries.

He knew something was trying to displace him from his own body, to force his spirit out so that it could possess his body and work evil. He knew that if it succeeded, he would become like it, a disembodied spirit slowly degenerating into a creature like this lost, mindless thing. Desperately, without knowing quite how, he fought back, seeking to push the thing out of him.

As he did so, he felt the fear begin to recede. His heartbeat slowed once more. His vision cleared. He saw the ghostly thing's horrifically distorted face before him. It was a ghastly parody of a man's, twisted with rage and a sickening desire for mortal flesh. Its mouth opened, distending far further than any human mouth, becoming so large it looked like it could swallow Felix's head in a bite. He snarled back at it, and swung his blade. It passed through the creature. The runes on its blade glowed and the hideous thing fell apart into dozens of smaller component clouds that slowly dissipated. As they did so the near overwhelming terror vanished as if it had never been.

He glanced around and saw that Gotrek stood in the middle of a cloud of shrieking spectres, his axe destroying them before they could get close to him. Max was nearby, encased in a shield of golden light that prevented the creatures from getting close to him. As Felix watched, Max gestured and incanted and the sphere surrounding him expanded, racing outwards into the night. Where it touched a ghost the thing disintegrated, unable to resist whatever magic the wizard had unleashed. Felix envied Max his powers. In a moment, the street around them was clear of the monsters, as was the sky above. From houses around them, Felix could hear shrieks and insane gibbering. He guessed that not all of the inhabitants of the houses has been as successful as he had at resisting possession by the ghosts. At that moment, another fear almost as overwhelming as the one the spectre had inflicted on him filled his mind. He glared over at Max: 'Ulrika – is she safe?'

Max's face went pale then he closed his eyes and made a complex series of hand-gestures. Behind his eyelids, Felix could see a molten golden glow. It was not a reassuring sight. The fire within had only just started to die away as Max opened his eyes once more. 'Do not worry. She is safe. The wards I left in place were more than enough to keep those creatures at bay.'

'What in hell were those things?' Felix asked, although already knew the answer. He needed to hear his own voice just to prove to himself he was still human.

'Ectoplasmic creatures, a psychic residue of the evil that once flowed over this city.'

'Once more Max, in language I might understand.'

'Ghosts, Felix. Spirits bound to the place of their death by the power of dark magic, and their own fears and hatreds. Praag is a haunted city.'

'How did the Chaos warriors free them? I thought you said their magic could not penetrate the warding spells in the city walls.'

Max shook his head, and all the light died from his eyes. He looked over at Gotrek and Felix. Heavy footsteps came closer in the night. Felix held his sword at the ready. Gotrek shook his head, telling him the weapon would not be needed. Max seemed oblivious to the potential threat. He kept speaking in a loud slightly theatrical voice, reminding Felix for all the world of his former professors at the University of Altdorf.

'Perhaps their magic has grown strong enough to pass through those spells. It is possible, but not likely. I do not think they are strong enough yet to manage that.'

'Then what did this?' As Felix watched glowing spheres of light began to expand outwards over other parts of the city. Felix did not need Max to tell him that other wizards were at work, doing exactly what Max had done.

'I don't think the Chaos horde freed these things exactly,' said Max. 'I think they were always here, always within the walls. I think that something the Chaos magicians have done woke them.'

'And what might that have been?'

'I don't know, but I sensed a mighty movement of the winds of magic not a watch ago. The Chaos moon waxes. The powers of evil magic grow strong. Let us go to the walls and see for ourselves.'

Even as Max finished speaking, Snorri Nosebiter emerged from the gloom and the snow. 'Funny ghostie things attacked Snorri. Stupid things kept hitting him. Nothing happened.'

'You didn't feel anything – fear, terror, pain?' Felix asked.

'No. Snorri didn't feel any such things.' Snorri sounded insulted by the very suggestion.

'That's because you need a brain to feel fear, manling,' said Gotrek. 'Snorri doesn't have one.'

Snorri beamed proudly at Gotrek's words. He looked pleased as punch as they rushed on towards the walls.

A MAN EMERGED from the snow. His features were pale, corpse-like. His eyes glowed with the same spectral luminescence that had surrounded the ghosts. Max knew instantly that here was one of those foul beings taken flesh. Embedded as it was on tissue and sinew, it could not now be disintegrated by the magical energies that Max had used to dispel its brethren. He summoned his energies, but it was becoming more difficult. He was numbed by the cold, and drained by the magic he had already wrought. The thing chuckled evilly and reached for him with long, cold white fingers.

Before it could reach him, Felix leapt past Max and slammed his sword through the creature's body. Blood seeped forth slowly, staining the snow. It was an unnatural response to so deep a wound, but the evil thing that had possessed the man was not giving up its life easily. The runes along Felix's blade glowed dully. Max did not sense any of the ancient sentience that had emerged when they had confronted the dragon Skjalandir. If it was still within the blade, it remained dormant.

As the creature fell, a long wailing shriek emerged from its mouth, and white mist bubbled out. At first Max feared that the ghost was going to attempt to possess either Felix or himself, but it did not. Instead, it began to disintegrate and blow away in the wind.

'Thank you,' said Max, and meant it. He was suddenly grateful that Felix, Gotrek and Snorri were there. They might not have been people who he would have wanted to spend time with under normal circumstances, but when you were trapped in a snowbound haunted city under siege by the powers of Chaos, they were exactly the sort you wanted by your side.

They continued to move on towards the walls. Max feared what they would find there. Overhead Morrslieb glowed fearfully. Its light was brighter than that of its larger brother, Mannslieb. He was not sure why this was happening but he knew from his reading of history that it was always a portent of dreadful things. In truth, he did not need the alteration to the moon to let him know this. His mage senses told him the same thing. The currents of dark magic swirled visibly beyond the city walls, a mighty tide of evil energy being drawn there for a reason. And he was sure that the reason was not a good one.

All around he sensed the pulse of magic. Other wizards were at work, and most likely some of the priests as well, doing their best to contain the evil spirits that had been unleashed. Even as he thought this, he sensed something else, a flow of dark magical energy through the night. It was potent and evil, and it came from close by.

'Gotrek! Felix! Turn right! Now! Beware! There is evil magic here!'

To their credit, the adventurers did not hesitate, or even question his instructions. They raced down the side street in the direction he had indicated with Snorri in their wake. As they did so, Max's magically attuned eyes picked up a strange, many-coloured gleam from up ahead. The currents of dark magic made his hackles rise. He muttered an incantation to strengthen his protective spells and prepared himself for battle.

What new madness was this, wondered Felix, as they ran towards the massive structure? He recognised the building as one of the fortified grain depots in which the city's foodstocks were stored. Normally the place was heavily guarded, but now the entrance was open and the way within clear. Where were the soldiers?

As he approached the arched doorway, he got his answer. They lay in the snow, with their throats cut, puddles of redness clotting all around them. Felix's mind reeled. This was not possible. Armed soldiers did not stand and let their throats be cut when they had the will and the means to resist. There was only one answer. Evil sorcery was at work here. The gargoyles above the entrance seemed poised to spring on him as he passed beneath them. He let out a sigh of relief as he stepped inside and nothing happened. For a moment he was glad to be out of the bitter cold, but when he saw what waited within he felt suddenly sick.

More guardsmen had been slaughtered. Their throats had been cut, and their eyes were wide and staring. Their weapons lay near at hand, unstained by the blood of their foes, obviously unused. Again, Felix felt a sick certainty that evil magic was at work here. These men had put up no resistance, and they could not have been anything but wary. Not with those shrieking spectres howling on the wind earlier. Dozens of them had died here, and their enemies, whoever they were, had not taken a casualty.

In a moment, Gotrek and the others were around him. 'They are here to destroy the food supplies,' said Max.

'Or poison them,' said Gotrek. Felix nodded remembering Sergei and Olaf and their tainted blades. Their employer certainly had knowledge of wicked alchemy.

'Snorri thinks we'd better stop them,' said Snorri.

'How?' Felix asked, fighting to keep fear from his voice. 'Three score of city guards didn't manage to.'

'I'm sure we'll think of something, manling,' said Gotrek running his thumb along the edge of his axe till a bright bead of blood blossomed forth. 'They are down in the silos. I can hear them.'

'Be wary,' said Max. 'They have strong magic. I can feel it.'

Gotrek looked at the corpses and snorted. 'I didn't need a wizard to tell me that.'

THEY CREPT FORWARD into the gloom. Felix caught the odd musty smell of grain in the air. Dust tickled his throat and made his mouth feel dry. They passed massive chutes designed to carry the grain down into the huge storage pits. It was gloomy here. The only illumination was the faint glow surrounding Max. He had muted it as much as possible to avoid warning any enemies of their approach, leaving only enough to let Felix see by. Felix suspected that the wizard had no more need of the light than the dwarfs, and he was grateful to Max for his concern.

'Do you think there is a connection?' Felix asked.

'Between what?' Max asked.

'The ghosts being unleashed, and now this raid on the grain stores?'

'I don't know. It's more likely an accident that the ghosts were unleashed and this happened at the same time. I think the raids were timed to happen on the same night as whatever is happening outside the wall, but that does not mean they are connected either.'

'What do you mean?'

'The Chaos moon is full. Dark magic is at its most powerful on a night like this. This is a holy night to the followers of the Ruinous Powers. It might just be that a number of things are happening concurrently because of that.'

'We can't be certain.'

'No. Maybe I am just hoping this is the case.'

'Why?'

'Because if it isn't it means that the attackers outside our walls have some method of communicating with the worshippers of Chaos within them. And if they have, maybe they have a way of getting more than messages through.'

'Not a reassuring thought.'

'This invasion has obviously been long planned, Felix, by someone, or a group of people with diabolical intelligence. Who knows what other nasty surprises they have in store?'

Felix stood on the edge of a loading ramp, looking down into the silo. About fifteen feet below, knee-deep in grain, he could see figures. There were a dozen robed and masked men. Some of them held lanterns whilst others moved in the storage bin, adding liquid from large vials and stirring it in to the grain. Felix knew Gotrek had been right. This was poison. What sort of men were these, he wondered, who could plot to kill their fellow citizens while outside an army of monsters waited? He already had the answer he realised. They were followers of the dark powers of Chaos. They probably did not even consider what they were doing as treachery. Unfortunately for them, he did.

Seeing how few their numbers were reassured him somewhat. They had used sorcery and dark magic to overcome the guards but, hopefully, Max could counter that. Unless they were quite extraordinary fighting men, Gotrek and Snorri would prove more than a match for them. And Felix would cheerfully help in that slaughter. They were obviously overconfident and would be easy enough to take by surprise. They had not even posted sentries.

'We were told not to kill the guards,' grumbled one of the men below. 'We were told but would you listen? No! When the higher-ups get word of this there will be trouble.'

'Better safe than sorry, that's what I say,' said another voice in a self-justifying tone. It was a nasty voice, with a slimy insinuating quality to it, and Felix did not doubt for a moment that its owner had been the one to start the slaughter of the guards, and had enjoyed doing it. 'Anyway, it's a few less blades for our brethren outside the walls to worry about.'

'Yes – but now everyone will know something happened here. This was supposed to be a surprise.'

'Hurry it up,' Felix heard a third voice say. This was the voice of a leader. 'The blizzard won't last forever, and the guard will be relieved in a couple of hours. We don't have all night.'

It was almost reassuring, hearing human voices after the spectral things they had encountered outside. Their foes were living, breathing people, and Felix knew that if he cut one, he would bleed. Suddenly he was glad.

As so often happened to him, his earlier fear had passed to be replaced with a smouldering rage. He was angry at those men below for what they had done. It was bad enough that they had slaughtered the guards by stealth, but they were planning the murder of hundreds, maybe thousands more people. Felix knew that if their plan was allowed to succeed, he or Ulrika or any of these others could easily be among the victims. What they were doing was wicked and cowardly as well as treacherous, and it had to be stopped.

'Looks like they've only managed to contaminate one bin so far,' whispered Max.

'Then let's stop them before they do any more,' Gotrek said. 'Oi! What are you doing down there?' he bellowed.

The masked cultists looked up. Felix could see feverish eyes gleaming. Several of them held knives or swords. One of them raised his hands, and began to incant. Without giving himself a chance to think, Felix launched himself into space, swinging his sword as he went. He landed near the Chaos sorcerer and split his skull with one blow. The impact of landing was cushioned by the soft grain in which he now stood almost up to his ankles.

The cultists yelled with dismay as Gotrek and Snorri dropped to join him. Gotrek's axe lashed out chopping the nearest cultist in two. The return swipe clipped the top off another's skull and sent brainstuff spurting over the grain. Snorri howled with glee as he lashed out with his axe and his hammer.

Felix's assessment of the cultists had been correct. It took them a moment to recover, and in that time, Felix launched himself forward to stab another in the stomach. As he did so he discovered one of the disadvantages of their situation. The grain slithered around underfoot. It was like wading through a slippery type of quicksand. It at once sucked you down and made it very difficult to keep your balance if you moved.

'Get them!' one of the cultists shouted. 'There's only three of them.'

The Chaos worshippers moved to engage them, slipping as they moved too. Only the dwarfs showed no signs of losing their balance. Of course, it was easy for them, thought Felix, with their short legs and broad feet. They strode forward to meet the enemy, barely impeded by their footing at all.

Felix found himself trading blows with a big man, larger than himself, armed with a heavy broadsword. The man was slower than he was, and not nearly as skilled, and under normal circumstances, Felix would have dispatched him in an instant. As it was the difficulty of moving without falling over, and the way the grain sucked at his legs and slowed his movements, meant that he was having some difficulty. It increased when the man was joined by two of his fellows. Wonderful, thought Felix. Why can't they go and fight with Gotrek instead of picking on me?

He parried one blow, barely turned another, and felt his arm being nicked by the edge of a sword. He prayed that the blade wasn't poisoned, and tried to keep the thought from freezing him on the spot as he blocked another blow. The force of the impact threatened to send his blade flying from his numbed fingers. He almost overbalanced in the slippery grain.

From above came a searing flash of golden light. One of the men's cowls caught fire, and the beam continued onwards, setting his hair alight and causing the flesh of his scalp to melt and run. As Felix watched his skull seemed to cave inwards, and his head sagged downwards as if made of melting clay. The man gave a horrible gurgling moan and collapsed. Another of Felix's assailants glanced upwards to locate the source of this new threat. Felix took the opportunity to slide his sword blade under the man's ribs, and send him headlong into Morr's realm.

The last man shrieked and leapt at Felix but as he did so, Gotrek's axe caught him on the back of his head, passed right through his torso and cleft him in twain. Felix glanced up and saw Max Schreiber standing there, a golden aura surrounding his right hand. Felix nodded his thanks and then glanced around the silo. It was like a scene from some hell of the Blood God's. Parts of dismembered bodies lay everywhere. Blood seeped into the grain. The alembics of poison lay there, their contents gurgling outwards.

'Snorri doesn't fancy eating any bread made from this stuff,' said Snorri.

For once in your life, Snorri, you just said something sensible, thought Felix.

'What are we going to do?' Felix asked worriedly. 'Wait here until the guards come?'

He had enough experience of these things to know that the guards might just take one look at the carnage they had caused and haul them off to the duke's cells. That's if any guards were coming. They might well not be, in the aftermath of the ghosts of Praag being unleashed.

'The question is whether this was the only granary being attacked,' Max said. 'The only reason these swine failed here is because we stopped them. If something similar is happening at every granary in the city...'

'We should warn someone,' Felix said.

'Who? If there is a traitor in the palace.'

'We should tell the duke in person. I doubt he's the traitor, and, if he is, we have an even bigger problem.'

'The duke would see me, I think,' Max said. 'He requested I attend his court earlier today. Of course, he would probably listen to Ulrika too, but she's not up and about.'

'He would listen to anyone who came here on the *Spirit of Grungni*,' Felix said, thinking quickly.

'Then let's not waste any more time debating about it,' said Gotrek. 'Let's go!'

The snow had stopped falling for the moment. The streets were eerily quiet beneath their blanket of white. The night air was cold and still. From somewhere off in the distance came a long high-pitched wail, and what sounded like a sob of grief. It seemed that the night's evil was unending, thought Felix. Max stood frozen for a moment, in the attitude of a man listening to some barely perceptible noise. After a moment, he said, 'The forces of dark magic are strong this night.'

'Easy to see who's the wizard here,' Gotrek said sarcastically. 'I don't think we need you to tell us that.'

'That's not what I meant,' Max said testily. 'Why don't you leave the divination to me, and I'll leave the axe work to you?'

'Sounds fair,' said Snorri.

'What did you mean exactly?' Gotrek said.

'There's something big going on out there,' said Max. There was no need to ask where out there was. They all knew he meant beyond the walls. 'Some mighty arcane ritual. They are gathering all the winds of dark magic from the north, channelling them into a mighty storm of magic.'

'To what end?' Felix asked. 'To overcome the city's spell walls?'

'Perhaps,' Max said. 'Or perhaps for some other reason.'

'What might that be?'

'Let me think about it.'

'Then think while we move,' said Gotrek. 'Come on!'

AS THEY RUSHED through the chilly winding streets, Max once more appreciated how cunningly Praag had been rebuilt. The city was a maze, designed to confuse any who did not know its layout already. Not that it would help much if invaders had cultist guides from within the walls. The guards at the gate of the inner wall let them pass easily enough, and they ran on up the massive stone outcrop on top of which the citadel rested.

Max was worried, more than he had been in his entire life. The full enormity of their situation was settling like a lead weight on his shoulders. He and Ulrika and the others were trapped here. Not only was the weight of foes without the walls near overwhelming, but also there were traitors within. Worse, the enemy army contained sorcerers more powerful than any Max had ever encountered, and they were, even now, engaged in some evil magical ritual the purpose of which he could not yet fathom.

Think, he told himself. What are they really doing? Gathering all the dark magical energy of an entire continent to them. Why? What can they achieve? They can power spells of enormous force. Or? Or, for a short time, they can raise the level of dark magical power in this area to that of the Chaos Wastes, or even higher. Suddenly, a sinking feeling settled in the pit of Max's stomach. All of his studies pointed to one thing they could do with that energy.

'I think they are going to raise an army of daemons,' said Max.

Felix let out a low moan. Snorri gave what might been a yip of glee. Gotrek smiled with grim mirth. 'What makes you say that?' Felix asked.

How could he explain this to them, he wondered? They were not sorcerers. They did not have the training or the knowledge that would let them appreciate the full enormity of the situation. He did. This was an area he had studied extensively. Daemons required the presence of enormous amounts of magical energy if they were to hold their forms in the mortal world for any length of time. Magic was to daemons what air was to humans or water to fishes. It was an element they needed to survive. Fortunately for humanity, in most areas of the world magic was relatively scarce and daemons could not be summoned for more than very short periods of time. Usually minutes, hours at most. Only in areas like the Chaos Wastes was there enough of the raw stuff of magic to enable them to permanently hold their forms. If the mages of the army out there could draw enough energy to Praag they could recreate those conditions. And once that was done, with all that energy loose, who knew what daemons were capable of? Not even the most powerful of the ancient wizards had any idea.

Max felt a chill worse than that of the night air pass into his very bones.

AHEAD OF THEM the citadel loomed out of the snow. It was huge, as large as any royal palace in the Empire, but, to Felix's mind, there was something odd about it. It looked subtly wrong. The doors were too massive, the wings subtly out of proportion, as if the architect had been eating weirdroot when he had drawn the schematics, and then labourers had actually gone out and built what he imagined.

For all that it had a disturbing beauty. Monstrous gargoyles clutched the roof eaves. Huge ornately carved stone balconies jutted out from beneath the window arches. Massive monsters had been carved in such a way as to suggest that they were emerging from the living stone to do battle with the sculpted heroes who confronted them. A huge statue of Magnus the Pious loomed beside the main door raising his hammer so that it met the blade of Tzar Alexander that rose from the other side. These two heroes of the Great War against Chaos stood eternal guard on the entrance. Felix wondered if there was any truth to the legend that they would spring to life again to defend the city if the need arose. Somehow, he doubted it. If ever the hour of that dire necessity was at hand it was now, and the two stone warriors showed not the slightest inclination to spring to life and join battle with the hordes of Darkness. Felix did not blame them. They had probably got enough of that during their own lifetimes.

The statues should have been heartening, a reminder of the fact that men had triumphed over Chaos before, but they were not. Felix suddenly realised why the architecture of the place seemed so mad, and the decorations were so disturbing. The palace had been built by those who had seen such monsters and who had fought against them. It was as much a memorial to that struggle as the great statue of the unknown warriors facing it across palace square. Perhaps his suspicions concerning the sanity of the builders were unfounded. Anyone who maintained enough grasp on reality to build anything after the Great War with Chaos was to be admired. Felix fervently hoped that some of the people here in Praag would be able to build something that their descendants could marvel at in two centuries. He fervently hoped that there would be descendants, and a world for them to live in.

The sentries at the gate crossed their halberds to deny the adventurers admittance. Felix could see that there were plenty more behind them. Hard-eyed suspicious men with a haunted look in their eyes. Hardly surprising under the circumstances. What had happened tonight was enough to make even the easiest going suspicious, and the guardsmen of Praag had never been famous for their tolerance.

'State your business!' said a tough-looking sergeant. 'And be quick about it!'

'I don't like your tone,' said Gotrek nastily, and raised his axe. Not now, thought Felix. We have enemies enough to worry about without getting into a brawl with the duke's personal guard.

'We bring a warning to the duke. There are traitors within the city. They sought to poison the Watergate granary.'

'The granary is guarded by a score of men,' said the sergeant. 'They would never get past–'

'There were a score of men,' Gotrek sneered. 'There's a score less now.'

'Dark magic was used to overcome them,' said Max. The sergeant looked at the wizard. He appeared to recognise him.

'You're the mage from the White Boar. The one who was too busy to see his grace. You changed your mind.'

Now it was Max's turn to sound testy. 'Be grateful I did,' he said, 'and be grateful to these brave warriors, for otherwise one of these days you would all be eating poisoned bread.'

Max's tone, and probably his reputation as a sorcerer, seemed to impress the sergeant. 'Get the captain,' he said. 'You can explain all of this to him. Get inside. Ulric knows we can use all the wizards we can on a night like tonight.'

For the first time, Felix noticed the very real fear in the man's voice. He like all the guards seemed strained to breaking point. It occurred to Felix that if the Chaos sorcerers had deliberately unleashed the ghosts to undermine morale in the city they could not have done a better job.

THE DUKE LOOKED tired, thought Max, and that tiredness had done nothing to improve his temper. Then again, all of them were the worse for wear. It had been a night to fray the nerves. Inwardly Max thanked the guard sergeant. The captain had been a reasonable and competent man, and he had listened to all they had to say, and sent them on to the duke's chambers where the ruler and his council were in emergency session.

'So glad you decided you could join us, Herr Schreiber,' said the duke. There was heavy sarcasm in his voice.

A hard man to like, the Duke Enrik, thought Max. There was something in his abrupt manner that brought out the worst in people. Max prayed to Verena that Gotrek would hold his tongue and his temper. He knew there was little enough chance of it, but if he could get in first… 'And nice of you to bring a retinue of armed bodyguards.'

Suddenly the duke smiled for the first time, and there was something almost likeable in his face. 'A man could probably not find better ones on this continent, or so I have heard.'

He looked at the Slayers for an instant, and said in dwarfish: 'Do you come to keep the ancient oaths of alliance?'

Max was startled. He doubted that there was anyone in the city save himself, a few scholars, the priests of Sigmar and the dwarfs themselves who could have made themselves understood in the old tongue of the elder race.

Enrik was making himself more than understood. He sounded positively fluent. It was a surprising achievement in a Kislevite ruler. Perhaps they were not all the barbarians Max had thought them to be.

'Yes,' Gotrek said in the Imperial tongue. 'That we do.'

'Then be welcome. What brings you here in the middle of the night?'

Swiftly Max outlined the events of the evening. The duke's visage became darker and darker as he spoke. When Max finished he barked out orders that guards be sent to each of the granaries and all of the wells. Then he turned to them and said: 'Foul deeds have been done this evening. We owe you a debt of gratitude for rooting out these traitors. I will think on your reward.'

'The only reward I need is a row of Chaos worshippers ahead of me, and an axe in my hand.'

Enrik gave one of his rare smiles. 'That should be easy enough to manage given our current situation.'

'And you, Herr Schreiber, you appear to know more of these matters than all the mages and priests on my council. I wish you had revealed your gifts sooner – I would have offered you a place on my council.'

'I would have been honoured,' Max said in turn.

'Then we must see that you are. Go now and sleep. I will speak with you again on the morrow.'

# NINE

GREY SEER THANQUOL stared out into the snow. He hated it. It got everywhere, melting and making his fur reek, turning his nose cold. The accursed stuff did not in any way, shape or form suit the skaven metabolism. He was miserable and ill. An icicle of snot hung from the end of his snout and he could not find the energy to break it off. For the hundredth time he longed for his nice warm burrow back in Skavenblight or at least for the security of the underways that he had left behind.

He glanced around. They had taken refuge from the blizzard in one of the deep, dark pine woods that provided the only relief from the monotony of the endless Kislevite plains. Snow made the branches droop and block out the light, giving a comforting dimness to the spot. Thanquol could hear hundreds of skaven paws softly crunching snow all around him. It was the only vaguely reassuring thing about the whole scene.

Part of him argued that it would be best for him to go back, that it would serve no purpose for him to remain here above ground in the freezing cold and dazzling whiteness. It would do skavenkind no good if he were to catch a chill and die. He desperately wanted to give in to this part of him but he could not. He needed to find out more about this huge surge of dark magic being drawn down from the north. To his mage senses the great current of dark magical energy was as visible as the snout in front of his face. It writhed across the sky, carrying within it an enormous charge of energy. Thanquol had not yet dared reach out and attempt to draw some of that power into himself. He suspected that if he did so he would come to the awareness of whatever powers had created that roaring river of power, and he was not sure he was quite ready for that encounter yet.

And there were other reasons to remain. His troops were here, scouting the land, looking for evidence of the forces of Chaos and their plans, and it was all too possible that if they encountered them without Thanquol's decisive leadership to guide them, they would do something foolish that would get them destroyed. He doubted that Izak Grottle, who had been assigned to be his second in command, could handle the threat posed by the Chaos warriors. But if he did, he would doubtless use any credit gained from the exploit to try and undermine Thanquol's authority.

Thanquol was having none of that. He was a past master of the politics of leading skaven armies, and he had a great deal of firsthand experience of Grottle's treachery. Thanquol still suspected Grottle had a hand in the destruction of his master plan to conquer the city of Nuln. Perhaps he had even betrayed Thanquol's infallible plan to the humans. What else could explain his survival when every other skaven leader in the great assault, save Thanquol, had been exterminated?

Besides, Thanquol was no longer sure even the underways were safe. Several times on the journey south they had encountered beastmen and mutant humanoids within the hidden tunnels. Thanquol was not sure how they could have got there. Was it possible that skaven traitors had shown them the hidden entrances? It seemed a far more plausible explanation than that they had simply stumbled into the secret cave mouths out of the snow. Thanquol dismissed Grottle's inane suggestion from his mind. He had found that in all things, the simplest explanation was rarely the best. In real life all things were complexly inter-related, usually by the scheming of his enemies.

Still there were some good things about the situation. He had replenished his supply of powdered warpstone back in Hell Pit. Indeed, he had managed to convince the Moulders that given the nature of the emergency, he should have a whole sackful of the stuff. It was the best and purest powder he had ever found. Thanquol wondered if the Moulders were secretly sending their warriors into the Wastes to acquire it, or whether they had some other source. He decided that when all of this was over, he would make it his business to find out.

He took a pinch of the powder and immediately felt its tingling warmth pass out of his mouth and into his bloodstream. He felt alive once more, and could ignore the crippling cold. Using the faintest hint of a spell, he blasted the snot icicle from his nose and freed his body from the taint of fever. It was good to be using his power once more. It was even good, he admitted, to be surrounded by so many skaven warriors. His long trek across the plains of Kislev with only the treacherous Lurk for company and dubious protection had made him more aware of such things. It was a good thing to have so many of his furry kindred to stand between him and any approaching enemies.

He wished that Clan Moulder had provided a larger force. He was uneasy with only the few thousand warriors he had at his disposal. The fools had maintained that they needed the bulk of their troops to hold their ancestral citadel at Hell Pit. They were passing up the chance of rich pickings and great glory following in the wake of the Chaos horde and waiting for the opportunity to strike. A burst of warpstone-inspired confidence and contempt surged through Thanquol. As if preserving that worthless pile of rock could be worth more than protecting the life of the greatest of all skaven geniuses.

Izak Grottle glared at him red-eyed. Had it not been for the warpstone in his veins the look would have filled the grey seer with justifiable caution. As it was, he half wished that the obese Moulder warlord would provoke him so he could blast him. In fact, thought Thanquol, why wait for provocation? Why not just avenge himself on the fat monster?

As if reading his thoughts, Grottle bared his fangs in a menacing snarl, and then gestured to the hundreds of massive Moulder stormvermin who surrounded them. Why not, thought Thanquol? That was a good reason. He did not doubt that with his awesome magical powers he could blast hundreds of these worthless vermin into oblivion should they prove troublesome but he could not kill a whole army of them. Not unless he reached out and grasped that awesome flow of power in the sky. He was almost tempted to do it. For moments he stood there, tail lashing, fangs bared, matching Grottle glare for glare. The urge to drawn on that power and slay became near overwhelming.

As quickly as it came, the warpstone-inspired fit passed and he shook his head. The red haze lifted from his mind. The desire to kill and maim subsided somewhat. He felt as if he had just thrown off some evil spell. For a moment, he had a brief intense awareness of something. All of his long training as a grey seer, and all his great experience of working magic, rushed forth to provide him with an extraordinary insight.

Something within the warpstone was responding to that current of Chaos magic, and he was responding to whatever it was that was in the warpstone. Just for an instant there he had almost lost control of himself, and destroyed a skaven force which, no matter how richly deserving of destruction, could still be used to serve his purposes. Worse than that, he had almost risked his own precious hide to do it.

He shivered and glared off into the distance. The world was changing. The Old Gods were putting forth their strength. They had somehow almost managed to influence even Grey Seer Thanquol. He knew that he would have to be very careful. He would not risk tapping into that river of power.

Not yet anyway.

'WHAT IS GOING on out there?' Felix asked, squinting out into the dawn light. Even as he watched the eerie glow around the menhirs and the war machines seemed to fade. He knew it was not gone; it had just faded to invisibility in the stronger light of the sun. Felix wondered how long that would last. Morrslieb was still a presence in the sky, a greenish smear of its light visible even through the grey clouds.

They stood once more on the great watchtower, overlooking the Gargoyle Gate. The walls below them were nearly ten strides thick. The tower was twenty times the height of a man, and bristled with ballistae and other siege engines. From somewhere a group of Imperial mercenaries had produced an organ gun and were manhandling it into position. It was hard work and the men were sweating profusely even on this wintery day. Felix drew his red Sudenland cloak tight about him and glanced over at the others. From somewhere the evil reek of alchemical fire rose to assault his nostrils.

Gotrek looked stern and sullen. Max looked disturbed. Ulrika looked wan but determined. The other Slayers looked hungover. 'The army is massing to attack. Even Snorri can see that is obvious, young Felix,' said Snorri.

'I meant what was that glow? What foul magic is being used out there?'

Max clutched at the stones of the battlements with his gloved fingers. The duke had asked him to come here and report on the activities of the army. It seemed that from somewhere he had acquired the idea that Max was the most powerful and best qualified magician in the city. Felix suspected that this might even be true.

'They are summoning daemons,' Max said, 'and a great deal of magical energy. I can only guess what they are going to do with them.'

'And what would that guess be?' Gotrek asked.

'I would say that some of the daemons will be bound into those siege engines to move them, rather in the way you use steam to power your own war machines. I have read that such things are possible.'

'Steam power has nothing to do with daemons,' Gotrek said.

'It was merely an analogy. I think the life force of the daemons will be used to allow those massive metal towers to move and use their weapons and perhaps do other things…'

'Like what?'

'Shield the occupants from magical attack.'

'You said some of those daemons would be used for that. What about the others?'

'They will materialise directly and be used as shock troops.'

Felix thought about the great bloodthirster at Karag Dum and shivered. He had hoped never to meet such a thing again in his life, and now they were facing the possibility of an army of them. He voiced his suspicions to Max who shook his head.

'I doubt that will happen. Such creatures are so powerful that even the huge pool of magical energy out there could not support more than a few of them.'

Felix wondered at the equanimity with which Max said a few of them. One of those creatures had been almost enough to destroy an army. A few of them would be more than capable of overwhelming all of Praag. After all, they did not now have the Hammer of Firebeard to help them. Max carried on speaking, unaware of Felix's dark thoughts.

'Besides, I think our Chaos-loving friends out there have other uses for the power they are gathering.'

'Such as what?' Gotrek asked.

'I think they will use it to overwhelm the defensive runes on part of the wall, then use their magic to cast down the towers and parapets so that their troops can come through.'

'Have you any idea where they will do this?' Felix asked.

'Not until they actually make the attempt. I will be able to sense the flows of power then. Still I would say it's a fair bet that it will happen where they mass their forces strongest.'

'Unless that is just a feint,' Gotrek said.

'Look at that army out there, Slayer. It has no need of subtlety. It needs only its strength.'

For once even Gotrek seemed abashed and fell silent. After a few moments he looked up and grinned, showing his rotten teeth. 'There will be good killing at this gate,' he said.

'That there will,' Max said with no great enthusiasm.

'WE ARE ALL going to die!' shouted the zealot. 'The end of the world is here. From the north the daemons have come. Death rides with them. Plague rides with them. Hunger rides with them. All manner of filth and foulness and abomination ride with them.'

Felix thought that it was a measure of the change of mood in the city that the scrawny fanatic had managed to get such an attentive audience in the crowded market square. A few days previously he would have been roundly jeered by the Kislevites. Now, people were really listening to his words.

'It is time to repent your sins, and cleanse your souls. Outside our gates the daemons wait. They have come because we were unworthy, because we betrayed the principles of our ancestors, and sank into licentiousness and debauchery. We have consorted with outlanders and failed to keep the true blood of Kislev pure.'

Felix frowned. The man had picked up a few more listeners. He could not be sure but he thought some of them were looking at him and Ulrika. He was, by his manner of speech, his clothing and his features marked as a non-Kislevite for sure. His nose was too long, his cheekbones were not high enough, and his features not flat enough. He was too tall to be mistaken for a citizen of Praag.

'The duke has encouraged this. His has been a rule of iniquity where houses of ill-repute have flourished, where outlanders have soiled the native daughters of Kislev into wanton ways, where all manners of foreign vice have undermined the strength and manhood of our nation.'

'He certainly has a bee in his bonnet about something,' Max muttered. 'Every lunatic in the city with an axe to grind seems to have come out today.'

It was certainly true, Felix thought, but not necessarily the most tactful thing to say under the circumstances, particularly not when some of the zealot's friends and supporters were in earshot. He glanced around. In the crowd he thought he could make out some of the faces of the fanatics who Gotrek had chased out of the White Boar a few nights ago. At that moment, he wished the Slayer was with them, but he had chosen to go off drinking with the other dwarfs, leaving Felix and Ulrika to accompany Max back to the citadel.

'Wizards are welcome in the palace now. Dabblers in dark sorcery. Weavers of wickedness, steeped in sin, depraved in demeanour, fiends of unspeakable foulness.'

Max made another mistake. He smiled, as if he could not take the whole thing quite seriously. The zealot was obviously working himself up to a pitch of fury, and he was carrying some of the crowd with him. He chose that moment to glance over at Max, resplendent in his gold brocade robes, leaning on his rune-carved staff.

We make the perfect tableau for him, don't we, thought Felix? A wicked wizard and a pure Kislevite maid besmirched by a debauched outlander. He forced a nasty grin onto his own face, and moved his hand to the hilt of his sword. The crowd followed the zealot's gaze and stared at them.

Felix could see pale frightened faces, pinched with hunger. These were scared people with an invincible-seeming foe outside their gate. Of course there would be a few of them just looking for something to vent their pent-up emotions on. It did not take Felix a lot of thought to work out who the most likely targets were going to be.

'There in our midst stands one of that evil brotherhood, one of those depraved dabblers in Darkness who have brought doom down on us. See how he smirks at the success of his sinister schemes. Witness the wanton wickedness of the wild woman with him. Look on his lust-filled lewd–'

'Perhaps you should use less alliteration,' Max said, 'and more thought.'

To Felix's surprise, the wizard sounded completely calm, bored almost. There was perfect confidence in his manner. He seemed to feel no doubt in his ability to handle the crowd around them and it showed in his face. The crowd sensed this too, and drew back. The zealot did not like being mocked. His thin features twisted, spittle poured from his mouth. He stabbed an accusing finger at Max, as if by the force of his gesture he could make a hole appear in the magician's chest.

'You dare! You dare to speak! You should crawl on your knees and grovel in the dirt before these good people. You should abase yourself in abject apology for your vileness. You should beg their forgiveness. You and your doxy and your mercenary outlander bodyguard should–'

'We should teach you a lesson for wasting the time of these good people! We should take you to the duke to explain your treacherous words. Our only desire is to help fight the forces of Darkness outside the walls. It seems yours is to spread dissension and discontent within them.'

Felix was surprised once more by the scorn and the power within Max's words. The wizard was angry but it was a controlled anger that seemed to fuel his power. Without in any way changing his appearance Max had somehow become larger, and more threatening. The power within him, normally veiled, was suddenly visible. He had become quite as menacing in his own way as Gotrek was in his. Felix was impressed. He could tell the crowd were as well. They had moved backwards to leave a space between Max and the zealot.

The fanatic climbed down from his perch, drew his ragged robes about him, and strode towards the wizard. He was a small scrawny man, and Max was far taller and broader. Whatever other flaws the man might have, Felix thought, cowardice was not one of them. Out of the corner of his eye, Felix could see some of the bully boys from the White Boar were moving into flanking positions. He nudged Ulrika to alert her, but she was already watching alertly.

The small man strode right up to Max, his chin out, fists clenched. His eyes were gleamed insanely. He stopped in front of the wizard and flexed his fingers as if considering strangling him. Max gazed back calmly.

'The gods will smite you down for your sins,' he said confidently.

'If they felt that way, they would have done so before now,' said Max with mocking reasonableness.

Swift as a snake the zealot reached within his robes and produced a dagger. He made as if to strike Max but before he could do so, a spark of power flashed from the magician to the blade. It glowed red hot in an instant. The zealot screamed as the weapon dropped from his scorched fingers.

The power within Max began to increase rapidly. He became a massive figure looming over the howling zealot like an angry god. He reached out gently and touched the man. Another spark of energy flowed out of him and propelled the fanatic twenty strides to lie, sprawled unconscious in the dirt.

The crowd muttered, at once awed and angered. Felix could understand their feeling. No matter how many times he had seen Max wield magic there was something deeply unsettling and frightening about it. It was all too possible that the crowd would either flee in panic or attack them in an overwhelming mass. The crowd of people stood glaring for a moment, undecided as to what to do.

'Go home!' shouted Ulrika. At that moment she sounded every inch the commanding Kislevite aristocrat. Her voice would have commanded instant obedience from a troop of winged lancers. 'Go home and prepare yourself for war! Tomorrow the forces of Darkness will attack and we will need every able-bodied citizen to help defend the walls. Do not listen to fools like this whipped dog,' she said, pointing to the unconscious zealot. 'They might mean well but they cause only fear and falling out between those who on the morrow need to stand together. All of us here, even him, will be needed come the dawn. And we will need every weapon, even sorcery, to withstand the forces that march against us!'

The crowd responded as much to her as to the reasonableness of her words. Like Max, she was showing a new side, one he had never really seen before. When she spoke in that tone, she had presence, an aura of command that made people listen to her words, and, as was becoming obvious, obey. The crowd began to disperse save for a few who came forward to bow to her and Max, and wish them well in the coming struggle. Even the bully boy fanatics had drawn back, though whether from fear or respect, Felix could not be sure. To tell the truth, he did not care why, he was just glad that it was so.

No one else hindered them as they made their way towards the ancient heart of the city.

AREK DAEMONCLAW GAZED down upon his warriors from the top of the highest siege tower. The air thrummed with energy. The great siege machines were coming to life, filled with the essence of bound daemons that would enable their enormous weight to rumble forward and crush the walls of Praag. He could feel the trapped creature's energy seething beneath his armoured gauntlet, imprisoned by his sorcerers' spells within the black iron walls of the tower.

All around him the vast horde moved with one purpose and one will, his purpose and his will. Soon he would smash the city before him, and offer up the souls of its citizens to his god. He vowed he would leave no stone standing. Never again would men build a city on this spot. Thus he would avenge the defeat of Chaos two centuries ago by the accursed Magnus the Pious. He was confident. The ring of standing stones around the city was channelling ever-greater amounts of dark magical energy to his army. Every day more and more warriors arrived from the Wastes drawn by the promise of blood and souls, death and glory, loot and slaughter. Massive beastmen, burly ogres, mighty black-armoured Chaos warriors, furious reavers and marauders from the northern tribes, all manner of twisted and mutated things were being drawn to his banner, following, sometimes consciously, sometimes not, the tide of power rushing down from the north.

Even as he watched a cloud of harpies rose in a flock and filled part of the sky over the army, their wings beating like a storm, their raucous wails and screams filling the air. They swept towards the city and were met with a cloud of arrows from the walls. Most fell short, a few found targets and the harpies wheeled and swirled away. It was not an attack; even the furious winged monsters knew their orders and would keep to them.

Arek was not entirely content. He knew that there were those within his army who plotted against him. It was no surprise. Such had been the way within Chaos armies since the dawn of time. It did not matter. There were always those who envied their betters and schemed against them. He knew that as long as his victory looked certain, the bulk of the army would remain loyal to him. They were all too filled with the prospect of smashing the hated city of Praag to risk pointless internecine strife.

There were other rumours that worried him a little more. Scouts had reported a human army approaching from the south-west. A pitiful thing, barely worthy to be called an army in comparison with his own mighty force, but it might prove troublesome if it appeared at the wrong time. Others had seen a force of the vicious ratmen the humans called skaven teeming down from the north. It appeared that Lhoigor and Kelmain's cunning scheme to destroy the ratmen city had failed, and the beasts perhaps sought vengeance. Yet for the moment they barely seemed worth the trouble either.

A little more worrying was the lack of reports from within the city concerning the fate of Gotrek Gurnisson and Felix Jaeger. He had expected his agents to have succeeded in their assassination by now. It would be nice to know that the wielder of that deadly axe had been removed. Who knew what such a weapon of power was capable of? The vision he had been granted still troubled him some times. On the other hand, if he did not enter the fray himself, it could not come true.

Arek glanced back over his shoulder and saw the twin sorcerers there. He was not pleased with them. They had been slow to obey orders recently, and quick to question his decisions. His spies reported that they had been seen in the company of his warlords, and he suspected that the twins might just be plotting against him. If so, he would soon show them the error of their ways. Actually, he was planning on doing that soon anyway. As soon as the spells were cast that would open his way into Praag, they would be consigned to the middenheap of history.

Lhoigor caught Arek's glance and smiled, revealing his glistening white fangs. It was a smile that would have made a lesser man than Arek uneasy. He merely thought, *smile all you like, magician, your smiling days will be over soon.*

LHOIGOR LOOKED AT his leader and smiled. It seemed like the best thing to do at the moment. Arek was becoming less and less stable with every day, but at least for the moment, he was the leader of the horde. That would soon change. The arrogant fool had made a suitable figurehead for this great dark crusade but his usefulness was just about ended, and with it, his life. It was his own fault too.

Neither Lhoigor or his brother would have objected to him remaining as the figurehead of the crusade for as long as he wished, if he had only bowed to their wishes. After all, someone had to lead the army and neither he nor Kelmain were warriors or generals. It was not what they had been born to do. Arek had been a good pawn for as long as he followed his instructions. He had danced like a puppet on the strings they had threaded around him but now he was too powerful and too full of himself to listen to reason.

Lhoigor clutched the golden staff tight in his hands. He could feel endless energy pulsing through it. Part of his mind was constantly occupied weaving and holding the spells that drew the great flow of power from the north together. He was such an accomplished mage now that he did not need more than part of his brain to do this, even though the effort would have blasted the sanity of lesser mages. He doubted that there were more than a few magicians on this pitiful world who could accomplish what he was doing now, and none of them could manage it so easily, he was sure. Perhaps Nagash at the height of his power, perhaps the Witch King of the Dark Elves, perhaps Teclis of the White Tower. Possibly they could do it. It did not matter, certainly he and his brother could. The blessing of Tzeentch was theirs, and there was little in the way of magic they could not accomplish if they set their minds to it.

It had always been their destiny. From birth they had been marked by the favour of the Changer of Ways. Their mother had lain with a daemon during the great winter solstice orgies in the caves of her tribe. As albino twins born with claws and fangs ready to eat meat at their first meal, they had come into the world marked for great things. The old shaman of the Weirdblood tribe had recognised them for what they were immediately and had taken them from their mother and put them under his own protection. They had learned all the old warlock had to teach them before they were six years old, and were respected in the councils of the tribe.

The Changer spoke to them in their dreams, whispering secrets of forbidden magic to them, and allowing them to guide the tribe to caches of ancient artefacts, long lost in the Wastes. Before they were ten, they had left the tribe to wander far across the lands of men. They had sought out the ancient holy sites in the Chaos Wastes, unearthed their staffs in the ruins of Ulangor, pledged their souls to the Lord of Mutation at the crystal altar of Nul. Everywhere the followers of Tzeentch were, they had gone, disguising themselves when they had journeyed in the lands of men,

They had walked cloaked and hooded through the streets of Altdorf, and bought tomes of forbidden lore in the bazaar of books in Marienburg. They had consulted with defrocked priests of Verena, and sailed as far as Tilea. Everywhere they had gone together, sharing the bond of magical power, and the ability to speak in each other's minds over a distance. With time, their spellcrafting skills had far outstripped those of their former masters and they had become ambassadors of Tzeentch supervising the organisation of cultists in many lands, fomenting rebellions, rousing the mutated, tempting the weak, intimidating the strong. Tzeentch had rewarded them with more gifts, and more power, and the most precious prize of all, enduring life. They had lived for centuries watching their contemporaries pass away, needing no company but each other's.

Eventually, their work among men completed, they had returned to the Wastes, to advance a plan they had conceived for themselves. They had decided that they would raise up a warleader and use him to spearhead a campaign to put the Old World under the dominion of Tzeentch. Arek had seemed like a good choice.

He was strong, he was intelligent, he was favoured by the Changer, and he was a formidable general and diplomat, a combination of qualities rare in Chaos warriors. It had been a useful alliance, and they had helped make him great, leading him subtly from triumph to triumph until his reputation had been enough to cement a massive alliance of warlords from the Wastes. It had all gone well for close on a decade. It was unfortunate that Arek had chosen this moment to try and ruin all their plans by his mulishness. He had attacked too early, before the paths of the Old Ones had opened, and let his troops run out of hand.

And now he was scheming to remove them from their place of power. It had not escaped Lhoigor's notice how he and his brother had been left out of the recent councils of war. Soon, he thought, Arek was going to find out who the real chosen of Tzeentch were here. And he was not going to like that one little bit.

THE STREETS WERE filled with marching men. Their manner spoke of quiet desperation. Felix could see that they did not have a great deal of hope of survival, yet their grimness told another story. They intended to sell their lives dearly. In the great square at the base of the citadel grandfathers and young boys drilled with ancient rusty weapons dragged from some hidden storehouses. Women carried loaves of bread from the bakeries. The ducal guard stood by each shop and made sure that prices were in line with the duke's orders. There was to be no profiteering here.

Enrik might not be popular or even diplomatic, Felix thought, but he knew how to run his city. It seemed that at least some of the people were starting to realise that too. He had overheard some washerwomen commenting on the business of bread prices with approval. The only people who did not seem too pleased with the situation were some of the merchants. They did not complain too loudly though. The duke had threatened to put the heads of any profiteers on a spike outside the palace gates. No one doubted that he would be as good as his word.

They passed into the citadel easily. The sentries recognised them and gave them no trouble. It seemed that there had been orders from the highest level to let Max through as soon as he returned. The right of entry seemed to have been extended to Felix and Ulrika.

Felix looked over at Max and Ulrika. Since he had healed her, the two of them had spent a great deal of time together, and they seemed to get on better than she and Felix ever had. Since her recovery she had been distant to him. Part of him was jealous, and another part of him was glad. He did not like the idea that she might prefer any other man to him, but at the same time, he was tired of the endless arguments and constant bickering. Now that she had passed the crisis stage of her illness, the deep love for her he had thought he felt seemed to have faded in the face of her coldness. He shook his head. He doubted that he would ever understand the nature of their relationship.

He wondered if she did.

ULRIKA STRODE THROUGH the corridor. The marble flagstones echoed beneath her boots. Despite the atmosphere of dread that surrounded her, she felt a strange contentment. She was alive, and she was healthy. The weakness the plague had inflicted on her was past. The nightmares that had filled the days of her illness were fading memories. Everything had a brightness and a clarity to it, and her heart was filled with a cold clear joy. She had returned from the gates of Morr's kingdom, and life seemed good to her.

She felt like a different person. Her eyes had been opened to many things, and she saw her life with a clarity that had been denied to her before. She glanced over at Felix and wondered at the power he had once held over her. It seemed like the person who had fallen for him had been someone else a long time ago, someone much younger and much more naïve. She still cared about him, but the powerful sweeping passion was gone. She had been cured of it, as she had been cured of the sickness.

She wondered about this. Was this, too, a result of Max's magic? Had he somehow interfered with her thoughts and her emotions as he had been healing her? If so, she found she did not mind quite as much as she thought she would have. It was almost a relief to be freed of Felix's constant intrusion in her thoughts, and the constant need to preserve her own identity and keep some distance between them by fighting. It seemed clear to her now that this is what she had been doing during all those arguments, and it was a good thing to feel free of it.

She glanced over at Max. He seemed different too. He had grown somehow over the past few weeks. He was more confident, more mature. He wore his power like a cloak now, and he seemed deserving of the respect the guards showed him as they entered the duke's council chambers.

She owed him for her life. It was a debt she felt sure she would be given a chance to repay in the coming struggle.

'Well,' the duke said as they entered, 'what did you find out?'

Felix managed to keep a pleasant smile on his face in spite of the duke's tone. Max looked a little put out by the brusqueness but then smiled anyway. Good, thought Felix, you're learning. He listened as Max swiftly outlined his theories as to what was going on. Undiplomatic he might be, but the duke was a good listener and his council took their cue from him. He waited for Max to finish before he spoke. Felix did not think he had ever seen quite so many wealthy and powerful people gathered together in one place before: guards, nobles, priests, richly garbed merchants were all present.

'It seems like we can expect the main attack to begin soon. So far all we have faced are a few raids. This will be the real thing. How ready are we?'

The question was directed at Boris, the captain of the ducal guard, the man who was directly responsible for overseeing the defences of the city. 'We have every able bodied man ready to fight on the walls. They have been divided into three watches that can relieve each other when necessary. The city militias have been mustered and can be summoned by the alarm bells. We have enough food to last the winter, if rationed, and if more granaries are not poisoned. The wells are under guard. The people are frightened but willing. We are ready to fight.'

The duke glanced over at the Archlector of the Temple of Ulric, an old man, with the powerful build and straight back of the warrior. He adjusted the wolf-skin cloak about his shoulders. 'Prayers are being said in the temple daily. The aid of the gods is being sought. The runes of protection on the walls remain strong, but our divinations tell us that our enemies are gathering an enormous amount of power. To what end remains unclear. Within the city we have some twenty priests and twelve wizards capable of working battle magic. It seems clear to me that we can and must resist.'

It was now the turn of a white-robed woman to speak. She was still beautiful though her hair was white and her face lined. Her hands played nervously with a silver dove amulet around her neck. 'The Sisterhood of Shallya has so far treated four hundred wounded, and many cases of the plague. Fortunately, for the moment, the disease appears to be under control. I think the snowstorms may have worked to inhibit its spread in some way. Or it may simply be that whoever summoned the plague magic has ceased their efforts or moved on to other things.'

One by one, the highest-ranking citizens of Praag were called on to speak: guildmasters, priests, merchants, builders. Slowly a picture emerged of the situation. Praag appeared as well prepared for a siege as it was possible for any city to be. Had it been any other army save the vast mutant horde sitting outside its walls, the city could have withstood an attack with certainty. As it was, no one really knew what the Chaos worshippers were capable of, and the uncertainty was provoking a deep-seated unease. Max's conclusions had done nothing to reassure the assembled council. Of all the people there, only the duke and to a lesser extent his brother did not seem bothered. They radiated a calm and decisive confidence that under almost any other circumstances might have been reassuring.

'When do you expect the attack to begin in earnest?' the duke asked Max.

'Very soon. They must plan on doing something with all the power they are gathering. I do not see how they can hope to keep it under control for any length of time, no matter how potent their sorcerers are.'

The duke nodded. 'Very well. We must expect an attack at any moment. I thank you for your presence. I suggest you all visit the temple of your choice and pray for our deliverance.'

I hope the gods can help, Felix thought. He could see no other source of deliverance.

THE GOSPODAR MUSTER was impressive, Ivan Petrovich Straghov thought. Hundreds of tents dotted the plain around Mikal's Ford. The air was filled with the scent of horseflesh and charcoal braziers. In the distance was the huge pavilion that was the Ice Queen's palace when she travelled. The tzarina must have stripped the realm bare to have assembled so many troops in so short a time. There was well over five thousand cavalry present: horse archers, winged lancers, light horse. As he rode through the throng, he shouted to many old comrades and waved his response to many more.

There was Maximilian Trask, the Count of Volksgrad, victor of over a thousand skirmishes with the orcs of the Eastern Steppes, a fact that the garland of orc ears around his neck was a testimony to. A bellow from his left drew his attention to Stanislav Lesky. Old One-eye still looked hale despite his sixty winters. He rode upright with a horsemanship that would have shamed the twenty grandsons who cantered along beside him, the sign of the grey wolf fluttering on their banners. Ivan waved and shouted: 'Tonight we drink vodka in my tent!'

Over there was his old rival, Kaminsky, with whom Ivan had fought many a border dispute – and drunk many a cup of peace when battle was over. Now Kaminsky was as homeless as he. Still it was good to see him here, even if his riders were as diminished in numbers as Ivan's own. What could one expect really? Like himself, Kaminsky had been right in the path of the advancing horde.

Ivan rode through the tents. The soft snow gave way beneath his horse's hooves. Beneath it the ground was iron hard. In front of his men, Ivan chose to interpret this as a good sign. Lord Winter was mustering his white troops to defend Kislev. In reality he was worried. Snow made it just as difficult for a Kislevite army to move and support itself as it did for anyone else. Perhaps the Chaos warriors were going to use magic to feed themselves. Ivan knew his countrymen could not. But there was no sense in worrying about that now. He needed to report what he had seen to his ruler.

A groom waiting outside the vast blue pavilion took his horse, and without formality, Ivan was allowed to stride into the tent. Inside it was cold, not quite as chilly as it had been in the snow, but it was far less warm that most people would have expected. Ivan chose to interpret this as a good sign as well. When the Ice Queen was exerting her formidable powers of sorcery, the air around her inevitably took chill.

Ivan drew his furs tighter around him and strode across a floor piled with carpets towards the distant throne. Large fur-clad men moved aside to let him pass. In a few heartbeats he stood looking up at his monarch.

She was tall, taller than he, and her skin was so pale that he could see the blue veins in her face. Her eyes were a startling chilly blue, but her lips and hair fiery red. Her nails were long and glittered like gems. Rich robes covered her full, sensuous figure. When she spoke her voice was low, husky and thrilling: 'Greetings, Ivan Petrovich. What news from the north?'

Ivan returned her greeting respectfully and told her of his journey, knowing even as he spoke that little of what he said would come as a surprise to her. The Ice Queen had her own ways of knowing what passed in her realm. It was said that she could see to its furthest reaches in the massive turquoise orb she kept beside her throne.

After he had finished speaking, he spoke openly and frankly to her as befitted a trusted Kislevite retainer speaking to his liege. 'But what of the Empire, my lady? And our ancient allies?'

'The Emperor musters his army to face the horde. But it is a long way from Altdorf to Kislev, and we cannot hope to see him before the spring. White Wolves ride from Middenheim, and we hope to see them sooner. The dwarfs of the World's Edge Mountains have also promised aid, though the roads through the peaks are hard at this time of year, and who knows when help may arrive from that doughty quarter?'

It was very much as Ivan would have expected. By attacking so late in the season, the Chaos warriors had gained an advantage. Had they attacked in spring, as any human army would have, then Kislev's allies could have come to her aid. Now, it was unlikely they would be of much help before winter's end. Ivan saw one small ray of hope.

'Perhaps with their airship the dwarfs might be able to get here sooner.'

'Perhaps. We have had no word of it since it departed for Praag. We can but hope that no mishap had befallen it.'

Ivan prayed fervently that was not the case. 'When do we ride for Praag?'

'On the morrow,' said the Ice Queen. 'Though my heart misgives me at the thought of what we will find when we get there.'

# TEN

HALEK LISTENED UNHAPPILY to his agent. Felix Jaeger had been to the Red Rose and had been seen talking to the girl Sasha, an associate of his late and unlamented henchmen Sergei and Olaf. He glanced around his richly furnished chambers, rose from his cushioned seat, and went to the door. He opened it, and checked to make sure there was no one listening. In the palace you could never be quite certain. There were servants everywhere. Normally, he would never have agreed to meet his underling in his own quarters, but the man had claimed the matter was urgent, and he was someone whose judgement Halek had learned to trust.

What could the girl have told Jaeger? Nothing too incriminating, he was sure. She had never seen his face, and he had never let the two assassins know who he really was. No, he was in no danger, of that he was certain. He rose and picked up a small ebony statuette, an exotic carving made in Araby or one of those other hot southern lands. He was sure his brother would know; it was the sort of scholarship in which he excelled. His hand tightened around the figurine with such force that he almost broke it.

Control yourself, he told himself. It was bad form to show any tension in front of his lackeys, something he would never normally do. It was a sign of the pressure he was under. His superiors, those who had progressed further in the hidden order than he, were holding him responsible for the continued existence of Gotrek Gurnisson and Felix Jaeger, and it did not help that the two of them had been instrumental in foiling the poisoning of the grain stores. The pressure to do something about them was really on him now. Halek shook his head, wishing for the thousandth time he had never accepted that first invitation to study secret alchemical lore.

Not that it all mattered. Soon the city would fall anyway. He took a deep breath to calm himself and fought to get his whirling thoughts under control. Even though he knew he was going to be on the winning side, the wait for victory was proving to be an enormous strain. He wished the waiting were over, and the city fallen. Only a matter of time, he told himself.

He forced his resentment-filled thoughts back to the matter at hand, the business with this bar girl. She was of no account. She could not harm him. Perhaps it would be best just to let the matter lie. That was most likely the best course. Certainly it would have been the one he would normally have favoured. But now, with the effects of his hidden mutation working on him, and the stress of all the waiting, and this constant feeling that he was betraying someone no matter what he did, he felt the need to do something.

After all, why take chances?

Quickly, decisively, he gave his agent instructions. It would perhaps be for the best if the girl quietly disappeared. He was sorry about her death, but he tried telling himself he was being merciful. She would most likely be dead in the next few days anyway.

THE WHITE BOAR was quiet. Everyone was moody and tense. The events of the past few days had unsettled them all. Ghosts, dark sorcery and rumours of traitors poisoning the granaries had done nothing to improve a level of morale already undermined by plague and the size of the besieging army. Felix glanced around, wondering where Ulrika was. She had been strangely distant recently. He was starting to think that even their fights might be better than this growing estrangement. At least part of him was. Another part of him felt a growing sense of relief, of freedom, even.

He wondered where Ulli, Bjorni and Snorri were. Most likely at the Red Rose again. Bjorni was certainly proving to be a bad influence on young Ulli, dragging him along to the joy-house every night. But, it wasn't as if he was holding a dagger to the younger Slayer's throat. Felix looked down into his goblet of wine, swirled the red liquid around and took a sip. He was too tense this evening, he told himself then smiled sourly.

Under the circumstances, it was hardly surprising. Assassins were looking for him. He was in a haunted, plague-ridden city under siege by a daemonic army, and he and his companions had insulted many of their fellow citizens including some nasty witch hunters. It was only natural to be tense under the circumstances. He tried to tell himself he had been in tighter corners, but it did not do much good. He looked over at Gotrek. The Slayer was glaring morosely into his ale. He looked around as if daring any of their fellow customers to look at him the wrong way. No one, not even the party of White Wolf templars, were foolish enough to do so.

'No need to look for a fight,' said Felix. 'There will be enough of that tomorrow.'

'Aye, most likely,' said Gotrek.

'And no doubt you will have a chance to find your doom.'

'There is that, manling.'

'You don't sound too pleased.'

'It galls me.' Felix was shocked. Was the Slayer having second thoughts about seeking a heroic death?

'What galls you?'

'That the forces of Chaos might conquer this place. That they might win.'

'What does that matter to you? It is death you seek.'

'Aye, it is. But a meaningful death. Not falling anonymously in some great ruck.'

'Somehow I doubt that will be your fate.'

'We shall see.'

'Perhaps you will get a chance to challenge one of the horde's leaders. That would be a mighty doom.'

Gotrek looked up, as if to see whether Felix was mocking him.

At that moment, the door of the White Boar opened and Snorri and Ulli hurried in. They came right over to the table. 'Best get over to the Red Rose!' bellowed Ulli.

'Snorri thinks there's something you might want to see.'

AMAZING, THOUGHT Grey Seer Thanquol, staring up at the sky. So much power. So much magic. The clouds were red. Not with the sort of ruddiness he had seen before when the sun set, but a bloody red in which swirled vortexes of pure mystical energy, and around which bolts of lightning flickered without ever discharging themselves to earth. The sun was pleasantly obscured, the snow gleamed bloodily. Thanquol's weariness evaporated as he surveyed the battlefield.

Another great victory, he told himself. A force nearly a quarter of our size annihilated with only a few hundred casualties to show for it. It was another testimony to his military genius. He could tell even Izak Grottle was impressed though he muttered sourly about their foes already having been exhausted by an earlier conflict.

As if that made any difference. Thanquol readily conceded that their foes had already seen combat. It was merely another testament to his tactical skill that he had chosen such a moment to attack them. Grottle might claim it was mere luck, but Thanquol knew that all great commanders made their own luck. So what if the Chaos worshippers had been harried by a few of the Kislevite horse soldiers? This in no way detracted from the magnitude of Thanquol's victory.

Sweeter still was the feeling that his power was growing, as this red storm from the north grew. Using magic had come easier to him than ever before, and he had barely needed his intake of powdered warpstone to cast even his mightiest spells. It seemed like the Horned Rat favoured him once more. And about time too, a deeply buried part of him thought. If only Felix Jaeger and Gotrek Gurnisson were put before him at this moment, he felt sure he would dispatch them with ease. How sweet that would be.

He fought off a feeling almost like drunkenness. He was giddy with so much power in the air. The winds of magic were blowing stronger than ever he had felt them. Morrslieb glowed so bright its green light was visible even through the ruddy clouds. Magic flowed through his fur and into his veins. Truly this was a fine time to be alive, Thanquol thought.

He gave orders for his army to hurry south, confident that he would be able to deal with any threat they might encounter. Behind him Izak Grottle groaned and wheezed as he gave the instructions to follow the grey seer's orders. Just at that moment, Thanquol stood dumbfounded, sensing an awesome gathering of power to the south of him. Suddenly he wanted to bury himself deep below the ground, and not emerge till he was certain whatever it was had passed. Since he could not do that, he decided it would be best to begin a tactical withdrawal away from it. He began to give the orders, but Grottle countermanded him.

'I was told to see you to Skavenblight, and that is what I intend to do.'

Thanquol almost blasted him then and there, but restrained himself from unleashing his righteous wrath. It was time to preserve his power, in case he needed to make a quick escape.

MAX SCHREIBER GAZED out from the tower. Soon the attack would come. It was obvious. As the sun set amid the eerie red clouds a strange mist gathered over the battlefield. It was almost the same colour as the clouds, and charged with the same evil energy. Max could see the lines of force swirling within it, and knew that a spell of awesome potency was being prepared. Even with his own new-found confidence in his powers, Max knew that he would not care to meet who-ever was casting that spell. The amount of power being gathered would need almost god-like strength to control, even with the backing of hundreds of acolytes. Max wished there was something he could do to disrupt it, but there was nothing he could think of. Even if he had all the mages in his college of magic behind him, he doubted there would have been anything he could do.

He turned to Ulrika. They had grown closer in the past few days. She was grateful to him for saving her life, but he sensed something more. He pushed the thought away, knowing it was more likely his own hope speaking than anything real. He gave a sour smile, thinking it was easier for men to comprehend the mysteries of potent magic than see into the human heart.

'Why do you smile?' Ulrika asked pleasantly.

'You most likely don't want to know,' Max replied. He was embarrassed. Most of his life had been spent in study, and in advising folk on how to protect themselves against evil magic. It was not something that had prepared him for dealing with a woman like Ulrika.

'I would not have asked if I had not wished to know.'

Max scratched his lengthening beard to cover his embarrassment. Sometimes she was disconcertingly literal minded.

'I… I am happy to be here with you,' he ventured. 'Even under such circumstances as this.'

It was her turn to fall silent. She glanced away, looking over the glittering rooftops of Praag, instead of out at the gathering Chaos horde. By the light of the setting sun, seen from the height of the wall, it was magical: a wide expanse of red-tiled roofs and whitewashed walls from which rose bell-towers, onion domes, and the gilded spires of the temples. Even the frosting of snow contributed to the beauty. Max walked over to her and laid his hand on her fur-covered shoulder. She did not flinch but she did not look at him either. 'Are you happy?' he asked.

'I don't know,' she said. 'I am confused.'

'About what?'

'About lots of things.'

'About you and Felix?'

'Yes. Among other things.'

'Is there anything I can do to help?'

She slipped out of his grasp, and walked over to the edge of the battlements once more. She leaned forward, putting her weight on the parapet and glanced out towards their enemy. The massive war machines, high as towers, carved like statues, shimmered in the gloom. Along their sides eerie red runes were springing to life, their balefires reflecting in the snow beneath them. They drew the eye naturally, such was their power. They seemed liked statues of evil gods. The small figures moving around their bases seemed more like insects than men.

'Felix told me that in the Wastes there are huge statues of the Lords of Chaos,' she said. 'They must resemble those machines, don't you think?'

'It is possible,' he said, noncommittally, a little hurt that she had avoided his question. 'But I think what he saw really were statues. Those things are machines of metal and sorcery.'

'Sorcery?'

'Daemons are being bound into them, to give them power. Soon, I fear they will spring to life.'

'And then?'

'And then they will roll over these walls and crush everything in their path.'

'Is there nothing we can do?'

'We can pray.'

'RECOGNISE HIM?' ASKED Bjorni, gesturing to the unconscious man. To his surprise, Felix did. He knew he had seen him somewhere before, he just could not recall where. The large bruise on his face might have something to do with that.

'He is somewhat familiar,' Felix said, leaning over and clasping the man's chin, then moving his face from side to side to get a better view. The man's hair was long and had flopped down into his face. His clothes were those of a nobleman, the fabric good, and the cut expensive. Felix had seen enough in his father's storehouses to know. He looked very out of place lying here on the floor of this seedy room in the Red Rose.

'What sort of company have you been keeping, young Felix?' Bjorni asked with a leer. He put his heavily muscled arm around the shivering figure of the girl, Sasha, and with surprising gentleness wiped away the tears from her face. Felix looked at the half-naked Slayer, and the racks of whips and chains on the walls, and wondered if what he suspected about Bjorni and Sasha could possibly be true.

'Nasty company,' Gotrek said, leaning over and picking up the dagger that had fallen near the man's hands. He sniffed it then thrust the blade in Felix's general direction. Felix could see a greenish paste crusting the sharpened steel.

'I am willing to bet that is the same poison that was on Sergei and Olaf's blades,' he said.

'I think that is a bet you would win,' Gotrek said.

'What happened here?' Felix asked, looking at Bjorni and then at Sasha. They both were in a state of considerable undress. The girl's bodice had been hastily pinned closed. She wore only the scantiest of night-shirts. Bjorni was clad only in his britches. His boots and weapons lay near the bed.

'Well, I thought maybe you hadn't gone about your questioning the right way, young Felix, so I thought I would... interrogate Sasha here in my own way.'

'That would be what the leather cords and the chains were for then,' said Felix, gesturing to the pile of mechanisms near the bed.

Bjorni looked up at the ceiling and then nodded. 'Something like that. Anyway just as we were getting down to business there was a disturbance outside the door and some men barged in. They were armed, and they obviously meant to do harm.'

'You stopped them?'

'I threw a sheet over a pair of them, and then head-butted another in the nadgers,' said Bjorni with some satisfaction. 'They obviously weren't expecting much resistance, and I think they panicked when they heard Snorri and Ulli coming. So they started to run. I brained this one with the lampstand.'

'Funny thing is, none of the bouncers came to investigate the noise, and you could hear the commotion all the way down the corridor,' said Ulli. His face was red and he looked very embarrassed for some reason.

'They were paid off, obviously,' Gotrek said.

'Such would be my guess,' Felix added. 'Did you know any of these men?' he asked the girl.

'They weren't customers here,' she said, 'if that's what you mean.'

Felix shrugged and looked at the unconscious man once more, thinking it was about time they woke him up. The only question was whether to hand him over to the authorities or leave him to the tender mercies of the Slayers. Under the circumstances, he felt like they didn't have much choice. He would much rather they did this interrogation themselves. He was not at all sure of what might happen if they handed this would-be killer over to the guards.

Even as the thought crossed his mind, Felix suddenly realised where he had seen this man before. On the first day of the siege, at the Gate of Gargoyles, he had been one of the young men riding with the duke's brother, Villem. Wonderful, thought Felix, wondering exactly how far this corruption reached. Just then the man groaned and began to stir.

He looked up and turned pale as he glanced into the nastily grinning faces of the Slayers surrounding him. 'Tell me,' said Felix. 'Does Villem know you're here?'

The man's response surprised Felix. 'He'll kill me if he finds out.'

'It's us you should worry about,' Gotrek said, raising his axe menacingly.

HALEK PACED BACKWARDS and forwards across the thick Arabian carpets of his chambers. All around him, he could hear the sounds of the palace. He strode to the window, pulled the thick brocade hanging aside and glanced out through the heavy leaded glass. A rim of snow clutched the window frame. Far below he could see clean across the Square of Heroes to the Temple of Ulric. Thinking about what happened to heretics in that place, if they were caught, made him more nervous still. Being handed over to the tender mercies of the Templars of Ulric was not a prospect to make any man cheerful.

He cursed Jan Pavelovich bitterly. *If ever you find your way back into my hands I will make you pay for this, you blundering fool.* He turned away from the window, and strode over to his bookshelves, took down the copy of the Deed of Magnus he had pored over as a boy, and told himself to remain calm. *It need not have been Jan Pavelovich's fault. Who could have told that one of those accursed Slayers would have been present during the attack, and could have fought off four armed men equipped only with improvised weapons?*

*No. These things happened. Sometimes the fates were unkind, or maybe the old gods of Kislev conspired to undo his work. It was no use blaming Jan Pavelovich. The youth* had served loyally and well for many seasons, ever since Halek had inducted him into the cult of the Changer of Ways. He was dedicated to the Great Cause. It was not his fault he had been left behind when the others fled. It was much more likely the fault of those other fools, the ones who had left him to the Slayer.

The words on the page were a blur. This was getting him nowhere. It did not matter who was to blame. The damage was done. The only question was how much Jan Pavelovich had told them. Halek cursed the day he had ever been so foolish as to let the young man know his true identity. Perhaps it would not matter so much. It would only be the word of Jan and his accusers against Halek's own. He was a man of great influence at court. He could most likely face down any accusations.

Unless the Templars were called in. Or someone demanded to examine him for the stigmata of Chaos. Or perhaps one of those wizards, like Max Schreiber for instance, might be able to incriminate him with a spell. That would not be good. What could he do? The Great Plan was so near completion. Soon the city would fall. If only he could last until then he would be certain of his reward. He could flee the palace and find a hiding place among his brethren until the great day dawned.

Or could he? He had failed to see to the deaths of Gotrek Gurnisson and Felix Jaeger. Perhaps the hidden masters of the cult would punish him for that. After all, they had their reasons for wanting those two dead and he had not managed it. And trusting himself to the tender mercies of the likes of Victor or Damien was not a prospect he enjoyed either. They might find it all too tempting to do away with a potential rival under such circumstances.

And then there was his own plan to contribute to the ultimate victory. At the height of the coming attack he had fully intended to open one of the postern gates to the Chaos horde. He had the authority and the means to do so. It was an act that would win him great favour in the eyes of Tzeentch. Did he really want to give that up? Did he have any choice?

Things did not seem quite as rosey as they had when he arose from his bed this morning. Don't panic, he told himself. Think; you will find a solution.

Suddenly a way to redeem himself struck him. It was a solution so simple, and yet so perfect, he was surprised he had not dared implement it before. He shook his head. He knew why.

This was a throw of the dice by a desperate man, and he had never been this desperate before. And he had never really wanted to kill his own brother.

FELIX LOOKED DOWN at the bruised and battered form of the heretic. In the end, under the less than gentle ministrations of Bjorni, he had told them all. Now he lay there, pale as a sheet, watching them with eyes filled with horror and pain.

Felix looked at the Slayers. He had no idea if they were as appalled by what they had found out as he was. They gave no sign of it on their faces. Gotrek looked grim. Bjorni looked satisfied. Snorri looked baffled. Ulli looked as queasy as Felix felt. His suspicions had been confirmed, if this was not all some cunning lie by the cultist. There was a traitor in the palace, and his rank was higher even than Felix's worst fears would have put him. Who would have thought the duke's own brother would stoop to such a thing? And why?

He looked down at the whimpering young nobleman, Jan Pavelovich, by name. He doubted the youth was in any condition to have made up such a daring lie. He simply did not look capable of it. On the other hand who knew what the cultists of Tzeentch were capable of? Perhaps he was able to resist a beating at the hands of a demented Slayer, even if he did not look it. Felix shuddered. The cult of the Changer of the Ways had managed to infiltrate even the highest levels of Kislevite society. They stood poised to reap the spoils of the great horde's victory, or so Jan Pavelovich had claimed. And they wanted him and Gotrek dead.

Why, Felix wondered? What had they ever done to aggravate the secret cult? Well, aside from foiling their scheme at the granary, and killing a few of their assassins. Felix wondered why he had ever bothered agreeing to accompany the Slayer on his quest.

He knew this was an unworthy thought, that he should be proud that the enemies of mankind considered him worthy of being singled out along with the Slayer as a dangerous foe.

He simply did not feel that way. He wondered what would happen when the horde broke into the city. Nothing pleasant, that was for sure. He pushed the thought aside and returned to the consideration of what they were to do.

Go to the palace and confront Villem? He doubted they would last very long if they did. After all, it was the word of this self-confessed heretic against that of the heir to the duchy. Who would believe them without additional proof? Maybe they could try something else – enter the palace and kill Villem. He could not quite bring himself to do that either. What if they were wrong? Perhaps the Slayers were capable of executing a man who might be innocent, but he was not. Where did that leave them then?

Felix felt well out of his depth. He needed advice from someone who knew more about mystical matters. Perhaps Max would be able to cast a spell that would compel the youth to speak the truth. And perhaps not. And even if he did, how could they be sure? The cultists obviously had magical ways of avoiding detection and baffling such spells. Max had said as much himself. Felix rose and stretched himself to his full height. He glanced over at the Slayer.

'What do you think?' he asked.

'I think we should kill this traitorous scum.' The other Slayers nodded agreement. A puddle of wetness marked the carpet around Jan Pavelovich's legs.

'We need him alive. We need him to tell his story to the duke.'

'Why should the duke believe him?' Felix shrugged. Despite his appearance Gotrek was far from stupid and his thoughts on the matter were obviously close to Felix's own.

'We could get Max to ensorcel him.' The Slayer shrugged.

'It might work. I know nothing of sorcery except that I don't like most of it.'

'Snorri agrees,' said Snorri. Another thought struck Felix. The would-be assassins must have brought word of their failure to their master by now. Doubtless he was cooking up some nasty surprise for them. Felix knew they'd better act swiftly but could not think of any brilliant plan. Lacking anything better he said: 'Snorri, Bjorni, stay here and make sure our friend doesn't go anywhere. Ulli, go find Max and tell

him what's going on. See if there is anything he can do.
Gotrek and I are going to the palace.'

Felix headed for the door. As he opened it he turned, and
said: 'And don't kill him. We need him alive.'

He could have sworn a look of disappointment passed
across Bjorni's face.

MAX SCHREIBER PACED through the streets towards the White
Boar, Ulrika by his side. The air was crisp and cold. His breath
came forth in plumes like smoke from the nostrils of a
dragon. His feet were chilled through his boots but he was
not troubled. He knew that people were staring at them but
he did not care. He was simply happy that they were together
on what might well prove to be the last day of their lives.
Ulrika stopped to look at a street stall where a man was
sharpening blades. Sparks flew from the grindstone as he
pressed a dagger to it. The high-pitched shriek of metal
against stone filled the air. Max was suddenly reminded of the
calls of the ghosts as they seeped from the stones of Praag and
fought back a shiver. In a lifetime filled with dealing with
what most people called the supernatural, he had seen little
to rival that spectacle for strangeness and terror. As long as
you did not count the army sitting in the snow beyond Praag.
He did not doubt that come dawn, they would see powers
unleashed that would be greater than anyone living had witnessed. The slow build-up of energies was as noticeable to his
mage senses as the tension before a storm would be to a normal man. Even so, he found it hard to be too unhappy. He
had spent most of the day with Ulrika and the natural magic
of her presence made him happy. It was something to be
grateful for. Even in the shadow of death and terror there
were simple pleasures to be found.

A squad of troops, local citizens drafted into the militia by
the look of them, hurried past, their faces pale with strain.
They were frightened boys and older men for the most part.
The professionals were already on the wall confronting the
enemy. A few cast envious looks at him, and Max was not sure
whether it was because Ulrika was with him, or because he
was a wizard, or simply because he did not have to march
towards the battle yet. Maybe it was a little of all three.

Max glanced around and saw a familiar figure moving towards him out of the crowd. It was the fresh-faced young Slayer, Ulli. Ulli just as obviously recognised him, and came ploughing through the mass of people. Something about his expression told Max that the idyll was over. His strong arm grabbed Max's wrist.

'Felix says you've got to come immediately. We have caught a traitor!' bellowed Ulli. His loud voice made dozens of folk turn to look. Max gave Ulli a hard glare. This was not the sort of thing you wanted to go shouting in a street full of scared people. It could all too easily lead to a riot or a lynch mob. Max glanced around to see that Ulrika had noticed what was going on, and indicated that she should follow. He prayed that no one in the crowd would decide to investigate the truth of the Slayer's words. Felix could have picked a more tactful messenger, thought Max, then realised that he probably only had the Slayers to pick from. None of them was a good choice.

'Lead on,' said Max. 'Tell me what is going on, and try not to shout.'

'Do you have a plan, manling, or are you just making this up as you go along?' asked Gotrek Gurnisson as they raced across the Square of Heroes towards the citadel.

'The latter,' Felix said. He was breathing easily. What was a fast run for the Slayer was but a trot for him.

'Good. I would hate to think we were about to do anything sensible.'

'It would probably be a good idea if you don't attack Villem as soon as we see him. He may be innocent after all.'

'I once heard someone say better ten innocents be punished than one guilty man go free.'

'He was a dwarf, I suppose.'

'He was the chief witch hunter of the Temple of Ulric.'

Felix glanced across the square at the huge temple of the Wolf God. He had been brought up in the Sigmarite faith of the Empire and had never particularly cared for that grim savage deity and his equally savage worshippers, but right now he would not have minded having a company of White Wolf templars by his side.

'Still, it might be a good idea to keep your axe unbloodied till we establish his guilt or innocence.'

'How are we going to do that?'

'I wish I knew.'

VILLEM STRODE THROUGH the ducal palace towards the main council chamber. Even at this late hour throngs of people were still coming and going. In a city under siege there was always someone who wanted to see the leaders. Villem returned the salutes of the guards and walked in. He touched the hilt of the poisoned blade just to reassure himself it was still there. He wondered if he would get a chance to use it.

Enrik still sat on his throne, listening to his councillors debate what was to be done. He massaged his temples tiredly. His thin face showed some signs of the immense strain he must be under. Good, thought Villem, at least he was not the only one feeling the strain. He wondered why his brother even bothered to put up with these fools. They were always clamouring to make their little points heard. As if it really mattered which troop held which tower, or how the supplies were distributed to the men on the front lines. Tomorrow they would all be dead. Of this, he was quite certain.

He wondered if his henchmen were in position. He hoped so. Maybe this way they could make up for their bungled attempt on the girl. This was one assassination attempt that must succeed. All he had to do was lure his brother into position. It should not be too difficult.

'Gentlemen, gentlemen,' he said in his suavest voice. 'Cannot you see your ruler is tired and must take some time to rest.'

Enrik looked up and gave him a wintery smile. Villem forced himself to clamp down on the sickness that gnawed at his guts and smiled back.

'There is no time for that, brother,' he said. 'We must see to the disposition of the troops, and decide how we will meet the Chaos worshippers on the morrow.'

'Surely that can wait for ten minutes, brother. After all, we do not even know for certain that they will attack tomorrow.'

The Archprelate of Ulric glanced at him scornfully. 'If you had bothered to attend the meeting earlier, you would know that all the portents point to an imminent attack.'

'Portents have been wrong before,' Villem said easily. 'I remember when the Lector of Sigmar was certain that a shower of falling stars foretold the end of the world.'

Not even the reminder of the discomfiture of his greatest rival thawed the look on the Archprelate's face. 'Brother Amos today also spoke of treachery among the highest,' he said darkly.

Villem cursed inwardly. That old madman had prophesied such things before and he was usually right. Someone should have stuck a knife in him long ago. Well, after this night it would not matter. There would be all the time in the world to deal with visionary ascetics… assuming they actually survived the coming bloodletting.

'Such accusations have been made before, usually by those trying to spread dissension in the ranks of all true men,' he said calmly.

'Are you suggesting one of our senior brothers could possibly be a heretic?'

Villem made his smile a little broader, as if trying to suggest he was making a joke. 'Well, he did warn you to beware of treachery in high places.'

A few courtiers, mostly from his own faction, sniggered at that. The Archprelate remained frosty. This was not good, thought Villem. He did not want to spend all night bandying words with this old fanatic. He needed his brother dead. It was regrettable, but necessary. And it needed to be done soon.

'Come, gentlemen, won't you allow me to have a quiet word with my brother while he eats? There are some things we need to discuss among ourselves.'

He saw a curious look pass across Enrik's face. Obviously his brother was wondering what they could possibly need to discuss in private at this late hour.

'His grace could use a little food,' said the chamberlain. 'He has had nothing to eat since this morning.'

Villem inwardly blessed the old man. There had been many a time when he could cheerfully have throttled the stuffy old mumbler, but he had just made up for all those long dull boyhood hours of protocol lessons.

'I suppose we could take a break for ten minutes,' said the duke. 'What is it exactly you want to talk to me about, Villem?'

'A private matter of some urgency,' Villem said, glancing around them mysteriously. Enrik merely shrugged, as if to say have it your own way then. The members of the council had already begun to file their way out of the antechamber.

'Come, let us walk to the dining hall, and you can stretch your legs.'

'Now that is not such a bad idea. I could use a little exercise. It will loosen me up for tomorrow.'

Villem threw his arm around his brother's shoulders and began to guide him towards the doorway that led to the dining hall. 'You worry too much about tomorrow, brother.'

FELIX LOOKED AROUND the antechamber, and recognised Boris, the captain of the ducal guard. So far, so good, he and the Slayer had managed to get this far without anyone attempting to stop them. Now all he had to do was find the duke. He gestured to get the guard captain's attention. Boris saw him and came striding over at once.

'What is it, Herr Jaeger?'

'Where is the duke?'

'He has retired to the dining chamber to get something to eat. The council will reconvene in a few minutes. Why do you wish to see him?'

Felix frantically searched for a reason that would enable him to speak to the duke in private. Inspiration suddenly seized him. 'I bring him an urgent message from Herr Schreiber about the daemonic forces laying siege to the city.'

He could see that he had got the interest of many of those present. Wizard or not, Max Schreiber was obviously well respected by these people. Well, the first hurdle was crossed. Now all he had to do was work out a way of breaking the news to the duke without losing his own head in the process.

'Where is the duke?' he asked out of idle curiosity.

'He's just gone off to the dining hall to have something to eat, and a quiet word with his brother.'

Felix exchanged a shocked look with the Slayer. This might be perfectly innocent – or it might be something much more sinister. 'Which way to the hall?' he asked. Seeing the quizzical look on the captain's face, he added, 'I have heard many tales of the beauties of the tapestries there.'

'It's beyond the main audience chamber, near to the great stairwell. Where is your brave companion going in such a hurry? I was hoping to talk to him about his work on the walls.'

'I think he seeks a jakes. He had a lot to drink earlier.'

VILLEM WALKED BESIDE his brother through the shadowy halls of the palace. He was glad it was night, and he was glad it was gloomy despite the torchlight. He did not want to look too closely at Enrik's face, and he did not want his brother to be able to see his. He feared that his intent and his guilt were written all too clearly there.

'So, brother, what is it you wish to talk to me about?'

In his mind, Villem tried to work out how close they were to the place where Lars and Pavel waited. Not too far now, he thought, maybe thirty paces. They should be waiting in the alcoves there. He hoped they remembered their instructions. Clean thrusts. He checked the poisoned dagger once more, remembering the part of the plan he hadn't told them.

It was going to be necessary for them to die, slain by the grieving brother after they had foully struck down their duke. A couple of nicks with his dagger would stop them. After that he could rip up their bodies at will, and make it look like there had been a suitably bloody battle. Even as the thought crossed his mind, he wondered if he could bring himself to lead his brother to his doom. Had he really sunk this low?

'You seem very preoccupied,' Enrik added. 'What is eating at you?'

His brother sounded concerned. It was actually a little touching. Now is the time to be ruthless, Villem told himself. You can't afford sentiment. It's him or you. It was an easy enough thing to think when he was dealing with strangers and rivals in the service of Tzeentch. It was a harder thing now. This was his brother after all, a man he had known longer than he'd known almost anybody else, who he had grown up with, whom he had played with as a child. A person who had known him in the old days before he had become entangled in the webs of Dark Gods and their followers, when life had been simpler and more innocent.

'Do you remember when we were boys and were taking sword fighting lessons with old Boris?'

'This is the important business you wanted to talk to me about?' Enrik asked softly. He didn't sound angry, he sounded surprised and a little affectionate. This was a side of him that most people did not see, who saw only the cold and haughty duke. This was a human being, Villem realised, that only he truly knew. He was a man whom Villem had served loyally for many years, and not all of that loyalty had been play-acting by any means, he now realised, even after he had entered the cult of the Changer. When he killed the duke's assassins, it would be in part a real vengeance by a grieving brother.

He really would miss Enrik, and part of him was truly sorry that things had ever come to this pass. However, it was impossible his brother would survive the next few days anyway. Arek Daemonclaw's horde would certainly take the city, and his brother would die along with all of his troops. In a way, Villem was doing him a favour by ensuring he did not live to see the bloodstained dawn.

Enough of this hypocrisy, he told himself. Your brother must die to ensure you receive eternal life at the hands of the Great Mutator. It is as simple as that. Yet, he knew it wasn't. Too often in the past he had regretted his decision to join the cults of Chaos, and wished he had been brave enough to refuse them, and damn the consequences. He was sure when the moment came for Tzeentch to judge him, the god would see this, and hold it against him. He did not possess the ruthlessness and the drive to succeed within the ranks of the Lord of Change. He was damned whichever way he jumped. He could not turn back from the path he had chosen, and the way forward led to perdition too. He shook his head and sighed.

'Are you ever going to let me in on this great secret you are keeping?' Enrik asked lightly.

He was joking, of course, but Villem felt a sudden, suicidal urge to confess all, to tell his brother exactly what great

secrets he had been keeping. He did not want to beg for forgiveness, he did not want to repent; he did not even want to
be understood. He simply felt weary, and bowed beneath the
weight of his forbidden knowledge. He wanted an end to this
secrecy and standing apart.

It no longer made him feel superior to the common herd.
It no longer made him feel like a member of a privileged elite.
It simply made him tired almost unto death.

'I've been thinking about that a lot recently, the fencing
lessons,' he said, just to end the silence and have something
to say. How far were they from the alcoves now? Ten paces?
Fifteen? It was hard to judge. 'I was thinking about the time
when I lost my temper, and hit you from behind and bruised
your head, and you told Boris that it was an accident. I never
thanked you for that.'

'Its been preying on your mind all this time, has it?' asked
Enrik and laughed. It was a healthy, hearty laugh, the laugh
of a man in his prime. It did not seem fair to cut that laugh
off, thought Villem sadly. It came to him now that nothing he
had done really mattered. He had killed a lot of people to no
purpose, to further an end in which he had never truly
believed, and now he was condemning his own brother for
the very same reason. It was time for this madness to stop.
Only how could he stop it now? Things had gone too far.
They were almost at the alcoves. He was certain he could see
the shadows of the waiting assassins. Suddenly Pavel sprang
forward.

Villem was not quite sure what drove him forward into the
way of the assassin's blade: regret, love, loyalty… or perhaps
a simple belief that his life had all gone wrong somehow and
now he must atone. A deep-seated urge for self-preservation
brought his knife from its sheath, and he shouted, 'Beware,
assassins!' and pushed his brother back out of the way, sending him tumbling headlong. A sharp sudden stab of agony in
his side told him that Pavel's blade had found a home in his
flesh. It would be a matter of moments before the poison finished him. Unless…

He reached down into his soul and found the spark of mystical power that had awakened so recently. It flickered feebly
but he grasped it and instinctively sent it racing to neutralise

the poison. He was aware that he had only partially succeeded, had merely bought himself a few more heartbeats of
life but perhaps they would be enough. He lashed out at
Pavel but the assassin was too quick. Villem watched surprise
flicker across his face when Pavel realised who it was that was
attacking him. It remained there only for an instant. All the
followers of Tzeentch were only too aware that treachery
ringed around them, and that the next blade that came at
them might be from one of their allies.

Pavel reacted instantly, ducking back and stabbing once
more. His blade pierced Villem's side again. He felt a muscular arm loop itself around his neck and was aware that Lars
had grabbed him and was holding him steady while Pavel
plunged the blade into his body again and again. The pain
receded. Strength drained from him. Everything in his sight
seemed to be growing dimmer. He watched the floor rise to
meet him and realised that his two erstwhile followers had
dropped him. All the red stuff around him was blood and it
was coming from his body. He had not realised that the
human body could hold quite so much.

He looked back and saw his brother still lay sprawled on
the floor. He had landed heavily when Villem pushed him
clear. Regret filled him. All of his efforts had gone for naught.
He had killed his brother, or at least made it possible for his
assassins to do so, by accident. As from a great distance he
heard a bellowed war cry and became aware of a large shadowy figure moving up the corridor. It was a dwarf, one he
recognised: the Slayer, Gotrek Gurnisson.

How ironic, Villem thought. I spent all this time trying to
have him killed and now I am praying for him to arrive in
time and triumph. How the gods must be laughing!

Even as he watched he saw the dwarf advance upon Lars
and Pavel. They turned to meet him but were no match for
the Slayer's ferocity. The axe flickered once, twice, and it was
over. The red ruins of his fellow cultists lay dismembered on
the ground beside him.

'Thank you,' Villem tried to say, but couldn't get the words
out because of the crimson tide that bubbled from his throat.

The darkness gathered round him, and he felt himself
drawn downwards towards what waited beyond the doors of

death. It was hot down there, and full of searing agony. The Lord of Changes waited there to greet him.

# ELEVEN

Felix looked out from the walls near the Gargoyle Gate. Today was the day, no doubt about it. The legions of Chaos worshippers knew it. All the soldiers on the wall knew it. All of the citizens behind them knew it too. There was something in the air that you did not have to be a sorcerer to spot that told you so.

The clouds in the sky were red, streaked through with occasional flickers of black and silver. A crimson haze hovered over the surrounding land, turning the snow the colour of blood, and obscuring the more distant elements of the Chaos army from sight. Something about that glow made the skin on the back of Felix's neck prickle. He did not need Max Schreiber to tell him that foul magic was at play here. Even as he watched, thousands and thousands of warriors moved to take up their positions.

Regiment was too disciplined a word to describe the mob out there, he decided. They were more like primitive tribesmen bound together in the service of some potent chieftain. They seethed around the base of the daemonic war engines, eerily silent in the ruddy light. How many tribes of the Chaos scum were there out there?

He could count at least a dozen different banners belonging to the fur-garbed humans alone. There was a flayed man. There was a face with the lips sewn shut. Above one force fluttered a symbol of a three-headed howling dog. Above the heads of others floated banners depicting some sort of daemon. Felix wished he could be certain that the only Chaos worshipping humans near him were those outside the wall. The events of the previous evening had left him shaken.

He guessed he would never know whether Villem was a traitor or not. He had certainly been a mutant, the stigmata had already appeared on his body. But, according to the duke and Gotrek, he had fought to save his brother's life when ambushed and had died in the attempt. I guess he was innocent, and it was all part of Jan Pavelovich's plan to sow dissension among the leadership of the city. That was if Jan Pavelovich was the highest ranking cultist, a fact which Felix frankly doubted. He wondered if the young noble had really thrown himself out the window when Snorri and Bjorni were drinking, or whether the Slayers had given him a little help. It did not seem politic to ask, and there was no sense in falling out with the others now the moment of battle was at hand. They would all need to stand together if they were to have the faintest chance of survival.

Felix shook his head wondering what he was thinking. Such thoughts would never occur to the Slayers. That was not why they were here. They were here to seek a heroic doom. There would be plenty of those to go around this morning, Felix reckoned. He glanced sidelong at the others to see how they were taking things.

Gotrek looked as grim as ever. His gaze never left the advancing horde; he seemed to be singling out individuals as if judging whether they would be worthy of his time in single combat. Felix smiled looking at the Slayer. There was one who was going to sell his life dearly, and drag dozens, at very least, down to hell with him.

Snorri clutched his head and groaned, apparently more concerned with his hangover than the prospect of death before them. Occasionally he would break off from his moaning long enough to shout what sounded like dwarfish obscenities in the direction of the Chaos worshippers for interrupting his slumber. Bjorni stood nearby with one arm round Sasha and the other round Mona. Felix wondered how he had managed to smuggle the bar girls onto the wall with him, and how he had managed to convince them to come with him to this place of imminent danger. Money most likely, although judging by the way they held him close, they seemed to feel some genuine affection for him. It was a funny old world, Felix thought.

Ulli stood nearby, looking pale and thoughtful. His hand played with his stubby beard and he looked up at the sky a lot as if not wanting to look too closely at the enemy. Felix could not blame him. Not too many people liked to watch certain death approach them. Not even Slayers.

Max and Ulrika stood near the duke and his retinue. Max peered off into the distance as if viewing things only he could see. Ulrika did not even look in Felix's direction. He felt he should have been hurt more than he was, but it was obvious that their affair had run its course now, and even in the unlikely event of both of them surviving this, it was most likely they would part. A shame, he thought, but there it was.

The duke looked stern and commanding, and his soldiers were doing their best to put a brave face on things. Under normal circumstances, they would have managed it too. The winged lion fluttered from every tower, and from the pennons of a hundred companies. Heavily armed men crowded the battlements: swords, spears, and halberds clutched in gauntleted fists. Units of archers made ready to fire as soon as the enemy advanced. Mangonels, ballistae and other war machines rose from the ranks every fifty paces or so. Felix knew that in the honeycombed walls beneath them, more archers made ready to fire out through the arrow-slits and murder holes. He could smell boiling oil being heated, and hot pitch being made ready to pour on the stumps of the wounded. The canisters of alchemical fire were in the open now, ready to be loaded into the siege engines. He wished he had eaten nothing this morning but now it was too late.

He saw more movement in the distance. A vast cloud of harpies rose from the mass of Chaos worshippers and seethed and wheeled above it like a flock of swallows circling a temple spire on a summer's evening. Not the most apt analogy, Felix thought. More like flocks of daemons rising from some fiery hell to seek prey among the lost souls beneath them. He hoped the archers and wizards were ready for them. He did not relish the prospect of fighting off a horde of those foul-smelling bat-winged fiends. Vivid memories of his narrow escape from them in the Chaos Wastes came back to his mind far too easily.

The harpies began to slowly circle around the city spiralling higher and higher until they were simply small dots in the vast blood-red sky. Obviously they were not planning on attacking just yet. Motion on the ground attracted Felix's attention once more. Hordes of beastmen were making their way through the humans and forming up slightly ahead of them, leaving gaps through which other units might pass. It was like watching a huge chessboard on which the pieces were made of flesh and blood and were constantly in motion. Now, the black-clad Chaos warriors advanced to the beating of huge drums. Ranks of cavalry rode over the ramps across the forward trenches of the Chaos lines. Massive war altars were carried on the shoulders of tattooed fanatics.

Suddenly there was a deadly silence. Felix raised his spyglass to his eye and focussed on the great silk pavilion in the centre of the army. From it emerged Arek Daemonclaw, his warlords and his wizards. Felix could see the two evil-looking albino twins, gold-robed and black-robed, and a horde of lesser mages, all clad in thick raiments covered in oddly glowing symbols and all bearing staffs that looked as if they had been carved from bone and topped with human skulls. Judging by appearances, Felix guessed that some sort of argument was taking place between the Chaos general and his wizards. He was gesticulating angrily and pointing at the city walls, while the mages at first shook their heads, and finally nodded.

What was going on over there, Felix wondered?

AREK DAEMONCLAW WAS livid. All night he had listened to the bickering of his warlords as each sought a prime position for himself and his followers in the coming assault, and attempted to persuade Arek to place them ahead of their rivals. All night he had listened to the foolish carpings of his wizards telling him that the time was not quite right for their spells, that the stars were not correctly aligned, that the ultimate force had not been summoned yet.

He was sure this was all just an excuse. His spies, and there were many of them, had brought him word that Lhoigor and Kelmain had been visiting many of his warlords. When challenged they had claimed they were simply doing their best to hold the army together and reassure his followers that all was going well. Arek was having none of it. He knew they were plotting against him, and that it would only be a matter of time before one or more of his generals rose against him. This constant inactivity, this protesting about stars and omens, was simply buying his enemies time during which the army was becoming bored and restless with inaction, and ripe for rebellion against their rightful leader. Worse than that it was giving his enemy time to gather against him. Scouts reported that the Ice Queen's army was but a few days away, and there was a force of skaven advancing from the north. True these forces were tiny, but Arek knew that many mighty armies had been routed due to being attacked from the rear at an inopportune moment. This was not going to happen to his force. All thoughts of rebellion and inaction were going to end today.

He was not going to give them time for that. Soon all his army was going to be too busy to be bothered plotting against him. Soon he would give them a victory that would unite the entire horde behind him once more, and give those who would challenge him pause for thought. Today they would sweep over the walls of Praag and claim final and total victory.

MAX SCHREIBER WATCHED the mages of the Chaos horde advance to the fore. He had a more than professional interest in this. Very soon his life and the life of the woman he cared about might depend on his understanding of what he saw here.

He watched the two twin albinos closest of all. There was something about that pair that set them apart. To Max's trained senses, they almost glowed with power. They were the mightiest mages he had ever seen, far stronger than any of his old

masters, or Max himself. The others with them were almost
certainly their acolytes. They watched the twins with a wary
respect, and seemed to hang on their every word and gesture.

The two mages advanced to the clear ground in front of the
horde, still well out of bowshot of the walls. They stood
silent, heads down for a moment, then glanced at one
another, raised their arms and began to chant. At first nothing seemed to happen. Max detected only the slightest
stirring of the winds of magic and then only because his
senses were keyed up to the highest pitch. One by one the
mages around the albinos bowed their heads and began to
chant too. And as they did so, Max began to feel a subtle
change in the air.

The winds of magic swirled stronger now, as did the real
breeze. Cool fingers of air touched Max's face. Tendrils of
power flickered out from the staffs of the twins and touched
the might war engines around them. Arcs of power jumped
from engine to engine forming a latticework almost too intricate for Max's eye to follow. As he watched beam after beam
reached upwards and outwards touching the glowing clouds
overhead. Thunder rumbled. Lightning flickered downwards.

It was no normal lightning, Max could tell. It was pregnant
with all the power the Chaos horde had drawn down from
the Northern Wastes. The huge bolts all lashed downwards
and struck the tips of one of the twins' staffs. As they did so,
the mages seemed to swell with ominous power. To Max's
trained eye their auras became ever brighter. Their voices
swelled until their chanting could be heard from the walls of
Praag. The words were full of evil import and repeated the
name of Tzeentch constantly. As Max watched, the snow
around the sorcerers melted away from around their feet until
an area fifty strides across was clear, and the brown earth was
visible beneath.

As the thunder rumbled, the clouds began to swirl, like
water in a whirlpool. In their midst a gap opened revealing
the sky above. Through that gap the evil Chaos moon
Morrslieb glared down. It glowed bright as a small sun, and
more than once the aura surrounding it seemed to form a
wicked leering face with a gaping mouth and a massive
tongue that gazed down hungrily on the city.

Max heard people close to him whimper and moan. He knew why. That wicked face was depicted on tapestries in the palace and in sculptures on many buildings. It was the same malevolent visage that had glared down on Praag during the last siege. The air vibrated with energy. A monstrous rumbling began as the light of the moon fell on the huge siege engines. Auras flickered around them. Their metal forms shuddered and vibrated and began to move. It was a terrifying and awe-inspiring sight, like watching a field of massive metal statues spring to life.

The sorcerers did not cease their chanting. The haze surrounding the army seemed to clot and congeal, drawing itself together into massive blocks of reddish light. Then these seemed to shrink and dwindle and at the same time concentrate. As they did so the outlines of humanoid figures began to appear. At first they were only vague, monstrous shapes, but as the long minutes went on, and the chanting of the wizards continued, they became solid featureless figures of light, then took on shape and definition until thousands of obscenely-shaped figures were present.

Max recognised many of them from the forbidden tomes he had studied. Those things which somehow suggested evil animated fungi were Flamers of Tzeentch, lesser daemons of considerable power. Pink beings with massive heads where their torsos should have been capered and danced on the open ground.

Now other mages in the vast army began to join in. Max guessed that it was the priests and sorcerers in the service of other powers, taking advantage of all the dark magic Arek's house wizards had summoned. As Max watched aghast more and more daemonic figures emerged from nothingness into being.

He recognised the Daemonettes of Slaanesh: odd androgynous figures with one bare breast, hairless heads, and one mighty claw like a crab's pincer. They had a strange and disturbing beauty. Some units of them rode on odd bipedal beasts with long flickering tongues, others marched afoot and brandished long blades.

Amid the ranks of black-armoured Chaos warriors, other figures were materialising. Mighty hounds with teeth of steel and great collars of flesh emerging from their necks. Huge

armoured warriors bounded onto the backs of mighty red
and bronze steeds far more massive than any horse, whose
eyes blazed with an eerie blood-red light. Strange slithering
slug-like things bubbled into being ahead of the diseased
ranks of the followers of Nurgle. All of them were surrounded
by a halo of power that told Max of their daemonic origin. In
all of his life, he had never witnessed such a potent summoning, or seen so much mystical power unleashed in one
spot.

He doubted he would live to see its like again.

FELIX WATCHED THE Chaos horde begin its advance. It was all he
could do to keep himself from whimpering with fear like
some of those around him. He wondered whether he would
survive an hour. Massive metal siege towers carved with the
effigies of hideous daemons began to rumble forward. Teams
of sweating, near-naked men drew some of them. Others
moved under their own sorcerous power, rumbling ever
closer to the walls. Huge trebuchet arms swung backwards
and forwards sending loads of massive stones tumbling
towards the walls. Felix heard screams and shrieks from a distant section of the line as their cargo of death descended
among the defenders.

Now tens of thousands of marauders, beastmen and Chaos
warriors began to charge forward, racing through the snow
towards the walls. Their shouts and screams were terrible to
hear. Mighty drums were beaten. Huge horns sounded. The
wind brought the odours of brimstone and corrupt bodies to
Felix's nostrils.

He gripped his sword tight and fought to steady himself. It
was difficult. He recognised some of the things racing towards
them from the time he had spent in the tunnels beneath
Karag Dum. Those hounds, for example, were daemonic
things whose flesh no normal blade could pierce. He wondered how the defenders were going to stop them. Gotrek's
axe was capable of killing them, but the Slayer could not be
everywhere at once, and not even he could kill the small army
of daemons advancing upon them.

'Ask them to keep the noise down. Snorri has a bit of a
hangover,' said Snorri.

Felix almost smiled. Some of the tension eased out of him. He decided that whatever approached and however powerful it was, he was going to give as good an account of himself as he could. If there was nothing else he could do, he was at least going to take some of those Chaos-worshipping bastards with him.

Overhead the harpies ceased to circle and began to spiral downwards. Their long descent was nothing like the swooping dives Felix had seen them perform in the Chaos Wastes. He could only guess that they had been instructed to time their attack to strike just as the siege towers were hitting the wall. They would provide an additional distraction that the defenders could not afford to ignore. Someone out there had indeed been planning this for a long time.

The Chaos horde moved ever closer. Most of the warriors and the daemons clustered around the mighty siege engines, seeking shelter in their shadow. A few bolder, more foolhardy or more desperate for glory rushed ahead. The defenders on the wall watched tensely. Soon, Felix knew, the Chaos worshippers would be in range. Now was the time to whittle away their attackers.

Felix raised his spyglass and ran it over the oncoming horde. Faces leapt into focus. Brutal barbarians, mouths open in screams of fury, froth spilling from their lips, veins standing out on their forehead, muscles distended, filled his vision. Beside them were massive beastmen, ram-headed, horned, furred, eyes filled with red malice, inhuman muzzles raised to bay their bestial cries. Black helms, rune-inscribed, hid the faces of the Chaos knights, all save their strangely glowing eyes. Daemonic visages shimmered in the wicked glow of the witch moon. Felix wrenched his sight away from them and studied one of the siege towers.

It was taller even than the walls of Praag, a structure built from wood, and sheathed in the black iron of the Wastes, doubtless drawn from the daemonic forges beneath the ruins of Karag Dum. The plates were moulded into the shape of leering daemon heads, or inscribed with unspeakable runes whose evil light hurt the eye. The tower that Felix gazed upon had a massive cast head of Khorne attached to its front. Its wheels were embossed with faces similar to that of the great bloodthirster he had faced in the lost dwarf city. It gave the impression of immense size and solidity. It seemed more like a mobile tower from some iron keep than a mobile engine of war. And yet it moved, powered by sorcery, lumbering forward as fast as a man might trot, bouncing on the rutted ground, crushing any beastman unfortunate enough to fall in its path.

A huge two-headed battering ram flickered from Khorne's gaping maw, for all the world like the tongue of some vast snake. At the tower's top a crew of tribesmen manned a small ballista, and were frantically bringing it to bear on the defenders. Through dozens of small windows in the machine's sides, Felix could see the shadow shapes of the warriors waiting within.

Felix heard the chant of prayer and spell close to him now. Fireballs erupted from the walls of Praag, arcing outwards and downwards into the oncoming horde. Bolts of lightning flickered out of the turbulent sky. Odd golden glows appeared over the heads of bellowing Chaos warriors. Most of the spells spluttered and died, absorbed by the eerie haze surrounding the evil army, or neutralised by the work of the horde's own sorcerers. One or two hit home though. As Felix watched a fireball exploded amid a regiment of beastmen. A score were blown to pieces where they stood. A dozen more caught fire and raced randomly among their brethren, blazing like human torches, till they were cut down or trampled underfoot. At the sight, a cheer went up from the warriors on the battlements. It was a first, small victory. Felix hoped there would be many more.

A creaking followed by a loud twang announced to Felix that one of the mighty catapults near him had been brought to bear. A mass of huge rocks arced out over the besiegers and then, with what seemed like appalling slowness to the distant onlooker, crashed down, killing anything beneath them. It heartened Felix to see that the catapult did not just kill its immediate targets. Many of the marauders who sought to avoid the stonefall were trampled under the hooves of their beastmen comrades. That section of the approaching line was thrown into disarray by the milling of the mob, and the advance slowed. Those coming on behind them trampled more, as the press of bodies caused a huge pileup of man and beast.

More and more catapults and ballistae opened fire from the walls. More and more beastmen and marauders fell to their projectiles. More and more crushed and maimed bodies blocked the advance of at least part of the Chaos army, causing eddies, currents in that vast sea of flesh to rival anything in a real ocean. Kegs of alchemical fire descended on the horde, turning men and beasts into blazing torches that not even the chill of the snow could extinguish.

The defenders were not having it all their own way though. The huge trebuchets at the back of the enemy lines lobbed their own cargoes of death at the walls of Praag. Felix ducked as a mighty boulder passed overhead, and flinched at the sound of it crashing through red-tiled roofs behind him. Shouts of alarm and the smell of burning told him that either it had upset some fire or stove within the broken building, or the stone had born some sinister enchantment that caused a blaze where it fell. Felix frantically hoped it was the former but suspected that it might all too easily prove to be the latter.

Amid the horde some mages, either forgetting what they knew of the defences of Praag or too filled with their own sense of superiority to care, sent spells hurtling towards the walls. As Felix watched a fiery ball in which was visible a leering evil face arced towards the defenders. The ancient enchantments held good and the spell fizzled out paces from the battlements, sending the sour stench of brimstone into the nostrils of the warriors manning them. Shouts of triumph and relief from along the line told him that the old enchantments still held there too.

Thousands of bows twanged. Thousands of arrows driven by all the power of short Kislevite composite bows and dwarf-made crossbows scythed through the attackers. Screams of agony mingled with shouts of bloodlust. Another volley and hundreds more fell. Officers shouted commands, archers reloaded and fired. Crossbowmen worked the mechanisms of their weapons. Corpses littered the snow, but were crushed to jelly beneath the wheels of the advancing siege towers. The lords of death stalked the battlefield, feasting hungrily on the souls of the slain.

A hideous stench, a crack of wings opening to slow a fast descent and the rough cawing of raucous voices all warned Felix that the harpies had at last begun their attack. He ducked the sweep of an iron-taloned claw and hacked right through the wrist of his attacker. Spurting black blood, the winged humanoid tumbled backwards away from the wall and fluttered downwards to be impaled in the spike-filled pits below. Felix wiped the ichor from his face and spat, then glanced along the wall.

Hundreds of the bat-winged humanoids wrestled and clawed at the defenders, distracting the archers and interfering with the work of the siege engines at this critical point in the battle. More and more of them surged overhead and descended into the city to spread fire and alarm. Felix watched with some satisfaction as archers from the streets below picked off a few of them but more and more descended from the blood-red heavens to continue the wicked work.

Gotrek's war cry got Felix's attention. A swipe of the Slayer's axe slew two of the vile creatures; its starmetal blade seeming to sear their flesh as it passed through it. Snorri pinned one down with his foot while he bashed out its brains with his hammer, all the while keeping the beast's companions at bay with his whirling axe. Bjorni had hidden the two girls somewhere and now was dealing terrible damage to the attackers with a military pick. Ulli wrestled with another on the blood-slick stone near Felix. The man raced over and with a lunge passed his blade through the harpy's back.

Ulli rose to his feet, glaring and spitting blood. 'I could have taken it,' he shouted.

Felix gestured around them. 'Plenty more where that one came from.'

Ulli nodded and plunged once more into the fray. A familiar searing gold light blazed along the battlements. Felix recognised that Max's magic was at work. Powerfully too. Half a dozen winged monsters shrivelled and fell under its impact. Felix looked around to see Max and Ulrika standing side by side, the area around them clear of monsters. He gave them a thumbs-up sign and was answered with nods.

Suddenly the harpies seemed to have had enough. They rose from the battlements, shrieking defiance, and surged on into the city. At least on this section of the line they had found the defenders too tough for them. Felix looked out at the advancing horde. They had made good use of the distraction to get ever closer to the city walls. Only a few hundred paces separated them from the stonework now.

He wiped sweat from his face and shouted to one of the water-carriers. His throat felt as dry as the sands of Araby. The boy brought him a waterskin and Felix hastily downed some of its contents. They felt sweet as wine sliding down his throat. He was taking advantage of the water while it lasted. Doubtless in a few hours, if he yet lived, he would be reduced to taking mouthfuls of the snow. He should be so lucky, he told himself.

A cheer from along the line got his attention. Under a relentless bombardment from the catapults on the walls, one of the great siege engines had ground to a halt and was now beginning to topple. It wobbled for a few moments, like a cart whose front wheels have gone over the edge of a ditch. There was a sound like a metal drum hit with a hammer only a hundred times louder as another massive stone smashed into it. It was too much for the daemonic engine. It heeled over like a ship in a storm and crashed down into the middle of a host of beastmen. Their screams and wails of agony told of hundreds of deaths. There was a mighty explosion, and in an instant the black structure appeared to expand, revealing yellow fires burning inside, like a mystic portal to some hot hell. Massive metal plates, knife-edged, hurled everywhere, decapitating Chaos marauders, cutting through the armour of the black-encased knights, taking an enormous death toll.

'One down, twelve to go,' Ulli muttered.

'I could show them a bigger tower,' growled Bjorni, 'and mine doesn't come down so fast either.' No one seemed interested. A company of fresh bowmen raced into position on the battlements near them. Their officer shouted instructions. The men knocked their arrows, drew their strings back to their ears and then let fly. More Chaos worshippers fell.

'We're slaughtering them,' crowed Ulli.

'This is the easy part!' Gotrek shouted back. 'Just wait till they get to the walls.'

The younger Slayer's face fell.

*Good for you, Gotrek Gurnisson*, thought Felix ironically. You can always be relied on to raise morale in a tight spot. But if any of the men were discouraged by the dwarf's pronouncement, they gave no sign. Probably too busy trying to pick new targets, Felix thought and offered up a prayer of thanks to Sigmar for small mercies.

Couriers raced past, bearing messages for the duke from other towers and other parts of the battlefield. Felix wondered that anybody could make any sense out of this maelstrom of combat but the duke sent all of the messengers away seemingly satisfied with the orders he had given. Felix supposed it was probably just the fact that he looked calm, and in control that did it. The men believed because they wanted to believe.

The first of the remaining siege towers was only a hundred strides away now. Huge fur-clad barbarians bellowed challenges from its roof, and brandished their weapons obscenely at the defenders. The Kislevites responded with arrow fire. Most of the marauders managed to duck down behind their parapets in time. Their kinsmen tossed those who did not off the top of their machine. No help for the wounded here, thought Felix. Khorne is probably hungry for their souls.

He strode across to Ulrika and Max. Woman and wizard were covered in gore. Felix had no idea how much of it was their own. 'Are you all right?' he asked.

'Fine,' she replied and looking closely at her Felix could see this was the case. She looked more than fine. She looked exalted, like someone in the throes of a powerful drug. Felix had seen many warriors get that way, had felt the same thing himself on many occasions, felt a touch of it himself now. There was nothing more thrilling than surviving mortal combat. She cast a glance out at the howling sea of Chaos worshippers.

'Bring them on,' she said and laughed. It was an eerie laugh, with more than a little madness in it. It reminded him of Gotrek in the throes of killing lust. Felix followed her gaze. He could see that many of those howling barbarians out there around the base of the war machines carried long siege ladders.

'They'll be here soon enough,' he said.

'Scared, Felix?' she asked mockingly. He smiled.

'Absolutely.'

She cocked her head to one side and looked him up and down. 'You don't fight like it.'

'I find being terrified gives me an extra incentive to fight well.'

'You are a strange man, Felix Jaeger. No Kislevite warrior would confess to feeling as you do.'

'Perhaps I am just more honest,' he muttered.

'What?' she shouted, obviously having failed to hear him over the tumult of the battle.

'Look out!' shouted Max and raised his hands. Golden spheres winked into being around them. Beams of energy speared upwards. Felix looked up in time to see a swooping harpy turn into a blackened, charred husk. It tumbled to the battlements at his feet and split open, revealing reddish meat and whitish bone within. Felix looked away with a grimace. A foul smell of burning flesh clogged his nostrils.

'A useful trick, Max,' he said.

'I've been getting a lot of practice recently,' replied the wizard and turning outwards, directed his ravening beams of coruscating energy at the nearest siege engine.

Something around that daemonic machine absorbed the power. Felix could see the air shimmering around it, as if some semi-visible shield were recoiling under the impact. The haze moved away from the point of impact, rippling like water in a pond disturbed by a thrown stone. Max drove his spell harder and the light crept slowly closer to the tip of the tower, touched a howling beastman, and caused his flesh to melt and run. Seconds later the ballista he was manning caught fire.

Felix could only hope the flames would spread to the rest of the structure. As he watched smoke continued to rise from the top of the tower and the flames leapt ever higher. It seemed that the wood, or whatever else the thing was made from was combustible. Felix watched, awe struck, as gates in the tower's side, obviously intended to be lowered to let those within assault the walls, were thrown open and men began to leap out, falling to their doom fifty strides below. Felix turned to Max.

'If only you could do that a few more times we might hold
them back.'

The wizard was bent double. He looked pale and sickly like
a man convalescing after a long illness. All of the strength had
gone out of him. Ulrika stood by his side, supporting him.
Felix wrestled with a surge of futile jealousy and went over to
see if there was anything he could do to help.

'I should… should not have done that,' Max gasped, sweat
running from his brow. 'There was something alive imprisoned
within the tower, something daemonic, wicked and older than
the world. The strain of banishing it nearly killed me. It was
just that I felt the protective spells going down, and thought if
I tried a little harder I might overcome them. I did, didn't I?'

'Yes,' Felix said, catching the wizard as he slowly keeled
over. Hastily he and Ulrika carried Max over and propped his
back against the parapet. The wizard looked as if he might
pass away at any moment.

'Will he be all right?' Ulrika asked. She sounded very concerned. Felix checked the wizard's pulse. It was fast but
strong. His brow felt very warm. 'I think so, but I am neither
physician nor wizard. I don't know how magic can drain you.
There's not a mark on him, and he seems all right…'

'I don't think he had fully recovered his strength from healing me,' she said. She sounded guilty. Felix looked up at her
and shook his head.

'Nonsense. He was fine when he helped us stop the attack
on the grain silos. Don't fret yourself. We have other things to
worry about.'

Despite his reassuring words, Felix was not so sure he was
correct. Max had been using a lot of his energies recently, in
combat, in healing, in banishing the ghosts that had attacked
them. Perhaps he had overspent his life force and was now
about to pay the price. Even as the thoughts crossed his mind,
he felt a tugging on his sleeve and looked down to see Max
smiling wanly up at him.

'I'll be fine,' he muttered. 'I just need a few minute's rest and
I'll be good as new.'

The wizard did not look that way, but his words seemed to
reassure Ulrika. She gave him a radiant smile, and touched
his face gently. Felix felt blood rush to his cheeks. Had there

been something going on between those two without him knowing? They looked more like lovers at this moment than he and Ulrika did. Get a grip on yourself, he thought. This is not the time nor the place for such thoughts.

Spells flickered between wall and siege tower. The air crackled as protective magic dampened them out. Clouds of dust rose from the oncoming units. The deadly hiss of arrows filled the air, almost drowned out by the screams of the wounded and the roaring of that onrushing sea of flesh.

Terrible frenzy filled the Chaos worshippers. The presence of the daemons in their midst obviously goaded them on as nothing else could. Despite the appalling casualties, they came on undaunted. No amount of killing seemed to dent their resolve. Felix knew that he was in for the fight of his life.

A company of beastmen in advance of the rest had reached the ditch at the foot of the walls. They had come prepared. A massive ladder was lofted, and even before it touched the walls, a goat-headed warrior was on it, climbing with surprising deftness in spite of its hooves. Even as the ladder hit the wall, it was twisted and pushed away. The beastman fell, caught a rung with one powerful hand and then continued his climb. He managed to get half way up the ladder, several of his cloven-hoofed brethren just behind him, when the defenders managed to topple the ladder. Instead of falling straight back it toppled sideways, sending the beastmen to their deaths on the sharpened stakes below.

The wall shook as the first of the mighty siege towers made contact. Felix leaned out over the battlements to see what was happening. The thing had driven right into the ditch, crushing the stakes beneath its weight. The battering ram in its belly smashed into the walls, sending chips of stone flying. Already a bridge had been lowered on the machine's top and warriors were starting to emerge from within the machine's body and pour across it. As Felix watched other Chaos worshippers, mad with battlelust, started to clamber up the side of the machine, using the embossed daemonic faces as handholds. Felix was reminded of ants swarming over a stump as more and more of them began the arduous climb.

All along the wall other siege towers were making contact, and more and more Chaos worshippers emerged, bellowing the name of Khorne and shouting his praises in their guttural tongue. Felix readied his sword, and looked around for the Slayers. Predictably they were rushing towards the thick of the fighting. Felix glanced at Ulrika who was bent over Max soothing his brow. He felt a surge of jealousy, annoyance, and battle lust.

'Keep an eye on Max,' he said as he sprinted towards the fray. 'I will be right back.'

Even as he ran, he wondered why was he doing this. Was he running to get away from them, or to try and impress the girl with his bravery? He wondered if he would ever know.

AREK WATCHED HIS warriors begin to reduce the walls of Praag. In some ways it was going better than he had expected. In some ways it was going worse. He had not expected to lose two of the towers before they even reached the walls. Curse that sorcerer and the siege engineers manning those catapults. On the other hand, the harpies had done an admirable job of distracting the defenders, and judging by the flames rising beyond the outer wall, were even now spreading havoc within the enemy city.

Arek watched enthralled as the huge siege towers disgorged their freight of warriors onto the wall. Northern tribesmen and snarling beastmen fought alongside each other, filled with a rabid desire to kill. Arek almost envied them at this moment. He had always found it deeply satisfying to triumph over his opponent in the heat of battle. There were times when he suspected that he might almost have enjoyed being one of the berserker followers of Khorne. He had never lost a single combat, and knew he was never likely to, with all the gifts the Great Mutator had heaped upon him. He was all but invincible when it came to a fray which was why none of the other warlords had ever challenged him to duel for leadership of the horde. If it had not been for that accursed vision...

Lightning flickered along the battlements, clearing away some of his men. Obviously the spell barriers that prevented his wizards casting spells at or through the walls did nothing to stop someone already there. Why was that, he wondered? Was it like being behind a wall or caught in a passage between two barriers? He would have to ask his pet

magicians about it when he got the chance. Perhaps before
he had them executed for showing insufficient zeal in protecting his troops. They had sworn the towers were totally
protected from enemy spells and invulnerable to enemy
weapons. Today's events had proven them wrong on both
accounts.

Still, the machines had worked and looked like they would
fulfil their purpose, and that was the main thing. He knew
they would have to do it today, all the vast energy so labori-
ously summoned from the northlands had been expended in
the animation of the towers, the summoning of the daemons,
and the weaving of the protective spells. He knew they were
going to be exhausted for days afterwards.

That would be the perfect time to round them up and make
an example of them, Arek thought.

FELIX FOUGHT HIS way along the battlements. The stone was
slippery with blood, and severed entrails. Puddles of red
stained the snow. He leapt to one side as a dying beastman
reached for him. The movement took him to the edge of the
parapet on the town side of the wall. He caught sight of red-
tiled roofs below him, and buildings blazing in the distance.
Men seemed to be fighting with men back there. Panicked
townsfolk, he wondered, or more cultists emerging to help
their fellows in battle?

Time enough to worry about that later. If he survived what
was going on around him now. The beastman had raised
itself on one hand and gathered itself in a crouch. Judging by
its wounds it was not far from death. Felix guessed that it
intended to take him with it, and he had a fair idea of how.
He was proven correct. The beastman sprang, spreading its
arms to make a grab for him. Expecting this, Felix crouched
and rolled letting the massive creature pass over him, and the
battlements, and fall to its doom far below.

The snow was cold on his hands, and was starting to seep
through his tunic where he had been lying in it. The chainmail shirt he wore beneath did nothing to help with the chill.
Might get a fever from this, he thought, and then laughed.
That would be the least of his worries. He grasped the hilt of
his sword, and pushed himself upright, rising to his knees

just in time to see another beastman swinging a monstrous spiked mace down on his head.

He threw himself to one side, bracing himself on one hand while swinging his blade at the creature. The mace passed just to one side of his head. His blow took the thing just behind the knee, drawing blood. The beastman threw back its goat head and bellowed in pain. Felix stabbed upwards, taking it in the groin. The bellow became extremely high-pitched and then tailed off into a piteous whimper. Felix withdrew the blade and rose to his feet, chopping half way through his foe's neck with another swipe. Its head flopped loose, still attached by tendons. Black blood boiled forth to melt the snow. Felix strode on. Snow had started to fall. Flakes blew into his eyes and partially obscured his sight. The wind seemed to be picking up. Was this more sorcery, he wondered, or just a natural effect of the weather in these chill northern climes?

Ahead of him he could see the Slayers, fighting amid a horde of beastmen and marauders and more than holding their own. Dead and dying foes lay all around them. The Kislevites, heartened by their presence, fought like men possessed. Here at least, it seemed possible to believe, if only for a moment, that victory might be theirs. Another monstrous siege tower crashed into the wall. A smell something like musk, something like perfume wafted into Felix's nostrils. For a moment, he thought nothing of it, but then his skin started to tingle, and a ticklish sensation started at the back of his throat. He felt all of the killing lust draining out of him, and turned to find the source of this delightful odour.

All around him, men and beastmen were doing the same, temporarily forgetting their enmity in their desire to find the source of the sweet perfume. Felix saw a massive iron drawbridge crash onto the battlements. Exotic, strangely beautiful, oddly familiar figures leapt forth from the siege tower, and raced into the fray. They looked like shaven-headed women. Despite the chill, they were near naked, wearing black leather tunics that revealed one perfectly formed breast. In place of one hand, they had crab-like claws. In the other hand some held long stabbing swords, some held whips, some held nets. Moving with an eerie grace they glided across the battlements. Wherever they went, men died. Felix recognised them as creatures of Slaanesh, Lord of Unspeakable Pleasures.

Felix watched one huge Kislevite warrior who had only moments before slaughtered three beastmen stand like a lamb waiting to be slaughtered while one of the beautiful woman things clipped off his head with a claw. Instead of avenging him the man's comrades calmly waited for death to come to them. Felix watched it all fascinated, and filled with an odd elation. There was something perfectly enthralling about the whole performance: the grace of the females, the way the red blood glistened in perfect droplets on the snow. There was something sensual and deeply arousing about it. He doubted he had ever seen anything quite so attractive as the daemon women. It would be a pleasure to die at their hands. In fact, he could hardly wait. He took a stride towards them, eager to feel death's embrace.

Part of him, deeply buried in his psyche, screamed that it was wrong. Those were not women. They were daemons. They were the enemy. Their musk or some other sorcery had him enchanted. Yet there was nothing he could do about it. His feet kept moving as if they belonged to someone else, the sword dangled limply from his fingers and it was all he could do not to let it slip to the ground. A smile was frozen on his face. He could see the same smile written on the lips of other enthralled defenders.

A beastman aimed a blow at him. He did not want this. It would prevent him embracing the woman-thing of his choice, an enchanting creature with pale white skin and ruby red lips. He ducked the blow and took his assailant's hand off at the wrist. As it fell backwards, he rammed his sword into its throat. Behind him he could hear the sound of running feet, and the sound of something heavy hacking through flesh like a butcher's cleaver. Felix sincerely hoped it wasn't another rival for the favour of his chosen one. He wanted to look back to make sure, but he could not keep his eyes off her. Look at the way her smile revealed those gleaming ivory fangs!

Something rushed past him, and he almost stabbed it before realising that it was Gotrek. Did the Slayer intend to challenge him for the she-daemon's favours? He would see about that. Felix aimed a stab at the Slayer's back but something restrained him. He seemed unable to move his arm. Looking down, he saw a massive hand was locked on his wrist. He tried to struggle but someone immobilised him with the same ease with which he might immobilise a child.

'Snorri thinks that's far enough,' said a deep voice from somewhere around the region of his lower back. Felix fought against the steely grip and raved curses as he saw what the cruel Slayer intended. Gotrek moved among the Slaanesh worshippers. Their light weapons could not withstand his axe, which now blazed lantern-bright with an evil red glow. One by one he chopped his way through them. They did not die as human warriors might have. Instead, as they fell their bodies disintegrated into showers of sparks and clouds of vile perfume. Smelling that stink broke the spell, and made Felix realise how close he had come to being slain by its evil enchantment. All around him other human warriors appeared to realise the same. They shook themselves, looked at their foes, and took up the fray once more.

Gotrek slew the last of the she-daemons, and leaping to the battlement struck at the lowered drawbridge with his axe. The powerful enchantment on the weapon, powerful enough to banish even the greatest of daemons, caused far more destruction on the siege tower than even the strength of Gotrek's blow would seem to warrant. Sparks blazed on the black metal where he struck, and instead of disappearing, flickered and grew larger, writhing around the hell-metal like tiny chains of blood-red lightning. In an instant they flickered outwards from the point of impact, until they covered the whole of the mighty siege tower in a display of dazzling pyrotechnics that hurt the eye.

Felix watched in amazement. The contact with Gotrek's mighty weapon had in some way disrupted the spell animating the siege machine, freeing the imprisoned daemonic energy. A smell like ozone mingled with brimstone filled the air, clearing away the stench of the slain daemonettes. Even Gotrek appeared stunned by the effect of his action. He stood motionless for a second watching the strange halo of lightning engulf the daemon tower. From within came screams and the stink of burning flesh and fur. Snowflakes sizzled into nothingness where they touched the light. Then the tower simply fell apart, its components raining to the ground below.

Felix wished Max Schreiber were here now to tell him what had happened. The wizard would know about such things for certain. All Felix could do was guess. He reckoned that the tower had been at least partially constructed with sorcery, and held together by magical energies. Gotrek's blade had disrupted the spell binding its components together, and thus ensured its destruction.

The Slayer shook his head, as if to clear his sight, and then, appearing to realise what he had done, let out a crazed laugh. He raced along the battlements, seeking another one of the towers. Felix swiftly moved to follow. He knew that at all costs the Slayer must be kept alive.

If anything could turn the tide of the battle it was his axe.

MAX SCHREIBER STARED in wonderment as the spell holding the tower together unravelled. To his mage's senses, even partially blinded as they were by the storm of dark magical energy raging about him, it was obvious what was going on. Gotrek's blade had been forged to be the bane of daemons. Max knew this for a certainty. Those towers contained and were animated by the imprisoned essence of daemons from the darkest hells. Max knew as much from his contact with the tower earlier when he had unwoven the spell binding the evil thing.

As the axe banished the daemons from the mortal plane, the vessel holding them fell apart, no longer bound together by their presence. Max watched in awe as the Slayers made their way along the battlements and in quick succession Gotrek reduced first one, then two, then three of the monstrous engines to flinders. It was an amazing thing to watch. It seemed that in some ways the gods themselves had decided to aid the defenders after all, by allowing the presence of such a potent weapon, and such a powerful wielder. Was this the destiny the Slayer had been spared for so long to meet? Max did not know.

Summoning the last of his magical energies he freed his senses from his body, allowing sight and mage vision to roam free along the walls and observe the struggle. Everywhere he looked he could see slaughter. Men and beastmen, Chaos warrior and human defender were locked in brutal combat. Along the wall, Gotrek and Felix and the other Slayers roamed like angry gods, seemingly killing at will.

Even as he watched though, he became certain that this would not be enough. Gotrek could not be everywhere, and the towers had already done their wicked work. At many points along the wall Chaos warriors, beastmen and vile tribesmen were present, holding small sections long enough for more and more of their brethren to swarm up ladders, and haul more normal engines into place. Despite the Slayers' efforts it looked as if the walls would be over-run.

But the attack had cost the horde dearly. Horns sounded from around them. Max sent his vision looking for the source and saw reinforcements sweeping up from the town to the walls. Fresh warriors hurled themselves into the fray, hacking at their hideous foes, chopping them down. One by one the beachheads established by the Chaos worshippers were overwhelmed, and the wall was cleared, stride by painful stride.

Max almost believed that they might be able to win this battle, and hold the wall for another day, but even as he thought this, he sensed sorcerous power being unleashed at a different section of the wall. Quickly he sent his spirit soaring in search of the disturbance. His vision ran around the perimeter, his magic still imprisoned by the binding spells along the outer and inner walls. As it did so, he saw what was going on.

At another section of the wall, far distant from where the Slayers were, more of the daemonic towers attacked. Max saw that they had reduced one section of the stonework to rubble. The protective spells in this spot had already unravelled allowing Max to shift his point of view to outside the confining perimeter. His gaze flickered over the horde of Chaos warriors and beastmen piling into the city through the gap. As he watched the largest of the towers used its ram to break through the mighty gateway. It would only be a matter of moments before the iron-clad wooden beams gave way completely. Max saw the wood splinter and the metal buckle and then the whole gate flew apart, letting the screaming horde into the city.

Max looked up at Ulrika. Concern was written on her face. 'Go and tell the duke that the East Gate has fallen,' he said. 'The hordes of Chaos are within the city.'

# TWELVE

THE HORNS SOUNDED loudly. The Kislevite troops on the wall began to panic. Felix knew what that signal meant: the enemy were within the walls. All the hard fighting they had done here had been for nothing. He gritted his teeth and spat into the snow. Somewhere, somehow, he had got blood in his mouth. Maybe he had bitten his cheek or tongue. Maybe one of his teeth was coming loose. He had been struck glancing blows a few times in the combat, and he bled from a dozen nicks on his arms, legs and face. He was tired, and filled with fear, and the sight of the hardened defenders around him starting to panic did nothing to reduce his own trepidation. He looked around to see how the Slayers were doing.

Gotrek did not look well. He swayed wearily on his feet and his features were pale. Felix had not seen him look quite this bad since after the battle at Karag Dum. It was apparent that whatever power the axe had, using it drained the Slayer of a great deal of his energy. He caught Felix's sympathetic glance and growled, 'I am not dead yet, manling.'

It looked only a matter of time though. Even a warrior as fearsome as Gotrek could not fight for long in the condition

231

he was in. The Chaos warriors so recently cleared from the walls were returning with renewed vigour, casting ladders up, and pushing more conventional siege towers into position.

Snorri, Bjorni and Ulli weren't in much better condition. All three looked as if they had been bathed in a pool of blood. Bjorni had a flap of skin loose on the side of his face which gaped open to reveal his teeth. Snorri's tattoos were near invisible against a dark background of bruises. Ulli looked as if he wanted to either burst into tears or berserk rage and was not quite sure which. All of the Slayers looked determined though, and it was obvious to Felix that they intended to make a last stand here on the walls against the oncoming horde. It would probably prove suicidal but that after all was their avowed aim in life.

Madness, Felix thought, simple madness. For a brief moment back there during the fighting, he had felt something like hope. The power of Gotrek's axe against the daemon towers, and the way the dwarfs had helped rally the weary defenders had almost made him believe victory was possible. A hopeless dream he could see now, watching the duke bellowing orders and getting his own guard to hold firm to cover the retreat of the rest of his men from the wall. It was only due to his presence of mind that things were not turning into a fully-fledged rout.

Ulrika and Max were already moving down the stairs, and he waved to them as they went. The woman supported the tired sorcerer, and Felix could not grudge him that. Max had earned a chance at life this day, and Ulrika owed him for saving hers. He knew that she would pay that debt whatever it took. He tried not to think jealous thoughts of any other reasons she might have. This was not the time.

Seeing the duke's banner still fluttering along the walls, some of the massive siege engines had started firing again, obviously aiming at the one proud banner still fluttering defiantly in their faces, oblivious to the peril in which they placed their own warriors. Felix ducked involuntarily as a huge stone went hurtling past overhead to crash onto the tenements behind them.

'Missed!' cackled Snorri.

'Not even close,' muttered Ulli without much conviction.

Gotrek limped back over in the general direction of the wall, and began to bellow challenges at the beastmen.

Don't do that, you idiot, thought Felix, but could not quite muster the courage to say it aloud. The duke's men were covering the stairway down from the tower now. The duke himself shouted, 'Come on! There is still time to go! We need every warrior now to help defend the city!'

His plea almost moved the dwarfs. He could see that it struck a chord within them. They knew his words were true. Ulli scuffed his feet and began to move in the direction of the stairwell. Bjorni shook his head. Snorri shrugged and rushed along the wall to send another ladder toppling backwards with one heave of his enormous shoulders. Gotrek did not even look back. Ulli shamefacedly stood his ground as if undecided as to whether to stay or go.

'Come on, Jaeger, we need you too!' shouted the duke. He obviously understood what was going on with the Slayers, and knew they were beyond either his pleadings or his commands. Felix looked at the dwarfs once more.

They are not going to come, he thought. This is it. The end of the road. They are going to wait here, fight the beastmen as they come over the walls, and die in the stupidly heroic manner they wanted to. Idiots. And he knew, to his own fury, that their madness had infected him. He was not going to move either. He had sworn an oath to record Gotrek's doom, and he fully intended to do it, if he had to stand in the doorway there and wait until the wall was seething with Chaos warriors. Only then would he see about trying to make his own escape, if that were possible. He looked at the duke and said, 'Go on! I'll catch up!'

The duke gave him a wan smile and ordered his troops to go. In moments the wall was clear. It seemed strangely quiet. Felix looked at the four dwarfs and realised that at this instant he was probably the only human being on the walls of Praag. He wondered how long it would take for the beastmen and the tribesmen to start clambering up the ladders, surely not long now.

What were they waiting for? Why did he have this sense of imminent danger? He glanced all around and saw nothing, then out of the corner of his eye was aware of something massive flashing through the air towards them. No, not at them, at the space the duke and his men had so recently left. One of the trebuchet engineers had finally got the range.

He flinched as the enormous stone came tumbling down towards them. It smashed into the stonework not a dozen feet from Gotrek and sent chunks of smashed masonry and clouds of snow flying through the air. When the wrack had cleared, Felix saw the Slayer was down, a pool of blood marking the snow around his head. His axe had slipped from his nerveless fingers. He glanced at the other Slayers and saw that they were just as appalled as he was. Perhaps they had all shared some secret belief in Gotrek's invincibility. He could see that they were shaken.

Damn, he thought, of all the incredibly stupid and utterly unworthy ways to die, that must take the prize.

GREY SEER THANQUOL glared at the red sky. Up ahead of him, not too far away, he sensed the unleashing of enormous magical energies. Whatever power had been drawn down from the Chaos Wastes was being discharged now, at an incredible rate. He tugged some of it down to him, determined not to let all of it get away, and then used the energy to cast his awareness ahead of the army. Never had it been so easy. It was almost as if his soul was being swept along by the currents of energy, towards the vortex into which it had been sucked.

Thanquol was amazed and appalled by what he witnessed. He saw the mighty Chaos army throw itself at the walls of Praag. He saw enormous towers full of pent-up daemonic energy rumble forward. He saw the mass of warriors around their wheels. Had he been occupying his physical body at that moment, he would have squirted the musk of fear. He had always thought the assembled hordes of skavendom must surely be the most numerous army in the world but now he was not so sure. The Chaos horde had grown since he had encountered it thundering across the tundra of northern Kislev and it had been mighty then.

He had wanted to send his spirit soaring over the city to investigate what was going on inside, but as soon as it neared the walls, he found himself repelled painfully by some mysterious force. Protective enchantments, for sure. Perhaps just as well. It might be best to send his spirit soaring high, out of the range of possible detection by the mages he sensed present below. Two of them were of such power as to give even Grey Seer Thanquol pause. Never in his life, not even in the hall of the Council of Thirteen, had he encountered such auras of power. It was quite possible, he was forced to admit, that those two beings down there were the most powerful magicians in the world, himself not excluded. It was a terrifying thought. More terrifying yet was that he recognised them. They were the albino twins he had met in the camp of Arek Daemonclaw.

He tried to console himself with the thought that it was only because they were filled with the energy they had drawn down from the daemon lands of the north that they were his superiors in magic, but somehow the thought did not reassure him. It was still appalling to contemplate the fact that there existed two beings capable of acting as vessels for such god-like power. Thanquol felt sure that not even he could duplicate the feat. Almost he considered returning to his fleshly shell then and there to avoid even the possibility of their notice. But something kept him from doing so.

It was evident to his keen mage senses that the spells they were weaving were so complex and powerful that all of their attention must go in to maintaining them. Thanquol swept his gaze over the battlefield and counted the number of daemons that were manifesting. Astonishing. He would not have believed it was possible so far south of the Wastes. Apparently he was wrong. Sheer terror gnawed at the pit of his stomach. Here was a threat to all skavendom, and perhaps even the wellbeing and future plans of Grey Seer Thanquol himself. At all costs something must be done about it. Preferably not by him, however.

He observed the mighty assault begin, and sheer skaven curiosity kept him watching. It seemed impossible to him that the humans on the wall did not immediately turn tail and flee at the first sight of the mighty war engines and the horde of men, daemons and monsters surrounding them. Then again, he had always thought there was no end to the witless folly of the hairless apes. He watched with even greater astonishment as the humans managed to slow down

and destroy one of the massive daemonic engines with catapult fire and then was even more amazed to see another
destroyed by a spell of unbinding. What was even more disturbing was that Thanquol recognised the magical signature
of the mage who had done it. He had fought with that wizard on two occasions at the horse-soldiers' burrow. It
appeared his power had grown since then though. How was
it possible, what was his secret? Thanquol sent his spirit-self
soaring even higher. There was another individual to be
avoided at all costs.

Thanquol contented himself with a bird's eye view of the
main action. From just beneath the clouds it was possible for
him to grasp the wide sweep of the Chaos army's strategy.
Most of the Chaos force was concentrated for a frontal assault
on the gargoyle-encrusted northern gate, but a significant
fraction of the numbers assaulted the eastern and western
gates. Such were the numbers of the horde that it was possible for it to make these attacks in a great sweeping crescent,
and still outnumber the defenders at any point. Mass attack
tactics worthy of any skaven army, Thanquol thought.

He watched the man-things die like ants below him. It did
not move him in any way. He was a skaven, and the deaths of
lesser races meant nothing to him. To tell the truth, the
deaths of most skaven meant nothing either. The only emotion he felt about death was a sense of triumph when it
happened to some sworn enemy of his. The battle raged for
long minutes. Siege engines exchanged shots. Arrows darkened the sky. The daemons entered the fray. Thanquol
watched astonished as something unexpected occurred.

Many daemons died. One of the great siege towers toppled,
the spells binding it unravelling. Now what could have
caused that, the grey seer wondered? Some magic of awesome
power.

He dropped his point of view towards the wall to get a
closer look. He was in no way surprised to see the accursed
Gotrek Gurnisson standing at the centre of the mystical con-
flagration, that terrible axe burning with energy in his hands.
Hatred and fear warred within Thanquol. He told himself
that it was impossible for the slow-witted dwarf to see him,
and maintained a sensible distance from the action.

The Slayer and his companions, more dwarfs and that wicked human Felix Jaeger, raced along the walls, bringing destruction to more of the siege towers. Thanquol watched in astonishment as that evil axe did its work. He could see the runespells laid on it quite clearly now. He had always known it was a potent weapon, but he had never guessed quite how powerful. Blazing within that starmetal blade was a power quite the equal of that wielded by those sorcerers back there amid the Chaos horde, greater even perhaps. A seer trained as Thanquol was had no trouble seeing that these two opposing powers could not possibly have come to the same place at the same time by accident. He guessed that they were all in some way counters in the game played by the gods. At this moment, he felt only gladness that his physical body was many leagues away.

A disturbance at the eastern gate drew his attention; he cast his mind swiftly in that direction in time to witness the fall of the gate. It looked like despite all the resistance put up by the human defenders the city was doomed to fall after all. Thanquol watched with a certain malicious pleasure as the beastmen and barbarian tribesmen poured through the gap in the wall and charged into the city.

Already part of him wondered if there was any way to turn this to his advantage. Perhaps he could come upon the Chaos horde after it had taken the city. Not while it was there in force, of course. That would be suicide. But perhaps the horde would move on, leaving only a garrison. That would be the time for a swift certain, strike in the true skaven manner. Yes. Yes. He could organise that.

Swiftly he sent his awareness flashing back to the area where Gotrek Gurnisson and Felix Jaeger were. With any luck they would be caught up in the rout and chopped down. He prayed to the Horned Rat that this would be the case. He watched as the humans abandoned the city's outer walls and only the foolish Slayers, and Felix Jaeger remained. This was getting better and better.

He saw the enormous stone, trebuchet-cast, tumbling head-long down onto the walls. He watched the explosion of flying masonry strike down Gotrek Gurnisson, and saw the Slayer slump forward into the snow. His whole soul exulted in an ecstasy of triumph. The Horned Rat had answered his prayers. He had seen with his own mage senses the fall of his most hated enemy.

It seemed certain that if he only waited a little while longer, he would witness the death of the loathsome Jaeger as well. Today was turning out to be one of the best of his life.

AREK SAW THE Slayer fall to the huge trebuchet stone. He kept watching until he was certain that Gotrek Gurnisson would not rise again. Long moments passed and he felt a huge weight lift from his shoulders. There was no way the vision the twins had shown him could be true. It was merely part of some cruel plot on their part. He could have shouted aloud with relief. He had not realised how much the vision had oppressed him until this moment. Now, he was himself once more. Now he could ride into battle like the conquering hero he was.

IVAN PETROVICH STRAGHOV touched his heels to the flanks of his horse. They moved wearily through the snow. It had been a long, hard ride under difficult conditions, and only the fact that the muster had driven a herd of remounts with it, had enabled them to make such good time towards Praag. Ivan studied the sky. Things did not look good. The clouds were a hideous red. Ivan had seen skies like that before, over the peaks that separated northern Kislev and the Troll Country from the Chaos Wastes, but he had never thought to see anything like it so far south, deep within his native land. Perhaps the seers were right, perhaps the end of the world was coming. He turned to the tzarina and said, 'I like this not. Such a sky is not a good sign. It is as if the Wastes themselves are moving southwards.'

The tzarina looked at him with her pale blue eyes. 'Such things have happened before, old friend. In the time of Magnus and Alexander, when last that fatal moon shimmered in the daylight sky.'

Ivan forced a smile. 'Such words do nothing to reassure me, highness.'

The tzarina shrugged. She rode better than most men, and her mount showed no sign of tiredness. Sorcery, he thought, but in her he could not resent it. Hers was the magic of winter and the old gods of Kislev. It had not the taint of Chaos about it. 'If anything, it is worse than you would think. Potent magic is at work ahead of us.'

'You think the horde expects us then?'

'I am certain of it, old friend, but I doubt those dire enchantments are intended to welcome us. I think they are directed at the walls of Praag, and the warriors who defend it.'

'My daughter is there,' Ivan said. 'And many of my friends.'

'Pray for her, and pray for them, my friend. I fear we will arrive in time only to avenge them, and even that might be beyond our strength.'

FELIX LOOKED AT the lifeless form of the Slayer. Part of him did not want to believe this was happening. Part of him could not believe it. The Slayer was invincible, and, despite the nature of his self-set quest, indestructible. It was impossible for Gotrek Gurnisson to be dead. Still, Felix doubted that anything could have survived being hit on the head by such a large piece of rock. Any human would have died instantly.

He bent forward and checked the Slayer's pulse, just to be certain. A wave of relief flooded through him. Gotrek's heart still beat, and beat strongly. There was something to be thankful for.

'He's alive,' Felix said. Smiles lit the faces of the dwarfs to be swiftly replaced by their usual sombre expressions.

'What do you want Snorri to do, young Felix?' asked Snorri Nosebiter.

'Perhaps give me a hand to move him from here.'

'What good would that do?' Bjorni asked. 'We have our own dooms to find here, Felix Jaeger.'

'Yes, what good would it do?' asked Ulli. He sounded like he hoped Felix could give him some good reason to get away. Felix looked at them in disbelief. Here they were debating while the beastmen clambered over the walls. He racked his mind for some reason that might cause these stubborn idiots to aid him.

'Well, for one thing, we might prevent his axe falling into the hands of the Chaos gods. Surely all of you can see that it is special. Perhaps even the key to victory here.'

Slowly, Bjorni and Ulli nodded. They looked as if they were thinking about it. 'And if he lives, you will surely have helped him greatly. This is not a doom worthy of the Slayer of the Great Bloodthirster, of the hero of Karag Dum.'

'Snorri thinks you have a point there, young Felix,' said Snorri. 'Plus he still owes Snorri for the beer Snorri bought last night.'

'Well, there you go then,' Felix said. 'What are you waiting for?'

He jerked his thumb in the direction of the great Chaos horde. 'After all, you can always return to seek your doom later. And, let's face it, there is every possibility we might not be able to escape anyway.'

Felix only wished that his words did not sound all too probable. Swiftly, he hoisted Gotrek's recumbent form up. It was not easy. The Slayer was very, very heavy. Snorri Nosebiter reached out and grabbed him with one mighty hand, holding the Slayer upright easily. 'Snorri will take him,' he said.

'One of you two get his axe,' said Felix. Ulli and Bjorni just looked at him blankly. 'It's his axe,' they said.

Exasperated Felix sheathed his sword and picked up the starmetal blade. It took him both hands to lift it, and he doubted he could wield it. 'Let's get out of here,' he said.

Already behind him, he could hear the curses and war cries of the barbarians about to clamber over the parapet.

LIFE WAS SO unfair, Thanquol was thinking. For one glorious moment, he had seen the Slayer fall, and thought him dead. And it looked certain that Jaeger and the demented dwarfs would soon be joining him. Then, in an instant, the whole wonderful dream had dissipated. He saw Jaeger bend over the Slayer and announce that he was alive, and the others move to aid him move the dwarf.

Thanquol felt like gnawing his tail in frustration. If only there was some way he could interfere, some way he could cast a spell, but it was not possible. The protective barriers still held on this part of the wall, and even if they did not, Thanquol would not have risked drawing the attention of those wizards back there in the horde. It was so frustrating, having such an easy shot at one of his most dangerous foes, and not being able to take it. One simple spell would be all it would take. The Slayer did not even have the power of his axe to protect him at this moment.

Thanquol heaped curses on the world, the gods, his enemies, and everyone else he could think of, himself excepted. The sheer unfairness of it all was shocking. Filled with the urge to howl with frustration, he decided he had seen enough here. It was time to return to his body and scheme. Perhaps there was some way he could get into the city and take vengeance on Gotrek Gurnisson while he was still unconscious.

Thanquol swore that if there was such a way, and it did not involve too many risks to his own precious hide, he would find it.

AREK RODE TOWARDS the Gate of Gargoyles. His warriors had taken and opened it, and were now flooding into the undefended city. All around him buildings blazed, wooden support beams catching fire, stonework falling to blackened ruin. Whooping wildly, beastmen and barbaric tribesmen roared through the streets of the city. Some of them had discovered ale barrels, doubtless in the remains of some tavern, and were pouring jack after jack down their throats.

Let the ignorant clods have their fun, thought Arek. Soon they will regret torching those buildings. Where did they think they were going to stay now that winter had set in? Their wild songs were most likely celebrating their own certain deaths, and they did not know it. He rode on, his daemonic charger responding instantly to his mental impulse, his bodyguard of Chaos knights gazing triumphantly on the wreckage of the city.

'We are victorious,' Bayar Hornhelm said. His voice sounded hollow. It echoed from deep within the chest plate of his incredibly ornate armour.

'Not yet,' Arek said. Ahead of him he could see the inner wall rising higher than the outer wall ever had, and beyond that the mighty bulk of the citadel of Praag stood defiantly. The battle would not be over, Arek knew, until both of those had fallen. 'This is only the beginning.'

'Surely they cannot hold out against us much longer.' Arek shook his head, astonished by the ignorance of even his own followers, the worshippers of Tzeentch. Surely they must know better. The casualties taking the outer wall had been greater than he expected, and now, fully two thirds of the enormous daemonic siege engines were destroyed. Mostly by that accursed dwarf, and his foul axe. Worse yet, despite the fall of the wall, no one had found the dwarf's corpse or his axe. The vision that his sorcerers had shown him returned to plague Arek. He saw the dwarf and the human standing triumphant over his corpse. It might still come to pass, he thought. No. He would not allow it.

'Spread the word, the blessing of Lord Tzeentch and the pick of the plunder to any who bring me the head of the Slayer Gotrek Gurnisson and that of his human companion, Felix Jaeger.'

His heralds instantly rode to obey his instructions. Despite his victory, Arek had an ominous feeling of foreboding. It seemed he had ridden forward too soon.

FELIX STAGGERED DOWN the narrow alleyway. The weight of the axe was murderous. He began to understand how the Slayer had become so strong. Just carrying the weapon for a few weeks would be enough to give anyone muscles like a blacksmith.

The stink of burning assailed his nostrils. He could hear the distant triumphant roar of the Chaos warriors and the crash of collapsing buildings. Off in the distance, he could see one of the gigantic daemonic siege towers looming over the red-tiled roofs of the buildings. The sun was hidden by smoke and the eerie red clouds, but the whole scene was given hellish illumination by the flames of burning tenements. At the end of the alley, he could see hordes of barbarians and beastmen revelling in the street. If he had not known better he would have thought he had died and been cast into one of the fiery hells beloved of the worst sort of Sigmarite preacher.

'Where to?' Ulli asked, licking his lips nervously. It was a good question. What they needed was to find Max Schreiber, if that was possible, or a healer if that was not. The best bet for that would be a Temple of Shallya where the priestesses of the dove goddess waited to grant their merciful mistress's blessings to the sick and the wounded. That was assuming any of the temples were left standing. They were most likely all burned and pillaged by the Chaos worshippers. Somehow he could not see them allowing the house of a rival god to stand.

'No sense in making for the inner city,' said Bjorni. 'The gates will be locked tight by now, if the guardians have any sense.'

'Not enough time,' said Felix. 'I doubt that the duke could have got all of his men back there in so short a time.'

'Won't make any difference,' said Bjorni with certainty. This was a side of the ugly Slayer's character he had never seen before. Bjorni in the heat of battle sounded like a real soldier, not the lecherous lout he normally was. 'If they are cut off, they are cut off. It's the duty of the troops on those gates to close them and hold them no matter who is left outside.'

'And where does that leave us?' asked Ulli. He sounded downright panicky.

'In the beastmen droppings, as usual,' said Bjorni, and cackled.

'You seem unduly happy under the circumstances,' said Felix. Bjorni looked at him and winked. 'Why not? I am alive when I expected to be making excuses to my ancestors in hell. And the prospect of doom is still in front of me. Why not make the best of these few extra minutes among the living.'

'Why not indeed? But we still have to get Gotrek to a healer.'

'There's a temple of Shallya down these back alleys somewhere,' Bjorni said. 'One of the priestesses cured me of a nasty little rash I picked up at–'

'Spare me the gory details,' Felix said. 'Lead on.'

MAX WATCHED AS the great gate of the inner city slammed shut behind them. He could not remember ever being this weary. He felt utterly exhausted and yet he also felt that he must do something. He looked around and saw the duke. He seemed angry but hid it well. Max had seen him hustled onto horseback by his personal guard once the outer wall was vacated. His bodyguards had almost ridden down anyone who got in their way. Max was just glad that he and Ulrika had been deemed valuable enough to go with them. He did not relish the idea of being trapped out there in the city with the horde of Chaos worshippers on the rampage.

Ulrika was looking back at the huge iron-shod wooden doors as if by looking hard enough, she might be able to see through them.

'What is it?' asked Max.

'Felix and the others are still out there.'

'It's too late to worry about that now,' he said. 'There's nothing you can do for them.'

'I know. It's just I wish we hadn't been separated.'

Despite his rivalry with Felix, Max felt the same way, and not just because of his comradeship with the man and the Slayer. He felt certain somehow, that if anyone were going to survive this mess, it would be those two. It might have been useful to be with them when they did.

The duke was already striding through the postern gate that led to the stairs into the watchtower. Going to watch his city burn, thought Max. I suppose we'd better join him.

IT WAS QUIET inside the temple and cool, Felix looked around at the icons showing the goddess and her saints on the wall, and the huge symbol of the dove carved on the altar. The place was packed with the scared and the wounded. Bloody, bandaged men lay on the floor. Weeping women and screaming children were everywhere. Obviously these unfortunates had not managed to make it to the safety of the inner city either.

Felix wondered if there was anything at all he could do for these people. He doubted it. They were probably doomed. It would only be a matter of time before the Chaos warriors got here, or the fire spread to the temple. He doubted this wooden structure would last very long in either eventuality.

Felix watched Snorri and the other Slayers carry Gotrek through the crowd towards the altar. He followed them wearily, glancing at the icons all the time. He had come to the temple of Shallya in Altdorf many times when still a very young child. His mother had been dying of the wasting sickness, and they had come to beg the goddess's intercession on her behalf. In spite of all his father's offerings, the goddess, for reasons of her own no doubt, had refused to intervene. Felix had been left with ambivalent feelings towards the temple after that. He had liked the kind, quietly spoken priestesses, but he could not understand why Shallya had not answered his prayers. After all, she was a goddess; almost anything was supposed to be in her power. He forced those thoughts to one side. Now was not the time to be wool-gathering.

A priestess rose to greet the Slayers. She looked tired, pale and drained of energy in the same way as Gotrek had looked after the destruction of the daemon towers. It looked like the priestesses of the merciful one contributed some of their own strength to work their healing. It seemed logical, given what Max had told him about the nature of sorcery. He only hoped the woman still had enough power left within her to help Gotrek.

'Lay him down near the altar,' she said. Without comment Snorri obeyed then stood to one side, holding his huge paw respectfully over his heart. The priestess passed her hand over Gotrek's forehead.

'This one's spirit is strong,' she said. 'He might live.'

'We need him on his feet now,' Felix said. 'Can't you do something?'

The woman looked up at Felix. He was sorry he had spoken so sharply to her. Huge fatigue circles darkened the skin under her eyes. She looked ready to drop from weariness. When she saw the axe in his hand, she gasped. 'Is that his axe?'

'Yes. Why?'

'It is a weapon of great power. I can feel its strength from here.' She turned to look at the recumbent form of the Slayer once more. 'I will see what I can do.'

She knelt beside Gotrek and placed her hand on his forehead. Closing her eyes, she began to sway from side to side, invoking the name of the goddess. A halo of light shimmered around her head and her hand. The flesh of Gotrek's scalp began to knit together, and after a long moment, his one good eye flickered and opened.

'You called me back,' he said. He sounded groggy and amazed. 'I stood at the gates of the Ancestral Hall and they would not let me in. I had not redeemed myself in battle, they said. My spirit was doomed to wander homeless in the eternal fog.'

'Hush now,' the priestess said, stroking his forehead as she might a child's. 'You were hit on the head. Often that brings strange dreams and visions.'

'This did not feel like a dream.'

'Sometimes they do not.'

'Nonetheless, I owe you a debt of honour, priestess. And it is one I will repay.'

'Don't forget you owe Snorri a beer as well then,' said Snorri.

Gotrek glared at him. 'Why?'

'I carried you here.'

Gotrek gave him a crooked smile. 'Then I will buy you a tankard or two, Snorri Nosebiter.'

'It's true what they say then,' Snorri said happily. 'There *is* a first time for everything.'

AREK CURSED AS he rode through the devastated streets of Praag. All was madness now. The horde had broken apart in a frenzy of looting and destruction. They drank and brawled and offered up the souls of those defenders they found to their patron daemons. It would take days to reinforce discipline now, and they might not have days. They needed to take and hold the city before the depths of winter settled in. They needed shelter, not a city that had been reduced to rubble.

He had started to feel that his god was mocking him. He had possessed no idea of the scale of the challenge of holding his force together. A few more victories like this would be as good as a defeat. He looked at the drunken warriors, the blazing buildings, and the sheer brute stupidity of it all, and fought down an urge to kill. The fires blazed furnace-like, out of control. He could feel the backwash of heat from here.

'Order the warriors to cease torching the buildings,' said Arek suspecting it was already too late, that the fire was beyond any attempt to control it.

'It wasn't our warriors,' said Bayar Hornhelm. 'It's the Kislevites. They did this. They set fire to their homes as they retreated into the citadel. A stubborn lot.'

Arek nodded. He should have expected it. The Kislevites were not fools. They understood the situation as well as he did. They knew that without food and shelter the winter would avenge them on their conquerors. Arek knew that he and his Chaos warriors would survive, most of the magicians too, but the beastmen and the humans would be reduced to cannibalism to see them through the cold season. The great horde would evaporate. He did not doubt that soon the various factions would fall out and start preying on one another. Either that or flee and hope to find the army of another great warlord.

Although he hated to admit it, the wizards had been right about the risks of attacking so late in the season. He had gambled and lost. Still, at the very least, he consoled himself with the thought that he would ensure that none of the Kislevites survived to enjoy their pitiful triumph. A courier rode up:

'A message, Lord Arek.' The warlord gestured for him to speak.

'A Kislevite army approaches from the west. The skaven host has emerged north of us. Morgar Doomblade has taken his troops to engage them.'

Arek cursed the Khornate warleader. Always seeking glory. Always seeking more victories and more blood and more souls to offer to his hungry howling god. It was not enough to finish mopping up the defenders of Praag first. He had to seek other battles. Arek forced himself to keep calm. Under the circumstances it might not be a bad thing. After all it would not do to have the ratmen attacking his army in the rear. The question of what to do about the approaching Kislevites vexed him. They must have ridden like daemons to get here so quickly. He doubted that his own warriors, intoxicated as they currently were with butchery, were in any condition to stop them.

Swiftly he thought through his options. He needed this blaze extinguished and the city preserved. Only magic could do that now. This was a job for Kelmain and Lhoigor, damn their unruly souls. If anyone could succeed it was them. The reserves waiting outside the walls could hold the Kislevites until he could organise the overwhelming mass of his men to throw at them. At least the cold waters of the river would hold

the Kislevites for a while. It would take time to get any army
across the bridges and fords.

He gave the courier orders quickly, then rode out into the
mob, bellowing orders in his most commanding voice.

'GREY SEER THANQUOL! Awaken!' bellowed a familiar deep
voice in his ear. Thanquol pulled himself from his trance, and
resisted the urge to blast Izak Grottle with his most devastat-
ing spell.

'Yes! Yes! What is it?' he asked.

'We are attacked,' Grottle said. 'Chaos Warriors, daemons
and beastmen approach from the south. Why did you not
warn us?'

Because I had more interesting things to look at, Thanquol
almost replied, but didn't. The import of Grottle's words
started to sink in. A force of Chaos warriors was about to
attack them! The situation was serious! Thanquol must
immediately take steps to preserve his precious life.

'How many? How close? Quick! Quick!' he chittered.

'Thousands. Almost upon us,' Grottle stammered.

'Why did you not rouse me sooner?'

'We tried but you were deep in your sorcery. We thought
you must have been communing with the Horned Rat himself.'

'We all might be very soon, if we do not get ready to defend
ourselves.' Hastily Thanquol barked out orders and instructions. Filled with apprehension his warriors rushed to obey.

GOTREK RAISED HIS axe and inspected it carefully. The edge glittered, as sharp as ever. The runes blazed brightly. The Slayer
seemed to draw strength from the weapon. He was still pale
as a ghost but he looked capable of fighting. A mad rage glittered in his one good eye. Outside in the distance, the sounds
of battle could be heard.

'Let's get going,' he said. 'We've killing to do.'

# THIRTEEN

'IT'S NOT THAT I in any way doubt your majesty's word, but do you think it will hold?' Ivan Petrovich Straghov asked carefully. The Ice Queen was usually a very cold and calm woman, but when she lost her temper it was as bad as a northlands blizzard.

'It will hold, old friend,' she replied, surveying her work with satisfaction. 'I guarantee it.'

The belief in her voice compelled him to believe it too, although, had he not witnessed this with his own eyes, he would have found the whole thing incredible. The Ice Queen's sorcery was potent indeed. Ivan had watched as she stood by the sluggish grey waters of the river, and incanted her spell. Spreading her arms wide she had called upon the east and west winds. Snow had fallen on the river; the air had become incredibly chill. As he watched, in heartbeats, a fine layer of frost had formed on the surface of the river, moving outward with incredible speed from the spot where the Ice Queen stood. Within a minute, massive blocks of ice had formed. Within ten minutes, the whole river had frozen solid. Now the snow lay atop it, were it not for the trench formed by its banks, Ivan would not have been able to tell the river was there at all.

'Go,' the tzarina said. 'It will hold our weight.'

Suiting action to words, she spurred her horse to a gallop and it raced out over the frozen waters. With a mighty shout, the Gospodar muster followed her.

'LOOK UP THERE!' said Ulrika pointing at the sky. Max looked up expecting to see harpies descending on them. He did indeed see some of the hideous beasts but they were fluttering upwards to attack something massive descending through the clouds.

'It's the *Spirit of Grungni,*' Ulrika said, her voice filled with wonder.

Sigmar be praised, thought Max somewhat ashamedly. At least we will have a way out of here. As he watched, brilliant flashes blazed from the airship's sides. The harpies plummeted earthwards as the *Spirit of Grungni's* potent weaponry scythed through them.

KELMAIN LOOKED AT his twin and saw his own weariness echoed in that familiar face. No living thing could withstand the stresses they had endured this day and remain untouched. They had wielded the sort of power normally reserved for greater daemons, and it had stretched them to the limit, and left them weary almost beyond enduring. Magical feedback from the destruction of the towers had almost driven them both insane. Many of their apprentices had not been so fortunate. They writhed gibbering in the snowdrifts nearby. So far neither he nor his twin had been able to spare the energy to kill them.

'You feel it too, brother,' Lhoigor said.

Kelmain could only nod. To the west, they sensed a mystical disturbance of great power, human magic of a powerful sort, drawing on the chill power of the Kislevite winter. To the north was another disturbance, different, touched by Chaos, also of great power. At a guess, Kelmain would have said they were skaven, and he was sure his twin would have agreed with him. Powerful as the disturbances were, under normal circumstances the twins would not have feared their cause.

Few indeed were the mages in the world they feared. But these were not normal circumstances. Neither of them would be able to wield their full power for days to come. The apocalyptic energies they had unleashed today had drained most of their strength.

A rider thundered closer. Kelmain looked at the Chaos warrior closely, noting the silvered helm that marked one of Lord Arek's personal couriers. The horseman rode right up to them and reared his mount, bringing it to a stop. 'The Lord Arek commands you to quench the blaze in the city,' he shouted arrogantly.

Kelmain looked at his brother. Lhoigor looked back at him. Simultaneously they began to laugh. 'Tell Lord Arek that regretfully we must decline his polite request,' Kelmain said.

'What?' spluttered the Chaos warrior.

'Sadly it is impossible at this exact moment,' explained Lhoigor.

'*Impossible?* Lord Arek will order you skinned alive.'

'It is a very bad idea to threaten us,' Lhoigor said.

'Very bad indeed,' Kelmain added. He summoned enough energy to reduce the courier's armour to molten slag. Droplets of metal sizzled in the snow.

'That was unwise, brother,' said Lhoigor, smiling approvingly.

'True, but he deserved it.'

'What shall we do now?'

'Watch and wait. I suspect that Lord Arek is about to discover that his fortunes have turned.'

'We did warn him that the stars were not right. But would he listen?'

'How long do you think the daemons can remain on this plane? They were your responsibility.'

'Another hour, at most. Quite possibly much less.'

'Well, there are other warlords in the south now, and the paths of the Old Ones will soon be open.'

'Then by all means let us see what happens.'

FELIX CHOPPED DOWN another beastman. He had lost count of the number they had killed since they emerged into the maze of side streets around the temple. He looked around. The dwarfs seemed to be enjoying themselves. They grinned like maniacs as they killed. He supposed it was only to be expected really. They were close to finding their long-awaited dooms.

He blocked the blow of a massive fur-clad barbarian. A necklace of still bloody ears hung round the man's neck. Felix could see that many of them were small enough to belong to children. The man bellowed something in his incomprehensible tongue and aimed another clumsy slash at Felix with his black iron blade. Felix ducked, and, with a cold cruelty he had not known he possessed, stabbed him carefully in the stomach and then turned his blade in the wound before withdrawing it. He kicked the screaming man in the mouth for good measure as he fell.

'Look up there!' he heard Ulli shout. Felix risked a glance upwards, and despite his despair felt his heart soar. Above them flew the well-remembered shape of the *Spirit of Grungni*. It appeared that Malakai Makaisson had returned. Felix could only hope he had brought reinforcements with him.

Although he doubted that the airship could possibly hold enough men to make a difference in this conflict.

THE BURNING BUILDING crashed down around Arek. A wall of flames licked out, driving him and his knights down another side street. Arek looked up at the sky and shook his fist. Another black bomb descended, tossed down from that flying ship. The explosion blew Arek from his mount. Where were the harpies? Why were his mages not blasting that accursed airship from the sky with lightning? He looked around and saw that the explosion had killed several of his bodyguards. The rest were riding off. Obviously they had missed him in the chaos of smoke and flames and explosions.

Not that it mattered. He could hear beastmen shouting war cries nearby. He would find them, rally them to his side, and return to the fray. When he saw them again he would have more than harsh words for his pet sorcerers.

THANQUOL WATCHED WAVE after wave of Chaos knights surge towards his force. Enormous warriors bellowing the name of the Blood god surged through the snow and threatened to overwhelm even the stormvermin. Twice now Thanquol had been forced to call on his sorcerous powers to throw them back, and twice it had been touch and go. He had used the dark magical energy around him to inspire his troops to feats of ferocity unprecedented by any skaven army before, and it still had proved barely enough. Thanquol would have used his escape spell to cast himself clear of the fray long ago, had he not been so certain that without him the Moulder army would collapse and he would swiftly be ridden down by the Khornate riders. It might come to that yet, he thought, chewing on a piece of purified warpstone and letting the unleashed power surge through his veins.

'They come! They come again!' Izak Grottle bellowed in his ear.

Thanquol made a mental note that if the worst came to the worst, he would blast the obese Moulder into his component atoms before attempting his escape.

IVAN PETROVICH STRAGHOV rode through the Chaos lines chopping at anything that got in the way with his sabre. Above him the blood red sky glowered down. The burning city of Praag fitfully illuminated the whole hellish scene of battle. Ahead of him, beastmen bellowed challenges and ran for their trenches. It was a mark of how overconfident they had been that all their earthworks faced the city. Well, thought Ivan, they were paying for it now.

Ahead of him someone had set fire to a massive trebuchet. The huge siege engine blazed like a gigantic torch. Beside him the Ice Queen and her bodyguard fought like warriors born. The tzarina's blade blazed in her hand. Ancient runes glittered along the length of the blade. Suddenly, the last beastman in the area was dead. In the lull, the Ice Queen spoke.

'This place stinks of evil sorcery. Such power had been drawn on here as has not been felt in centuries. Daemons have been here, aye, and, worse than daemons.'

'What could be worse than daemons, majesty?' Ivan asked curiously.

'The men who would summon them.'

Ivan was not sure about that, but he was not about to argue. Ahead of them, he could see new enemies emerging from the gates of Praag, thousands upon thousands of them, frothing with battle lust, and ready to die in combat.

'It seems we must worry about these wicked men later, my queen,' he said.

'Aye, old friend, for now we must face daemons in earnest.'

Looking at the glowing shapes in the middle of the oncoming horde, Ivan knew exactly what she meant. He took a moment to commend his soul and the soul of his daughter to Ulric, and then prepared to charge once more.

MAX SWARMED UP the swaying rope ladder into the airship's cupola. The wind tore at his face, and he took a last look down. It was a long drop. The streets of the burning city were a long way below. Ulrika waved up at him and then raced off to join the duke's force. He prayed she would be all right. She meant as much as life to him. Still, he could not see what harm could come to her now. No one was leaving the inner city and venturing out into that inferno.

The squat leather-clad form of the Slayer Engineer, Malakai Makaisson, was there to greet him. His leather flying-helm with the slit cut in it for his dyed crest of hair was on his head. The crystal goggles he wore when flying his gyrocopter were pushed back onto his forehead.

'You took your time, Malakai,' said Max. He found he was grinning nonetheless as he stretched out his hand to grasp the Slayer's.

'Aye, weel, we had a wee bit o' mechanical trouble an' then some bother wi' the headwinds, an' it took some time tae get ah the lads the gither,' said Makaisson. He actually sounded a little embarrassed about it. 'An' the Spirit is joost a wee bit overloaded tae.'

'Well, better late than never.'

'That's what ah always say. Whaur's Gotrek and the lad Felix Jaeger? They no wi' ye?'

It was Max's turn to sound embarrassed. 'I don't know where they are. I last saw them on the outer wall. They're probably fighting in the city right now. They were not in the citadel.'

'Well, if onybody is gannae be fine in this mess, it's that pair, so ah better get doon tae bizness.'

'What would that be?'

'The Slayer King asked me tae ferry his warriors here. Got aboot a hundred stuffed intae every nook and cranny. Some are even upstairs in the gasbag. We'd better get the lads ontae the grun so they can start fightin' an' ah can get doon tae the serious bizness o' killin' beastmen.'

Even as Max and the Slayer spoke, hard-faced dwarf warriors were pushing their way down the passage, and swarming down the rope.

'Ah wuz gannae gaun back an' bring the rest, but it looks like ah neednae bother. The fightin' might well be ever by the time ah got back.'

'Every little helps, Malakai.'

'Aye, weel, ah built some new weapons onto the *Spirit of Grungni* here. Ah'll show them in a wee minute, yince the boys are doon. That was yin o' the things that kept me awae so laung. Ah thocht I might need something special for this.'

Max wondered what Malakai Makaisson could possibly have brought that was deadly enough to turn the tide of this conflict. He knew that if anyone could build such a thing it was the Slayer Engineer.

'Is that the last of them?' Felix asked.

'Snorri doesn't think so!' said Snorri peering into the gloom. Snow, melted by the heat of the burning buildings, was starting to puddle round his feet. Blood mingled with the water. The reflected flames looked odd in the ruddy mess.

'Where have they all gone then? There seems to be less of them than there was a minute ago.'

'That's coz we killed so many, young Felix,' said Snorri. Felix shook his head. Was it really possible for any creature to be as stupid as Snorri Nosebiter and still live he wondered?

'The manling is right,' said Gotrek. 'Something has drawn them off, and it's not just the *Spirit of Grungni.*'

'What does Makaisson think he's playing at?' asked Ulli. 'One minute he was overhead, bombing the Chaos lovers, and the next he's vanished.'

'We just can't see him from here,' said Felix. 'My guess is that he headed for the citadel. Must have brought some warriors or some weapons.'

'We'll find out soon enough,' Bjorni said. 'Come on. Let's go and see if we can find some more beastmen to kill.'

'Snorri thinks that's a good idea,' said Snorri.

'AND IF YE pull this lever,' Malakai Makaisson said, pulling the lever, 'it drops alchemical fire on the wee basturds. Like so!'

Max knew enough to understand what was going on. It was the same stuff the siege engines on the walls had used, the ever-burning fire of the ancients. Not even water or snow could put it out. It would burn for days. Screams rising from below told the wizard that the beastmen were discovering this the hard way.

'Malakai, isn't it dangerous to carry alchemical fire on an airship? You are always talking about the fire hazard and it's one of the most inflammable substances known to magecraft.'

Malakai tugged at another control lever, and swung the wheel, bringing the *Spirit of Grungni* around for another pass over the Chaos horde. 'Aye, weel… ye're right, ye ken, but ah thocht, joost this yince, it would be worth the risk. Ah coodnae think o' onythin' else that would even the odds. Except maybe this,' he added, pulling another lever.

'What is it?' The sound of enormous explosions rose from beneath him.

'Bloody big bombs. Gunpooder an' lots o' it. Cost a fortune tae make but the Slayer king was footin' the bill so why no?'

'Malakai, you are insane,' Max said, shuddering. Alchemical fire and tons of gunpowder on an overloaded airship, flying through a storm. It was a miracle that they had arrived at all. If he'd known, he would never have volunteered to come aboard and brief the Slayer as to the situation. This was quite possibly the most dangerous place in the battle right now.

All it would take would be for one fireball spell to break through the wards he'd placed on the machine before it went off into the Chaos Wastes, and everyone on the airship would be blasted to Morrslieb by the power of the explosion. No wonder Malakai was flying with a skeleton crew. It was a wonder anyone had elected to remain on board at all.

'Ah'll tell ye somethin' though, Max, there were a few times this past flight when ah damn near cacked ma britches. Ah will never dae this again. No if ah live tae be five hundred.'

'Glad to hear it,' said Max. He wondered how Ulrika was doing. Was she fighting down there in the city even now? Malakai pulled the lever again. There was a long whistling sound and then a huge explosion.

'Excellent,' said Malakai peering backwards and downwards. 'Got yin o' those big siege towers.'

'SOUNDED LIKE AN explosion,' said Felix. 'A big one. What new deviltry is this?'

'If you ask me it's that Malakai Makaisson up to his tricks,' said Bjorni. They had all seen the airship go sailing overhead a few minutes ago, and they all knew what the Slayer Engineer was capable of dreaming up.

'Sounds like lots of explosions,' said Snorri. He was right too. It sounded like a continuous rumble of thunder in the distance. The ground shook, and some of the blazing buildings threatened to topple. As they ran for an open plaza, a strange chemical stink assailed their nostrils. Gotrek sniffed at it loudly.

'Alchemical fire. Only a maniac like Makaisson would think of taking that on an airship.'

He sounded almost as if he admired the engineer's insanity.

KELMAIN AND HIS brother watched the huge airship passing over the Chaos horde as it poured from the blazing city.

'Protected,' he said. To his mage senses, the runes protecting the flying machine blazed like beacons.

'Powerfully,' Lhoigor agreed. 'Given time we could overcome them though.'

'Given time, and a period of recuperation, you mean brother,' Kelmain said, grinning wickedly at his twin.

'Do you think we should try?'

'No. Whatever happens, Arek's army is doomed. The fool should have listened to our advice. Why waste our strength trying to stave off the inevitable? We will need it to get ourselves away.'

'You are correct, I fear,' said Lhoigor.

'There's always next spring,' said Kelmain. 'Once the paths of the Old Ones open we will be able to do what we wish. We can unite the other warlords and move the great plan forward.'

'Arek might win yet.' Kelmain laughed.

'Do you really think that's likely? I suspect the old powers oppose him here. I am starting to feel the daemons fade.'

'Then perhaps we should be going – before we get caught up in the rout.'

The two sorcerers gestured. The air shimmered and, in a moment, they were gone, leaving behind the dozen or so corpses of the apprentices they had drained of their power.

AREK LED HIS beastmen along the street. He was filled with a seething annoyance. He could sense that somehow things had turned against him, and he was not where he ought to be. Right now, he should be leading his army against the Kislevites. Looking at the massive airship raining death down on his army from above, he knew they would need someone to hold them together in the face of the assault.

Where were the magicians, he asked himself again? Surely they should have blasted it out of the sky by now. He cursed again. If only he had not thrown away the harpies in the earlier assault, they might have swarmed over the airship and torn it from the sky despite its deadly armaments. As it was, they were just too few to get past those deadly cannons. Well, live and learn, he thought. Next time he would know better.

Ahead of him, he could see a massive ruck. Beastmen were fighting with humans and dwarfs. He braced himself for the coming combat. He was enjoying the slaughter. It had been some time since he had indulged his taste for carnage and he had almost forgotten just how pleasurable exercising his physical superiority could be. There was something primal in the hack and slash of battle. It was at times like this he could understand why men followed the Blood God, Khorne.

A human warrior wearing the winged lion tabard of Praag charged at him. The man's face was pale and his eyes were wide and mindless. Froth erupted from his lips. It was obvious to Arek that the man was berserk, near mindless with rage and fear. He charged at the Chaos warrior, howling barely coherent challenges. Behind his helmet, Arek's face twisted into a grim smile. This was almost too easy.

The human guardsman aimed a blow straight at Arek's head. He parried it easily with his runesword, chipping away bits of steel from his opponent's blade. A blow from Arek's axe separated the man's head from his shoulders. Arek leapt forward into the fray, hacking as he went. Every blow struck home, pruning away limbs, shearing heads from necks, leaving twisted torsos dripping blood and entrails onto the cobblestones.

He gave himself up to the joy of combat, fighting with the icy precision characteristic of the followers of Tzeentch. This was a game to be enjoyed. Every blow was a move, every parry a counter-move, every footstep and every shift of weight a thing to be calculated precisely. He evaluated the situation around him with lightning speed and mathematical precision. He moved like a whirlwind of death through the melee, sweeping away the tiny motes of flesh and blood and life surrounding him. He reaped souls with each passing heartbeat.

He felt almost grateful to the chain of convoluted circumstances that had brought him to this out of the way place, in the darkest heart of the battle. He had stayed in his command throne too long, he thought. He needed this baptism of blood to remind him that he was a warrior as well as a worshipper of Tzeentch.

Nearby he sensed something; a mighty mystical force he knew was inimical to him and his kind. Suddenly the vision of the Slayer and his axe passed through Arek's mind. Was it possible that the dwarf had survived and was somehow back in the combat? If so, it was too late to do anything about it.

Part of him warned him to shy away, to get away from whatever it was, knowing that here was something that could end his immortal existence. The part of his mind that had enabled him to live so long and rise so high knew that it was not worth taking a risk, that small though the probability was of his being defeated, it was still there. He had not reached where he was today by not listening to this part of his mind. Immortality, after all, was reached in part by playing the odds, and minimising the risks. If you lived long enough, even a one in a million chance was bound to come up some day.

At the same time, part of him recognised the fact that here was a foe worthy of being overcome, a challenge greater than

these puny mortals represented. The part of him that had lain
so long dormant, and which had woken to the thrill of combat,
wanted to face the threat, and overcome it. And Arek was wise
enough to realise that the challenge appealed to another facet
of his personality too. Part of him, more deeply buried than all
the rest and yet still there, was sick of his long life, weary of eternal warfare, bored with the eternal repetition of his daily
struggle. He recognised this part of himself for what it was, the
true enemy within, the weak human part that still sometimes
felt fear or guilt, and which simply wanted an end to it all.

He knew that this part of him would have to be destroyed.
It was a weight holding him back, anchoring him to his mortality that made failure and destruction a temptation. He
knew that he should walk away from this battle, avoid the
power that was coming ever closer. And yet he could not. The
deeply hidden part of him, the weak, mewling pathetic thing
that he despised still had some strength, so did the lure of
combat, so did the desire to prove himself worthy. They all
conspired to keep him moving forward, killing as he went,
when the wisest part of him knew that he should be doing his
best to get away.

Felix Jaeger wiped sweat from his forehead. As he did so he
noticed his sleeve was red. Blood, he thought. The question
was: did it belong to him or someone else? He did not know.
He could not feel anything. There was no pain. This in itself
meant nothing. Many times before, he had endured wounds
in battle without even realising that he had taken them till
after the fight was over. He wanted to reach up and touch his
forehead to see if he felt torn flesh or exposed muscle or
bone, but he did not dare. All around him was the howling
madness of battle, and it would be suicidal to allow himself
to be distracted for even a split second.

Off to his right, he saw Ulli surrounded by a squad of beastmen. The young dwarf was covered in a hundred nicks and
cuts. His jerkin was torn. Somehow he had lost one boot, and
there was a long gash on his exposed leg, pumping a slow
flow of blood onto the stones. Nonetheless he fought on. His
hammer smashed the skull of a beastman, sending splinters
of bone and gobbets of brain flying everywhere.

'Take that, beast!' he bellowed, even louder than usual. 'What are the rest of you waiting for? Come on and die!'

The beasts did not need a second invitation. Howling with bloodlust they threw themselves forward at the young dwarf, who kept himself alive only by dint of desperate parrying. Felix could see that he was not going to last much longer. Not caring whether the dwarf would thank him or not for interfering with his heroic doom, Felix launched himself into the fray. His blade took one surprised beastman in the side, the creature lashed out reflexively as it coughed blood and died, and only ducking swiftly kept Felix's head on his shoulder.

A low blow hamstrung another beastman. A swift stab in the throat killed it as it fell. A hail of blows aimed in his direction told Felix that he had gotten the beast's attention. Suddenly it did not seem like such a good idea. He fell back parrying desperately, praying to Sigmar that no beastman would attack him on the blindside as he had just attacked them. Where was Ulli, he wondered? Now would be a good time for him to repay Felix's help.

The beastmen were far stronger than he was, and it was only his speed and experience that were keeping him alive in the face of their multiple attacks. He blocked another blow and the force of the impact almost took his sword from his hands. Cursing, he returned the stroke, and was rewarded with the sight of two of the beastman's fingers being sheared away. It dropped its huge bludgeon in surprise, and Felix took advantage of the moment to spear it in the groin, before continuing his fighting retreat.

He felt like he was caught in a raging sea now, being tossed around by waves of furious combat, and dragged away from his comrades by the currents of the battle. Sweat almost blinded him. He felt curiously disengaged from his body now. He fought mechanically, knowing that weariness was slowing him down, and that there was nothing he could do about it. He knew that if he lived, and kept on fighting, the weariness would pass, and his strength would return. It was curiously reassuring knowing this. Once he would have been terrified at being in the middle of this storm of blades, but somewhere along the line in his long travels with Gotrek, he had become a veteran.

Suddenly two of the beastmen ahead of him toppled forward, and he had to stay his hand before he chopped down Ulli. A look of ferocious joy was in the young Slayer's eye. It was the sort of expression Felix had only seen on the face of dwarfs lost in the contemplation of gold. At this moment, however, he doubted that coin was what was on Ulli's mind.

'Got two more of the bastards!' he bellowed and spread his arms exultantly, brandishing his weapon at the sky, as if challenging the gods themselves. 'Come and get dead!'

They were the last words he ever spoke. A beastman's axe descended on his head from behind. Fragments of bone and flesh splattered Felix's face.

A red rage descended on Felix Jaeger. He leapt forward into the fray, fighting with renewed energy and a desperate desire to slay. He had not particularly liked Ulli but they had shared a desperate adventure together. Seeing someone he had known killed before his eyes was far more personal than watching the death of a stranger. It was a terrifying reminder of his own mortality, one that he could only blot out in a furious quest for vengeance.

Beastman after beastman fell before his blade. Felix fought as he had never done before, reaching a new peak of skill, speed and fury in his bloodlust. Barbaric tribesman after barbaric tribesman went down under his lightning-swift blade. He saw fear enter men's eyes moments before they died, and cut them down with no hint of mercy. All sympathy he might have felt had been burned out of him. His mere presence started to fill his foes with fear. The expression on his face was enough to make hardened warriors back away. The moment of panic was often enough to cost them their lives. They froze rather than parried as he struck at them, and an instant of advantage was all a swordsman of Felix's skill needed.

He noticed that his ferocious onslaught had attracted the attention of a motley band of humans: guardsmen, militia and citizens armed with pickaxes and rakes and household implements. The men threw themselves into battle at his side, cheering and groaning as they came.

Out of the corner of his eye, he caught a flicker of red. A howling dwarf battle cry reached his ears, and he saw Gotrek wading through the mass of beastmen, axe held high, as unstoppable as the sea. There was a better rallying point than himself, Felix realised.

'Follow me!' he bellowed, and began to cleave his way through to the Slayer's side. With a ragged cheer the embattled defenders followed him.

ULRIKA LOOKED DOWN from the walls, searching for targets. There were certainly enough of them. The Chaos horde rampaged through the burning city, killing and maiming as it came. She drew the string back to her cheek, loosed a shaft and was rewarded by seeing a burly, bearskin-cloaked marauder fall to her shaft. Automatically, she drew another arrow, nocked and searched for another target.

She was not sure where she had gotten the bow. Snatched it from the hands of a wounded defender perhaps. It did not matter. What did was that she had the weapon and could kill the monsters defiling the streets of Praag. She intended to make them pay for this sacrilege in blood.

As her body responded to its long years of training, part of her mind wondered where Felix was, and where Max was. She even would have been glad to see Gotrek or Snorri or any of the other Slayers. They would have provided familiar points of reference in this world gone mad. She had never quite experienced anything like this. Her whole world and her whole life seemed to have shrunk to just this moment, and just this place. It was as if everything that had gone before was just a dream. There was no future. There was no past. There was only this crazed inferno of death and destruction.

The strange thing was that she did not care. It was exhilarating, oddly liberating, to have no cares other than those of the moment, not to have to worry about anything other than the now. She could understand now with perfect clarity why some men loved combat more than they loved wine or women or any other pleasure. She along with everyone around lived now only a heartbeat away from death, and she held the power of life or death in her own hands, wielded it with every arrow she loosed. It was a sensation that could only be described as god-like.

Perhaps this was why some of those evil men down there followed Khorne, she thought. Perhaps they were no more evil than she, merely addicted to the thrill of mortal combat. Perhaps this was the lure of the Blood god. Even as these thoughts flickered through her mind, she wondered if they were part of some strange spell laid on the battlefield, meant to lure mortal warriors to the side of Chaos.

She dismissed the idea. Right now it did not matter. She had her bow. She had targets. While her heart beat and her eyes could see there was work for her here.

SOMEHOW AREK REALISED he had fought his way out into the main streets again. All around bodies were pressed close against each other. He could smell sweat and blood and burning. It was impossible to tell who was winning from here. The beastmen and the northern tribesmen sounded trapped and panicked. That meant nothing. Arek knew all too well that warriors in one part of a battlefield responded differently from those in another. It was perfectly possible that overall the forces of Chaos were in control of the city even while this small group of them were cut off and surprised. Arek knew he could change that.

'To me!' he shouted. 'Stand firm! We *will* prevail!'

Such was the confidence and power in his voice that hundreds of eyes swung towards him. He saw the Chaos warriors take heart and fight with renewed vigour. They knew him by sight and by reputation and had every confidence in his awesome power. Just his simple presence made them feel as if victory was once again within their grasp.

Even as those around him gained heart, Arek felt himself losing it. He felt somehow that things were slipping out of his control, that events had turned against him. It was a sour feeling, a sense that his gods had turned their face from him. He did not quite know how or why things were like this, but he felt it was the case. He tried to tell himself that it was all in his mind, but he knew that it was not. His sense of the flow of events had been made keen by his centuries of experience, and he knew he perceived the ebb and flow of battle with senses other than human.

For himself, he would have felt no real fear, had he not still been aware of that terrible inimical presence nearby. He knew his armour was all but unbreachable by mortal weapons, and such was his strength and power that no ordinary warrior could stand against him even without it. But there was something disquieting about the power he felt close by. It was the same feeling he had felt when he saw that dwarf on the walls of the city. A long forgotten sensation started to work its way into his brain. It took several heartbeats for Arek to recognise it.

It was *fear*.

SIDE BY SIDE, Gotrek and Felix fought their way to the very heart of the battle. Killing as they went, they hurled themselves wherever the fighting was heaviest. Wherever they appeared, their presence gave heart to the defenders, rallying them as they wavered, inspiring them to ever fiercer assaults where they were confident. Sometime during the desperate melee Felix became aware that Snorri and Bjorni had joined them. Both dwarfs looked as if they had been working in a slaughterhouse. Blood painted their faces and arms. Matted filth covered their torsos. But they smiled as they fought, and laughed as they killed.

In the furious berserker joy of combat they seemed to have forgotten all about seeking their doom, and set out to kill as many of the enemy as they could. Almost as much as the appearance of Gotrek the sight of them dismayed the superstitious tribesmen, and seemed to cause even the beastmen unease. The Slayers stopped for nothing, feared nothing, were undaunted by superior numbers or size. Nothing slaked their thirst for killing. They seemed like avatars of their ancient gods brought back to life to slaughter the ancestral enemies of their kind.

Felix followed them, feeling like he was moving in the wake of a whirlwind of destruction. His earlier fury at the death of Ulli had passed to be replaced by a cold calculation. He fought now as much to stay alive and witness the Slayers' deeds as to kill his enemies. All fear had passed from his mind. It was not that he did not want to live. If he thought about it, he would have said that the fear was still there, but he had become so used to it that it seemed normal. It was simply something that sharpened his wits, and speeded his reflexes.

Ahead of him now, he sensed the resistance of the daemon worshippers stiffening. He saw black-armoured forms moving amid the masses, and realised that there were Chaos warriors present, and it seemed most likely that Gotrek and the others were about to meet foes more worthy of their steel.

Briefly Felix wondered how the battle was going, before losing himself again in the howling sea of battle.

IVAN STRAGHOV WATCHED bombs and alchemical fire rain down from the airship, turning the oncoming wave of beastmen into a mass of fiery flesh. Their screams were horrifying even to the ears of the men who hated them. Only the daemons continued to move closer, ignoring the flames that blazed around them.

As the first wave of creatures emerged from the inferno, the Ice Queen gestured and a searing wave of utter chill blasted towards them. Ivan sincerely hoped it was enough to stop them. He was getting too old to face daemons.

AREK SAW THE Slayers coming towards him through the gloom. The snow had started to fall heavily again. Footing was treacherous. Dead bodies lay partially buried where they fell. He recognised the scene at once. It was the same as the vision his mages had showed him. No. Not quite the same. Some elements were different. There were more dwarfs, and he was surrounded by more of his own people.

He recalled what the twins had told him. The future was not certain. They dealt only in probabilities. He knew then that there was a chance. The mocking foresight the Lord of all Change had provided him with need not come true. Already things were different enough for him to change the vision. He hoped so.

Looking at the Slayer he felt less fearful. Unlike in his vision the dwarf was already wounded. He did not move with quite the brutal ferocity Arek would have expected. The Chaos warlord knew he had faced more dangerous foes. He did not see how one lowly warrior could possibly stand against him.

As though he felt Arek's gaze upon him, the Slayer looked up. An electric spark of recognition passed between the two of them. Arek knew that they both knew who was their true foe in this battle.

Shouting his war cry, Arek strode towards the demented dwarf.

FELIX SAW THE Chaos warriors coming towards them. He recognised the one in the lead. It was the warlord who had shouted such a brutal challenge on the first day of the siege, the one who had told the whole city that he was going to kill them all.

Felix had to admit, Arek had made a fair effort to make good on that promise. The dead lay all around, only slowly being concealed by flurries of fresh snow. Here and there the white was stained with the red of blood, the black of bile or the brown of piss. Not even the fury of the gathering storm could entirely conceal the stench of death.

Felix took a deep breath, wondering if he was already dead and in hell. Buildings still burned. In the distance he could hear the sound of titanic explosions and smell the reek of alchemical fire. White flakes evaporated as the wind carried them into flames. All around men screamed and wept and died. And not just men. He could see daemons and beastmen and other things he did not want to look at too closely moving through the murk. Overhead, patches had appeared in the clouds and the hellish glow of the Chaos moon glared down, eclipsing the feeble stars.

The Chaos warriors were moving towards them now, the massive warlord in the lead. It was all the provocation that Gotrek needed. Howling madly he raced to meet them.

Oh well, thought Felix, where else have I got to go? He charged forward following the Slayers towards what he felt was certain death.

MAX SCHREIBER LOOKED down from the airship. He watched as the Ice Queen's spell smashed through the oncoming units of daemons. He doubted that under normal circumstances even so potent an onslaught could have held them, but the daemons were weakened, the dark magic saturating the area was draining away swiftly, and the spells binding them to this plane had unravelled. Max could no longer sense the presence of the mages that held the intricate skein of power together. Was it possible they had fled? Was it possible that the men of Kislev might yet, against all odds pull off a victory here?

Certainly the airship had wreaked terrible havoc on the Chaos horde. Huge craters spoke of the power of Malakai Makaisson's bombs. Glowing pools filled with melting corpses testified to the sheer destructive power of alchemical fire. Looking at the Slayer, Max realised that in his own way Malakai Makaisson wielded as much power as any mage, perhaps more. If a fleet of these airships could be manufactured they could change the course of history. Not that the engineer intended to do that. He did his best to share his secrets with no one. In their way magicians and engineers were perhaps not all that different. They were all jealous of their lore. And why not, thought Max? After all, knowledge is power.

He realised that he was only trying to distract himself from the destruction raging below. He could see the Kislevite cavalry surging through the remains of the horde. The airship's attack had levelled the odds. The horse warriors had a chance now, but only a chance. The battle was still in the balance, and Max knew that the least little thing could tip it one way or the other.

Flakes of snow whirled across his field of vision. The airship shuddered in the turbulence. The wind keened through the struts and hawsers binding the cupola to the gasbag. Makaisson turned the nose around and Max caught sight of the city.

It was an eerie sight. Towers and temples blazed. Huge tenements collapsed as fire ate away at their innards. Gusts of snow obscured everything for moments at a time. The citadel of Praag still rose above the inner city unassailed as yet and holding the promise of safety for some. Fiery arcs and explosions spoke of siege engines still being used from within.

'Weel, weel,' Malakai Makaisson said, 'that's the last o' the bombs. Ah suppose we'd better haid back and git doon tae some serious fightin.''

Max looked at the dwarf with something like wonder. This maniac had done as much as an army to turn the course of the battle. His genius might just have saved the city, and perhaps the whole of this part of the world from the threat of Chaos – and now he wanted to risk himself in the maelstrom of battle below. He regarded that as the real struggle! Max grinned at him and Malakai Makaisson grinned back.

'I suppose you're right, Malakai! I might as well come with you and see what I can do myself.'

'Rightie oh! Enough talk. Time for killing!'

AREK GRINNED AS his first blow sent the dwarf reeling backward. The Slayer seemed sluggish. He had barely managed to get that fearsome axe in the way. Arek told himself not to be overconfident. It was still a weapon of enormous power. If anything was capable of breaching his invincible armour, this was, and he had no wish to put that particular theory to the test.

He strode on, confident now. The Chaos warriors and beastmen at his back chanted loudly, certain of victory. Arek realised how much they had come to fear the Slayer over the past few days. Certainly the sight of him doing his bloody work on the walls had not been good for morale. He had become a symbol of the city's stubborn resistance, as well as a deadly killer to be feared by all who crossed his path. Well, that was going to end now, Arek thought. He had never lost a fight against any foe, and he was not going to start today.

He stepped forward calmly, and decided where to place his next blow. A feint with the sword, he thought, should leave his foe open to a killing blow from the axe. He aimed a cut directly at the Slayer's head. The dwarf ducked at the last moment, and Arek's razor-sharp sword chopped off a large swathe of his dyed crest of hair. His follow-up blow, intended to cave in the dwarf's ribs and place his axe blade in his heart, was met by the Slayer's axe. Sparks flew as hell-steel smashed into ancient starmetal.

The dwarf was a better fighter than he had given him credit for, Arek thought, calmly stepping back and parrying two thunderously powerful blows with his sword.

The Slayer was fighting on instinct and reflexes but was nonetheless deadly as a wolf at bay. Arek was pleased. It would make his inevitable victory all the sweeter.

* * *

FELIX CAUGHT A glimpse of the duel out of the corner of his eye. The two combatants were moving almost too fast for him to follow. Their weapons were merely flickers of light, whose contact ended in sparks and the ring of steel on steel. It was like watching gods fence with lightning bolts, he thought, and then gave his attention back to the beastman who was trying to chop his head off.

Felix ducked the blow and lunged forward, driving his blade into the beastman's stomach. With a flick of his wrist, he altered the angle upwards to seek the heart or some other vital organ. In the long run it would not matter much. A gut wound like this was inevitably fatal unless magic was used. In the short run though, an instant kill might save Felix's life. Many a wounded man had dragged his foe down to hell with him. Felix wanted to avoid that, if possible.

He stepped back as bile and blood fountained outwards, and turned just in time to block a blow from a massive Chaos warrior armed with a spiked club. Felix saw that the man was off-balance, and took advantage of it to kick his legs out from beneath him. Once the warrior was on his back, Felix brought his blade smashing down through the chink in the warrior's visor. He felt bone crunch, and hot blood spurted from the gap in the helm.

Felix saw Snorri and Bjorni battling side by side, trying to hack their way towards Gotrek and the Chaos warrior. Felix was sure that Gotrek would not thank them for interfering in his doom, but he was currently in no position to object. After all, the warlord of this horde was a prize for any Slayer. Falling in combat with him would be a doom they would all prize. Frankly it was one that Felix would be happy to avoid, but he knew if the three Slayers fell it was one he would most likely share, unless he was spectacularly lucky.

He risked another glance back at the duel. It was not going well for Gotrek as far as Felix could tell.

AREK HAD THE measure of his foe now. The Slayer was fast and the weapon was powerful. More than that, to Arek's altered senses, it was obvious there was some sort of link between the dwarf and the weapon. It fed him strength and vitality in some arcane manner. He guessed that, as the twins had surmised, over the years the Slayer had wielded it, the weapon had altered him, making him stronger and more resilient even than a dwarf would normally be. Arek had plenty of experience with weapons like that. Chaos had gifted them to many of his foes.

Only this was not a weapon created by the followers of the Dark Gods. It was something else. Something old and something potent had created it. The runes that blazed on its starmetal blade augmented its power, guiding perceptible flows of magical energy into it, adding keenness to its edge and swiftness to its wielder. More than that, it seethed with a baneful power, something inimical to Arek and all his kind.

Not that it mattered now. Arek knew he was the dwarf's master. No mortal was his match for speed or guile, and Arek's armour and weapons were just as powerful as the Slayer's. In a few more heartbeats he would be gazing down on the dwarf's corpse.

He moved forward once more, smashing his sword down, aiming for the Slayer's head. The dwarf moved aside slower this time, and Arek opened a cut on his temple. His axe smashed into the Slayer's weapon again, forcing the dwarf back another step. Soon they would be at the entrance to a burning building, and there would be nowhere else for the dwarf to retreat.

Arek saw rage and something like fear burning in the mad dwarf's one good eye. His opponent knew he was doomed. Now was the time when he would be most dangerous. Soon the dwarf would throw all his strength into one last desperate attack. Arek focused all his concentration on his foe, readying himself for the moment of supreme victory.

It came as a complete surprise to him when he felt something barrel into him just behind his knee. His leg started to give way. He heard a voice bellow, 'This one is Bjorni Bjornisson's!'

He looked around and down and saw a second, repulsively ugly Slayer glaring up at him. Reflexively he brought his sword smashing down. Out of the corner of his eye, he caught sight of something metallic, covered in baleful runes, flashing towards his head.

It was the last thing he ever saw. As he died, the realisation that Lord Tzeentch had played a terrible trick on him flared through his mind.

TO FELIX IT looked like everything happened at once. One moment, Arek stood triumphant, about to slay Gotrek with one blow. In the next, Snorri and Bjorni had barrelled into the warrior, upsetting everything.

Bjorni hit the warlord just behind the left knee, throwing him off-balance. His weapon bounced from the ornate Chaos armour but the force of the blow was still enough to upset Arek.

In the same instant, Snorri lashed out with both hammer and axe. The sheer power of his blows started the warlord toppling.

Even so, Arek was still deadly. As he fell, his savage slash smashed through poor Bjorni's skull, splitting his head in two, and giving Felix the sort of view of the dwarf's teeth, brains and skull that he could cheerfully have lived without. At the same time, he twisted to his right, attempting to catch Snorri with his axe. The Slayer managed to get both his weapons in the way, but the power of Arek's blow sheared through the hammer head, and chopped through the haft of the axe, before carving a slice from Snorri's chest.

At the sight of this, Gotrek howled a curse and lashed out with his axe. The mighty starmetal blade shrieked as it hit the neck guard of Arek's armour. Sparks flared. The runes on the axe-blade blazed bright as miniature suns. Then the axe cut right through the armour like a knife through rotten cheese. Arek's head parted from his shoulders, hit the ground, bounced once and rolled to land at Felix's feet.

Caught up in the moment, not quite knowing why he did it, Felix picked the helm up and brandished it aloft.

'Your warlord is dead!' he shouted. Droplets of black blood dripped from Arek's severed neck. Where they fell, the snow sizzled and melted. *'Your warlord is dead!'*

The beastmen looked upon him and fell back in dismay, as if unwilling to believe the evidence of their eyes. Felix looked over at Gotrek. The Slayer spat on the red-flecked snow in disgust.

'Once again it seems I am robbed of a mighty doom, man-ling!' he shouted, glaring at Snorri as if he held the other dwarf personally responsible. Snorri shrugged, looked at the remains of his weapons, and gently leaned down and picked up Bjorni's axe.

'Still plenty of killing to be done, Gotrek Gurnisson,' he said quietly.

'By Grimnir, you're right there!' Gotrek said. With that, he turned and lunged into the panicking beastmen like a swimmer diving into an ocean of blood.

SLOWLY AT FIRST, then more swiftly, word of Arek's fall passed through the remains of the Chaos army. Fleeing beastmen spread panic and disorder among their comrades. Without quite knowing why, those comrades also joined the general rout. The embattled defenders, sensing a real change in their fortunes at last, fought back with renewed fury.

Seeing the tide of battle turn, Duke Enrik led the remainder of his forces from the inner citadel, helping to drive the mutants and monsters back towards the gaps in the walls.

With the departure of the sorcerers, the spells binding the energies of dark magic unravelled and failed. The daemonic war engines lost power and became lifeless hulks. The last of the ravaging daemons thinned, faded and vanished into clouds of brimstone reek.

At the Gate of Gargoyles, the duke and his men linked up with the riders of the Ice Queen. Amid the destruction they saluted each other for a moment, then led their armies forth to complete the first victory in the Second Great War Against Chaos.

# ABOUT THE AUTHOR

William King was born in Stranraer, Scotland, in 1959. His short stories have appeared in *The Year's Best SF, Zenith, White Dwarf* and *Interzone*. He is also the author of three previous Gotrek & Felix novels: *Trollslayer, Skavenslayer, Daemonslayer* and *Dragonslayer*, and two volumes chronicling the adventures of a Space Marine warrior, Ragnar: *Space Wolf* and *Ragnar's Claw*. He has travelled extensively throughout Europe and Asia, but he currently lives in Prague, where he is now neck-deep in a new Gotrek & Felix adventure, *Vampireslayer*!

More Warhammer from the Black Library

# TROLLSLAYER
## A Gotrek & Felix novel
## by William King

HIGH ON THE HILL the scorched walled castle stood, a stone spider clutching the hilltop with blasted stone feet. Before the gaping maw of its broken gate hanged men dangled on gibbets, flies caught in its single-strand web.

'Time for some bloodletting,' Gotrek said. He ran his left hand through the massive red crest of hair that rose above his shaven tattooed skull. His nose chain tinkled gently, a strange counterpoint to his mad rumbling laughter.

'I am a slayer, manling. Born to die in battle. Fear has no place in my life.'

*TROLLSLAYER IS THE first part of the death saga of Gotrek Gurnisson, as retold by his travelling companion Felix Jaeger. Set in the darkly gothic world of Warhammer, Trollslayer is an episodic novel featuring some of the most extraordinary adventures of this deadly pair of heroes. Monsters, daemons, sorcerers, mutants, orcs, beastmen and worse are to be found as Gotrek strives to achieve a noble death in battle. Felix, of course, only has to survive to tell the tale.*

More Warhammer from the Black Library

# SKAVENSLAYER
## A Gotrek & Felix novel
## by William King

'BEWARE! SKAVEN!' Felix shouted and saw them all reach for their weapons. In moments, swords glittered in the half-light of the burning city. From inside the tavern a number of armoured figures spilled out into the gloom. Felix was relieved to see the massive squat figure of Gotrek among them. There was something enormously reassuring about the immense axe clutched in the dwarf's hands.

'I see you found our scuttling little friends, manling,' Gotrek said, running his thumb along the blade of his axe until a bright red bead of blood appeared.

'Yes, Felix gasped, struggling to get his breath back before the combat began.

'Good. Let's get killing then!'

*SET IN THE MIGHTY city of Nuln, Gotrek and Felix are back in SKAVENSLAYER, the second novel in this epic saga. Seeking to undermine the very fabric of the Empire with their arcane warp-sorcery, the skaven, twisted Chaos rat-men, are at large in the reeking sewers beneath the ancient city. Led by Grey Seer Thanquol, the servants of the Horned Rat are determined to overthrow this bastion of humanity. Against such forces, what possible threat can just two hard-bitten adventurers pose?*

More Warhammer from the Black Library

# DAEMONSLAYER
### A Gotrek & Felix novel
### by William King

THE ROAR WAS so loud and so terrifying that Felix almost dropped his blade. He looked up and fought the urge to soil his britches. The most frightening thing he had ever seen had entered the hall and behind it he could see the leering heads of beastmen.

As he gazed on the creature in wonder and terror, Felix thought: this is the incarnate nightmare which has bedevilled my people since time began.

'Just remember,' Gotrek said from beside him, 'the daemon is mine!'

*FRESH FROM THEIR adventures battling the foul servants of the rat-god in Nuln, Gotrek and Felix are now ready to join an expedition northwards in search of the long-lost dwarf hall of Karag Dum. Setting forth for the hideous Realms of Chaos in an experimental dwarf airship, Gotrek and Felix are sworn to succeed or die in the attempt. But greater and more sinister energies are coming into play, as a daemonic power is awoken to fulfil its ancient, deadly promise.*

**More Warhammer from the Black Library**

# DRAGONSLAYER
## A Gotrek & Felix novel
## by William King

THE DRAGON opened its vast mouth. All the fires of hell burned within its jaws.

Insanely, Felix thought the creature looked almost as if it were smiling. Some strange impulse compelled him to throw himself between Gotrek and the creature just as it breathed. He fought back the desire to scream as a wall of flame hurtled towards him.

*DRAGONSLAYER is the fourth epic instalment in the death-seeking saga of Gotrek and Felix. After the daring exploits revealed in Daemonslayer, the fearless duo find themselves pursued by the insidious and ruthless skaven-lord, Grey Seer Thanquol. Dragonslayer sees the fearless Troll Slayer and his sworn companion back aboard an arcane dwarf airship in a search for a golden hoard – and its deadly guardian.*

More William King from the Black Library

# SPACE WOLF
## A Warhammer 40,000 novel
## by William King

RAGNAR LEAPT UP from his hiding place, bolt pistol spitting death. The nightgangers could not help but notice where he was, and with a mighty roar of frenzied rage they raced towards him. Ragnar answered their war cry with a wolfish howl of his own, and was reassured to hear it echoed back from the throats of the surrounding Blood Claws. He pulled the trigger again and again as the frenzied mass of mutants approached, sending bolter shell after bolter shell rocketing into his targets. Ragnar laughed aloud, feeling the full battle rage come upon him. The beast roared within his soul, demanding to be unleashed.

*IN THE GRIM future of Warhammer 40,000, the Space Marines of the Adeptus Astartes are humanity's last hope. On the planet Fenris, young Ragnar is chosen to be inducted into the noble yet savage Space Wolves chapter. But with his ancient primal instincts unleashed by the implanting of the sacred Canis Helix, Ragnar must learn to control the beast within and fight for the greater good of the wolf pack.*

More William King from the Black Library

# RAGNAR'S CLAW
### A Warhammer 40,000 novel
### by William King

ONE OF THE enemy oficers, wearing the peaked cap and greatcoat of a lieutenant, dared to stick his head above the parapet. Without breaking stride, Ragnar raised his bolt pistol and put a shell through the man's head. It exploded like a melon hit with a sledgehammer. Shouts of confusion echoed from behind the wall of sandbags, then a few heretics, braver and more experienced than the rest, stuck their heads up in order to take a shot at their attackers. Another mistake: a wave of withering fire from the Space Marines behind Ragnar scythed through them, sending their corpses tumbling back amongst their comrades.

FROM THE DEATH-WORLD of Fenris come the Space Wolves, the most savage of the Emperor's Space Marines. Ragnar's Claw explores the bloody beginnings of Space Wolf Ragnar's first mission as a young Blood Claw warrior. From the jungle hell of Galt to the polluted cities of Hive World Venam, Ragnar's mission takes him on an epic trek across the galaxy to face the very heart of Evil itself.

More Warhammer from the Black Library

# HAMMERS
# OF ULRIC

## A Warhammer novel by Dan Abnett,
## Nik Vincent & James Wallis

ARIC RODE FORWARD across the corpse-strewn ground and helped Gruber to his feet. The older warrior was speckled with blood, but alive.

'See to von Glick and watch the standard. Give me your horse,' Gruber said to Aric.

Aric dismounted and returned to the banner of Vess as Gruber galloped back into the brutal fray.

Von Glick lay next to the standard, which was still stuck upright in the bloody earth. The lifeless bodies of almost a dozen beastmen lay around him.

'L-let me see...' von Glick breathed. Aric knelt beside him and raised his head. 'So, Anspach's bold plan worked...' breathed the veteran warrior. 'He's pleased... I'll wager.'

Aric started to laugh, then stopped. The old man was dead.

*IN THE SAVAGE world of Warhammer, dark powers gather around the ancient mountain-top city of Middenheim, the City of the White Wolf. Only the noble Templar Knights of Ulric and a few unlikely allies stand to defend her against the insidious servants of Death.*

More Warhammer from the Black Library

# THE WINE OF DREAMS

## A Warhammer novel by Brian Craig

THE SWORD FLEW from Reinmar's hand and he just had
time to think, as he was taken off his feet, that when he
landed – flat on his back – he would be wide open to
attack by a plunging dagger or flashing teeth. As the
beastman leapt, Sigurd's arm lashed out in a great
horizontal arc, the palm of his hand held flat. As it
impacted with the beastman's neck Reinmar heard the
snap that broke the creature's spine.

As soon as that, it was over. But it was not a victory.
Now there was no possible room for doubt that there
were monsters abroad in the hills.

*DEEP WITHIN the shadowy foothills of the Grey Mountains, a
dark and deadly plot is uncovered by an innocent young
merchant. A mysterious stranger leads young Reinmar
Weiland to stumble upon the secrets of a sinister underworld
hidden beneath the very feet of the unsuspecting Empire –
and learn of a legendary elixir, the mysterious and forbidden
Wine of Dreams.*

More Warhammer from the Black Library

# REALM OF CHAOS

An anthology of Warhammer
stories edited by Marc Gascoigne
& Andy Jones

'MARKUS WAS confused; the stranger's words were baffling his pain-numbed mind. "Just who are you, foul spawned deviant?"

'The warrior laughed again, slapping his hands on his knees. "I am called Estebar. My followers know me as the Master of Slaughter. And I have come for your soul."'
– **The Faithful Servant,** *by Gav Thorpe*

'THE WOLVES ARE running again. I can haear them panting in the darkness. I race through the forest, trying to outpace them. Behind the wolves I sense another presence, something evil. I am in the place of blood again.' – **Dark Heart,** *by Jonathan Green*

*IN THE DARK and gothic world of Warhammer, the ravaging armies of the Ruinous Powers sweep down from the savage north to assail the lands of men. REALM OF CHAOS is a searing collection of a dozen all-action fantasy short stories set in these desperate times.*

Also from the Black Library

# INTO THE MAELSTROM

## An anthology of Warhammer 40,000 stories, edited by Marc Gascoigne & Andy Jones

'The Chaos army had travelled from every continent, every shattered city, every ruined sector of Illium to gather on this patch of desert that had once been the control centre of the Imperial Garrison. The sand beneath their feet had been scorched, melted and fused by a final, futile act of suicidal defiance: the detonation of the garrison's remaining nuclear stockpile.' – **Hell in a Bottle** by Simon Jowett

'Hoarse screams and the screech of tortured hot metal filled the air. Massive laser blasts were punching into the spaceship. They superheated the air that men breathed, set fire to everything that could burn and sent fireballs exploding through the crowded passageways.' – **Children of the Emperor** by Barrington J. Bayley

*In the grim and gothic nightmare future of Warhammer 40,000, mankind teeters on the brink of extinction. INTO THE MAELSTROM is a storming collection of a dozen action-packed science fiction short stories set in this dark and brooding universe.*

Also from the Black Library

# DARK IMPERIUM

## An anthology of Warhammer 40,000 stories, edited by Marc Gascoigne & Andy Jones

'DE HAAN REALISED someone had set off the Frenzon too early. Their thralls ran to and fro, shrieking and swinging their clubs, pistols spitting and making the stone chambers a hell of sparks and ricochets. Bullets spanged off De Haan's armour as he shouldered his way through the crowd of naked, bleeding berserkers.' – from **Snares and Delusions** by *Matthew Farrer*

'SHE WORE ARMOUR only to display her body, which was lithe and supple to an extent which no human could match. Her long red-black hair flowed out in a stormy trail behind her as she moved, along with the glistening metallic net that she held in one hand. In the other, twirling like a rotor blade, was a halberd, as long as she was tall and tipped with a broad, wickedly curved blade.' – from **Hellbreak** by *Ben Counter*

*IN THE WAR-TORN 41st millennium humanity stands on the shores of damnation. Its only saviour is the immortal God Emperor and the massed armies of the Imperium, in this searing anthology of Warhammer 40,000 stories torn from the pages of Inferno! magazine.*

INFERNO! is the indispensable guide to the worlds of Warhammer and Warhammer 40,000 and the cornerstone of the Black Library. Every issue is crammed full of action packed stories, comic strips and artwork from a growing network of awesome writers and artists including:

- William King
- Brian Craig
- Gav Thorpe
- Dan Abnett
- Barrington J. Bayley
- Gordon Rennie

and many more

Presented every two months, Inferno! magazine brings the Warhammer worlds to life in ways you never thought possible.

# LET BATTLE COMMENCE!

NOW YOU can fight your way through the savage lands of the Empire and beyond with WARHAMMER, Games Workshop's game of fantasy battles. In a world of conflict, mighty armies clash to decide the fate of war-torn realms. In Warhammer, you and your opponents are the fearless commanders of these armies. The fate of your kingdoms rests on your shoulders as you control regiments of miniature soldiers, to do battle with terrifying monsters and fearless heroes.

*To find out more about Warhammer, along with Games Workshop's whole range of exciting fantasy and science fiction games and miniatures, just call our specialist Trolls on the following numbers:*

## IN THE UK: 0115-91 40 000

## IN THE US: 1-800-GAME

*or look us up online at:*

## www.games-workshop.com